FLESH HOUSE

By Stuart MacBride

Cold Granite
Dying Light
Broken Skin
Flesh House

STUART MACBRIDE

Flesh House

HarperCollins*Publishers*

HarperCollins*Publishers*
77–85 Fulham Palace Road,
Hammersmith, London W6 8JB

www.harpercollins.co.uk

Published by HarperCollins*Publishers* 2008
1

Set in Meridien
by Newgen Imaging Systems (P) Ltd, Chennai, India

Printed and bound in Great Britain by
Clays Ltd, St Ives plc

Mixed Sources
Product group from well-managed
forests and other controlled sources
www.fsc.org Cert no. SW-COC-1806
© 1996 Forest Stewardship Council
FSC

FSC is a non-profit international organisation established to promote the responsible management of the world's forests. Products carrying the FSC label are independently certified to assure consumers that they come from forests that are managed to meet the social, economic and ecological needs to present and future generations.

Find out more about HarperCollins and the environment at
www.harpercollins.co.uk/green

For my mother and father
Stuart and Sheena MacBride

Without Whom...

Many people helped (intentionally or otherwise) with the writing of this book by answering questions, asking them, or just saying bizarre things that sounded interesting within earshot.

I have to thank (because they'll arrest me if I don't) Grampian Police for all the help they've given me, not just with this book, but all the previous ones. A special nod goes to Chief Inspector Jim Bilsland, for pointers and some stories of what it was like in the force back in the 1980s – none of which I can repeat here – and Linda Cottriall for putting me straight about what a Family Liaison officer actually does.

That doyenne of the mortuary, Ishbel Gall, was once more unbelievably helpful, especially when it came to some of the more... *cannibalistic* aspects of the story. If she wasn't so nice, she'd be scary.

Any procedural stuff that I've got right is down to the input of these people. The bits I've got wrong are all my own work.

I want to thank Frank Clark and Bruce Fraser of McIntosh Donald for showing me how a *proper* abattoir works, and Keir

Allen and Duncan Oswald for talking them into it. Thanks guys, it was an eye-opener.

More thanks are due to Danny Stroud for the fascinating tour of Aberdeen Harbour; Szymon Krygiel for the lesson in Polish swearing; Christopher Croly for some interesting historical facts; everyone at Trinity Hall; and let's not forget Val McDermid, Tammy Jones, Mark Billingham, Bernard Cornwell, John 'Spanky' Rickards, Allan Guthrie, Stuart Singer of the Redgarth, and the late great R.D. Wingfield (who'll be sorely missed). Inspiration, beer, and abuse in equal measure.

Yet more thanks go to: Philip Patterson − not just a great agent, but a friend and top-notch monkey impersonator − Luke, Isabella, Jacquie, and everyone else at Marjacq scripts. HarperCollins: especially the brilliant Jane Johnson and dazzling Sarah Hodgson; the superb Amanda; Fiona, Louisa and the Publicity crew; Lucy, Airlie and the Rights gang; Clive, Wendy and the UK Sales team; Sylvia, Damon and the Export Sales guys; Leisa and the Marketing maestros; and Andrew and Dom for design interior and exterior. Kelley Ragland at St. Martin's Press. And James Oswald for his unusually bearded insight.

I also want to thank Tom and Hazel Stephen who donated a large sum of money to Books Abroad, so that they could appear as victims in this book − brave choice!

In order to make the newspaper clippings look as real as possible I had to twist some family members' arms to let me photograph them: my brother, Christopher appears as Ken Wiseman; my sister-in-law, Catherine plays Catherine Davidson; and a strange lady from Fife pretended to be Valerie Leith. (All the businesses and locations in the book were faked up using Adobe Photoshop.)

Lastly, but not leastly, I have to say thanks to my naughty wife, Fiona for random cups of tea and putting up with a succession of bizarre, rambling questions; and my little girl, Grendel for all the half-chewed bits of mice.

And now a message for the Aberdeen Tourist Board: I promise to set the next one in Summer, OK?

The World Is Shaped
By Fear

30 October 1987

'No, you listen to me: if my six year old son isn't back here in ten minutes I'm going to come round there and rip you a new arsehole, are we clear?' Ian McLaughlin slapped a hand over the mouthpiece and shouted at his wife to turn that bloody racket down. Then he went back to the idiot on the other end of the phone: 'Where the hell's Jamie?'

'*When I got back from the pub they were gone, OK? Catherine's not here either ... maybe she took the boys for a walk?*'

'A walk? It's pissing down, pitch black, freezing cold—'

'What? What's wrong?' Sharon stood at the door to the living room, wearing the witch costume she'd bought from Woolworths. The one that hid her pregnant bulge and made her breasts look enormous.

Ian grunted, not bothering to cover the phone this time. 'It's that moron Davidson: he's lost Jamie.'

'Jamie's missing?' Sharon clapped a hand to her mouth, stifling the shriek. Always overreacting, just like her bloody mother.

'*I never said that! I didn't say he was lost, I just—*'

'If we're late for this bloody party, I'm personally going to see to it that—'

The doorbell: loud and insistent.

3

'—your life is going to be—'

The doorbell again.

'For God's sake, Sharon, answer the bloody door! I'm on the phone . . .'

There was a clunk and a rattle as Sharon finally did what she was told, and then she shrieked again. 'Jamie! Oh Jamie, we were so *worried!*'

Ian stopped mid-rant, staring at the soggy tableau on the top step: Jamie and his best friend Richard Davidson, holding hands with some idiot in a Halloween costume. 'About bloody time,' said Ian, slamming the phone down. 'I told you to be home by five!' The two small boys looked wide eyed and frightened. And so they bloody should be. 'Where the hell have you two been?'

No reply. Typical. And look at the time . . . 'Jamie!' Ian hooked his thumb in the direction of the stairs. 'Get your backside up there and get changed. If you're not a Viking in three minutes you're going to the party as a kid in his vest and pants.'

Jamie cast a worried look at his partner in crime, then up at the stranger on the doorstep – the one wearing the blood-stained butcher's apron and Margaret Thatcher fright mask – before slinking up to his room, taking Richard with him.

Great, now they'd have to drop the little brat off at his parents' house.

Today was turning into a *complete* nightmare.

'House of Blood' parents missing

EXCLUSIVE
by Martin Leslie

A MAJOR police operation was launched last night to try to locate [I]an McLaughlin (27) and his wife [S]haron (22) who disappeared from [t]heir house on Seafield Drive in the [l]ate hours of Friday.

In a statement issued to the press [D]etective Chief Inspector Gary [B]rooks claimed that the police [w]ere "significantly worried" for [t]he McLaughlins' safety.

The alarm was raised when [f]riend of the family Christopher [D]avidson became concerned after [h]is six-year-old son failed to return [h]ome after visiting the McLaughlins.

"I went round to check if [e]verything was all right and the [p]lace was a mess," Davidson said, [there] was furniture overturned in the lounge and the kitchen was covered in blood."

Speaking from outside the Children's Hospital, where both his son and Jamie McLaughlin (6) are being treated for shock, Mr Davidson was clearly distressed.

"My wife was with the children when they left our house. Something terrible must have happened – she would never have left them unattended!"

Police refused to comment on rumours that the two boys could have witnessed the assault, but stressed the need to locate Mr and Mrs McLaughlin, and Catherine Davidson, as soon as possible.

DCI Brooks said, "We are concerned that one or all three of them may have suffered a significant medical trea[tment] It is u[n]

The McLaughlin Household in Seafield Drive – Polic

McLaughlin, who works for the oil   Aberdeen

The Aberdeen Examiner

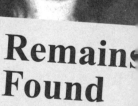

THREE DEAD IN [T]ENEMENT HORROR

[GLA]SGOW police issued [an] urgent plea for [infor]mation last night, [follow]ing an anonymous tip[off t]hat led them to a [tene]nt flat soaked in blood. [C]an't tell for certain," [said D]I Simon Ridley of [Cl]yde police, "but it [look]s very much as if Mr and [Mrs Suth]erland have been the [victims] of a viciou[s]

similarities to a recent case i[n] Aberdeen. The killer, dubbed "The Flesher" (the old Scots term for Butcher) is believed to be responsible for up to a dozen murders all over the United Kingdom.

A special task force made up of officers from e[very] region where [the]

Fears for mother's safety

EXCLUSIVE
by Martin Leslie

THE HUSBAND of Catherine [D]avidson spoke last night of his [fea]rs that his wife will never be [fou]nd.

Speaking exclusively to the [Ab]*erdeen Examiner*, Christopher [Da]vidson (27) shared his thoughts [on] his wife's disappearance: "I am [ver]y worried about her. She is a [dev]oted mother and our son, [Ric]hard (6) has had nightmares [eve]r since she disappeared."

[*]All we know is that she walked [Ric]hard and his friend Jamie home [the] night before Halloween. I can['t] [beli]eve she's gone."

Whatever happened that night[, he] said, "has left its mark on m[y fam]ily. The police have done the[ir]

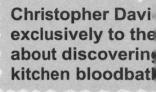

Remains Found

POLICE have confirmed tha[t the] remains found in a derelict sho[p on] Palmerston Road are human.

Sources within Grampian Police [have] hinted that the remains may belong [to Ian] and Sharon McLaughlin, missing [since] the 30th of October, but they we[re] unable to confirm this until furthe[r tests] are carried out.

A nationwide manhunt was spa[rked] when the McLaughlins disappeared [from] their Mannofield home on the night be[fore] Halloween.

The McLaughlins' son, Jamie (6) [was] discovered hiding in his bedroom clo[set] with his friend Richard Davidson. [...] Neither boy was able to close[ly]

Flesher [a]rrested

[A]berdeen killer caught

[po]lice suspect more deaths

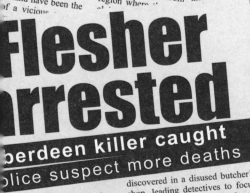

[A] DAWN RAID yesterday [Gram]pian Police arrested the man [knowi]ngly known as "the Flesher". [It] was the night before [Hall]oween, but little did Ian and [Shar]on McLaughlin know that [some]thing more terrifying than

discovered in a disused butcher's shop, leading detectives to focus their enquiries on Aberdeen's meat trade.

Missing body parts

DCI Brooks, who led the 50-man strong taskforce said that the arrest "represents a significant [...] after three years of

[W]hen bi[g]

[RES]IDENTS of a small North [com]munity have been stunned b[y]

20 Years Later

1

Detective Sergeant Logan McRae winced his way across the dark quayside trying not to scald his fingers, making for a scarred offshore container pinned in the harsh glow of police spotlights. The thing was about the size of a domestic bathroom – dented and battered from years of being shipped out to oilrigs in the middle of the North Sea and back again – its blue paint pockmarked with orange rust. A pool of dark red glittered in the Investigation Bureau's lights: blood mingling with oily puddles on the cold concrete, while figures in white oversuits buggered about with cameras and sticky tape and evidence bags.

Four o'clock in the morning, what a *great* start to the day.

The refrigerated container was little more than a metal box, lined with insulating material. Three wooden pallets took up most of the floor, piled high with boxes of frozen vegetables, fish, chicken bits and other assorted chunks of meat, the brown-grey cardboard sagging as the contents slowly defrosted.

Logan ducked under the cordon of blue-and-white POLICE tape.

It was impossible to miss Detective Inspector Insch: the man was huge, his SOC coveralls strained to nearly bursting. He had the suit's hood thrown back, exposing a big bald head that glinted in the spotlights. But even he was dwarfed by the looming bulk of the *Brae Explorer*, a massive orange offshore supply vessel parked alongside the quay, all its lights blazing in the purple-black night.

Logan handed one of the Styrofoam cups of tea to Insch. 'They were out of sugar.' That got him some rumbled swearing. He ignored it. 'Sky News have turned up. That makes three television crews, four newspapers and a handful of gawkers.

'Wonderful,' Insch's voice was a dark rumble, 'that's all we need.' He pointed up at the *Brae Explorer*. 'Those idiots found anything yet?'

'Search team's nearly finished. Other than some incredibly dodgy pornography it's clean. Ship's Captain says the container was only onboard for a couple of hours; someone noticed it was leaking all over the deck, so they got onto the cash and carry it came from. Shut. Apparently the rigs throw a fit if they don't get their containers on time, so the Captain got someone to try fixing the thing's refrigerator motor.'

Logan took a sip of his scalding hot tea. 'That's when they found the bits. Mechanic had to shift a couple of boxes of defrosting meat to get at the wiring. Soggy cardboard gave way on one of them, and the contents went everywhere.' He pointed at a small pile of clear plastic evidence pouches, each one containing a chunk of red. 'Soon as he saw what was in there, he called us.'

Insch nodded. 'What about the cash and carry?'

'Firm called Thompson's in Altens: they supply a couple of offshore catering companies. Frozen meat, veg, toilet paper, tins of beans ... the usual. They don't open till seven am, so it'll be a while before—'

The large man turned a baleful eye in Logan's direction. 'No it won't. Find out who's in charge over there and get the bastard out of his bed. I want a search team up there now.'

'But it—'

'NOW, Sergeant!'

'Yes, sir.' Arguing with Insch wasn't going to get him anywhere. Logan pulled out his mobile phone and wandered off to call Control, getting a search team and warrant organized between mouthfuls of tea. Doing his best to ignore the cameraman circling him like a short, balding shark.

Logan finished the call, then scrunched up his polystyrene cup and . . . there was nowhere to get rid of the thing, unless he just chucked it down on the dockside, or over into the water. Neither was going to look good on the television. Embarrassed, he hid it behind his back.

The shark lowered its HDV television camera – no bigger than a shoebox, with the BBC Scotland logo stencilled on the side – and grinned. 'Perfect. Thought the sound was going to be a bit ropey there, but it's not bad. This is dynamite stuff! Dismembered bodies, boats, tension, mystery. Ooh,' he pointed at the crumpled-up cup in Logan's hand, 'where'd you get the tea: I'm gasping.'

'Thought you were meant to be a fly on the wall, Alec, not a pain in the arse.'

'Aye, well, we all have our—'

Insch's voice bellowed out from the far side of the quay: 'SERGEANT!'

Swear. Count to ten. Sigh. 'If this programme's a success, can I come work for you guys at the BBC instead?'

'See what I can do.' And Alec was off, hurrying to get a good angle on whatever bollocking the inspector was about to dish out.

Logan followed on behind, wishing he'd been assigned to a different DI tonight, especially as the news from Control wasn't exactly good. These days, talking to Insch was like trying to do an eightsome reel in a minefield. Blindfolded. Still, might as well get it over with, 'Sorry, sir, they don't have any bodies spare – everyone's down here and—'

'Bloody hell!' The fat man ran a hand over his big, pink face. 'Why can no one do what they're told?'

'Another hour or so and we can free up some of the team here and—'

'I told you, I want it done now. Not in an hour: *now*.'

'But it's going to take that long to get a search warrant. Surely we should be concentrating on doing a thorough job here—'

The inspector loomed over him: six foot three of angry fat. 'Don't make me tell you twice, Sergeant.'

Logan tried to sound reasonable. 'Even if we pull every uniform off the boat and the docks, they're going to have to sit twiddling their thumbs till the search warrant comes through.'

Insch got as far as 'We don't have time to bugger about with—' before he was tapped on the shoulder by someone dressed in a white SOC oversuit. Someone who didn't look particularly happy.

'I've been waiting for you for fifteen minutes!' Dr Isobel McAllister, Aberdeen's chief pathologist, wearing an expression that would freeze the balls off a brass gorilla at twenty paces. 'You might not have anything better to do, but I can assure you that *I* have. Now are you going to listen to my preliminary findings, or shall I just go home and leave you to whatever it is you feel is more *important*?'

Logan groaned. That was all they needed, Isobel winding Insch up even further. As if the grumpy fat sod wasn't bad enough already. The inspector turned on her, his face flushing angry-scarlet in the IB spotlights. 'Thank you *so* much for waiting for me, Doctor, I'm sorry if my organizing a murder inquiry has *inconvenienced* you. I'll try not to let something as *trivial* get in the way again.'

They stared at each other in silence for a moment. Then Isobel pulled on a cold, unfriendly smile. 'Remains are human: male. Dismemberment looks as if it occurred some time after death with a long, sharp blade and a hacksaw, but I won't be able to confirm that until I've performed the post mortem.' She checked her watch. 'Which will take place at eleven am precisely.'

Insch bristled. 'Oh no it won't! I need those remains analysed now—'

'They're *frozen*, Inspector. They – need – to – defrost.' Emphasizing each word as if she were talking to a naughty child, rather than a huge, bad-tempered Detective Inspector. 'If you want, I suppose I *could* stick them in the canteen microwave for half an hour. But that might not be very professional. What do you think?'

Insch just ground his teeth at her. Face rapidly shifting from angry-red to furious-purple. 'Fine,' he said at last, 'then you can help by accompanying DS McRae to a cash and carry in Altens.'

'And what makes you think I—'

'Of course, if you're too busy, I can always ask one of the other pathologists to take over this case.' It was Insch's turn with the nasty smile. 'I understand the pressure you must be under: working mother, small child, can't really expect the same level of commitment to the job as—'

Isobel looked as if she was about to slap him. 'Don't you *dare* finish that sentence!' She flung an imperious gesture in Logan's direction. 'Get the car, Sergeant, we've got work to do.'

Insch nodded, pulled out his mobile and started dialling. 'Now if you'll excuse me, I've got a call to make ... Hello? ... That West Midlands Police? ... Yes, DI Insch: Grampian CID, I need to speak to Chief Constable Mark Faulds. ... Yes, of course I know what time it is!' He turned his back on them and wandered away out of the spotlights.

Isobel scowled after him, then turned and snapped at Logan, 'Well? We haven't got all night.'

They were halfway to the car when a loud, 'WILL YOU FUCK OFF WITH THAT BLOODY CAMERA!' exploded behind

13

them. Logan looked over his shoulder to see Alec scurrying in their direction while the inspector went back to his telephone call.

'Er . . .' said the cameraman, catching up to them by Logan's grubby, unmarked CID pool car, 'I wondered if I could tag along with you for a while. Insch is a bit . . .' He shrugged. 'You know.'

Logan did. 'Get in. I'll be back in a minute.'

It didn't take long to pass the word along: he just grabbed the nearest sergeant and asked her to give it forty-five minutes, then tell everyone to finish up and get their backsides over to Altens.

Alec was in full whinge when Logan got back to the car. 'I mean,' the cameraman said, leaning forward from the back seat – knee-deep in discarded chip papers and fast-food cartons, 'If he didn't want to be in the bloody series, why'd he volunteer? Always seemed really keen till now. He shouted at me – I had my headphones on, nearly blew my eardrums out.'

Logan shrugged, threading the car through the barricade of press cameras, microphones and spotlights. 'You're lucky. He shouts at me every bloody day.'

Isobel just sat there in frosty silence, seething.

Thompson's Cash and Carry was a long breezeblock warehouse in Altens: a soulless business park on the southernmost tip of Aberdeen. The building was huge, filled with rows and rows of high, deep shelves that stretched off into the distance, miserable beneath the flicker of fluorescent lighting and the drone of piped muzak. The manager's office was halfway up the end wall, a flight of concrete steps leading to a shiny blue door with 'YOUR SMILE IS OUR GREATEST ASSET' written on it. If that was the case, they were all screwed, because everyone looked bloody miserable.

The man in charge of Thompson's Cash and Carry was no exception. They'd dragged him out of his bed at half four in the morning and it showed: bags under the eyes, blue stubble on his jowly face, wearing a suit that probably cost a fortune, but looked as if someone had died in it. Mr Thompson peered out of the picture window that made up one wall of his office, watching as uniformed officers picked their way through the shelves of jelly babies, washing powder and baked beans. 'Oh God . . .'

'And you're quite sure,' said Logan, sitting in a creaky leather sofa with a cup of coffee and a chocolate biscuit, 'there haven't been any break-ins?'

'No. I mean, yes. I'm sure.' Thompson crossed his arms, paced back and forth, uncrossed his arms. Sat down. Stood up again. 'It can't have come from here: we've got someone on-site twenty-four-seven, a state-of-the-art security system.'

Logan had met their state-of-the-art security system – it was a sixty-eight-year-old man called Harold. Logan had sneezed more alert things than him.

Thompson went back to the window. 'Have you tried speaking to the ship's crew? Maybe they—'

'Who supplies your meat, Mr Thompson?'

'It . . . depends what it is. Some of the pre-packaged stuff comes from local butchers – it's cheaper than hiring someone in-house to hack it up – the rest comes from abattoirs. We use three—' He flinched as a loud, rattling crash came from the cash and carry floor below, followed by a derisory cheer and some slow handclapping. 'You promised me they'd be careful! We're open in an hour and a half; I can't have customers seeing the place in a mess.'

Logan shook his head. 'I think you've got more important things to worry about, sir.'

Thompson stared at him. 'You can't think we had anything to do with this! We're a family firm. We've been here for nearly thirty years.'

'That container came from your cash and carry with bits of human meat in it.'

15

'But—'

'How many other shipments do you think went out to the rigs like that? What if you've been selling chunks of dead bodies to catering companies for months? Do you think the guys who've been eating chopped-up corpses offshore are going to be happy about it?'

Mr Thompson blanched and said, 'Oh God . . . ' again.

Logan drained the last of his coffee and stood. 'Where did the meat in that container come from?'

'I . . . I'll have to look in the dockets.'

'You do that.'

The cash and carry's chill room sat on the opposite side of the building, separated from the shelves of tins and dried goods by a curtain of thick plastic strips that kept the cold in and the muzak out. A huge refrigeration unit bolted to the wall rattled away like a perpetual smoker's cough, making the air cold enough that Logan's breath trailed behind him in a fine mist as he marched between the boxes of fruit and vegetables, over to the walk-in freezer section.

Detective Constable Rennie stood beside the freezer's heavy steel doors, hands jammed deep in his armpits, nose Rudolf-red, dressed like a ninja version of the Michelin Man in layers and layers of black clothing.

'It's freezing in here,' said the constable, shivering, 'think my nipples just fell off.'

Logan stopped, one hand on the freezer's door-handle. 'You'd be a lot warmer if you actually did some work.'

Rennie pulled a face. 'The Ice Queen thinks we're all too thick to help. I mean, it's not my fault I don't know what I'm looking for, is it?'

'What?' Logan closed his eyes and tried counting to ten. Got as far as three. 'For God's sake; you're supposed to be looking for *human remains*!'

'I *know* that. I'm in there, standing in a sodding freezer the size of my house, looking at rows and rows of frozen bits of bloody meat. How am I supposed to tell a joint of pork from a joint of person? It all looks the same to me. A hand, a foot, a head: *that* I could recognize. But it's all just chunks of meat.' He shifted, stomping his feet and blowing into his cupped hands. 'I'm a policeman, not a bloody doctor.'

And Logan had to admit he had a point. They only knew that the joint of meat found in the offshore container was human because it had a pierced nipple. Farmers were an odd lot, but not that odd.

Logan hauled open the heavy metal door and stepped into the freezer . . . Dear God it was cold – like being punched in the chest by a bag of ice. His breath went from mist to impenetrable fog. 'Hello?'

He found Dr Isobel McAllister on the other side of a stack of cardboard boxes, their brown surfaces sparkling with a crisp film of white ice. She'd traded in her white SOC oversuit for a couple of dirty-blue parkas and a set of padded trousers, the ensemble topped off with a red and white bobble hat bandaged onto her head with a tatty maroon scarf. Not exactly her usual catwalk self. She was picking her way through a mound of frozen mystery meat.

'Anything?'

She scowled up at him. 'Other than hypothermia?' When Logan didn't answer, Isobel sighed and pointed at a big plastic crate stacked with chunks of vacuum-packed meat. 'We've got about three dozen possible pieces. If it was on the bone it'd be a lot easier to spot; cows and pigs have a much higher meat to bone ratio, but look at this,' she held up a pack labelled 'Diced Pork'. 'Could be anything. I'd expect human meat to be redder – based on the amount of myoglobin in the tissue – but if it's been bled and frozen . . . We'll need to defrost and DNA-test all of this before we'll know for sure.'

Isobel pulled over another cardboard box, sliced through the plastic strapping, and started picking her way through the contents. 'You can tell *Inspector* Insch it'll take at least two weeks.'

Logan groaned. 'He's not going to like that.'

'That's not my problem, Sergeant.'

Oh, when she wanted someone to babysit her kid, or suffer through her endless digital camera slideshows of the sticky-fingered, dribbly little monster, he was 'Logan', but when she was pissed off at work he was 'Sergeant.'

'Look,' he said, 'it's not *my* fault Insch had a go at you, OK? You think he's bad tonight? I get him all bloody day—' Clunk. Logan froze, eyes sweeping the shelves of frozen goods, hoping it wasn't Alec with his camera. Things were bad enough without being caught complaining about Insch on national television. 'Hello?'

'Sergeant McRae?' Mr Thompson peered around a stack of boxes marked 'Fish Fingers'. 'I've found the dockets . . .' he trailed off and stared at the pile of meat as Isobel added another chunk to the crate, the frozen pieces clattering against one another like ceramic tiles. 'Is . . . is that all . . . ?'

'We won't know till we test it.' Logan held out his hand, and the rumpled man looked puzzled for a moment, then tried to shake it. 'No,' Logan took a step back, leaving him hanging, 'the dockets?'

'Oh, right. Right. Of course.' He handed over a crumpled sheet of yellow A4, covered with biro scribbles. 'Sorry.'

Thompson fidgeted nervously as Logan read.

'What's going to happen? I mean if that . . .' He swallowed. 'What am I going to tell my customers?'

Logan pulled out his mobile phone and scrolled through the contacts list. 'We're going to need names and addresses for everyone who has access to this freezer. I want staff records, customers, suppliers, the lot.' An electronic voice on the other end of the line told him the number he was dialling was busy, please try again later.

The man in the crumpled suit shivered, wrapped his arms around himself and looked as if he was about to cry. 'We're a family firm, been here thirty years ...'

'Yes, well,' Logan tried for a reassuring smile, 'you never know: the tests might come up negative.'

'I wouldn't go getting Mr Thompson's hopes up,' said Isobel. She sat back on her haunches, breath a cloud of white around her head as she lifted something out of the box at her feet. From where Logan was standing it looked just like another chunk of pork, and he said so.

'That's true ...' she turned the joint of meat over, 'but pigs don't usually have tattoos of unicorns on their backsides.'

2

Insch was in the sweetie section, surrounded by catering-sized packs of Crunchies, Rolos, Sports Mixture, and fizzy flying saucers – eyeing them up as he spoke on the phone, 'Yeah, I'm sure.' The inspector listened for a moment, chewing on the side of his thumb, 'No . . . no . . . if the bastard sets foot outside his house I want him picked up. . . . What? . . . I don't care what you arrest him for, just bloody arrest him! . . . No, I don't have a warrant . . . '

Insch's face was starting its all too familiar slide from florid pink to angry scarlet. 'Because I bloody well told you to, that's why!' He snapped his phone shut and glowered at it.

Logan cleared his throat, and the glower turned his way. 'Sorry to interrupt, sir, but Iso . . . Dr McAllister's found at least one piece of human remains in the freezer. And about another forty possibles.'

The inspector's face lit up. 'About time.'

'Only trouble is, some of those are catering packs of diced meat. She says they'll have to defrost and DNA-test every chunk, otherwise there's no way of telling if a pack's got bits of one, two or a dozen people in it.' Deep breath. 'It's going to take at least a fortnight.'

And Insch went straight from angry scarlet to furious purple. 'WHAT?'

'She . . . it's what she said, OK?' Logan backed off, hands up.

Insch gritted his teeth and seethed for a moment. Then, 'You tell her I want those remains analysed and I want them analysed *now*. I don't care how many favours she has to call in, this takes top priority.'

'Ah ... maybe that'd sound better coming from you, sir? I—' The look on Insch's face was enough to stop Logan right there. 'Fine, I'll tell her.' Isobel was going to kill him. If the inspector didn't do it first. The big man looked like an unexploded bomb.

Logan had a bash at defusing him. 'According to the cash and carry's records the meat in the container came from a butcher's shop in Holburn Street: McFarlane's.'

'McFarlane's?' A nasty smile twisted Insch's face.

Logan pulled out the docket. 'Two sirloins, half a dozen sides of bacon, a pack of veal . . . '

But the inspector was already marching towards the exit, uniformed constables and IB technicians scurrying to get out of his way. 'I want a search warrant for that butcher's shop. Get everyone over there soon as it's organized.'

'What? But we haven't finished *here* yet.'

'The remains came from McFarlane's.'

'But we don't know that. This place isn't exactly difficult to get into. Anyone could have—'

'And I want an arrest warrant for Kenneth Wiseman.'

'Who the hell is—'

'And tell the press office to get their backsides in gear: briefing at ten am sharp.'

An hour and a half later Logan and Insch were sitting in a pool car outside McFarlane's butcher's shop, 'Good Eats Good Meats' according to the sign above the big dark window.

Holburn Street was virtually deserted, lonely traffic lights changing from red to green and back again with no one to watch them but a couple of unmarked CID Vauxhalls, a police van full of search-trained officers, a once-white transit van belonging to the Identification Bureau, and two patrol cars. All waiting for the Procurator Fiscal to turn up with the search and arrest warrants.

Insch scowled at his watch. 'What the hell is taking so long?'

Logan watched him fight his way into a small jar of pills – thick, sausage-like fingers struggling with the child-proof lid – then throw a couple of the small white tablets down. 'Are you OK, sir?'

Insch grimaced and swallowed. 'How long's it going to take you to get to the airport from here?'

'Depends if the Drive's busy: hour, hour and a half?'

'There's a Chief Constable Faulds coming in on the BMI red-eye. I want you to pick him up and bring him back here.'

'Can we not just send one of the uniforms? I'm—'

'No, I want *you* to do it.'

'I should be helping organize the search, not playing taxi driver!'

'I said NO!' Insch turned on him, voice loud enough to make the car windows rattle. 'Faulds is a slimy tosser – a two-faced, backstabbing bastard – but he's a Chief Constable, so everyone scurries round after him like he's the bloody Messiah. I do *not* want some idiot PC in the car with him telling tales out of school.'

'But—'

'No. No buts. You go pick him up and you don't tell him any more than he needs to know. And with any luck we'll have this whole thing wrapped up before he even gets here.'

Anderson Drive stretched across the city: from a horrible roundabout at Garthdee to an even more horrible one at the other end. Half past seven and Logan was stuck in the middle of a snaking ribbon of scarlet tail-lights shuffling their way towards the Haudagain roundabout. Dawn was little more than a pale yellow smear, its faint light making no difference to the thick pall of grey cloud that loomed over the city.

Some halfwit had broken the car's stereo, so all he had to listen to was the clack and yammer of the police radio – mostly people hustling to and fro, trying to keep out of DI Insch's way as 'Operation Cleaver' was thrown together. The fat git had been a pain in the backside ever since he'd started on that stupid diet. Eighteen months of tiptoeing about, trying not to set the man off on one of his legendary rants.

'*This is Alpha Nine One, we are in position, over.*'

It sounded as if they were ready to go.

'*Alpha Three Two, in position.*'

'*Aye, 'is is Alpha Mike Seven, we're a' set tae go too. Just gie the word.*'

Logan should have been with them, kicking down doors and taking names, not babysitting some tosser from Birmingham.

By the time he was leaving the city limits a light drizzle had started to fall, speckling the windscreen with a thin, wet fog, making the tail-lights of the taxi in front glow like volcanic embers as DI Insch gave his motivational speech.

'*Listen up: I want this done by the numbers, understand? Anyone steps out of line, I'll tear their balls off and shove them up their arse – do I make myself clear?*'

No one was daft enough to answer that one.

'*Right. All units, in five, four, three, two . . . GO! GO! GO!*'

And then there was shouting. The sound of a door being battered off its hinges. Bangs. Thumps . . .

Logan turned the radio off, sat in the long line of traffic waiting to turn towards Aberdeen airport, and sulked.

The airport was busy this morning: the queue for security backed up the length of the building – nearly out the front door – business commuters and holidaymakers nervously checking their watches; clutching their boarding passes; worrying about missing their planes while the tannoy droned on about not leaving baggage unattended.

The BD672 was supposed to have landed eight minutes ago, but there was still no sign of anyone getting off the thing. Logan stood on the concourse, next to the twee tartan gift shop, holding up a sheet of paper with 'CC FAULDS' scribbled on it in big biro capitals.

Finally the doors at the far end opened and the passengers on the 07:05 flight from London Heathrow staggered out.

Logan didn't think Faulds would be too hard to spot, he was a Chief Constable after all. He'd be in full dress uniform – hoping it would let him cut through security and get extra packets of peanuts on the plane – with some obsequious Chief Superintendent in tow to carry his bags and tell him how clever and witty he was.

So it came as something of a surprise when a gangly man in jeans, finger-tip, length black leather jacket, Hawaiian shirt, shark's tooth necklace, and a little salt-and-pepper goatee beard stopped, tapped the sign in Logan's hands and said, 'I'm Faulds. You must be . . . ?'

'Er . . . DS McRae, sir.'

Was that an earring? It was: Chief Constable Faulds had a diamond earring twinkling away in his left ear.

Faulds stuck out his hand. 'I take it DI Insch sent you?' The accent wasn't marked, just a hint of Brummie under the received pronunciation.

'Yes, sir.'

'So let me guess: you're not to tell me anything, and basically keep me out of the way. Yeah?'

'No, sir. I'm just to give you a lift into town.'

'Uh-huh. And that needed a detective sergeant?' Faulds watched Logan wriggle for a moment then laughed. 'Don't worry: I used to do the same thing when top brass descended on me from other divisions. Last thing you want is some desk-jockey coming in and telling you how to run your investigation.'

'Ah . . . OK . . . The car's—'

'Do you have a first name, Sergeant, or would that spoil your air of mystery?'

'Logan, sir.' He moved to pick up the Chief Constable's bag, but Faulds waved him away.

'I'm not a senior citizen yet, Logan.'

They crawled back into Aberdeen through the rush-hour, with Faulds on the phone, drawing Logan into a strange three-way conversation about the body parts they'd found the previous night.

'What? Of course it's raining: it's Aberdeen. ... No, no I don't think so, hold on ... ' The Chief Constable stuck his hand over the mouthpiece. 'Do you have an ID for any of the victims?'

'Not yet, we—'

'Not gone through the missing persons' database, or the DNA records?'

'We only just found the remains, sir. They're still frozen solid. The pathologist—'

And Faulds was back on the phone again. 'No, they've not done the DNA yet. ... I know. ... You heard? ... Yes. That's what I thought.' Back to Logan again. 'You don't need to defrost the whole thing – the sample you need for a DNA test should be small enough to come up to temperature in seconds. I'd better have a word with this pathologist of yours when we get in.'

'Actually, sir, that might not be—'

But Faulds was back on the phone again. 'Uh-huh ... I think you're right ... Did he?' Laughter. 'Silly sod ... '

He'd hung up by the time Logan was fighting through the long queue that trailed back from the Haudagain roundabout. Two lanes packed solid with cars and a bus lane full of orange cones. Faulds looked around at the collection of shiny new vehicles full of bored-looking people investigating the insides of their noses, while the drizzle drifted down. 'Is this going to take long, Logan?'

'Probably, sir. Apparently this is the worst roundabout in the country. Been questions raised about it in the Scottish Parliament.'

Faulds smiled. 'About a roundabout? You whacky Jocks: and they said devolution wouldn't work.'

'They estimate it costs the local economy about thirty million a year. *Sir.*'

'Thirty million, eh? That's a lot of deep-fried haggis pies.'

Logan bit his tongue. Calling the Chief Constable a condescending wanker probably wasn't the best career move.

They sat in uncomfortable silence, just the squeak of the windscreen wipers interrupting the stop-go of the motor as Logan inched the car forward. At least the bloody roundabout was in sight now.

And then Faulds burst out laughing. 'You are *so* easy to wind up!' He settled back in his seat. 'Come on then, I know you're dying to ask.'

'Sir?'

Faulds just smiled at him.

'Well … I was …' Logan snuck a glance at his passenger: the clothes, the earring. 'You're not exactly what I expected, sir.'

'You heard the words "Chief Constable" and you thought: doddery old fart with no sense of humour, who dresses up like a tailor's dummy because he's got an embarrassingly small penis and truncheon envy.'

'Actually, I was wondering why someone as senior as you would come all the way up here to sit in on a local murder enquiry.'

'Were you now?'

'Yes, sir.' Logan accelerated into the maelstrom of traffic, swung round the roundabout – trying not to get squashed by the articulated lorry heading straight for them – and finally they were on North Anderson Drive. Halleluiah! He put his foot down, overtaking a doddering old biddie in a clapped-out Mercedes. 'I mean, why not send a DI, or a Superintendent?'

There was a pause. 'Well, Logan, there are some things you just can't delegate.' He checked his watch. 'This raid DI Insch is on?'

'That's where we're going now.'

'Excellent.' Faulds pulled out his phone again and started dialling. 'Don't mind me, just got a couple of calls to make, we— Fiona? . . . Fiona, it's Mark: Mark Faulds . . . course I do, darling . . . '

They abandoned the pool car down a little side road and hurried out into the drizzle.

'You know,' said Faulds as they crossed at the traffic lights outside Country Ways, collars up and heads down, 'I've been to Aberdeen about a dozen times, and it's always sodding raining.'

'We do our best.'

'You buggers must be born with webbed feet.'

'Only the ones from Ellon, sir.'

Holburn Street had been brought to a virtual standstill – two uniformed officers pretending to be traffic lights as they funnelled the backed-up traffic down one side of the road. The butcher's shop had been hidden behind a cordon of eight-foot-high white plastic screens that reached out into the middle of the street.

A BBC outside broadcast van was parked on the double yellow lines just down from the scene, a woman with a pony tail, an umbrella, and a strange orange tan trying to convince a traffic warden not to give the van a ticket. There was a strobe-light flicker of flash photography and shouted questions as Logan and Faulds ducked under the blue-and-white Police tape, then they were through and behind the wall of plastic sheeting.

The IB's filthy Transit van was parked inside the cordon, its back doors open while someone rummaged about inside for SOC suits for Logan and the Chief Constable.

Inside, the shop walls were peppered with recipe cards hung at jaunty angles: goulash, rib roast, minty lamb kebabs... A deli section and a mini greengrocer's sat opposite an empty glass-fronted counter festooned with colourful stickers. The place was full of people in white paper oversuits and the smell of meat.

They found DI Insch in the cold store through the back, with a pair of IB technicians and Isobel, examining yet more chunks of meat.

Faulds took one look at the inspector in his bulging SOC outfit and said, 'Good God, David, you're huge!' He stuck out his hand to shake, but Insch just looked at it. 'Yes, well...' Faulds reached up and adjusted his suit's hood, as if that was what he'd meant to do in the first place. 'Have you picked up Wiseman yet?'

Insch scowled. 'Kicked his door down at seven forty-five this morning. He wasn't there.'

'You let him *escape*?'

'No I bloody didn't: I had an unmarked car sitting outside his house from the moment we found the remains down the docks. He never went home, OK?'

'Oh God...' Faulds closed his eyes and swore quietly. 'OK, right, fair enough, too late to worry about that now.' Sigh. 'So what are we looking at here?'

'That.' Insch pointed at the far corner of the cold store, where Isobel was examining a cut of meat hanging from a hook. It was about two foot long, seven inches wide: the flesh a dark rose colour, the fat a golden yellow, the surface punctuated by pale bones. No skin.

'Loin of pork?' asked Faulds, inching forwards.

'Close: long pig.' Isobel stood, rubbing her latex-gloved hands down the front of her coveralls. 'The meat's darker than pork, more like veal – definitely human. The ribs have been severed halfway down their length, but the shape's unmistakable.'

The Chief Constable thought about it for a moment, then asked, 'Care to hazard a time of death?'

Isobel stared at him. 'And you are?'

Faulds turned the full power of his smile on her. 'Mark Faulds, West Midlands Police. DI Insch asked me to come up and take a look at the case.'

Which sounded incredibly unlikely to Logan: Insch wouldn't ask for help if his crotch was on fire. From the look on her face, Isobel didn't believe it either.

'I don't know what kind of pathologists you're used to dealing with down there, *Mr* Faulds, but in Aberdeen we don't rush to conclusions before we've carried out the post mortem.' She went back to her slab of meat, muttering, 'God save us from bloody policemen, think we're all clairvoyant . . .'

'I see.' Faulds winked at Logan, whispering, 'I love a challenge.' He cleared his throat. 'Actually it's "Chief Constable", not "mister".' If he expected that to impress Isobel, he was in for a disappointment. She didn't even pause, just unhooked the chunk of meat and slipped it into a large evidence bag.

'Right,' she handed it to one of the IB technicians, 'I want every piece of meat in here taken down to the mortuary. Mince, sausages, everything.' She snapped off her gloves then nodded at Insch. 'Inspector, a word please.'

Faulds watched them march out of the cold room. 'Is she usually that welcoming?'

Logan smiled. 'No, sir. She must like you: normally she's a lot worse.'

The shop's owner – the eponymous Mr McFarlane – lived in a large flat directly above the butcher's, so it hadn't exactly taken Operation Cleaver long to track him down. He was a chunky blob with a worried expression, thinning hair, a red-veined nose, and bags under his eyes. He'd clarted himself in aftershave, but it still wasn't enough to cover the smell of stale sweat and last night's alcohol.

McFarlane sat behind the desk in a little office at the back of the shop, watching as an IB technician dismantled a yellow-grey computer and stuck it in an evidence crate.

'I . . . I don't understand,' McFarlane said, looking around with watery pink eyes, 'we're supposed to be open at nine . . . '

Insch leaned over the desk, looming over the butcher. 'Do you have any idea what they do to people like you in prison?'

McFarlane flinched as if he'd been slapped. 'I . . . But I've not done anything!'

'Then why have you got a slab of human flesh HANGING IN YOUR FRIDGE?'

'I didn't know! I didn't! It wasn't me! I never did anything, I've not even had a parking ticket, I'm law-abiding citizen, I do barbeques for charity, I don't even overcharge people! I've not—'

'You sold human remains to Thompson's Cash And Carry. *They* sold it on to catering companies.'

'Oh God . . . ' McFarlane had gone a deathly shade of white. 'But—'

'PEOPLE HAVE BEEN EATING IT!'

'David,' Faulds laid a hand on Insch's arm. 'It might help if you let the poor man complete a sentence.'

The Chief Constable perched himself on the edge of the desk, SOC oversuit rustling as he moved. 'You see, Mr McFarlane, you own a butcher's shop that sells chunks of dead bodies. Can you see why we might have a bit of a problem with that?'

'I didn't know!'

'Uh-huh . . . Mr McFarlane, you're a professional butcher, yes?'

The man nodded, setting his jowls wobbling, and Faulds gave him an encouraging smile. 'And you expect us to believe you can't tell the difference between pork and people?'

'I ... I ... I don't do a lot of the actual butchery anymore ...' He held up his trembling hands. 'Can't hold a knife still.'

'I see.'

Insch placed a massive paw on the desk. 'You don't remember me, do you, Mr McFarlane?'

'What?' He frowned. 'No. What are you—'

'Twenty years ago. Three people hacked up and fed—'

'Oh, no!' McFarlane clamped one of his quivering hands over his mouth. 'Not ... I'm not! I never did anything! I...' His frantic eyes locked onto Faulds. 'I never! It's not me! Tell him it's not me!'

'Where's Ken Wiseman?'

'Oh God, this isn't happening, not again...'

'WHERE – IS – HE?'

And suddenly all the colour rushed back into McFarlane's face. 'I don't know! And even if I did, I wouldn't tell you.' The butcher clambered to his feet. 'I remember you now, you and that bastard ... what was it...? Brooks! Ken never did anything, you fitted him up!'

'Where is he?'

Logan listened to Faulds and Insch playing Bad Cop, Worse Cop for a while, then let his attention wander round the little office. A couple of empty display stands were piled in the corner, next to a stack of dusty wicker picnic hampers; two filing cabinets beneath a barred window – Logan poked through one of them, keeping an ear on the conversation behind him.

Insch: 'Tell me where the bastard is.'

McFarlane: 'I've no idea, I haven't seen Ken in years.'

Insch: 'Bollocks.'

The filing cabinet was full of accounts, bills, payslips – nothing really jumped out. Logan pulled a ledger marked 'Overtime' from the drawer.

Faulds: 'You have to see it from our point of view—'

Insch again: '—going to send you down for a long, long—'

Faulds: 'Better if you just tell us everything you know—'

McFarlane: 'But I don't know anything!'

The ledger was nearly indecipherable, page after page of dates, hours, payments, and names in the butcher's trembling scrawl. Logan skipped to the most recent entries.

Insch: '—people like you in Peterhead Prison, with the—'

'Sir!' Logan cut across the inspector, and there was an ominous silence as Insch turned to glare at him. Logan held out the ledger. 'Last page. Third name from the bottom.'

Insch snatched it off him and read, his brow furrowed, lips slowly twitching into a smile. 'Well, well, well.'

Faulds: 'What?'

The inspector slammed the book down on the desktop, then tapped the page with a fat finger. 'Thought you said you'd not seen Ken Wiseman for years.'

McFarlane wouldn't look at the book. 'I ... I haven't.'

'Then why does this say he did two hours overtime, day before yesterday?'

3

There was a pause, and then a voice from the doorway said, 'Sorry guys, I ran out of tape. Any chance we could do that last bit again?' It was Alec, standing in the doorway with his HDV camera.

Insch rolled his eyes, sighed, then asked, 'From where?'

'Finding the book.'

Faulds looked confused, until Logan introduced the cameraman. 'He's from the BBC, they're doing one of those observational documentaries: *Granite City 999*. Going out next summer.'

'Ah . . . ' Faulds ran a hand through his hair, then snapped on the same smile he'd tried with the pathologist. 'Chief Constable Mark Faulds, West Midlands Police. Believe it or not I used to be on telly when I was younger. It was a children's show, sort of William Tell meets *The Muppets* only more—'

'Can we get on with this please?' said Insch.

'I was only—'

'McRae,' Insch handed the book back to Logan and told him to put it in the filing cabinet and find it again.

Logan groaned. 'But we're in the middle of—'

'Sergeant, this is a key discovery in the case: you're going to be a hero on national television. Now put the bloody book back and remember to act all surprised when you find it!'

'You know,' Faulds said, 'if you feel uncomfortable faking it, Logan, I'm sure DI Insch, or myself would be happy to do it for you. We—'

'No. DS McRae found the thing: he should be the one getting the credit for it.'

'Oh, well, of course ... I never meant that we'd take the credit for his hard work, I just thought ... if he wasn't comfortable—'

'He's comfortable. Aren't you, Sergeant.' It wasn't a question.

'Yes, sir.' Logan stuck the overtime ledger back in the filing cabinet, waited for Alec to shout 'ACTION!', then did the whole thing again.

'Terrific!' The cameraman gave them the thumbs up when they were done. 'Now all I need is for someone to explain who this Wiseman bloke is and we've got a great scene. Just try not to make it too expositiony, OK? I want it to look nice and natural.'

'Of course you know what this means?' said Insch, as McFarlane was stuffed into the back of a patrol car with a blanket over his head.

Faulds nodded. 'We've got a chance to do it properly this time.'

Two constables pulled back the barrier and the patrol car drove out into a barrage of flash photography and shouted questions.

'We did it properly *last* time.'

'Then why did it get thrown out on appeal?'

The inspector sighed. 'Because the jury were idiots. McRae!'

Logan held up a hand, mobile phone clamped to his ear, listening to Alpha Seven Two reporting back on their search of Wiseman's street. 'OK, yeah, thanks.' He hung up. 'Couple of neighbours think they saw Wiseman going out last night around ten. Not seen him since. They say he stays out pretty regularly.'

Insch swore. 'I want every uniform out there looking for him. Roadblocks on all major routes out of Aberdeen. Get onto the port, the bus station, railway and the airport. Search his house – I want a recent photo, circulate it. Posters up in all the usual places. Send out a notice to every police force in the UK.'

Logan groaned. 'But it's nearly eleven; I've been on duty since two yesterday afternoon!'

'Eleven?' Insch peered at his watch, frowned, rubbed a fat hand over his face, and swore again. 'Post mortem starts in three minutes.' He turned and marched off towards the barricade, peeling off his SOC suit and thrusting it into the arms of a spotty-faced PC.

Faulds watched him go, then placed a hand on Logan's shoulder and gave it a reassuring squeeze. 'You did well there, Sergeant. Good work.'

'Er ... thanks.' Logan shifted out of range, just in case the Chief Constable went in for a teambuilding hug. 'How come McFarlane's so upset about this Wiseman bloke?'

'"This Wiseman bloke"?' Faulds shook his head. 'Didn't they teach you anything in school? Andrew McFarlane was married to Ken Wiseman's sister when all this happened first time round. Which is why he's not too keen on your DI Insch.'

Logan tried to stifle a yawn, but it ripped free anyway. 'God ... Right, search teams ...'

Faulds did the shoulder squeezing thing again. 'Delegate. Pass that lot onto someone else and go get some sleep. You're no use to Insch, or anyone else if you can't function.' He smiled. 'Now if you'll excuse me, I think I'll nip along to that PM and take another crack at your lady pathologist friend.'

Logan didn't have the heart to tell him he was wasting his time.

4

INTERIOR: *a cramped office. Two figures out of focus in the background, one emptying a filing cabinet. Chief Constable Faulds stands centre shot wearing a white SOC suit.*

TITLE: *Chief Constable Mark Faulds – West Midlands Police*

FAULDS: There were corpses all over the country: London, Birmingham, Glasgow, even Dublin. It was like nothing we'd ever seen. He'd break into the victim's houses and butcher them. And I don't mean hack them up, I mean he'd take them apart, turn them into joints of meat. And there was never any clues ... should that be "there *were* never any clues"?

VOICEOVER: *Whatever you're comfortable with.*

FAULDS: Feels strange doing this without a script.

VOICEOVER: *If you're worried about it, I'm sure DI Insch can—*

FAULDS: No, no. Used to do this all the time when I was young. Like riding a bike ... OK, let's take it from "joints of meat". [gives himself a small shake] Every time he struck the papers would give him a new name: the Birmingham Butcher, the Clydeside Ripper. It wasn't till they found Ian and Sharon McLaughlin's remains that he finally got his true name: the Flesher.

[pause]

Does that sound too melodramatic? It does, doesn't it? Shit... Sorry, I'll start again.

[clears throat]

There were cases all over the country...

The room smelt of Pot Noodles. It was a small office at the back of FHQ, half-heartedly converted into a makeshift editing suite. Logan stifled a yawn and gazed out of the tiny window. It wasn't much of a view – just a small square of waterlogged car park and the stairs down to the mortuary. You couldn't even see the sky from here.

He'd managed to grab a couple of hours sleep back at the flat, all alone in a cold and empty bed. The place just wasn't the same without Jackie.

There was a strangled *vwipping* noise as Alec rewound the tape and then Faulds' voice crackled out of the TV monitor: '*Shit ... Sorry, I'll start again.*'

Alec hit pause, scribbled something down on his notepad, then shovelled another forkful of rehydrated noodles into his mouth. 'Mmmph, mmmph, mmm?'

Logan turned away from the window. 'You've got juice all down your chin, and I can't understand a word.'

Alec chewed, swallowed, then went in for another forkload. 'I said, "do you want to see the press conference?"'

'Not really.'

'No?' Alec tapped a couple of buttons on his bizarrely coloured editing keyboard and Faulds' face was replaced by a crowded room full of journalists. DI Insch, one of the media officers, and Aberdeen's very own Chief Constable were sitting at the front of the room, fielding questions like, '*Why was Ken Wiseman ever released?*', '*How many people has the Flesher killed?*', '*Why didn't Grampian Police make a stronger case against Wiseman in 1990?*' and that perennial favourite, '*Will there be a public enquiry?*'

The camera panned to focus on DI Insch's big pink head. He did *not* look happy.

Alec pointed at the screen with his fork. 'Look at the expression on his face. Enough to give you nightmares.'

'Welcome to my world.'

'He always been a grumpy fat bastard?' Alec scraped out the last of the noodles, then upended the plastic container into his mouth, sooking out the juice.

'I'm not answering that on the grounds he'd have my balls if he found out.'

'Is it just me,' said Alec, 'or does Insch have a thing for bollocks? Every time he threatens anyone it involves their testicles.' The cameraman dropped his empty Pot Noodle carton in the bin. 'Just between you and me, I think he might be a little repressed.'

'Yeah, you tell him that. I'm sure he'll love to hear it.'

'Spoke to my Executive Producer this morning: they're upping my budget. Couple of extra camera crew, more editing time. Think we might even get David Jason to do the voiceover.'

'You must be so proud.'

Alec sighed. 'You're a right ray of bloody sunshine today.'

'So would you be – I've got to go tell Insch we've no idea where Ken Wiseman is.'

There were times when living in Fittie was a pain in the backside. Yes it was all quaint and historical – a tiny seventeenth-century fishing village at the mouth of Aberdeen harbour, the little granite homes arranged around three small squares, facing inwards. Huddling together for warmth. A little slice of history, surrounded by warehouses and mud tanks on two sides, the harbour on the third, and the North Sea on the fourth. Beautiful . . . But not being able to park anywhere near the front door was an absolute sod. Grumbling, Heather lowered her bulging plastic bags to the cobbled street and tried to rub some feeling back into her hands. She *should* get herself a bike, one of those little-old-lady ones with the basket on the front. Then she could just cycle up to the supermarket and kill two birds with one stone: get the shopping done, and get rid of some of this bloody baby fat. If you were still allowed to call it baby fat *three years* after giving birth.

She rummaged around inside one of the bags and came out with a bar of Dairy Milk, taking a big bite out of the chocolate and chewing unhappily.

Get a bike and go to Weight Watchers. Maybe that would stop her bloody mother banging on about how fat she looked every time the old bag came to visit. Heather picked up the shopping again.

Tonight she was going to treat herself to a bottle of wine and sod the antidepressants. Maybe there'd even be something good on the telly?

A loud shout sounded somewhere back along the beach, and she sighed. Stupid kids getting into stupid fights over who had the stupidest car. Out Bouley bashing: racing up and down the Beach Boulevard at all hours, in the souped-up hatch-backs their mummies and daddies bought for them. Like chimpanzees marking their territory to the constant back-ground *bmm-tshhhh, bmm-tshhhh, bmm-tshhhh* of their stupid car stereos. And there was no point complaining to the bloody police: dispersal zone her arse . . .

God, twenty-five and she was already middle-aged. Wasn't so long ago that she'd been the one out Bouley bashing with her girlfriends, and now look at her: whinging on about loud music and dangerous driving. That was what having a three-year-old did for you. Knackered all the time with no sex-life. Looking forward to *Celebrity X-Factor* on the TV.

One more pause to put the bags down – and then she was outside the front door, rummaging through her cavernous rubbish-tip of a handbag for the house keys.

Justin's pumpkin was sitting on the windowsill, a tealight flickering between the pointy teeth. Of course, she'd done the actual carving, but he'd drawn the face on in blue biro, his tongue sticking out the side of his mouth in concentration.

Strange how one little person could bring so much joy, and so much misery, into the world...

One more bite of chocolate then she hid the bar away – not wanting Duncan to know she'd been naughty – and let herself into the house.

'Duncan?'

No answer, but she could hear the telly on in the kitchen. Maybe he was making tea for a change?

'Duncan, can you give me a hand with these bags? Sodding things weigh a ton.' She dumped them in the hall and closed the front door behind her. 'You'll never guess who I ran into in Asda: Gillian. You remember? The one who married that guy from the radio and went off to live in Edinburgh?'

Heather shucked off her coat and hung it up, pausing to examine the mess that stared back at her from the mirror. 'Well, he only upped and left her for that bloke who used to do the weather on STV. *And* she's got three kids!'

She grabbed one of the carrier bags and wandered through into the kitchen. 'Talk about overcompensating . . . '

Heather dropped the bag. It hit the deck with a clattering thud, tins of Cock-a-Leekie rolling out across the tiles.

Duncan was on the floor, slumped back against the kitchen cabinets, face bruised and bloody, mouth hanging open, dark crusts of red around his lips and nostrils.

'Oh God, Duncan!' She ran to him, grabbed his shoulders and shook. 'Duncan, what did you do?'

His hands were curled in his lap, the wrists held together with cable-ties.

'Duncan? Duncan: where's Justin? DUNCAN! —'

Something slammed into the side of her head and she sprawled across the tiled floor. Someone was in the house! Another blow to the ribs. Heather dragged her hands up, covering her head as a boot connected with the small of her back.

40

She tried to scream, but no sound came out. Pain stabbed through her head as someone grabbed a handful of her hair and dragged her backwards and—

THUMP – her head battered into the kitchen cupboards. Blood on the handle: she could see it glinting in the spotlights as her head smashed against the cupboard again. The room spun.

Warm.

She spiralled backwards, teeth rattling as her head connected with the tiled floor. Justin... Her little boy was upstairs... She'd bought Ready Brek for his breakfast. Justin liked Ready Brek.

CRACK. And her head was bounced off the floor again.

Justin... A spark went off in the middle of her head. JUSTIN! She had to save Justin! She had to get up right now and—

Black.

—right now. GET UP! She struggled and something heavy landed on her chest. Focus! Get up! Justin needs—

Hands wrapped round her throat and squeezed. She tried to fight back, to pull the hands away, but they were too strong. They—

Black.

—Eyes, go for the eyes! She clawed at her killer's face, but it was smooth, hard. The eyes just holes into nothingness. The thing had no eyes! The thing—

Black.

—NO! Justin needed her! Heather flung a hand out, fumbling across the terracotta tiles. Nothing. Nothing. Nothing. Tin! A tin of soup! She grabbed it and swung with all her might.

But her fingers wouldn't work. The can barely moved.

It rolled off quietly to lie beside Duncan's foot.

The world got darker, and darker, and darker, and—

Black...

...ETITION TIME

of Mackie's Ice-cream ■ A weekend break for two in P

...EVIL

Potty for Potter...

News in ...

...ATH W...

WRONG WITH THE SCOTTISH

...E F...

...eman, pictured before his trial in 1990

...iller Strikes Again as Cannibal Terror Returns to Aberdeen

THE PARENTS of Peter (32) and Mary Collier (35) launched a candle-lit vigil last night outside the headquarters of Strathclyde Police.

"It's been four months," said Peter's mother, "we're all very worried about them. They are a loving and devoted couple, and they wouldn't not call for this long.

Peter and Mary went missing while on holiday in the Lake District.

Mary's father said, "We want anyone who's seen them to get in touch with the police. We just want to know that they're all right."

Strathclyde Police issued a statement saying that enquiries had so far yielded no results, but that they remained hopeful.

EXCLUSIVE
By Colin Miller
C.Miller@Aberdeen-Examiner.com

HISTORY has a nasty habit of repeating itself. Twenty years ago Aberdeen was rocked by the discovery of human remains in a small, disused butcher's shop on Palmerston Road. And yesterday it happened again.

Customers and staff at McFarlane's on Holburn Street were shocked to find that police had uncovered a grisly cache of body parts.

Speaking to the P&J, part-time butcher's assistant Simon Patterson said, "We had no idea anything like this was going on. It's come as a horrible surprise."

More surprising was the fact that Ken Wiseman, arrested in

tip-off and later convicted of the murders of Ian and Sharon McLaughlin, was working at McFarlane's butcher shop and had been for a number of years.

Although suspected of committing up to 15 other killings in Glasgow, Dublin, B... London and Newcas... were unable to prove a...

Sentencing Wiser... imprisonment, She... Hodgson described t... "the most despicabl... been my displeasur... [Wiseman] are a ... heartless man, wh... mercy and no remo...

A high court ... overturned the c... "significant short... investigative proc... honesty". But t... was implicated ... fellow inmate a... further 15 years

'good behaviour'.

Although Police refused to comment on Wiseman's guilt, his disappearance following the discovery yesterday morning at McFarlane's has drawn considerable comment from the local community.

Nationwide hunt for 'the Flesher'

POLICE forces up and down the country were put on alert yesterday looking for Ken Wiseman (46).

Wiseman was found guilty in 1990 of a number of gruesome murders across the UK, but later had his conviction overturned on appeal.

Police sources warned that Wiseman was considered armed and dangerous and should not be approached

5

DI Insch looked like an over-inflated marshmallow in his white SOC oversuit. He pretty much filled the tiny lounge on his own, leaving Faulds to perch on the edge of a creaky sofa, while the Identification Bureau finished up in the kitchen. It was only a tiny house in Fittie, but it was stuffed with police photographers, IB technicians, and fingerprint specialists – turning a crime scene into a disaster area.

Logan dug out his notebook. 'Door-to-door turned up nothing – no one saw anyone coming or going from the house last night. Closest we've got are the next-door neighbours: they heard the kid, Justin, crying from about three o'clock this morning. When he hadn't stopped by noon they tried the doorbell. No reply. They've got a key in case of emergencies so they let themselves in . . . ' Logan's gaze drifted past the inspector's bulk to the blood-spattered kitchen. 'No sign of Mr or Mrs Inglis, but Justin was upstairs in his room. He'd barricaded himself in with a rocking chair and his toy box.'

Faulds picked a silver photo frame off the mantelpiece: mother and child grinning at the camera, the not-so-golden sands of Aberdeen beach stretching away behind them. 'They didn't hear anything last night?'

'Neighbours say the Inglises weren't exactly the most stable of couples. They'd be OK for a couple of months, then they'd go ballistic at one another. Throw things, screaming rows – usually about money – she put him in hospital once with concussion.'

'Hmm... so we *could* be looking at a domestic here. Fight gets out of hand, someone gets seriously hurt.'

'I've been on to the hospital, no one called Inglis admitted.'

Faulds put the photo back where he'd found it. 'Perhaps she's killed him this time? She needs to get rid of the body, so—'

'Sorry sir, their car's parked about a two-minute walk away. The boot's still full of shopping and there's no sign of blood.'

'Well...' The Chief Constable thought about it. 'The harbour's at the bottom of the road, isn't it? She could have dragged her husband's body down there and thrown him in.'

Insch didn't quite laugh, but it sounded close. 'And then vanished into thin air, leaving her three-year-old son trapped in his bedroom with no food, water or access to a toilet? The poor wee sod had to crap in his wardrobe. No, this was Wiseman. He knows we're on to him and he's escalating again. Just like last time. The Inglises are already dead.'

Darkness. Darkness and slow, numbing pain. God, everything hurt! Her skull throbbed, her throat was full of burning sand ... cramp rampaged down her left leg and she choked back a scream as the muscle convulsed. Screaming only made her throat feel worse.

She rode it out, face screwed up in agony, then tried to work some life back into her limbs. It wasn't easy, not with her ankles strapped together and her wrists bound behind her back. Curled up on a filthy mattress that stank of fear and piss. And meat.

'Duncan?' it came out as a painful croak. 'Duncan, you've got to stay awake...'

Duncan didn't say anything. He hadn't said anything for at least – what, an hour? Two? It was difficult to tell in the foetid darkness. 'Duncan, you've got a concussion: you have to stay awake!'

They were going to die. They were going to die in the stink and the black and no one would ever find them... Heather blinked hard. Tears weren't going to help anyone. She had to get out of here. Had to save Justin. Had to find and save her son. And tears weren't going to help.

But she cried anyway.

INTERIOR: *small house in Aberdeen, festooned with ornaments. Two men in the background wearing white SOC coveralls dust for prints.*

TITLE: *Chief Constable Mark Faulds – West Midlands Police*

VOICEOVER: *So what do you think the chances are of finding them alive?*

FAULDS: Well, obviously we have to hope, but the reality of the situation is that killers like Wiseman... I'm allowed to call him a killer on television, aren't I?

VOICEOVER: *I think he was acquitted wasn't he?*

FAULDS: Yes, but that doesn't really mean anything, does it? Let out on appeal because of a technicality isn't the same as being found not guilty. And he was given another fifteen years for beating that rapist to death in the prison showers.

VOICEOVER: *Yeah, but probably better safe than sorry. Or we can film two versions: one where you name Wiseman, one where we just say 'The Flesher'. How about that?*

FAULDS: OK. Ahem. [coughs] The reality of the situation is that serial killers in this kind of situation ... hold on, I said situation twice. Can we start over?

Logan and Insch stood in the kitchen, listening to Faulds making a mess of his third take. The inspector shook his head, then closed the door, saying, 'Bloody amateurs...'

The IB had left the place in a mess, as usual. All the surfaces were covered in a thin film of fingerprint powder – black on the kitchen units, white on the granite worktop. Little yellow tags marked the drops of drying blood, a smeared handprint on a kitchen cabinet, a clump of human hair stuck to a door handle, a broken tooth by the fridge-freezer . . .

'Look at him, can't even get a simple speech to camera right. How the hell was he ever a professional actor? Unbelievable.' Insch shut the door as Faulds launched into yet another take. 'What's he been saying about the case?'

Logan shrugged. 'Not much. We spent the morning in the morgue watching them poke little chunks of meat. And then we dug out the Flesher files from the archives. There's bloody heaps of—'

'What about me?'

'You? . . . er . . . nothing.'

Insch scowled at the ruined kitchen, chewing on the inside of his cheek. Logan could almost hear the Machiavellian wheels turning inside that huge pink head.

'I don't get it:' said Logan, 'if you can't stand Faulds, why did you ask him up here in the first place?'

'Because that was the deal. If you get a Flesher case, you call in the old investigating team – doesn't matter if you want their "help" or not, the useless sods turn up anyway. And lucky old me: Chief Constable Faulds had nothing better to do.' The inspector brooded for a moment, then seemed to come to a decision.'Call Control: get someone going through the CCTV footage. Whoever took the victims used a car, or a truck, or a van. Find it. And you'd better get the press office to set up a conference. Circulate the Inglises' photos. See if anyone saw anything.' He stopped for a moment, staring at a child's drawing of a ghost surrounded by happy skeletons, pinned to the refrigerator.. 'Poor wee sod . . . We'll need to talk to the kid. Find out if he saw— Bloody hell.'

His phone was screeching out 'The Lord High Executioner' from *The Mikado*. Insch pulled the thing out, groaned, then hit the button. 'Hello Gary ... Yes ... Yes I know you did, but— Because it's an ongoing investigation, that's why ... No ...' he rolled his eyes and stomped out of the kitchen, barging past Faulds and the cameraman on his way to the front door.

He slammed it behind him.

Faulds sighed. 'I see his temper's not improved much.'

'Yes ... well, he's under a lot of pressure, sir.'

'He a good governor?'

Logan thought about it. 'He puts a lot of criminals behind bars.'

'Which is a diplomatic way of saying, "utter bastard".'

He couldn't argue with that.

The press conference was not a happy place. As soon as the prepared statement had been read the savaging began: Wiseman was on the loose, people were dying and apparently it was all Grampian Police's fault. The Chief Constable went straight into damage limitation mode, but it didn't take a genius to tell what tomorrow's headlines were going to be like.

When the briefing was finally over, Logan told Insch the good news: 'Social says we're OK to speak to the Inglis kid, but we need to keep it brief.'

'Good. You can—' Insch's phone was ringing again. 'Bloody hell, leave me alone!' He pulled it out and took the call. 'Insch ... Yes, Gary we're sure it's him ... no, we— No. I can't. You *know* I can't, we went over this! ... But ... I don't see what that could—' The fat man sighed. 'Yes, yes I'll try ... I said *I'll try*, Gary. OK.' He hung up and swore.

Logan waited for Insch to explain, but the inspector just stuffed the phone back in his pocket and lumbered off towards the lifts.

It was meant to be a non-threatening environment: the walls painted a cheerful shade of yellow; Monet prints; two comfy sofas; a coffee table; a standard lamp; a widescreen television; and a box of battered plastic toys. But it still managed to be bloody depressing.

Back in the early days people would sneak down here in their breaks to sit on the sofa, drink their coffee, and watch reruns of *Columbo* on the telly. Then one by one they stopped coming, preferring the scarred formica of the canteen to the soft furnishings. There was something about listening to someone sobbing as they tried to tell you about the man who raped them, or the grown-up who made them do dirty things, that really took the 'happy' off a room.

A small boy in pirate-print pyjamas was sitting in the middle of a bright green rug, holding onto a tatty stuffed dog as if his life depended on it, and sneaking glances at the video camera in the corner. A child psychologist slumped on one of the couches, half-heartedly trying to build a house out of Lego. She didn't stop when Logan and Insch entered.

The kid froze.

'Hello,' said Insch, easing his massive bulk down till he was sitting cross-legged on the rug, 'my name's David. What's yours?'

Nothing.

So Insch tried again, 'I'm a policeman.' He pulled a handful of bricks and a little blue Lego man from the box, clicking them together surprisingly quickly for someone with such huge fingers. 'Do you like boats? I'll bet you do, living down in Fittie. Bet you see lots of boats.'

Justin looked up at the dead-fish eye of the camera, then back at Insch and nodded.

'Good,' the inspector smiled, 'I like boats too.' He grabbed another lot of little plastic bricks, a passable fishing trawler taking shape in his hands. 'So, do you want to tell me your name, or shall we call you . . .' Insch thought for a moment. 'Logan? Would you like that?'

The wee boy shook his head.

'Quite right too, it's a poopy name.' said Insch, ignoring the mutters of protest behind him. 'I bet your name's much cooler.'

'Justin.' Barely a whisper. But at least the kid was talking.

And slowly the inspector teased the story out of him: how his daddy had picked him up from day-care, because his mummy was out shopping. They'd had fish fingers and beans and mashed potatoes for tea and done the washing up, then daddy was going to cook something for mummy called 'beef burnt onions'. Then the doorbell went and daddy answered it and someone came in and daddy fell over and hit his head on the coffee table. Then the someone gave Justin a whole packet of Maltesers and sent him to bed. Then the bad thing happened and Justin had to hide in his wardrobe till it got stinky, because his doggie did number twos in there. He held the stuffed dog up so Insch could see how naughty it had been.

'And what did the someone look like?' Insch asked, after telling the dog it shouldn't poop in people's wardrobes.

'He looked like a stripy man with a scary face.'

The inspector produced a sheet of paper, unfolding it to reveal a picture of ex-Prime Minister Margaret Thatcher. 'Is this—'

Justin screamed and hid behind his naughty dog.

'Yeah,' Insch put the picture back in his pocket, 'she has that effect on a lot of people.'

6

The major incident room was too noisy for a meeting, so Insch, Faulds, and the Procurator Fiscal commandeered a small office on the second floor of FHQ, then sent Logan off to get the coffees.

He was halfway up the stairs, making for the canteen, when the voice of doom sounded: 'Where the hell have you been?'

Logan froze, swore quietly, then turned to see DI Steel standing behind him, hands on her hips, face pulled into a scowl. God knows what had happened to her hair, but it sat on top of her wrinkly head like an electrocuted badger. 'I,' said the inspector, shaking a nicotine-stained finger at him, 'have been waiting for that bloody vandalism report for a week now.'

'Ah,' said Logan, 'I've been seconded to this new Flesher investigation. Didn't Insch tell you?'

Steel's scowl got even worse. 'Well that's just sodding perfect. I mean, it's no' like *my* caseload's important is it? No' as long as Fat Boy Insch is happy.' She let loose a string of foul language, then stared at the ceiling for a moment. 'So when, *exactly*, am I going to see my report?'

'They've got me babysitting this Chief Constable from Birmingham, I—'

'I didn't ask for excuses, Sergeant, I asked when you'd have that bloody report finished.'

'This isn't my fault! I'm only—'

'You remembering you're supposed to be in court tomorrow?'

'Of course.' Which was a lie: he'd forgotten all about it. 'I'm probably not even going to get called, though, you know what these indecent exposure cases are—'

'Ten thirty on the dot, Sergeant.' Steel turned and marched off, calling back over her shoulder, 'And don't forget that bloody report!'

Logan waited for her to disappear round the corner before sticking two fingers up in her direction.

Steel's voice echoed through the stairwell: 'I saw that!' Then the doors to the corridor slammed shut and Logan was on his own again.

By the time he got back to the little office, Insch, Faulds and the PF were gathered round a desk, discussing Justin Inglis's statement – the inspector casually doodling glasses and blacking out teeth on his photo of Margaret Thatcher. 'Of course, it's not conclusive,' he said, 'how could it be? The kid's only three, but I'm pretty sure he's telling the truth.' Insch helped himself to one of the mugs on Logan's tray, sniffed it, and wrinkled his nose. 'I asked for a double mochaccino with extra cinnamon and chocolate – what the hell is this?'

'Machine's broken, so everyone's got instant.'

'Typical...'

The PF reached for the vandalized ex-Prime Minister. 'This could still be a copycat.' She held up a hand before Insch could complain. 'Playing Devil's advocate: ever since that damn book came out everyone knows the Flesher wears a butcher's apron and a Margaret Thatcher Halloween mask. On its own it means nothing.'

'It means,' rumbled Insch, 'that Wiseman is up to his old tricks again. We found a package of human meat in the Inglises' freezer for God's sake!'

'That's exactly the kind of thinking that scuppered the original investigation – people leapt to conclusions, didn't keep an open mind, didn't follow procedure. Wiseman would still be in jail if the case had been airtight. I agree that it's highly unlikely this is a copycat, but I want *every* possibility investigated.' She took one of Logan's coffees. 'What do we know about the Inglises?'

'Duncan Inglis works for the Council's Finance Department. He's twenty eight. Got admitted to hospital last year when his wife cracked the toaster off his head. She's twenty five; diagnosed with postnatal depression after the birth of their son, been on medication ever since.'

'Interesting.' The PF took a sip of coffee, shuddered, then put her mug back on the tray. 'So we have a history of violence.'

'We're looking into it.'

'And the butcher, McFarlane?'

'Went up before the Sheriff this morning: remanded in custody, no bail. He's sticking to his story: no idea how all those bits of dead body ended up in his shop, and we're all a bunch of bastards for picking on Wiseman again.'

'My heart bleeds. How many search teams?'

'Three, and roadblocks on all major routes out of Aberdeen. We've got posters up at the train station, harbour, airport, and nearly every bus stop in the city.'

Logan chimed in with a report on the Automatic Number Plate Recognition System: 'No sign of any vehicle he's got access to leaving Aberdeen. And we've warned all the rental places.'

The PF nodded. 'CCTV?'

'Nothing. All the cameras down the beach were pointing the wrong way – big fight outside that new nightclub.'

'Right.' She stood, hoisted her handbag over her shoulder, and made for the door. 'Make sure you catch Wiseman, and *soon*. I don't want anyone else turning up in bite-size chunks.'

Half past eight and Logan was slumped at his desk in the pigsty masquerading as a CID office, trying to work up some enthusiasm for DI Steel's vandalism report. And failing. Somehow it was difficult to care about a bunch of keyed cars and some graffiti in Rosemount when Ken Wiseman was out there turning people into joints of meat.

Stifling a yawn, he printed out all the crime reports and started sticking figures into a spreadsheet. God knew when he'd actually get home tonight. Bloody DI Bloody Steel and her Bloody Report.

'All on your lonesome?'

Logan turned, and there was Doc Fraser looking more like someone's granddad than a pathologist – beige cardigan, glasses, bald head, and hairy ears.

'You want some coffee?'

The pathologist held up a manila folder. 'I won't come in, I've got shingles. Give this to Insch when he gets in tomorrow, will you?'

'Uh-huh.' Logan took the folder and flipped through the contents – sheet after sheet of forms and ID numbers.

'Tell him it's the preliminaries on all those chunks of meat you dug out of the butcher's, cash and carry, and that container.'

'Logan was impressed. 'Already? That's—'

'I wouldn't go getting your hopes up – this is just the indexing. It'll be weeks before we get the proper results in.' The pathologist sighed. 'And don't look at me like that, we've got five hundred and thirty-two individual lumps of meat and they all need to be DNA-tested. Like the bloody EU corpse mountain down there.'

The pathologist reached in under his cardigan and started scratching. 'We're farming out samples to Tayside, Strathclyde,

Lothian and Borders, Highlands, you name it. If they've got DNA-testing facilities they're getting bits...' He trailed off, looking out of the CID window at the bleak, spotlit square of car park. 'We never used to get stuff like this. Back in the good old days it was one or two murders a year, all nice and neat.' Another sigh. 'Anyway ... better get back to it. The Ice Queen may rule the day, but *I* command the children of the night!' He pulled up one corner of his cardigan, pretending it was a cape, then stalked from the room like a hunched, beige Dracula. Who'd really let himself go.

7

Hot white blobs of light picked their way through the trees in the background, then the camera panned round to an over-weight reporter as he told the nation that this was the second night Ken Wiseman remained at large. '... *increased manpower, combing through woods and industrial units all over Aberdeen. Halloween is traditionally a time for trick or treating—*'

'Guising!' Logan shouted at the television. 'In Scotland we go guising, not trick or treating!' He snatched his second tin of beer off the coffee table and drank deep.

'*—but this year the streets of the city are empty, left to the cold and the mist. Because this year, there really is a monster out there—*'

'Oh for God's sake!' Logan excavated the remote control from the sofa's cushions and stabbed the button, hunting through the channels for something decent to watch and coming up empty.

Nothing to help him ignore the little red light on the answering machine.

Another mouthful of beer and the tin was empty. Logan stifled a belch and got to his feet. Should probably get something to eat . . . The little red light blinked at him.

He walked over, and pressed the button.

'*MESSAGE ONE: Hi Logan, it's me . . .* ' Jackie, the words alcohol-slurred and fuzzy. '*I miss you, OK? I do. I miss you . . .* ' He could hear raised voices in the background, a jukebox, a bandit pinging and bleeping to itself. '*Just thought you should know.*' *Beeeeeeep.* And the tape rewound itself.

He pressed the button again.

'*MESSAGE ONE: Hi Logan, it's me . . . I miss you, OK? I do. I miss you . . .* ' Pub noises. '*Just thought you should know.*' *Beeeeeeep.*

RRRRRRRRRRinggggggggggggggg – the flat's doorbell.

'*MESSAGE ONE: Hi Logan, it's me . . . I miss you, OK? I—*' *RRRRRRRRRRinggggggggggggggg.*

'Oh . . . bloody hell. OK, I'm coming.'

There was a short, stocky Glaswegian waiting outside, clutching a couple of plastic bags as a thin drizzle oozed down out of a dirty orange sky. 'Laz, my man! Trick or treat?'

Logan scowled at him. 'Don't you bloody start.'

'Aye, and a happy Christmas to you too. You look like shite, byraway. C'moan, shift over, curry's no' gettin' any warmer here.'

'Colin, I . . .'

But the reporter had already shouldered his way past. Sighing, Logan closed the stairwell door and followed him up. Colin Miller: even dressed casually, the wee man looked like a deranged, muscle-bound clothes model. God alone knew what Isobel saw in him.

'You seen those arseholes on the news, but?' Miller stuck his plastic bags on the kitchen table, then dug into one and tossed a cold bottle of Kingfisher beer in Logan's direction.

Logan caught it just before it hit the kitchen floor. 'Don't you ever ring first?'

'Aye, you're right,' said the wee man, pulling a plastic takeaway container out of the second bag, then stacking another five beside it, topping them off with a bag of poppadoms, 'what was I thinkin'? You could'a had a hot date!'

'Very funny.'

'Ah come on, Laz, lighten up. I've got the evenin' off, She Who Must's catching up on her beauty sleep, her mum's got the wain till tomorrow, an' you're all on yer tod. So: boys' night in!' He rummaged in Logan's cutlery drawer and produced the bottle opener, fumbling the top off his beer with stiff, gloved fingers. 'Get blootered, curry-out from the Nazma, watch some footie on the telly, and break wind to our hearts' content.'

Logan popped the top off his Kingfisher, then helped himself to a poppadom. 'You *do* know I can't talk about the Wiseman case, don't you?'

The reporter froze. 'Wiseman case? Never crossed my mind! I'm no—'

'Oh come off it Colin, you're trying to bribe me into talking about an ongoing investigation with Indian beer from...' Logan checked the label. 'Kent?'

Miller grinned. 'And curry. Don't forget the curry.'

'Fat chance.'

'Oh come on, man! Throw a freelancer a bone, eh? Those BBC bastards've got exclusive access to everythin'.'

'Thought you were going back on staff.'

The reporter shrugged. 'Nah, freelance pays better. Doing a fair chunk for the *Examiner* though.'

'Bet the *Journals* like that.'

'All's fair in love and journalism. Lime pickle?'

'Cupboard above the kettle. Anyway, it's an observational documentary, not a news programme. Not even going to be out till next year.'

'But—'

'*And* it's a pain in the backside. Everywhere you turn someone's sticking a camera up your nose. You try it for a week, see how you like it.'

'Chicken Jalfrezi, Lamb Biryani, Prawn Rogan Josh, or a bit of everything?'

'Everything.' He watched Miller serving up, the reporter's leather gloves struggling with the clear plastic containers. It would have been much easier to just take the gloves off, but Miller was too vain for that.

Logan scowled into his beer. 'I mean they didn't even ask if I wanted to be in it—'

'I get it. Fuck's sake: enough!' He licked a dob of bright red sauce from his leathered thumb. 'Every time I come over here . . . '

'I was only saying—'

'And would it kill you to get some decent cutlery? Izzy carves up deid people with better silverware than this.'

There was a noise in the darkness, like metal scraping on metal. Heather froze, lying on her side on the cold floor.

Count to a hundred.

Silence.

She went back to wriggling along the invisible line of steel bars. It wasn't easy with her hands tied behind her back; the cable-ties round her wrists and ankles dug into the skin as she felt her way to the end wall. There was something square here, a plastic box with a lid . . . Heather retreated when she realised what it was: a chemical toilet – its harsh disinfectant reek overlaid with something altogether less pleasant. The bars stretched all the way across the little metal room, dividing the pitch-black prison in two. Her on one side, Duncan on the other.

'Duncan?' She sounded like a frog, her throat dry and sore. 'Duncan, can you hear me?'

There was some shuffling, then Duncan moaned. Coughed. Hissed in pain.

'Duncan, we need to get out of here!'

A grunt, then his voice, sounding thin and weak. 'I . . . I'm not . . . ' Another cough: wet and rattling. 'Ahhh . . . Jesus . . . ' He was moving: she could hear him struggling along the floor

60

on his side, like a dying caterpillar. Making sounds of pain all the way.

'Duncan, are you OK?'

'I'm so tired . . . ' He coughed again in the darkness, and she heard him spit. Then gurgle. Then swear. And then he was still. Panting in the darkness. Weeping quietly. 'I'm so *tired*, Heather. I . . . I'm . . . '

'You're going to be fine! You hear me?' She was sobbing now, the words burning out of her. 'You hear me Duncan Inglis? You're going to be fine. Stay awake!'

'I love you. I just wanted you to know before . . . '

More ragged breathing.

'Duncan! DUNCAN, WAKE UP!'

Something brushed her hands. 'Duncan?' It was his hair, matted and sticky. 'Duncan you can't leave me. *Please* don't leave me!'

'I'm so sorry . . . ' Sounding far away, even though he was just on the other side of the bars.

'Don't leave me.'

When Miller was gone, and there was nothing left but the smell of old curry and stale beer, Logan stood in the lounge, in the dark.

'MESSAGE ONE: *Hi Logan, it's me . . . I miss you, OK? I do. I miss you . . . '* The swell of background noise as she took another drink. *'Just thought you should know.'* Beeeeeeep.

He hit delete and went to bed.

8

Hanging about in Court One, waiting to be called, wasn't exactly Logan's idea of a good time: an endless procession of Aberdeen's dispossessed, unlucky, or downright stupid, being hauled into the dock to find out if they'd be going home with a fine, or a getting a few weeks free B&B at Her Majesty's Pleasure. In a strange way it was a bit like a dentist's waiting room – unhappy people sitting about waiting for something nasty to happen – only without the ancient copies of *Woman's Realm* and dog-eared *Readers' Digest*s.

At least it was better than humping dusty file boxes up from the archives. And it gave Logan a chance to read some of the old case notes.

By the time Grampian Police arrested him, Ken Wiseman had eighteen notches on his belt – a string of bodies that stretched all the way across the UK. Eighteen people and the most they'd ever found were a few chunks of meat.

Logan flicked through the names and dates. All those deaths...

According to the notes, everyone knew Wiseman was responsible, but couldn't prove it, so in the end they'd had to settle for the only ones they *could* prove: Mr and Mrs McLaughlin, Aberdeen, 1987. And even then—

'Sergeant McRae!'

Logan looked up from his pile of paperwork to find the whole court staring at him. He clambered to his feet, blushing. 'Ah ... yes, sorry Milord ... ' and it sort of went downhill from there.

The light was blinding, streaming in from an open door on the other side of the bars. Heather screwed her face shut, one hand over her eyes for added protection. After all this time in total darkness it was just too painful.

Her head throbbed, her throat ached, she felt dizzy and weak. Her wrists burned where she'd scraped them up and down against the rough edge of the bars, till the cable-ties snapped.

Gradually her eyes got used to the light and the room faded into focus. They were in a small metal space, no bigger than their tiny bedroom back home – the floor red with rust and dried blood... Oh God ... Duncan was dead. She reached through the bars with a trembling hand and stroked his forehead. It was hot, not cold: he was still alive!

She croaked through the bars at him: 'Duncan! Duncan wake up!'

Nothing.

'Duncan! Someone's found us, Duncan! It's going to be all right!'

A shadow blocked the light, then a loud metallic clang rattled the walls.

Heather tried to shout, but her throat was too dry to do much more than whisper, 'My husband needs medical...' There was a figure standing in the doorway: butcher's apron, white Wellington boots, grubby rubber mask, the eyeholes two black voids with nothing human behind them.

'Please,' Heather tried again, 'please, we won't tell anyone! Please, Duncan needs help!'

The man in the butcher's apron stood with his head on one side, watching her cry, the way a cat watches an injured bird.

'Please! I'll do anything you want! PLEASE!' She scrambled to her knees and fumbled at the buttons on her blood-soaked blouse, tears rolling down her cheeks as she exposed her pale body. 'Please don't hurt us . . .'

The Butcher turned and pulled an old tin bath into the room.

Heather knelt there in her grey, mumsy bra. 'Whatever we did, we're sorry!'

He stooped and pulled two lengths of chain out of the bath, and threaded them through a pair of pulleys bolted to the ceiling. Then he dragged Duncan into the middle of the room.

She lunged forwards, hands scrabbling between the bars, clutching at her husband's ankles. Holding on for dear life.

'NO! You can't have him! You can't!'

The Butcher let go and Duncan clattered to the ground. Heather hauled him back towards the bars, screaming at the top of her lungs, 'HELP! HELP! WE'RE IN HERE! SOMEBODY HELP!'

The Butcher grabbed her wrists, yanking her forward and bashing her head into the metal bars. Pain closed her eyes, burning iron filled her nose. Heather opened her mouth to cry out and tasted blood. She tried to break free, but he held her firm . . . and then he let go. She lurched backwards, but something jerked her to a painful halt – there was a fresh set of cable-ties around her wrists, binding them on either side of a rusted metal bar. 'NO!'

She lunged back and forth, ignoring the pain. 'LET HIM GO!'

The Butcher fastened the chains around Duncan's ankles, then pulled – the links rattling through the pulleys as her husband's limp body was hoisted upside-down, dangling over the tin bath. Something flickered in his pale face, and his eyes opened. Confused. 'Heather?'

'Duncan!' She dropped her shoulder and slammed into the bars, too close to get up any real momentum, but enough to make the metal groan.

'Heather...'

This time the whole room shook as she slammed into the bars. 'LET HIM GO!'

The Butcher took a long, green rubber apron from the bucket and pulled it on. Then a pair of elbow-length green rubber gloves.

'Give me back my fucking husband!' BOOM – she threw herself at the bars again, tearing the skin on her naked shoulder.

An axe came out of the bucket, followed by what looked like a torch, or a lightsaber. The last thing was a set of knives. The Butcher selected one and sliced Duncan's clothes off, running the blade up the seams, peeling him like an orange.

And when Duncan had been stripped naked – his pale skin fluorescing in the harsh electric light – the butcher twisted the lightsaber in half, slipped a tiny green cartridge into it, and screwed it back together.

'LET HIM GO!' She slammed into the bars again.

'Heather...'

Click, and the lightsaber was given another small twist. The man grabbed a handful of hair and dragged Duncan's head up.

'Heather ... Heather, I love y—'

He brought the blunt end of the lightsaber down hard, right on the top of Duncan's head. A loud CRACK reverberated round the metal room and Duncan convulsed; a thin plume of blood pulsed from the new hole in his scalp. Heather screamed. The Butcher calmly picked up a thin wire rod and slid it into the little geyser of blood: jerking it in and out, then jamming it so far in that only the wooden handle protruded. Duncan stopped moving.

The Butcher slit Duncan's throat vertically from clavicle to chin, opening his neck. Then the blade disappeared up inside the cut, twisted, and a huge rush of bright scarlet deluged into the tin bath.

Duncan hung naked and still as the grave. Dripping and swaying gently.

Heather sank to her knees and sobbed. She didn't watch the man skin and gut her husband.

9

DI Steel was waiting for Logan when he got back from court. 'Well?'

'Two months.'

'Is that *all*?'

'Sheriff said he'd shown real remorse and didn't present an immediate danger to the public. We were lucky he got banged up at all.'

'Why do we even bother arresting the bastards?' Steel hitched up her trousers. 'Right, I want you to—'

'Scuse me,' DC Rennie staggered to a halt, clutching a dusty cardboard box full of case files. 'Bloody thing weighs a ton . . .'

The inspector stood to one side and Rennie lurched past.

The constable paused. 'You two coming tonight?'

Steel shrugged. 'Ah, why not? Laz can bring his new boyfriend from Birmingham.'

'He's not my boyfriend!'

'That reminds me,' Renne shifted his grip on the box. 'Chief Constable Faulds's been looking for you.'

'Oh aye?' said Steel, 'Well he can kiss my—'

'No, not you: DS McRae. Something about retracing the original investigation.'

Logan closed his eyes. 'Oh God . . .'

Steel slapped him on the back. 'Never mind, Laz, you'll get your reward in heaven. But before you get there I want that vandalism report, or you're going the other way, understand?'

The setting sun made the grey buildings glow peach and gold as Logan locked the pool car and waited for Faulds to finish his anecdote about a seventy-two-year-old prostitute he'd arrested in the middle of Birmingham town centre wearing nothing but a nun's wimple and a surgical truss. Alec the cameraman waited till the Chief Constable got to the punch line, then confirmed the sound levels were perfect.

'Good.' Faulds ran a hand through his hair and looked up at the sparkling granite tenement. Cleared his throat. Marched up to the door.

Logan leaned over and whispered to the cameraman, 'So ... Insch tell you to get lost again?'

Alec pulled a face. 'He's a nightmare. Thought he was going to smack me one this morning. All I did was ask how his diet's going.'

They followed Faulds into the building. It was dark inside: a welcome mat smeared with mud and the faint smell of dog shit; a mountain bike chained to the banisters; a stack of junk mail slowly festering in a dirty puddle on the tiled floor. Faulds started up the stairs.

'Anyway,' said Alec, 'this is going to be great for the Flesher special – revisiting the original case, talking to the witnesses, walking the crime scenes.'

Faulds paused on the first landing, leant on the balustrade and called down to them: 'Something wrong?'

'With you in a second.' Alec lowered his voice. 'Just between you and me: what do you reckon to Faulds, then?'

Logan shrugged. 'He's OK, I suppose. Fancies himself a bit. I was expecting him to be more of an arse, pull rank the whole time ... you know: your average Chief Constable.'

'You remember that Birmingham Bomber case? Well Faulds was the one who—'

'You two asleep down there?'

Logan sighed and started for the stairs. 'Our master's voice.'

Flat six was on the top floor, the door painted dark red with a little brass plaque above the letterbox: 'JAMES MCLAUGHLIN PHD' engraved at the top, 'CERBERUS, MEDUSA & MRS POO' underneath. Logan rang the doorbell.

It was answered two minutes later by a young, bearded man in his pyjamas, dressing gown and slippers. Mid twenties. Cup of tea in one hand, slice of toast in the other. Glasses perched on the end of his nose. He took one look at the three of them standing in the hallway, saw Alec's camera, and said, 'Ten minutes. I get to plug the book twice. It stays in shot the whole time. Agreed?' He stuck the toast in his mouth then offered his hand to seal the deal. There was jam on it.

Logan didn't shake it. 'We're not from the television, Mr McLaughlin.' He dug out his warrant card. 'DS McRae: Grampian Police, this is Chief Constable Faulds: West Midlands. We're here to ask you a few questions about the night your parents disappeared.'

'It was twenty years ago!' McLaughlin rolled his eyes. 'Look, read the book, OK? It's all in there. I can't remember anything else.'

'We'll try not take up too much of your time, sir. It *is* important.'

Sigh. 'OK, OK. You can come in. But watch where you're walking. I'm pretty sure Medusa's been sick, but I haven't found out where yet ...'

James McLaughlin's living room was littered with books. A computer desk sat in the bay window, covered in bits of paper and more books. A typist's chair sat in front of it, a large, grey, furry cat watching them from the seat, master of all it surveyed.

McLaughlin shooed it off. 'Come on Cerberus, that's daddy's chair.'

Logan couldn't see anywhere to sit himself, so he moved a pile of paperbacks from the settee to the floor. 'Sorry if we got you out of bed.'

The man shrugged. 'Nah, you're all right: I was working.' He swept a hand down the front of his pyjamas. 'Standard writers' uniform.'

Faulds picked his way round the room, peering at the framed photographs on the wall. 'I read your book,' he said at last. 'Very good. I especially liked the bit about all the fancy policemen coming up from down south.'

McLaughlin beamed. 'Glad you liked it. It was...' He frowned. 'Detective Superintendent! Thought I recognized you. Jesus, you've not changed much.'

'Chief Constable now. For my sins.' Faulds picked up a little wooden plaque, read the inscription and put it back down again. 'I'm really glad you did something with your life, Jamie. Some people would have curled up in a little ball and never come out again.'

'Yes, well, I was always good at English and my therapist thought writing the whole thing down would be ... well ... *therapeutic*. And now look.' He smiled, indicating the four framed covers on the wall – all bestselling children's books. Aberdeen's answer to J.K. Rowling, only nowhere near as famous. Or rich. 'But you're not here to talk about *Simon and the Goblins*, are you?'

'You've seen the news?'

McLaughlin shuddered and pointed at a copy of the *Daily Mail* sitting on a pile of encyclopaedias – 'CANNIBAL KILLER STILL AT LARGE'. 'Difficult to miss it. Been having nightmares ever since I heard about those body parts down the docks. Last night I dreamt Wiseman came back to finish me off... Took half a bottle of Macallan to make that one go away.' He wrapped his dressing gown around himself, tying the chord tight.

Logan pulled out his notebook, flipping through the pages till he got to the bit about McLaughlin's parents. 'We've been reviewing the old case files. They're a bit vague about what happened before you got to the house.'

Faulds nodded. 'And you don't say much about it in your book either.'

McLaughlin opened his mouth to say something, then changed his mind. He stood. 'Anyone fancy a drink? I've got gin and I've got whisky. Drank all the wine last night . . .'

'Sorry, sir, but we're on duty. Tea would be nice, though.'

'Right, tea it is then.' And he was off into the kitchen.

The Chief Constable stopped on his tour of the living room, selecting a book from a low shelf: *Smoak With Blood – The Hunt For The Flesher*. It had a photo on the front of someone dressed in a butcher's apron and Margaret Thatcher fright mask. Not surprising there wasn't a framed version up on the wall – who wanted to look at the man who killed their parents every day?

By the time McLaughlin returned with the drinks Faulds was reading aloud:

'"For some reason, it's one of my earliest memories – walking through the dark and rain-swept streets with my best friend. Heading back to my house. Hand in hand with a killer. Everything before that is lost to me, as if the first five years of my life never happened. As if I only came into being at that moment. Sparked into existence minutes before the death of my parents . . . "'

McLaughlin blushed. 'Yes, well . . . I was reading a lot of Dickens at the time. Can't believe I wrote anything so pretentious.'

'What happened to Catherine Davidson? She was supposed to be walking you home.'

The young man handed over Logan's tea, then poured himself a large measure of eighteen-year-old Highland Park. 'Wish I knew. When I was writing the book I tried everything:

71

word association, hypnosis, the works. I know it sounds like a load of old wank, but everything before that walk home is a blank. It's like my childhood never happened.' He took a deep drink from his whisky, holding it in his mouth for a thoughtful pause, before swallowing.

'What about your friend: Richard Davidson?'

'Ah, yes ... Richard. We don't talk these days. Last I heard he was in Craiginches doing three years for possession, perjury, and aggravated assault. Like you said, Superintendent: some people never come out again. Wiseman took my parents and my past, he took Richard's mum and his future.' Another mouthful of whisky. 'I don't know which is worse.'

'And then he made you both dinner.'

'Yeah. Findus Crispy Pancakes with fried onions, mashed potatoes and peas. I wanted fish fingers.' A shallow laugh. 'Good isn't it? My mum and dad are being dismembered in the kitchen and I'm whinging about Captain Sodding Birdseye ... I'd never seen so much blood...' The last of McLaughlin's whisky disappeared. 'Who's for another one?'

Rush-hour was in full swing as Logan drove them back to the station – roads packed with nose-to-tail traffic beneath the yellow streetlight. Muttered swearing came from the back seat; Alec checking the messages on his mobile phone. 'Bloody hell, why can no one get anything right? ... Delete ... Don't care ... Delete ... Holy shit!' The cameraman scooted forward, sticking his head between the front seats. 'You're not going to believe this—'

Faulds' mobile phone started playing Phil Collins: 'In The Air Tonight'. 'Hello?'

'I've just got a call from the BBC News Department—'

'Hello?' The Chief Constable stuck one finger in his ear, 'Yes ... No, we'll be right there!'

'—Wiseman's been on the phone.'

Logan took his eyes off the road for a second, then had to slam on the breaks to avoid rear-ending a Porsche. 'You're kidding!'

'Wants to set up an interview, like that Ipswich guy.'

Faulds hung up. 'Any chance you can put your foot down? We've got a briefing to get to. Wiseman's—'

'Been on the phone to the BBC. Yes, sir, Alec was just telling me about it.'

Faulds frowned. 'No. He's grabbed someone else.'

10

'Right, settle down.' There was a sudden stillness in the briefing room. The place was packed with uniformed officers, support staff, and CID. Alec and his mate with the very big camera had set up so one of them could film the crowd while the other one focused on DI Insch, standing at the front of the room, telling everyone about the latest disappearance.

'Valerie Leith.' *Click* and a woman's face filled the projection screen: mid thirties, slightly overweight, brown hair cut in an unflattering bob, pretty green eyes. 'Approximately half four this morning her husband hears a noise downstairs. He goes to investigate and is attacked. By the time he regains consciousness, his wife is missing and the kitchen's covered in blood.'

Click – the cover of James McLaughlin's book appeared, *Smoak With Blood* written in white on a lurid red cover featuring the photo of someone dressed as the Flesher. 'This is who Leith says attacked him.' Insch went for a big dramatic pause. 'This makes William Leith the first person *ever* to survive a confrontation with Wiseman.'

DC Rennie leant over and whispered in Logan's ear: 'What the hell does "smoak" mean when it's at home?'

'No idea. Shut up.'

'Only asking . . .'

Click – and a battered man's face filled the screen, half his head hidden behind a swathe of bandages. 'Thirty-four stitches,' said Insch, 'three units of blood. Leith's now under protective custody at Aberdeen Royal Infirmary – I have no intention of Wiseman coming back and finishing the job.'

Click – Ken Wiseman scowled out from the projection screen. Time and HM Prison Peterhead hadn't been kind: what little hair he had left was close cropped and greying, his goatee more salt than pepper. Big ears, big hands, big all over; overweight, but still powerful with it. A long scar ran from the top left of his forehead, through his right eyebrow and down to the middle of his cheek, pulling the eyelid out of shape. Not a pretty face.

'He's been on the run since Tuesday morning, but this afternoon he called the BBC.' Insch gave the nod and a uniformed PC set the tape running.

A woman's voice, friendly: *'Hello, BBC Scotland, can I help you?'*

Some crackling. A pause. Then a man's voice, deep, with just enough Aberdonian in it to be noticeable: *'I want to speak to someone about the Flesher.'*

'Just a moment and I'll see if anyone's free . . . ' the line went silent for a moment, then hold music, then another woman's voice:

'News desk – can I help you?'

'Do you know who I am?'

Another pause, probably filled with rolling eyes and theatrical sighs. *'Are you calling about anything in—'*

'Ken Wiseman. They're looking for me. They're lying *about me.'*

Some frantic scrabbling and the woman's voice suddenly got a lot more interested. *'I see. And you want to set the record straight? Let people hear your side of the story?'*

'They did it before – they're not doing it again. They're not sending me back to that fucking prison!'

It went on, Wiseman ranting about what a bunch of bastards Grampian Police were, while the briefing room listened in silence. Then Insch told the PC to pause the tape. 'Right,' he said, rummaging absentmindedly through his pockets on the never-ending quest for sweeties that weren't there, 'we've played this to his social worker and two people from his work: it's definitely Wiseman's voice. Call came from a public phone box in Tillydrone, so we know he's still in the city. But this is the interesting bit . . . '

The tape started up again. There was more ranting, and then the woman asked, *'Would you like to put your case in person? A televised interview? Tell the whole country?'*

This time the pause was so long, Logan began to think Wiseman had hung up. But finally that dark voice came back on the line. *'The whole country?'*

'We could do it today! Is today good? You could come into the studio: we're on Beachgrove Terrace and—'

'You think I'm stupid? I say when and where. Understand?'

'OK! OK, whatever you say. You tell me where, and we'll come to you. Not a problem. You're the boss. I didn't mean to—'

'I'll be in touch.' Then the soft burr of a dead line.

'Hello? Hello? Holy shit . . . Steve! Steve, you'll never guess who I just—' Clunk. And the recording ended.

'Right,' said Insch, 'any questions?'

'Good God.' Faulds stopped dead in the middle of the Leiths' kitchen and did a slow three hundred and sixty degree turn. 'It's like *Reservoir Dogs* in here . . . ' The little metal walkway the IB had put down to stop people trampling through the evidence creaked under his feet as he picked his way across to the sink.

There was blood everywhere: all over the floor, up the units, smears on the work surfaces, splashes on the walls, spatters on the ceiling. Someone had decorated the place in eight pints of Valerie Leith.

The Chief Constable looked down at the sticky tiles. 'First impressions?'

Logan stared at a stalagmite of congealed haemoglobin hanging from the cooker hood. 'There's a lot more blood than last time.'

Faulds nodded. 'We found the same pattern twenty years ago. Sometimes Wiseman butchers them on site, sometimes he takes them away and kills them elsewhere. Anything else?'

'Well . . . They're obviously not short of a bob or two.' William and Valerie Leith had a Porche 911 in the garage and a huge Lexus four-by-four parked outside the house. It was one of those converted steadings on the outskirts of Aberdeen that always cost a bloody fortune: ramshackle farm buildings, snatched up by some developer and turned into 'luxury country homes for the discerning executive' – as exclusive as they were expensive.

Faulds leant an absentminded hand on the black granite work surface, grimaced, and pulled it away again, his latex glove making a sticky screltching sound as it parted with the tacky blood. 'Damn . . . ' He wiped it down the front of his white SOC suit, leaving a dark red smear.

Logan opened the patio doors and stepped out onto the decking. It was pitch dark outside, the surrounding country-side little more than grey-brown silhouettes against the backdrop of Aberdeen at night. Little blobs of torchlight worked their way across the field behind the house, silent except for the occasional bark of a police dog.

The view was spectacular – on the other side of the South Deeside Road the lights of Cults, Garthdee, and Ruthrieston glittered. A lone rocket zwipped up into the November sky, exploding in a shower of red. Four seconds later the BANG arrived, but by then the sparks were long gone.

'Can you imagine being up here on Monday? You'd see every firework in the city.'

The Chief Constable joined him at the rail. 'God it's freezing.' He shivered. 'If you were Wiseman, would you hang around waiting to speak to the BBC?'

'Would I buggery. I'd be on the first boat out of the UK.'

'Which begs the question: why is he still here?'

Logan pushed away from the rail as another rocket screeched up into the sky. 'Unfinished business.'

Faulds nodded. 'That's what worries me.'

Heather mashed the heel of her hand into her eye, wiping away the tears. It was a nightmare, that's all. A bad dream. She'd wake up and everything would be OK and they'd have Boeuf Bourguignon for tea and drink some wine and Duncan would still be alive.

Duncan . . . she'd cried till her whole body ached, screamed till she couldn't breathe. And now there was nothing left, but a dull numb pain that wrapped around her heart like poisoned barbed wire.

She laid her head back against the dark metal wall and moaned.

There was a noise outside and light flooded her prison, sparking off the puddles of blood that littered the rusty red floor. All that was left of Duncan.

Heather closed her eyes. This was it – the Butcher had come back for her. It was her turn to be hung upside down over the tin bath and gutted. In a way it was a relief; at least she'd be with her husband and son again.

The Butcher stepped into the room and Heather scrabbled back, terrified.

She tried to plead for her life, but her mouth was too dry, her lips cracked and bleeding. She'd changed her mind: she didn't want to be with Justin and Duncan. She didn't want to die!

But the Butcher wasn't carrying a knife, he was carrying a hose. Cold water battered against the floor, bouncing off the hard metal surface to shower everything with droplets of pink liquid as the last remnants of Duncan were washed down the drain.

When there was nothing left, the Butcher disappeared, only to return thirty seconds later with a tinfoil parcel and a bottle of water. He placed both on the floor – just within arms' reach of the bars – then stood there, staring at her.

God she was thirsty.

Trembling, Heather inched forwards and snatched the bottle, scurrying back till she was in her corner again. The bastard hadn't even moved. She wrenched the top off the bottle and drank, coughing and spluttering as it went down too fast. Nearly bringing it all back up again.

The Butcher nodded, then pointed silently at the tinfoil bundle. Then at the mask's mouth. Then rubbed his stomach.

Heather stared at the parcel, too scared to pick it up.

He gently peeled back a corner of the foil and the smell of hot food filled the room. Her stomach growled.

She peered between the bars. It was just black pudding. Normal, everyday black pudding. And she was so hungry . . .

The Butcher backed off to the door again and Heather darted forwards, snatching the parcel back to her side of the bars. Breathing in the heady aroma of hot food. With trembling fingers she crammed the first disk of pudding into her mouth, closed her eyes and chewed. Her family was dead and she was eating black pudding as if nothing had ever happened.

Heather almost spat it out, but it was food and she was hungry and she felt miserable and she didn't have any pills with her. So she did what she'd done all her life: self medication through comfort eating.

She ate every last scrap, till there was nothing left, but greasy tinfoil.

And all the time the man watched her in silence. Then, when she was all finished, he nodded, stepped back outside and closed the door. Leaving her to the darkness.

Logan cupped a hand around his ear and asked DI Steel to say that again. The nightclub was far too busy, far too noisy, and far too hot. That's what they got for letting that idiot Rennie organize a staff night out. The carpet was sticky; the place stank of stale beer, sweat, aftershave and perfume; and the music was loud enough to make his lungs vibrate.

'I said,' Steel shouted, 'I wouldn't kick that lot out of bed for farting.' The inspector pointed at the group of girlies up on the dance floor: long blonde hair, short skirts, skimpy tops, the pulsing disco lights glittering off the jewellery in their pierced bellybuttons.

As Logan watched, Detective Constable Simon Rennie boogied his way past them, doing a pretty good impersonation of a octopus being electrocuted. One of the girlies laughed and joined in, bumping and grinding.

'Jammy bastard.' Steel took another swig of her vastly overpriced beer. 'I'm no' surprised he wanted to come here.'

Rennie wasn't the only off-duty police officer up there, strutting his funky stuff – even Faulds had gone up when they'd put on an old Phil Collins number – but Logan wasn't in the mood. 'I hate nightclubs.'

'So you keep saying.'

Three songs later and a sweaty Rennie was back, handing out another round of drinks. 'Is this not *brilliant*?'

Logan scowled at him, but it didn't seem to dent the constable's enthusiasm.

'Oh, 'fore I forget,' Rennie pulled out his wallet and produced a folded-up postcard of a naked bodybuilder with a strategically placed police helmet. 'This came yesterday.'

It was from Jackie, telling the muster room what a great time she was having on secondment to Strathclyde Police's Organized Crime and Gang Violence Unit.

Rennie nodded in time to the music as one song ground to a halt and another deafened its way out of the speakers. 'Sounds like a right laugh down there— Ooh, I love this one!' And he was back on the dance floor.

Twenty minutes later he was still up there, slow dancing with one of the blonde girlies from earlier, mouths locked, eyes closed, groping away.

'Makes you sick.' Steel sniffed, watching the detective constable and his friend trying to crawl inside one another. 'I'm much sexier than he is.'

Faulds leant on the rail that separated the drinkers from the dancers and fondlers. 'So,' he shouted, 'what's with all this "Laz" business then?'

Logan sighed. 'Just a stupid nickname. It's nothing—'

'Laz – short for Lazarus.' Steel grinned and clinked her latest bottle of beer off of the Chief Constable's pint, 'DS McRae here came back from the dead, didn't you?'

'It wasn't—'

'Oh aye, our wee boy's a bona fide police hero!' She wrapped her arm round Logan and gave him an affectionate shoogle. 'Shame he's so bloody ugly.'

EXTERIOR: *A graveyard in Aberdeen – Union Street. Church in background. Noises of traffic and seagulls.*

CAPTION: *Detective Sergeant Logan McRae*

McRAE: I'd rather not, to be honest.

VOICEOVER: *But you were instrumental in catching The Mastrick Monster?*

McRAE: Do we have to do this, Alec?

VOICEOVER: *Come on, it'll make for good telly. And if you don't tell us we'll just get it from someone else.*

McRAE: *[shifts uncomfortably]* Look, there's nothing to tell. It was a joint operation, I just happened to be there at the end. Now can we just drop it?

[end tape]

INTERIOR: *An untidy office in Grampian Police Headquarters.*

CAPTION: *Detective Inspector Roberta Steel.*

STEEL: *[finishes a cigarette and flicks it out of open office window]* Right, where were we?

VOICEOVER: *We've done Insch, Rennie and McInnis. That leaves DS Beattie, Doctor McAllister, Inspector Nairn and DS McRae.*

STEEL: Right, we'll do McRae next. My hair look OK to you?

VOICEOVER: *Well ... it'll be fine.*

STEEL: Good, got my public to think of ... you'll edit out that bit with me smoking, aye? I'll no' hear the end of it otherwise. OK, June 2004, and we've got fifteen women in the morgue. The press are calling him the Mastrick Monster – he stabs his victims, then rapes them while they die. Sick bastard. Anyway, the investigation's going nowhere when up pops Detective Constable Logan McRae. He goes digging and unearths Angus Robertson – turns out Robertson works in a sandwich shop that delivers all over Aberdeen, that's how he was picking his victims—

[loud rattling cough – goes on for nearly a minute]

Ah ... fucking hell ...

[presses hand to chest]

Bastard ...

Anyway, something happens and Robertson finds out he's a suspect: he goes bonkers, snatches McRae's girlfriend, and there's a big showdown on the roof of this tower block. All very dramatic. McRae takes Robertson down, but gets himself stabbed about twenty times in the stomach doing it. Robertson gets thirty to life; McRae gets a year in hospital and promoted to DS.

[clears throat and spits into wastepaper basket]

OK, who's next? Beattie? Useless, fat, beardy arsehole. Next!

11

The Press Liaison Officer slammed the incident room door. 'Bastards!'

Logan looked up from a pile of search reports and watched her march up to DI Insch and wave a newspaper in his face.

'Have you seen the front page? Have you? They're eating us alive out there!' Which was a pretty unfortunate choice of words. This morning's *Aberdeen Examiner* had, 'CANNIBAL HORROR FOR HUNDREDS OF NORTH EAST RESIDENTS!' plastered all over the front page. Colin Miller strikes again.

Insch snatched the paper and skimmed the article, face rapidly darkening to a furious scarlet. 'MCRAE! My office: NOW!' He stormed out, nearly flattening a constable carrying a big stack of actions from the Home Office Large Major Enquiry System.

Logan slumped back in his seat, stared at the ceiling, and swore. Then followed in the inspector's wake.

Insch's office wasn't its usual tidy self: the floor was littered with screwed-up bits of paper and sweetie wrappers. The inspector's bin lay on its side against the wall, with a dirty big dent in it. He didn't even wait for Logan to close the door. 'WHY THE HELL DIDN'T YOU TELL ME ABOUT THIS?'

'I thought you knew! It's not—'

'How did your bloody Weegie friend know people have been eating . . . ' he narrowed his angry, piggy, eyes. 'Did you—'

'I never said a word! He—'

'That two-faced cow!' The inspector's face got even uglier. He stabbed a button on his phone and demanded to be put through to the mortuary.

It wasn't long before Isobel's voice crackled out of the speakerphone: *'This had better be important! Do you have any idea—'*

'WHAT THE HELL WERE YOU THINKING?'

'What? I—'

'Did you really think I wouldn't find out?'

Isobel's voice dropped about twenty degrees. *'If you've got something to say to me Inspector, you'd better say it, because I will not have you shouting down the phone at me like some sort of petulant child, do you understand?'*

'Your boyfriend. The front page of the *Examiner*. I expected you to act like a professional—'

A loud *brrrrrrrrrrrrrr* came from the speaker: she'd hung up on him.

Insch stabbed the off button hard enough to make the whole phone creak. 'You . . . ' He screwed up his face, grimaced, held two fingers to the side of his throat and tried to breathe slowly. In and out. In and out.

Logan watched him do his Zen breathing thing, wondering how much mess it was going to make when the inspector's head finally exploded. 'Er . . . do you want me to get you a glass of water, sir?'

Insch didn't open his eyes, didn't stop his slow, shuddering breaths.

The office door slammed open. 'How dare you!' Isobel stormed into the room, still dressed in her white paper SOC suit, green plastic apron, hairnet, and white morgue clogs. She snapped off her surgical gloves and hurled them onto the inspector's desk. 'If you *ever* speak to me like that again—'

Insch slammed a fat fist down on the newspaper. 'How did he know? Your "boyfriend"? How did he get sensitive information about an ongoing investigation? One *you*'re involved in? One—'

Isobel slapped him, hard, leaving a perfect white handprint on his florid face. She snatched the phone off the desk and dialled. Probably making a complaint to Professional Standards. 'Hello? . . . Yes.' She pressed the button and asked, 'Can you hear me?'

Colin Miller's broad Glaswegian accent blared out into the room, *'Aye, is this goin'* . . . *Am I on a speakerphone? Izzy, you know I'm no'* —'

'Colin, did I tell you anything about the Wiseman case?'

'Eh? What's going—'

'Did I tell you?'

A small pause, then. *'What? No, you know you didn't.'*

Isobel stared at Insch, triumph written all over her face, but the inspector wasn't finished yet: 'Do you really expect me to believe he just *happened* to come up with this all by himself?'

'Who's that? Is that DI Fatbastard?'

Insch looked as if he was about to burst. 'Just answer the bloody question: who told you?'

'I don't believe this . . . You lot are down the docks crawlin' all over a container that's meant to be goin' offshore; next thing you're screamin' off tae a cash and carry; couple hours later you raid a butcher's shop. It's a fuckin' supply chain isn't it? What you think people were doin' with all that meat they bought? Givin' it a decent burial? Course they've been eatin' the fuckin' stuff!'

'Are you—'

'It's no' exactly rocket science, is it?'

Isobel folded her arms. 'Well, inspector? I think you've got something to say, don't you?'

Insch did, but not to her: 'Do you have any idea how much trouble you've caused? Printing that? The bloody switchboard's jammed with people complaining their sausages taste funny! How are we supposed to conduct a murder enquiry when—'

'*Aye, right. It's my fault you can't catch Wiseman. I told people they were eatin' deid bodies, because – it's – the – truth. 'Stead of blamin' me, you should be out there doin' somethin' about it. And if you ever talk to Izzy like that again, I'm gonnae come down there and punch your fat fuckin' lights out!*' And he was gone.

Richard Davidson wasn't the sort of person you'd leave your children with. Not unless you really, really didn't like them. Five foot eleven of tattooed resentment, he wore the standard institution-grey 'HMP Aberdeen' T-shirt, stripy shirt and blue jeans with all the panache of a grumpy rottweiler. He scowled at Logan and Faulds from the other side of the tiny table in the prison interview room.

The Chief Constable tried his disarming smile. 'Do you remember me, Richard? I was—'

'I know who you was. OK? Answer's still fuck off.'

'Richard, I'm sorry it's all worked out like this for you, but—'

'Aye, well that's just great. Makes everythin' all better that does. You're sorry. Jamie's mum and dad get kilt and *he* goes to live with his Nan. Goes to university. Writes a fuckin' book. What do I get? A father who drinks himself to death; foster parents who're bastards; and a criminal record.' He stabbed himself in the chest with a thumb. 'Where's my fuckin' publishin' deal?'

'Richard, I—'

'*And* his books are shite.'

Logan watched the pair of them staring at each other. 'Look,' he said, 'we just want to ask you a couple of questions about what happened twenty years ago. OK? Nothing else.'

Richard Davidson scowled. 'I didn't do nothin' else. Whatever they told you, it's a fuckin' lie.'

'Fine. Don't care. We just want to know what happened in 1987.'

'Nothin' else?'

'Nothing else.'

Davidson shifted in his seat, then stared at the camera bolted high in the corner of the room. 'We're walkin' Jamie home, in the dark, me and Mum. And we get to the jungle – just this wee bit of park, couple of trees and some shitey bushes, but Jamie and me played Japs and British there the whole time.' He looked down at his hands, flexing them open and closed, open and closed, like a heartbeat, the knuckles bruised between the DIY prison tattoos. 'Jamie and me run off into the jungle . . . Mum tries to call us back, only we don't listen. Jamie's got some crappy fancy-dress party to go to for his dad's work and Jamie don't want to go, 'cos his dad's a dick.'

He sighed. 'After a while we get bored bein' soldiers, but we can't find Mum anywhere. We shout, look all over the place . . . ' Davidson bit his bottom lip. 'Can't find her. Nowhere . . . She's gone.' He rubbed a hand across his eyes. Deep breath. 'And then he turns up: Wiseman, in his fuckin' butcher's costume. And he takes our hands and . . . and we walk back to Jamie's house . . . Never saw my mum again.'

Logan let the silence go on for nearly a minute. 'What happened at the house?'

'Stupid, isn't it? All this time and I still miss her . . . ' Davidson shook his head and wiped his eyes again. 'Jamie's dickhead father was on the phone, shouting at my dad, then he shouted at us and we ran upstairs and . . . and Jamie put on this stupid Viking costume and we sat there. We could hear more shouting and we didn't want to go downstairs in case we got into even more trouble – Jamie's dad was one of those wankers didn't worry about clobbering other people's kids. So we just sit there for ages, waiting for him to come get us. Only he doesn't . . . '

Davidson shuddered. 'Eventually we give in and go down-stairs. The kitchen was clarted in blood . . . and Wiseman . . . Wiseman made us sit in the lounge while he cooked tea . . . ' He looked up at them, his eyes rimmed with red. 'Jamie's book says Crispy Pancakes, but it was liver. His dad couldn't stand the stuff, wouldn't have liver in the house. So where do you think Wiseman got it from?' There was another long pause. Then Richard Davidson stood and wrapped his arms around himself. 'I'd like to go back to my cell now.'

'So,' said Logan, when a prison officer had taken Davidson away, 'what do you want to do now?'

Faulds checked his watch. 'Nearly ten. While we're here, how about we take a crack at the butcher – McFarlane?'

'Ah . . .'

'What?'

'Maybe not the *best* of ideas, sir. DI Insch can be a bit—'

The Chief Constable waved him down. 'Nonsense. We're just going to have a little chat with the man, where's the harm in that?'

'But—'

'Good, then it's settled. You get someone to bring him up from the cells and I'll sort us out a nice cup of tea.'

Five minutes later Logan had held up his end of the bargain, which was more than Faulds had done. Whatever was in the three Styrofoam cups he'd turned up with could only be described as 'nice' if you were a lying bastard. It was barely tea – just a watery brown substance with suspicious-looking froth round the edges.

But it wasn't the least attractive thing in the room: that honour went to Andrew McFarlane. The butcher was like one of the damned. Sweat beaded on his balding forehead, his baggy face swollen in places, bruises beginning to spread across his pale skin. His big, bloodshot nose had developed a list to the left, a sticking plaster crossing the bridge from one blackened eye to the other. And he stank. BO and desperation mingling with the sour tang of TCP.

Twitching.

'You have to get me out of here!'

Faulds passed him one of the polystyrene cups. 'It's all right, Mr McFarlane. No one's going to hurt you here.'

'No one's going to... WHAT ABOUT THIS?' He pointed a trembling finger at his battered face. 'They put my photo in the papers! Everyone thinks I killed those people...'

'I'm sure it's not—'

'He wouldn't stop hitting me! Said I'd killed his mother! I never touched her! It wasn't me!' McFarlane started to cry. 'All I wanted was to run a little butcher's shop, somewhere nice and local, where people would come and buy their meat...'

'Then why were you selling bits of dead body?'

McFarlane wiped his nose on his sleeve. 'I *told* you: I don't know how that stuff got into my shop.'

'So you're saying it was all Wiseman—'

'No. He didn't kill anyone, he—'

'When he was in Peterhead Prison, he beat a man to death in the showers.'

'Because you bastards put him there! It wasn't his fault.'

'I can't believe you gave him a job when he got out. Wiseman in a butcher's shop? Like giving Gary Glitter the keys to a children's home.'

'He's my *brother-in-law*, what was I suppose to do: abandon him? He didn't kill those people!'

'Come off it, Andrew.' Faulds sat back in his chair and tried his friendly Chief Constable smile again – the one that hadn't worked on Richard Davidson. 'When he was arrested they found a lot of blood in the boot of his car, it—'

'It – was – his! He cut himself. We went through all this at the appeal. You fitted him up.'

'He confessed.'

'You beat that out of him!'

'Oh please.' Faulds picked up his tea, then put it down again. 'You know, I always suspected he had an accomplice.

89

Someone to help him. Someone with their own butcher's shop. Someone—'

'No you bloody don't! I didn't do *anything*.'

The Chief Constable leant across the table and poked McFarlane in the chest. 'You were helping him dispose of the bodies twenty years ago, and you're helping him now.'

'I never—'

'Where were you on the fourteenth of October 1982?'

'What? I don't remember, it was twenty-five years—'

'Were you in Birmingham, Mr McFarlane?'

'No!'

'Shirley Gidwani was pregnant, did you know that, when you and Wiseman carved her up?'

'We didn't—'

'Stuffed chunks of her in the freezer like she was nothing more than joints of bloody meat.'

'I never—'

'I had to tell her parents!'

McFarlane slapped both hands over his ears. 'Stop it!'

'You didn't even leave them enough for a decent burial.'

'I DIDN'T KILL ANYONE! It wasn't me! Ask him! Ask Ken! He'll tell you—'

'Oh we intend to, Mr McFarlane, soon as we catch him. And we'd also like a word with your wife ...' Faulds checked his notes, 'Kirsty.'

McFarlane's face went fish-belly pale between the bruises. 'She left me.'

'We know that: where is she now?'

'I ... I don't know.' He stared at the tabletop. 'She ran off with an electrician called Neil, OK? You happy?'

'Not even vaguely.' Faulds pushed his chair back and stood, towering over the shivering butcher. 'I hope you've got a good lawyer Mr McFarlane, because you're going to need one.'

12

'You really think he's involved?' asked Logan as they drove back to FHQ.

Faulds didn't look round, watching the grey granite buildings drifting past instead. 'Don't tell me you bought all that, "It wasn't me" crap.'

The radio was on in the background: Jamie McLaughlin being interviewed on Northsound 2 about his book and the hunt for Ken Wiseman. *'Did you ever dream when you wrote* Smoak With Blood *that it would all happen again?'*

'McFarlane just doesn't seem . . .' Logan frowned. 'I don't think he'd be any use. And from what I hear, Wiseman's not the kind to carry passengers.'

'Not in my worst nightmares. You know, Damien, when the appeal court overturned his conviction in 1995—'

'And if McFarlane is involved, why didn't we find any forensics in his flat, or his car? The amount of blood at the scene – we should have found *something.*'

'—it was like everything I'd ever believed in was a lie. And now here we go again, right back where we started.'

Faulds sighed. 'I know.'

'Right, I suppose we'd better have a record, then well be back with Jamie McLaughlin, author of Smoak With Blood . . .'

Logan joined the tail end of a queue of traffic, shuffling its way down Market Street. 'What does it mean, "Smoak"?'

'Soak, I think. Or something like that. Comes from a painting in Trinity Hall, where the Aberdeen trades meet. We interviewed pretty much everyone involved there during the original investigation – bizarre place, full of all this historical stuff and ancient paintings. We should probably pay them another visit, see if any of the 1990 suspects are still around...' And then he started humming along to the song on the radio, just off-key enough to set Logan's teeth on edge. The torture didn't stop till the record did.

'You're listening to Northsound Radio Two, and I'm in the studio with Jamie McLaughlin—'

'You know,' said Faulds, 'you should read Jamie's book. It's a good insight into what happened in eighty-seven. Remind me when we get back to the station, I'll lend you my copy.'

'And I understand sales of the book have rocketed?'

'Then we'll get that trip to Trinity Hall organized.'

'—guilty about it, but the publishers have been swamped. There's talk of a television series on Channel Four, and a new book to accompany it.'

Faulds drummed his fingers on the dashboard. 'And we should try a search for McFarlane's missing wife as well. PNC, census records, Friends Reunited: the usual.' He started up the painful humming again.

'It's weird, I don't want to profit from other people's misfortune, but ... but it feels like my whole life's been shaped by Ken Wiseman and the murders he commits.'

'Dig out her statement when you get a minute. Should be on file somewhere. Probably a load of old bollocks about how her brother wouldn't hurt a fly, but you never know. And then we're going to book a restaurant; haven't had a decent curry since I got here.'

'I just have to pray that they catch him before he kills again—'

Amen to that.

'God, look at them,' said Rennie, whispering like some sort of naughty schoolboy, talking behind the teacher's back, 'I'll bet they're figuring out how to blame this on someone else.'

DI Insch, DI Steel and CC Faulds, stood at the front of the incident room arguing quietly amongst themselves.

Rennie sniffed. 'Not like it's our fault is it? Insch should have called in the Environmental Health people from the start.'

He was right, but Logan didn't want to be overheard agreeing with him. 'What happened to you last night then?'

The constable grinned. 'Wouldn't you like to know?'

Logan thought about it, said, 'Not really,' and went back to his paperwork.

'OK, OK, I'll tell you.' Rennie scooted his chair closer. 'Her name's Laura and we were at it *all night*. It ever becomes an Olympic sport, that girl could bonk for Scotland. She could suck a bowling ball through a garden hose.' He sighed, happily. 'Think I'm in love.'

'It's like Romeo and Juliet.'

'Only with lots and lots of condoms.'

The discussion at the incident board was getting heated, DI Insch heading his usual shade of beetroot.

'What's the book at?' asked Logan, as Insch placed a huge finger in the middle of Faulds' chest and poked.

'Six hundred for lamping someone, three hundred for a heart attack.'

'You're taking bets on when Insch'll have a heart attack now? What the hell is wrong with you people?' Logan shook his head. Then put ten quid on the inspector punching someone before the week was out. From the look of things, it was probably going to be Chief Constable Mark Faulds.

Insch turned and stormed out of the room, followed a beat later by DI Steel and an angry-looking Faulds. Maybe the end of the week was a little conservative: Logan doubted Insch would last till the end of the day.

'Three cups of tea, two rowies and an Eccles cake.' DC Rennie stuck the tray on top of a mound of dusty archive boxes, then helped himself to one of the cowpat-shaped disks of flour, lard, butter and salt, chewing as he handed out the mugs.

Faulds accepted his with an exasperated smile – still on the phone with his Deputy Chief Constable. 'I know it is, Arthur, but it's the same every year . . . ' He grabbed the other rowie, lumbering Logan with the Eccles cake.

The room looked even smaller than it had when Faulds had claimed it for his own yesterday, marking his territory with a laminated sheet of A4 taped to the door: 'FLESHER HISTORY ROOM'. Someone kept sticking Post-it notes on it with, 'ABANDON HOPE ALL YE WHO ENTER HERE' scrawled on them – it looked like DI Steel's handwriting. The walls were lined with stacks of file boxes going back twenty-five years, each one representing another Flesher victim. Newcastle, Glasgow, London, Dublin, Manchester, Birmingham: they'd all sent up everything they had, and now Logan, Faulds and Rennie were sifting through the lot, looking for anything that might help catch Ken Wiseman.

Rennie parked his backside on one of the three desks squeezed in between the case histories, and munched his way through his rowie, staring at the death board as Logan pinned up another victim in chronological order.

'So,' said the constable, pausing to sook his fingers clean of grease, 'Wiseman's a chubby chaser then?'

Logan pulled out the crime scene photo that went with the face – another kitchen splattered with blood – and stuck it on the board. 'What?'

Rennie pointed at the photos. 'All the women: chunky. Most of the blokes too. Not wanting to speak ill of the dead and that, but the whole lot look like they could have done with a few less pies.'

Logan opened a box file from Northumbria Police and dug about for the next victim. 'If he's killing them for meat, he'll want a reasonable covering of flesh, won't he?'

Rennie shook his head. 'Fat people got the same amount of muscle as thin ones, it's just buried under lots of lard. I saw a programme on it. Mind you, my mum always says that when you're cooking stuff, fat's where all the flavour is.'

'Thank you for that startling insight.'

Logan looked at the Chief Constable, but he was still on the phone, laying on the calm and reasonable with a trowel: 'Arthur, you're perfectly capable of making the decision on your own . . . No . . . Arthur, if I didn't think you were the best man for the job I wouldn't have picked you . . . '

'Do you think he roasts or fries them?'

'You're supposed to be going through the door-to-doors.'

'Yeah, but it's all twenty years out of date.'

'Don't whinge.'

'But I'm *bored*.' Rennie struck a pose. 'Shouldn't be in here, pawing through ancient history, I should be out there: fighting crime! I'm a lean, mean, detecting machine!'

'You're an idiot.' Logan went back to the box and pulled out the coroner's report. A small stack of glossy eight-by-tens slithered out, scattering across the grubby carpet tiles. Logan swore and started picking them up – each one showed a joint of meat, photographed from various angles as it defrosted.

The victim's picture was paper-clipped onto the scene of crime report. Logan put it up on the board with the others. Rennie was right – twice in one day, something of a record – every one of Wiseman's victims was overweight. Not *obese*, but not skinny either.

He worked his way through all the case files until the wall of death was complete. A collage of blood and pain that stretched all the way from a Glasgow shopkeeper in 1983 to Valerie Leith yesterday. All overweight. Other than that, Wiseman's victims had nothing in common. They weren't all blonde or brunette, nearly fifty per cent were men, some were Asian, one couple in Newcastle were from Trinidad, and yet something had brought them all into contact with Ken Wiseman. Something that meant the difference between a long and happy life, and a chunk of flesh in a morgue photograph.

The crime scenes were a lot more regular – soaked bright red, or just signs of a struggle. A joint of meat left in the freezer as a parting gift.

Logan stopped at the photo of the Leiths' kitchen, remembering the hot copper smell. How could one person contain so much blood?

'Bloody hell...' Faulds flipped his mobile phone shut and stuck it back in his pocket. 'Never become a Chief Constable, Logan. Yes, it *sounds* like a bundle of laughs: fancy uniform, people saluting, dancing girls, but it's a royal pain in the backside.' He covered his face with his hands and slumped back in his chair. 'I have to go back to Birmingham. Tonight.'

'But Wiseman's—'

'I know, I know: he's going to call the BBC back and set up that interview, and we'll come down on him like a ton of bricks. And I won't be there, because no one wants to be responsible for policing bonfire night.' He pulled his hands away, swore, and put them back again. 'I am a lily, floating on a cool pond...' Faulds sat up. 'It's no good; I'm going to have to go. The buck stops here, after all. Can you get someone to run me over to the airport?'

Rennie nearly exploded out of his seat. 'I'll take you!' Anything to get out of going through mounds of dusty paperwork.

Logan went back to his post mortem report.

The incident room door nearly banged off its hinges as DI Insch barged into the room. Glaring. 'Where the hell's that useless bastard Rennie?'

Logan closed his eyes and counted to three, but Insch was still there when he opened them again. So much for wishful thinking. 'He's taking Faulds to the airport.'

'He's supposed to be reviewing case files!'

'The Chief Constable pulled rank.' Not strictly true, but it might save Rennie an ear-bashing when he got back. 'You want me to pass on a message?'

'Tell him *I'm* running this investigation, *not* Faulds. *Remind* him that I'll rip his balls off and stuff them down his throat if he *ever* disappears without my say so again! Understand?'

Logan held up his hands. 'Nothing to do with—'

'In the meantime I want a rundown of all sex offenders over forty with a history of serious assault.'

Logan checked the clock on the wall. Twenty past four, forty minutes to go till he was off duty. 'Actually, sir, I'm in the middle of something for—'

'Did that sound like a request to you, Sergeant?'

Getting together a list of sex offenders over forty years old was only the start of it: Insch wanted them all cross-referenced to see who'd done time in prison since 1990 – when the first batch of murders stopped – and he didn't just want them for Aberdeen either, Logan had to do it for the whole of the UK.

He sent another query running on the computer, then pasted the results into a spreadsheet. Now he had data from every police force in the nation with electronic records going back far enough to be of any use; the others would take days, if not weeks to respond to the inspector's request. But right now it was twenty past five.

Logan sent the list of names to the CID office printer. He'd dump them on Insch's desk and slope off before anyone noticed.

Chance would be a fine thing.

DI Steel stopped him on the stairs. He was going down: clutching his folder full of sex offenders, she was going up:

clutching her left breast through her charcoal-grey blouse. 'Where's your boyfriend, Faulds then?'

'He ... er ...' Trying not to watch what she was doing.

'Got this new bra from Markies, it's all weird bits of plastic. Feels like a ballistic missile.'

'Er ... he's off back to Birmingham. Rennie's taking him to the airport.'

'Oh aye?' She stopped fiddling with herself. 'So how come you've no' sloped off early then?'

Logan held up his folder. 'Going through the sex offenders list for Insch, trying to find an alternative suspect.'

'Bloody hell,' said Steel, faking a swoon, 'Fatty McFatfat's considering other suspects? Did a herd of pigs just fly by the station window?' She helped herself to the folder and riffled through the printouts, then tossed the lot back at him. 'Waste of sodding time, but I suppose it'll keep Chief Constable Knobjob happy.'

She turned and started back down the stairs again. 'Well, come on then – after you slap your pervy bastards on Insch, you and me are going on a little field trip.'

Logan followed her, trying to get his list back in some sort of order. 'Is it to the pub? Because if it isn't—'

'Have I ever steered you wrong?'

He didn't answer that.

Insch was in the main incident room, surrounded by a blizzard of paperwork. The phones were going non-stop, harassed support personnel answering them, taking details, and moving onto the next caller.

DI Steel skulked in the doorway while Logan snuck in, slipped the file into Insch's in-tray, and turned to leave.

A deep bass rumble caught him before he'd gone more than a couple of feet: 'And where do you think you're going?'

Damn. 'My shift finished twenty minutes ago, sir.'

'Ah, I see,' Insch opened the folder and pulled out the list of names. 'You *are* remembering that there's a madman out there, aren't you, Sergeant?'

Oh for God's sake. 'Yes, sir. I am remembering. But this—'

'Good, then you can get onto INTERPOL – I want the search widened to include other countries. We're looking for anything that matches the MO between 1990 and 2006. And while you're at it—'

Steel settled herself on the edge of Insch's desk. 'Nice to see you're taking Faulds' suggestion to heart. All that fixation on Wiseman's no' healthy.'

The inspector scowled. 'Wiseman is *still* my chief suspect. I'm just—'

'Doing what you're told. Good for you.'

Insch was starting to go scarlet. 'This investigation—'

'Nice to see you taking guidance for a change. Doesn't make you any less of a man.' She stood. 'You'll no' mind if I borrow McRae here, will you?'

'You . . .' Scarlet was turning to purple.

'Thought no'.' A saucy wink. 'When Faulds gets back we'll put in a good word for you.' She dragged Logan away, before Insch could do anything more than splutter.

13

DI Steel waited till they'd got all the way down the stairs before hooting with laughter. 'Did you see the look on his face? Thought he was going to have an aneurism.'

'But...' Logan looked back over his shoulder. 'What did you have to go winding him up for? He's bad enough as it is.'

'Ah, relax.' She hauled one of the double doors open and made for reception. 'I like to see how fast I can get him to change colour. He's like a really angry chameleon. Besides...' the inspector paused at the end of the corridor, peering through the glass at a crowd of people in the front lobby, all looking very, very upset. 'Second thoughts...' She turned round and headed back towards the stairs. 'You got any money on the sweepie?'

'Tenner on him punching someone Saturday.'

She nodded. 'I've got Monday. It's no easy keeping him at just the right level of pissed-off-ishness. Too much and he snaps early – no dosh for Auntie Roberta. Too little and the bugger won't lamp anyone.'

'What if you're the one he thumps?'

Steel grinned. 'I'll fucking kill him.' She marched out onto the rear podium car park, sparking up a cigarette and blowing out a cloud of smoke that glowed in the security spotlights. 'Oh, Christ I needed that.' She shuddered happily and puffed her way over to an unmarked pool car. 'Right, we're off up the hospital.'

'You said we were going to the pub!'

'Oh come on, no' like you've got anything better to do is it? Go home and mope in an empty flat? Wah, wah, wah, my girlfriend's in Glasgow playing cops and robbers and I'm not getting any. Wah, wah, wah . . . '

Silence.

She tapped ash from the end of her fag, little flecks of orange sparkling amongst the grey. 'It'll be good for you, get you out a bit, stop you developing wanker's elbow.' Still nothing. 'OK, OK. Insch'll no' admit it, but he's up to his ears in shite and sinking fast. He needs a hand. The ACC wants us to go up to A&E and interview that bloke whose wife disappeared yesterday. Take a bit of the pressure off.'

Logan kept his mouth shut.

'Buy you a pint after?'

As the inspector said, what else was he going to do?

They'd put Mr Leith in a semi-private room, between a man with lymphoma and a boy with two broken legs. According to the ward sister Leith was doing better than expected – given the shock and his injuries. They'd probably be letting him out in a couple of days. Steel gave the PC stationed outside the door permission to sod off to the canteen for a cuppa, then got Logan to pull the curtains round Leith's bed.

The man's head was nearly invisible beneath a thick layer of white bandages, a faint yellow stain leaking through where Wiseman had tried to open his skull with a cleaver.

Steel settled herself down on the visitor's chair, and asked Leith if he was awake. The man groaned, opened a pink eye and blinked. A morphine drip snaked into the back of one hand. A tremble, then he was still again.

'We need to ask you some questions about what happened yesterday, Mr Leith.'

'I ... I told the other one. You know ... ' he frowned, trying to remember, 'Big. Bald. Fat ... ' The words slurred and mis-shapen by drugs.

'I know, but you need to tell me as well.'

'Out shopping ... Sainsbury's, something for tea ... came home ... he was waiting for us ... ' It took a while, but eventually they got the whole story. How Valerie had unpacked the shopping from the car while he checked the answering machine. And then she was screaming and he ran into the kitchen and there was Wiseman, *killing* her ...

Leith stopped, hand fumbling for the button that would pump another dose of morphine into his veins as he told them how he'd tried to stop Wiseman, but the man was too strong. The flash of a meat cleaver, blinding light, darkness ... When he came round he was alone in the house, and the kitchen was covered in blood.

Steel checked with Logan, making sure he was getting all of this down. 'And did you hear him say anything?'

'He said ... he said we were smoak with blood ... we'd be sacrificed on the altar ... ' Leith's thumb hammered the button again, but it didn't seem to do any good. 'Oh God, Val ... I should ... I should have fought harder! I never should have let him take her ... '

'Christ that was depressing.' Steel took a deep swig at her white wine, sat back and watched Logan work his way through a bag of Scampi Flavour Fries. Half past eight and the pub was starting to liven up, the murmur of conversation rising as more people drifted in out of the rain. 'What do you think Wiseman does with the bones?'

Logan shrugged. 'Buries them somewhere?'

'I tell you Susan wants to get married?'

102

'Congratulations.' Logan raised his glass. 'About time she made an honest woman of you.'

Steel squirmed in her seat. 'I'm in my sexual prime here, and Susan wants to tie me down.' She gazed morosely into her half-empty glass. 'And no' in the good way, either.'

'Yeah, well . . . ' That was an image Logan *really* didn't want. 'You want another one?'

By the time Logan got back from the bar, Detective Constable Rennie had turned up. He was sitting at the table, interrogating a pint of lager and a packet of cheese and onion, while Steel told a filthy joke about two farmers and a bisexual sheep.

No more talk of marriage.

Two pints later and they were bitching about Insch behind his back. Two more and Rennie was beginning to make giggling noises. By then Logan was ready to call it a night, but he had another pint anyway. He walked, a little unsteadily, back from the toilets to find the constable holding forth on the Wiseman case.

'I'm just saying, OK? I mean . . . I mean,' Rennie was having difficulty staying upright on his stool, 'if this was a book, right? If this was a book, or a film, or something . . . then . . . ' He burped. 'Scuse me . . . If this was a book, it'd be one of us, wouldn't it? The Flesher? He'd be . . . he'd be the *last* person you'd expect!'

He nodded, had another drink, then waved a finger at them. 'Faulds! For example . . . Chief Cons . . . Consable Faulds – we've only got his word he's a Chief . . . Consable, don't we? And where is he now? Vanished!'

Logan smiled. 'He's flying back to Birmingham. You took him to the airport, you idiot.'

'Ah! Ah . . . ' Rennie tapped the side of his nose. 'But we don't *know* that for sure, do we? Hmmm? He could've . . . could've turned round soon as I was gone and scarpered. Could be out there right now: killing peoples.'

'You're pished.'

'Pished like a FOX!'

Steel banged her hand on the table, making all the empty glasses rattle. 'Karaoke!'

That was it – *definitely* time to go home.

A clunk, and Heather sat bolt upright on her stinky mattress, eyes straining in the dark. Heart hammering against her ribs. Maybe he'd come back? Maybe he'd come back with more food and water?

Her stomach growled again: a huge angry animal clawing its way through her innards. She'd never been so hungry in her life.

Another clunk, and a thin sliver of yellow light raced across the rusty metal floor. Heather scooted forwards on her hands and knees, peering through the bars.

The Butcher's shadow blocked out the light for a moment, then he stepped inside, walked over to the bars and placed a bottle of water and another tinfoil parcel where Heather could reach them.

She didn't even wait for him to back away this time, just grabbed the plastic bottle. The water was cool and sweet in her mouth. Like the tears of angels. She drank half of it in one go before ripping the foil package open. There was a paper plate inside, full of breaded escalopes, so hot she nearly burned her fingers.

God it was delicious. The best veal she'd ever tasted.

The Butcher stood and watched her eat. Nodding.

She chewed and swallowed. 'Can ... can I have more water? Please? I get so thirsty.'

There was a moment's silence, and then the Butcher turned his back and walked out, closing the door behind him. The darkness closed around her.

Heather started to cry. All she wanted was some water. She just wanted some bloody water! She screwed up her face, fists curled over her eyes, rocking back and forth. Just some fucking water . . .

Worthless, stupid bitch can't even ask for water properly. Can't do anything properly. Can't die with her family, has to get herself trapped in the dark, all alone.

She pulled one of the fists from her face and punched herself in the stomach as hard as she could.

Stupid.

Punch.

Useless.

Punch.

BITCH!

CLUNK and the door opened again. Heather froze. The Butcher was back, with a multi-pack of bottled water. He put it on the floor, then tore it open and started passing the individual plastic bottles through the bars.

He came back.

'Thank you . . .' She was crying again. He came back. 'My . . . my name's Heather.' She reached out and took one of the bottles from him. The Butcher froze for a moment. Then snatched his hand back. 'Did I say something wrong? I'm sorry! I didn't mean to . . .'

He backed up against the wall, staring silently down at her.

'I'm sorry! Please, don't leave me in the dark! Please! I—'

But he was gone, slamming the door. BOOOM.

Alone in the dark, Heather curled up in a little ball and screamed herself hoarse.

Aberdeen Bloodba...

Flesher Kills Wife and Leaves Husband for De...

By James Oswald

VALERIE LEITH was 35 when her path was crossed by the most notorious serial killer in Scottish history. The Flesher broke into her South Deeside home last night in what is becoming a chillingly familiar pattern.

Emergency Services received a 999 call just before midnight. An ambulance rushed to the scene and the crew arrived to find the kitchen awash with blood and Valerie's husband, William Leith (39), seriously injured.

He was rushed to Aberdeen Royal Infirmary and is understood to be in critical condition.

Patients awaiting treatment at Accident and Emergency were shocked by the severity of William Leith's injuries.

Blood Everywhere

"It was horrific," one woman said, "he had this huge gash in his head and there was blood everywhere. They rushed him straight through, but you could hear him screaming about his wife."

Grampian Police were reluctant to release any details, but sources (who

Aberdeen Book is UK Bestseller

They say it's an ill wind that blows no good, and for James McLaughlin that's certainly true. His first book, SMOAK WITH BLOOD, was published in 2001, but this week it went into the national bestseller charts at number 3, spurred on by the recent spate of gruesome murders in Aberdeen.

"It's a bizarre feeling," says James, "I wrote the book as a way of working through the events of 1987 and the hunt for my parents' killer. I feel quite uncomfortable that this upsurge in interest comes at the cost of human lives."

McLaughlin (26) belongs to a very exclusive club – people who have survived an encounter with the Flesher. The only oth... member is his childhood frie... Richard Davidson. The Fle... made dinner for the two... before making his escape, le... the kitchen drenched in bloo...

The Aberdeen author h... been approached by... Hollywood studios. "My... a couple of call from...

James McLaughlin
SMOAK WITH BLOOD
The Hunt for the Flesher

...erial kil...

Thinn
Winne...

EXCLU...
By Colin Mi...
C.Miller@Aberdeen...

TWO DUNDEE slimmers are... the pops. Maureen Taylor an... sister Sandra lost a combined w... of eight stone in a bid to r... awareness of juvenile onset diabet...

"I never thought we'd manage... said Maureen (25). "But loads... people sponsored us, and I'm rea... glad the money's going to such... good cause.

"We've both still got a long way to... go though," she joked.

Sandra (23), who was diagnosed... diabetic on her sixth birthday, was... delighted. "I've never really been... proud of the way I look, but this has... been a real boost." The pair plan to... lose another five stone each.

...LESH
...ibal Horror for Hundreds of N...

NE residents... **eating human flesh,** the *Examiner* can exclusively reveal.

Following the discovery of body parts in a container bound for offshore, medical experts are convinced that human meat has entered the food chain.

The meat in the container was traced back to McFarlane's butcher shop on Holburn Street, where Ken Wiseman is known to have worked.

Convicted of the murders of Ian and Sharon McLaughlin in 1990, but released on appeal only ten years later, Wiseman always denied...

...human.

How many more... went off to North Sea oi... without anyone knowing...

And it's not just thos... offshore who have t... Thompson's Cash an... supplies many local re... shops, and bakers with m...

Ken Wiseman was... seven years ago. Could... NE residents have been... their fellow citizens for tha... In addition to the moral... associated with cannib...

McFarlane's the Butcher
Good Eats Good Meats

...EADLY
...RADE

...n's Cash and Carry
...ans sold meat from
...e's butcher shop to

14

Hot water, soothing away a hangover brought on by too many beers and too many vodkas. Logan stood with his forehead against the cool tiles and let the shower wash over him. What the hell had he been thinking? 'Summer Nights' from *Grease* was *not* a good song to duet with DI Steel, no matter how drunk you were. His arse was still tender from where she'd pinched it during the caterwauling finale.

Woman had fingers like bloody pliers—

The phone's shrill ring invaded the steamy peace of the bathroom. Logan shouted, 'Go away!' at it, but it just kept going. Only stopping when the answering machine picked up.

He strained his ears, trying to tell who it was, but the ringing just started up again. 'Oh, for God's sake...'

Logan wrapped himself in a towel and dripped his way through to the lounge, snatching the phone out of its cradle. 'What?'

DI Insch's voice blared in his ear: *'You were supposed to be at work hours ago!'*

'It's my day off. So's tomorrow. I've been on since—'

'Listen up and listen good, Sergeant: you want a nine to five, Monday to Friday job? Go work in a bloody office. You're supposed to be a police officer!'

Logan closed his eyes and tried counting to ten.

'Hello? You still there?'

'Yes, sir.'

'Good. We've had a call from an old friend of yours: Angus Robertson.'

Logan froze. 'What does that little shite want?'

'Says he's got information about Wiseman. Said he'll only talk to you.'

'Tough: I don't want to talk to him. Little bastard can rot in his—'

'Get your arse up to the station, we're going to Peterhead whether you like it or not.'

The inspector's Range Rover had developed an overwhelming reek of dog. Lucy, the spaniel responsible, lay behind the grille that separated the boot from the rear seat on a tatty tartan blanket, snoring and twitching as Insch drove them up the A90 to Peterhead. Logan in the passenger seat, Alec in the back, fiddling with his camera.

'So . . .' Alec plugged in a couple of radio mikes. 'I know this is just meant to be you and him, one-to-one, but think Robertson will let me film it?'

Logan scowled at the scenery drifting past. 'It'll all just be bollocks anyway. He's a nasty, ignorant, murdering wee shite; he doesn't know anything. This is a complete waste of time.'

Alec scooted forwards, till his head was poking between the driver and passenger seat. 'But he's the Mastrick Monster! This'll make a *brilliant* scene for the documentary. Fancy doing a quick piece to camera when we get there? Go over the background: why he'll only speak to you?'

'No.'

'Oh, come on, *please*?' The cameraman turned to Insch for backup. 'Inspector, you understand dramatic narrative, we—'

Insch just growled at him: 'Sit back and put your bloody seatbelt on. I won't tell you again!'

'And how come,' said Logan, poking the dashboard, 'Robertson *suddenly* has information about Wiseman? Why should we believe anything he says?'

'Because they were on the same wing for nearly a year.' The inspector was starting to go red, but Logan didn't care.

'Doesn't mean they were friends!'

'You don't get it, do you?' said Insch, biting off the words, 'You're so wrapped up in your petty little world—'

'The fucker stabbed me twenty-three times. I *died* on the operating table!' Logan wrapped his arms around himself and glowered out the window. 'Sorry if you think I'm being *irrational*, but that sort of thing kind of puts a shitter on your day.'

An uncomfortable silence settled into the car. Outside, the green-brown landscape roared by, punctuated with little floral tributes, marking where people had died in road accidents. Insch cleared his throat. 'Look, I understand this is going to be hard for you, but it happened six years ago: Wiseman's out there killing people *right now*. And we need all the help we can get.'

Peterhead Prison wasn't the prettiest of buildings: an old-fashioned Victorian lump of concrete and barbed wire, home to three hundred and twenty of Scotland's worst sex offenders and other vulnerable prisoners. People who'd get the shit beaten out of them in any other prison. People like Angus Robertson.

Logan paced back and forth in the little office with 'THERAPY ROOM – 3' on the door, trying not to hyperventilate. He wiped his sweaty hands on his jeans. Christ it was hot in here, even with the window open.

He turned and looked out through the bars. From here you could see over the high outer wall with its festive topping of razor wire, across the south breakwater of Peterhead harbour, and past that to the North Sea. Dark grey water flecked with

111

white. Sky the colour of ancient concrete. And between the two, seagulls wheeled in lazy circles, waiting for the fishing boats that were becoming rarer every year.

What the hell was taking so long?

His hands were damp again.

Logan nearly jumped out of his skin when the door opened. It was a prison officer with a plastic cup of water. She handed it over. 'Right,' she said, 'I want you to know we don't approve of this. We've worked too long and too hard to get Angus where he is. But I'm agreeing to this meeting because there's a clear and immediate danger to human life. I need you to understand that if you reinforce his negative behavioural patterns, it could put him back years.' She paused, giving Logan a chance to say something, but he didn't. 'I'll bring him up from the cell block.' She paused, halfway to the door. 'We don't like to handcuff them when they're in the treatment rooms. Are you going to be OK with that?'

'Not really. No . . . ' Logan took a sip of water. 'We . . . didn't get on too well last time we met.'

'I know. He's still got the scars.'

Logan tried for a smile, but it wouldn't stick. 'Snap.'

She looked him up and down, her voice softening. 'He really has made a lot of changes. The STOP programme—'

'I just want to get this over with. OK?'

She shrugged. 'You're the boss.'

No he wasn't – because if he *were* the boss he wouldn't bloody be here.

Angus Robertson really *had* changed. The scruffy man in the boiler suit was gone, replaced by an HM Prison mannequin: blue and white striped shirt buttoned up to the chin, a sharp crease in his jeans, black shoes polished till they shone. He'd even slicked back his thinning brown hair.

Robertson sat perfectly still in one of the room's two soft armchairs, hands folded in his lap. Face expressionless. And when he spoke it was as if something dead had slithered into the room. 'You're looking well.'

Logan just stared at him.

'Why thank you,' Robertson gave a fleeting smile. 'I've been working out.'

'I didn't say anything.'

'Please, I've rehearsed this conversation so many, many times. It would be a shame to waste—'

'What's with the fake English accent?'

Robertson smiled. 'Accent?'

'Fine, I don't care.' Logan's palms were sweating again; the man made his skin crawl. 'You said you had information—'

'Ah yes, Kenneth Wiseman. He was in the cell next door. Lovely man. We had many interesting chats about...' Robertson made a tiny hand gesture. 'Life and death.'

'Where is he?'

'Now, now, now, let's not get ahead of ourselves. What are you going to give me in return?'

'Do you, or don't you know where Ken Wiseman is?'

'Quid pro quo, Sergeant McRae: I want my own meals. Prepared by someone who understands the needs of a gourmet like me, not the boiled crap they serve—'

'You're kidding, right? Gourmet? The closest you ever got to being a gourmet was saying "aye tae a pie". You're not Hannibal Bloody Lecter: you're a nasty wee shite from Milltimber.'

'I want my own chef!'

'Get fucked.' Logan stood. 'We're done here.' He was beginning to tremble – adrenaline priming the fight-or-flight mechanism. And right now 'fight' was winning – grab the little bastard by the throat and batter his head off the floor till it burst.

'But ... but I *made* you! I ... if it wasn't for me—'

'You're pathetic. A slimy piece of shite who had to kill women before you fucked them, because nothing living would have anything to do with you!'

Robertson clamped his hands over his ears. 'I didn't—'

'WHERE'S WISEMAN?'

'Stop shouting at me! Stop shouting!' The fake English accent was beginning to slip, exposing the Aberdonian underneath. 'I'm no' a bad boy! I'm no'!'

'WHERE'S FUCKING WISEMAN?'

'He told me stuff . . . about the woman he killed . . . and the man in the showers . . . at night, when everyone else was asleep . . . '

Logan took a deep, shivering breath. 'I'm not going to ask you again.'

Insch put his foot down, the windswept countryside flying past in shades of grey and miserable. Gusts of wind raked the trees and hedges outside the Range Rover's windows, making the car shudder as they flew down the A90 to Aberdeen.

'God that was bloody brilliant!' Alec, fiddled with his camera and grinned. 'It's going to look great when it goes out.'

'Oh Jesus . . . ' Logan turned round in his seat. 'You *can't* put that on the TV!'

Alec grinned. 'They're going to send me a copy of the treatment room's CCTV tape.'

'But—'

'*And* Angus Robertson signed a release.'

No surprise there: the little bastard would be desperate for another fifteen minutes of fame.

'I'll look like an arse!'

Insch nodded. 'Yup.'

'Nah,' Alec flipped the camera's tiny viewing screen round so Logan could see it. It was a shot of the CCTV monitor in the security room – where everyone else had gone to watch the interview. 'We'll slap in a bit of narration about how you're playing "bad cop" to get round his defences . . . maybe get a psychologist in . . . ' On the screen a little Logan exploded out of his seat and started shouting, his voice tinny through the

114

camera's built-in speaker. Then a prison officer barged in, claiming that this was setting Robertson's rehabilitation back years. Alec shrugged. 'You'll be fine.'

Logan groaned and went back to scowling at the scenery.

Heather lay back on the smelly mattress and stared up into the blackness. Dark. No sound. No light. No idea of time. Beginning to wonder if she was already dead – if she'd passed away and just not noticed.

She couldn't even cry any more. She'd lain for what felt like years, bawling her eyes out, sobbing for her husband and child, until there was simply nothing left. Not even—

'*Are you OK?*'

Heather screamed, scurrying back into the corner, flailing her arms around, trying to ward off the voice.

'*Jesus, Heather, you look like a complete spaz. Calm down for fuck's sake.*'

'D ... Duncan?' She peered into the dark. 'But ... you can't be ...'

One minute there was no one there, and the next: Duncan, wearing that goofy smile that always appeared when he thought he'd just done something awfully clever. Like coming back from the dead. '*Ta-da!*' There was a hole in the top of his head. It glowed bright red, glittering in his hair, making it shine like a scarlet halo.

Heather closed her eyes and punched herself in the stomach again.

'*Come on, Honey, stop it.*'

Teeth gritted. Another punch, torturing the already bruised skin.

'*Heather! Stop it! Stop!*' Duncan grabbed her hand. '*Stop.*'

'Let go of me – you're dead!'

'*Shhhh ... it's OK, it's OK.*'

'No it isn't! I—'

'*Justin misses his mummy.*'

'He . . . ' Tears ran down her cheeks. 'He's alive? Oh thank—'

'*I'm sorry, Honey: everybody's dead, but you.*'

'Noooooo . . . ' She went limp and let her dead husband rock her in his arms.

'*Shhhh . . .* ' He kissed the top of her head and she found her tears again. '*You've been through a lot, and you've not been taking your pills, have you?*'

Heather could barely get the words out: 'Duncan . . . I'm . . . so sorry . . . ' She cried and cried and cried. Then the sobbing trailed off and she just lay there, being held.

'*There you go, feel better?*' He smiled down at her wet face. '*I meant what I said: everything's OK, really.*'

She almost laughed. 'I'm trapped in a little metal box, everyone I love is dead, and I'm talking to a ghost. How is that OK?'

'*I'll look after you.*'

Heather smiled, blinked, wiped her nose on the back of her hand, enjoying the warmth of Duncan's body. 'Is this what going mad feels like?'

There was a moment's silence, then Duncan said, '*Yes, you're finally turning into your mother.*'

'You're such an arsehole.'

'*Don't you know it's bad luck to speak ill of the dead?*' But he kissed her head again.

'You're still an arsehole.' She closed her eyes and snuggled into Duncan's shoulder. He smelt of Old Spice and fresh blood. 'Did it hurt? Dying?'

'*Shhhh . . . go to sleep.*'

And she did.

Insch leant on the horn again. 'Get out the bloody way!' Up ahead the tractor took no notice, just continued to trundle down the A90 at thirty miles an hour, huge globs of mud flying from its rear wheels.

Logan turned up the volume on his mobile phone and stuck a finger in his other ear, trying to hear the voice of Control as Insch launched into another bout of horn blowing.

BREEEEEEEEEEP!

'—three cars and—'

BREEEEEEEEEEP!

'What?'

'Shift it! POLICE!'

'—no one there when—'

BREEEEEP BREEEEEEEEEEEP!

Logan slapped a hand over the mouthpiece. 'Will you lay off it for five minutes? I can't hear a bloody word!'

The inspector's face took on its familiar about-to-explode tinge, but at least he was quiet in the run-up to detonation. Logan asked Control to go back to the start, then gave Insch the edited version: 'They've got two cars at the address Robertson gave us.'

'And?'

'The bastard lied to us. Wiseman's not there.'

The inspector swore. 'Tell them I want the place watched – twenty-four-seven. At least two teams, low profile.' BREEEEEEEEEEP! 'Move that bloody tractor!'

Logan passed on the instructions and hung up as the tractor finally indicated and pulled into a rutted, muddy track, the farmer giving them the one-fingered-salute as they roared past.

'You really think Wiseman's still got keys to the place?'

Insch shrugged and put his foot down. 'He better, it's the only bloody lead we've got.' The inspector's trousers started singing at them. Insch dragged his mobile phone out, and handed it over. It was all warm. 'Don't just sit there: answer it!'

Logan hit the button. 'DI Insch's phone.'

A man's voice, old, rough round the edges. *'Who's this?'*

'DS McRae. Who's this?'

'Put David on.'

'He's driving.'

'Oh for goodness sake: half the country uses their mobile phone while driving!'

Now that they weren't stuck behind four tons of farm machinery the Range Rover was tearing down the road.

'Well?' said Insch, 'Who is it?'

'No idea.'

'Tell him it's Garry Brooks.'

'It's a Garry Brooks?'

The inspector groaned. 'What does he want?'

'I want to know what he's doing to catch that bastard Wiseman. Tell him no one down the station'll talk to me!'

Logan did as he was told. And Insch swore quietly. 'Tell him we're working on a couple of leads. I'll give him a shout when we have something more concrete.'

'He says—'

'I heard him! I'm retired, not deaf. Tell him: tonight. Redgarth. Half seven. He's buying.' And then the crotchety old man was gone. Logan shut the inspector's phone and handed it back.

'He says you've got to buy him a pint tonight.'

Insch's fat hands tightened on the steering wheel. 'Why didn't you tell him I couldn't make it? We're going to be watching Wiseman's bolthole! You *knew* that!'

'I didn't get the chance! The old git hung up on me.'

'That "old git" was policing Aberdeen before you were born!'

Alec scooted forward again. 'Brooks? Not *DCI* Brooks? The guy who—'

'I'm not going to tell you to sit back again, I'm going to slam on the brakes and send you flying through the bloody window!'

'Come on, you've got to meet with him! The continuity's great – Brooks heads up the investigation in 1987 and now he hands over the torch to his protégé, twenty years later. We get Logan there too and we've got three generations of policemen, all dedicated to catching the Flesher, discussing the case over a pint . . . '

'No.'

'Please?'

'No!'

'Oh Christ,' said Rennie, hiding behind a stack of missing persons reports, 'don't look now: it's Grumpy and Grumpier.'

DI Insch and DI Steel were at it again, arguing in front of the big map of Aberdeen that dominated one wall of the main Flesher incident room. From the sound of things Steel wanted to go into the address they'd got from Robertson with all guns blazing. Insch wanted to keep it under surveillance. And while the two of them fought, Alec filmed the whole thing from less than three feet away.

Finally Steel threw her hands in the air and marched out, banging the door behind her.

Insch stood for a moment, like a gathering storm, then marched out after her, with Alec hot on his heels.

'Bugger . . . ' Logan got the nasty feeling he was about to win his bet.

He watched the door swing shut, and then Rennie elbowed him in the ribs.

'Ow, what was that—'

'Aren't you going to do something?'

'Are you *crazy*? He'd kill me.'

'But you're supposed to be—'

'Fine! OK, *I'll* go.' Logan hauled himself to his feet and out the door, muttering under his breath the whole way.

There was no sign of Insch in the corridor outside, but Logan could hear the stairwell doors battering back and forth on their hinges. He broke into a jog as raised voices echoed down from the floor above.

Insch: 'You're being ridiculous, we—'

Steel: 'God's sake, I'm just saying, OK? He could still be in there!'

Logan took the stairs two at a time.

Insch: 'If we tear the place apart, he'll know. This discussion is over – we're not going in ... Will you get that bloody camera out of my face!'

Alec: 'I'm just doing my job ... hey ... where are—'

Logan pushed through the stairwell doors just in time to see Steel march into the gents' toilet, shouting, 'Don't you walk away from me! We're not finished.'

Logan hurried in after her.

The toilets were a depressing shade of green: three walls painted a nasty institutional spearmint; the fourth – where the long, trough urinal was – done in the same speckled green terrazzo as the floor. But unlike the floor, years of police officer's piddle had bleached white streaks into the surface, looking disturbingly like dried milk. Or sperm.

Steel stood by the line of cubicles, arms outstretched, preventing DI Insch from disappearing inside. 'No – we are going to talk about this like adults!'

'Get out of my bloody way.'

Alec shifted to get a better angle and Insch turned on him: 'WHAT DID I BLOODY TELL YOU?'

'I'm just—'

Insch stuck a hand against Alec's chest and shoved – sending the cameraman clattering back into the urinal trough.

'Aaaah! Fucking hell—'

Steel stared. 'Have you gone *mental*?'

Snarl. 'GET OUT!'

'You can't just—'

'Jesus ... I'm covered in piss!'

Insch turned, grabbed Steel by the lapel and shoved her back against a cubicle door. 'Listen up and listen good, you foul-smelling—'

Logan stepped forwards. 'Excuse me, sir!'

'I'm *busy*, Sergeant.'

'The Assistant Chief Constable wants to see you in his office.'

'Tell him I'll be there in a—'

'Get your fat hands off me!'

'He did say it was urgent, sir.'

Silence.

'Fine.' The inspector stepped back and let go of Steel. 'I'm finished here anyway.'

She straightened her jacket. 'You ever grab me like that again and you will be – I'll tear your fucking balls off!'

Alec was back on his feet, face a picture of disgust as he shook one foot and then the other, sending little droplets flying onto the grubby, green floor. 'Fucking piss everywhere! I was only trying to do my job!'

He picked up his camera and wiped it on his sleeve. 'You any idea how much these bloody things cost? I'm making an official complaint, you can't treat me like I'm some sort of—'

'Oh God . . .' Logan saw the punch coming long before anyone else: Insch curled one huge hand into a fist and swung.

Alec didn't stand a chance. So Logan lunged forwards, shoving him out of the way. The cameraman went sprawling, right back into the urinal again – and that was when Logan realized he'd not thought this through properly.

Insch's fist whistled through the gap where Alec used to be and clattered into Logan's face.

15

Everything smelt of burning copper. Logan sat in an uncomfortable plastic chair with his head thrown back and a clump of soggy paper towels clamped to his nose.

'Still bleeding?' Chief Inspector Napier – head of Professional Standards – was probably doing his best to sound concerned, but it wasn't working. Hook-nosed ginger bastard.

His office was crowded and noisy. Big Gary – huge, uniformed and covered in biscuit crumbs – sat in the corner, next to Napier's colleague, taking notes while Steel and Insch lied about what had happened in the toilets. Everyone doing their best not to get too close to Alec, who was starting to smell.

Logan pulled the compress away and dabbed at his nostrils with a finger. It came away covered in blood. He tipped his head back again and applied a fresh wodge of paper towels.

'As I see it,' said Napier, treating them all to his fish-like gaze, 'no one is denying DI Insch hit DS McRae in the toilets. Correct?'

No one said anything.

'I see . . .' Napier picked up a silver pen from his neat-freak desk and pointed it at Alec, as if it were a magic wand and by some miracle of prestidigitation he could make the cameraman not stink of piss. 'And did you manage to film this "assault"?'

Alec looked at Insch and Steel, then blushed and stared at the carpet instead. 'My ... my camera wasn't working because it fell in the urinal ... when I ... tripped.'

'Really?' The chief inspector pulled a notebook from his drawer and read aloud. 'He attacked me – he shoved me into the urinal. He tried to—'

Alec went even redder. 'I was wrong. I slipped and fell.'

'You slipped and fell.'

'I slipped and fell.'

'I see . . .' Napier put the notebook back in the drawer. 'And this sudden change of opinion wouldn't have anything to do with being threatened by DI Insch?'

The inspector lumbered to his feet. 'Are you suggesting I tampered with a witness? Because if you are—'

Napier didn't even look at him. 'Spare me the indignant act, you're in enough trouble as it is. Half the station heard you and DI Steel screaming at one another.'

'Friendly disagreement,' said Steel.

'Quite.' Napier turned a reptilian smile on Logan. 'I'd like to hear what DS McRae has to say for himself.'

Logan blanched. 'Whad? I did'n do adythig! It wasn't—'

'You must have done something for the Inspector to punch you.'

'He . . .' Logan snuck a glance at the pair of them – Insch and Steel, sitting there as if butter wouldn't melt. 'I slibbed and fell against the cubigle door.'

Napier took off his glasses and squeezed the bridge of his nose. 'Do I look stupid, Sergeant?'

Logan didn't want to answer that one.

'Very well,' said Napier at last, 'McRae, Steel, you may go. And take ... that,' he pointed at the smelly cameraman, 'with you. DI Insch and I have some things to discuss.'

Without Faulds and Rennie making the place look untidy, the Flesher history room was nice and quiet, giving Logan peace to groan and dab at his blood-encrusted nostrils. The whole front of his head felt like a bouncy castle full of rats.

Technically he should have gone home after being dismissed from Chief Inspector Napier's Lair of Doom, but he wanted to know what Professional Standards had in store for Insch. Unable to decide if he wanted the fat git suspended or not. Loyalty to your superior officer was all well and good, until they punched you on the nose.

A knock at the door and one of the station's Family Liaison officers stuck her head into the room. 'Rennie says...' she trailed off, staring at Logan's puffy face. 'Damn, I had a tenner on Wednesday.' She held up a small sheaf of paperwork. 'Are you in charge till Insch ... you know?'

Logan sighed and stuck out a hand. It was the initial victimology report on the Leith attack, trying to build up a picture of Valerie Leith's life before Wiseman put an end to it. It wasn't easy to concentrate with both nostrils stuffed full of tissue paper, but he did his best.

The FLO couldn't stop staring at Logan's nose. 'Haven't got any ibuprofen have you? Six hours in a hospital visitor's chair and my back's sodding killing me.'

Logan pointed at a desk in the far corner. 'Tob left drawer, helb yourself.' He'd already had four.

According to the FLO's report, Valerie Leith was a creature of habit: shopped at Sainsbury's every Saturday, Debenhams every Tuesday; worked in a solicitor's office doing house sales; had no close friends, but did have a number of people she spoke to on a regular basis. It would take a while, but the Family Liaison officers would interview each and every one of them.

Logan pulled out the rough family tree they'd managed to piece together – other than the husband: William, there was a brother in Canada and an aunt in Methyl. Not much help there.

So he flicked through the day-to-day stuff, trying to figure out what Wiseman had seen in Valerie Leith that made him want to chop her into little pieces. Ten years they'd had Wiseman in Peterhead Prison, and still no one had been able to figure out what made him do it. What made him pick one person over another.

'I think he's still in shock, by the way.'

'Who?' It took Logan a second to realize who the FLO was talking about. 'Oh, the husband. Not surprisig.'

'Poor bastard. Physically he's doing OK, doctors say it looks worse than it is, but emotionally . . . ' She swallowed a couple of pills. 'We've been up to our sodding ears trying to keep the press away. Can you believe they offered some nurse two thousand pounds to sneak a video camera in and film him talking about his wife? How sick is that?'

'What aboud the timbline?'

'Still working on it. No pre-cursor incidents that we can see so far. Loving couple, married for fifteen years, and then bang: Wiseman.' She stretched, puffed out her cheeks, sagged . . . 'Better get back to it I suppose. Don't want to leave Norman up there on his own for too long with all them pretty nurses. You know what he's like.'

Logan didn't, but he nodded anyway and stuck the FLO's report away with the ones on the Fittie family. One for each victim.

The way things were going there would be a lot more of these before they finally caught Ken Wiseman.

'Six hundred twenty, six hundred thirty, six hundred forty,' Rennie counted out the ten pound notes into Logan's out-stretched hand, 'six fifty, and one more makes it six sixty. And I still say you cheated.'

Logan ran his fingers through the stack of cash. 'Don't be such a bad loser.'

'Getting him to punch you on *your* day in the sweepie. Should be ashamed of yourself.' The constable scrunched up the brown envelope the money had been in, then lobbed it at the bin. 'Goal!' He stood there, looking pointedly at the pile of ten pound notes in Logan's hand. 'So, your round tonight then?'

'No chance. My head feels like a brick in a cement mixer.' He reached up and delicately teased one of the tissue paper plugs from his nostril. At least the bleeding had stopped. 'Home, bath, bed.'

'Ah, well, I've got a hot date tonight anyway: Laura again. Going to take her out for a pizza and then back to my place for a night of hot monkey love!' He lowered his voice to a stage whisper. 'Going to get some of that chocolate body paint from Ann Summers after work. We're going to—'

'You're a pervert, do you know that?'

'You're just jealous, 'cos I'm having wild passionate sex with a foxy babe and you're stuck on your tod till Christmas.' Rennie turned, flopping a theatrical hand across his brow. 'It's sad really.' Then he flounced off, to the sound of Logan calling him an utter, utter bastard.

'Hoy, Laz, where you think you're going?'

Logan finished signing out, then turned to see DI Steel standing at the back door in all her wrinkled glory – packet of cigarettes in one hand, cup of coffee in the other. She nodded her head in the direction of the rear podium car park. 'Come on, you can hold the brolly while I have a fag.'

'I'd really like to just go home. Nose is killing me.'

'Aye, well, that's what happens when you get yourself punched in the face. Come on, you can spare five minutes for your new Senior Investigating Officer.'

Trying not to groan, Logan joined her out in the rain, holding the umbrella so the inspector could smoke and drink her coffee at the same time.

'So,' she took a sip and a puff, 'you hear about Insch? Two days suspension and a slap on the wrist. No bad going when you think about it. Two days for lamping a Detective Sergeant ... Tempted to try it myself – Beattie's been getting on my tits.' She grinned at him through a plume of cigarette smoke. 'Oh, cheer up, you grumpy old bugger. Here – got a present for you ...'

She stuck the fag in her mouth and pulled out a battered paperback from the pocket of her jacket. 'Fusty Faulds said to give it to you when I'd finished.'

It was a well-thumbed copy of Jamie McLaughlin's book. Logan turned it over and read the blurb on the back.

'It's no' bad, bit longwinded, but what do you expect from a beardy weirdo?'

'"Follow James McLaughlin as he comes to terms with the loss of his parents and the hunt for their killer ..." Sounds like a bag of laughs.'

'Aye, wait till you get to the photographs.' She took a deep drag on her cigarette and blew the smoke out into the rain. 'Tell you, Laz, this is a golden opportunity. Wiseman turns up at that address you got from the Mastrick Monster, we catch him, cover ourselves in glory, and dance the dance of a thousand pints.' She took another slug of coffee. 'Speaking of being covered in stuff, where's Wee Fat Alec?'

'Last I heard he was off home to shower and chuck his clothes in the washing machine. Why?'

'Because when Wiseman turns up I want Mr Stinks-of-Piss filming as you and me arrest him.'

Logan sighed. 'It's supposed to be a low-key operation. Flood the place with parked cars full of CID and BBC cameramen, Wiseman'll run a mile.'

She wrinkled her face at him. 'You're no fun.'

'I'm knackered: haven't had a day off in weeks.'

'Oh?' Steel sooked the last gasp from her cigarette and pinged it out into the rain. 'Well, tell you what, why don't you take a couple of days at home. Put your feet up. Don't worry your pretty little head about a thing.'

'Sarcasm. Nice. It was my day off *today*, and where was I?'

'I'm sure that wee boy they found barricaded in his room in Fittie is over the moon you're prepared to put your social life on hold for two minutes while we try find the man who butchered his bloody parents.'

Logan handed her the brolly. 'Good night, Inspector.' And marched off into the night.

She shouted after him: 'Seven – sharp! And it's your turn to get the bacon butties!'

Jamie McLaughlin's book wasn't anywhere near as bad as Logan had expected. OK, so Jamie had a tendency to use three words where one would do, but other than that it was pretty good. Logan sat in the lounge, with the radiator and electric fire going full pelt, a cup of tea balanced on the arm of the settee, and a packet of Jaffa Cakes on the coffee table, reading about the hunt for Ken Wiseman, AKA: the Flesher.

Every now and then he'd come across a few pages of photographs, usually of the investigative team. Some were lifted from newspaper cuttings, but others were more candid: a uniformed officer standing outside the McLaughlin house while an SOC team shuffled by in the out-of-focus background; Jamie's bedroom; the pathologist having a sneaky cigarette in the back garden; a thin man with thick, dark hair deep in conversation with a statuesque redhead; a clunky looking, old-fashioned patrol car with... Logan flipped back a page. According to the caption it was 'DC DAVID INSCH (GRAMPIAN) AND DS JANIS MCKAY (STRATHCLYDE) DISCUSSING THE CASE'.

'Bloody hell...' Logan had never seen the inspector with hair before. And he didn't look like an angry, pink dirigible either, he was actually *smiling*!

There was a sight you didn't see every day.

Logan flipped to the index and went looking for more about Detective Constable David Insch.

He was in the kitchen, making another cup of tea when the doorbell rang. Logan thought about ignoring it – probably kids dressed up in black bin-bags and cheap plastic masks. Halloween was four days ago and the little bastards were still shouting 'Trick or treat?'

RRRRRRRRRRIngggggggggggggggg

Logan stuck the milk back in the fridge.

RRRRRRRRRRinggggggggggggggggg

He went through to the lounge and peered out of the window at the street below. There was a darkish Volvo estate illegally parked on the other side of the road, it's hazard lights flashing orange in the rain, the BBC Scotland logo stencilled on the driver's door.

RRRRRRRRRRingggggggggggggggg

'OK, OK, I'm coming.' Logan hurried down the communal stairs and opened the building's front door.

It was Alec, standing on the top step. 'Sorry I'm late,' he said, sticking his hands in his pockets, 'you ready to go?'

'Where?'

Alec looked puzzled. 'We're going for a pint with ex-DSI Brooks, remember? You and me; Oldmeldrum? Meeting Insch and Brooks? Remember?'

'Oh for God's . . . You still want to go, after everything—'

'I'm a professional: the Ob Doc comes first.' He frowned at Logan. 'Don't tell me you're bailing!'

'Well—'

'You can't! You promised!'

'No I didn't. And in case you didn't notice, I got clobbered in the face today.'

'I got pushed in pish. Twice!'

'That's not my fault—'

'You bloody did it the second time.'

'Saving your arse.'

The cameraman frowned, obviously trying to think up his comeback. 'Yeah? Well . . . I lied for you.'

'No, you lied for Insch.'

'Fuck . . . ' He tried on a winsome smile. 'I promise I won't let them make a tit out of you when we do the voiceover for the series.'

There was a stunned silence. 'What?'

'When they do the voiceover, they usually want someone to come across . . . well . . . you know what can happen when people start editing stuff. Amazing how you can make one thing look like another.'

'This blackmail?'

Alec grinned. 'Coercion. Maybe. At a push . . . please?'

Logan closed his eyes, swore, then went inside and fetched his coat.

16

Ken Wiseman was not a happy man. Hadn't been for many, many years. It wasn't his fault: life conspired to fuck him over at every available opportunity. Good things would happen to other people, but nothing good ever happened to him. Because life was a bastard and it hated him.

Some days it was all he could do to fuck it right back.

Everything had been OK for a while. Calm. Back to normal . . . and then it all started to unravel again. Just like it had last time. Taking a human being apart . . . the chunks of meat . . . the spiral into darkness.

He tightened his grip on the holdall. It was a lot heavier than it looked, knives and saws were funny like that. They looked so pretty, and sparkly, but the legacy of blood weighed them down. Made them deceptive. Made them lie . . .

Wiseman paused for a moment, looking up and down the quiet forecourt, making sure no one was watching, then opened the door and stepped inside.

It was time to fuck with life again.

The rain started to peter out somewhere after Newmacher, and by the time Alec was parking outside the Redgarth Inn it had stopped altogether. The view from the pub car park would have been perfect for Halloween: looking out across Old-meldrum's ever-expanding waistline, lights glittering yellow, orange and white; past fields as dark as coal; the faint glow of Inverurie eight miles away; and beyond that the asymmetric anvil of Bennachie reaching up into the night sky. There was even a gibbous moon, casting a waxy grey light that made greasy shadows between the muck-encrusted four-by-fours. Logan almost expected to see a witch on a broomstick, cackling her way across the moon's pitted face. But his mother was probably miles away.

Inside it was fairly busy, the happy murmur of Saturday-night conversation competing with vintage Rolling Stones on the stereo. Logan squeezed through to the bar and waved down a gangly man with white hair and a smile that made him look as if he was eating a coat hanger sideways. Logan smiled back. 'You haven't seen . . . ' it felt weird using the inspector's first name: 'David Insch around, have you? About six-three, this wide, bald—'

The man pointed at an empty barstool and an unattended pint of Guinness. 'Aye, he's sitting there. You gentlemen wanting something to eat? Or is it just a drink this evening?'

Logan thought about the Marks and Spencer ready meal sitting at home in the fridge, and asked to see the menu. They'd ordered by the time Insch appeared, stomping in from the cold night, wrapped up in a huge padded overcoat, muttering under his breath.

'No luck?' asked the barman.

Insch unbuttoned his coat. 'No answer, no lights on, no car in the drive.' He stopped when he saw Logan and Alec standing drinking at the bar. 'You're late.'

Logan was tempted to tell the grumpy fat sod he was lucky they were there at all. Punching someone in the face, or shoving them into a urinal, wasn't exactly motivational.

Insch levered himself up on his stool, his massive buttocks enveloping the seat, and took a big bite out of his Guinness.

132

'Well,' the barman poured a couple of pints for a hovering waitress, 'maybe he forgot. You know what he's like these days. Grandson's over from Canada, isn't he?'

Insch grumbled and threw back the last of his stout. 'That was last week.' He held up the empty glass. 'Same again, Stuart.' Then he looked at Logan and Alec. 'And whatever they're having.' Which was probably about as close as they were going to get to an apology.

They took a table in one of the large bay windows, overlooking the post-witching night. Alec collapsed into his seat. 'I can't believe he didn't show! It was going to be a great piece too . . .'

The hovering waitress arrived with placemats and cutlery.

Insch waited till she'd gone before asking, 'Who've they put in charge of—'

'DI Steel.' Logan sipped at his pint. 'Just till you're back.'

'*Wonderful*. So when Wiseman turns up she'll take all the credit.'

'Maybe Wiseman will lie low till you're back on duty? It's not as if he's in any hurry, is it?'

'Yes, and maybe he'll kill a couple more people while he waits. Wouldn't that be nice?'

Logan blushed. 'I was only saying.'

Alec pulled a brand-new HDV camera from its carry case and set it on the table so he could hook up the receivers for a pair of radio mikes. 'Just because Brooks hasn't turned up, doesn't mean the night's a washout.' He unpacked two small clip-on microphones and handed one each to Logan and Insch. 'Noise levels aren't bad in here: the pair of you can go over developments in the case.' He switched the camera on, fiddled with the settings, then pointed it at them. 'And, *action*!'

There was an uncomfortable silence.

'That means you have to start doing something.'

Logan groaned. 'Bugger off, Alec, eh?'

The cameraman stared at them. 'After all that shite this afternoon, you two *owe* me.'

'It wasn't shite,' said Insch with the faintest trace of a smile, 'it was pish.' Then he cleared his throat and asked Logan what was happening at the address they'd got from Angus Robertson.

'Nothing.'

Alec made 'more detail' hand gestures until Logan, reluctantly, started talking again. 'The building's pretty much derelict. Used to be a halfway house in the seventies, but there was a scandal ... look we already know all this.'

'Yes,' said Alec, never taking the camera off them, 'but the viewers *don't*.'

Sigh. 'There was a scandal: two of the "guests" took turns raping their social worker. The investigation turned up some questionable practices, financial irregularities, unsanitary conditions and dodgy wiring. So they shut it down... Aren't people going to notice I've been bashed in the face?'

Alec gritted his teeth. 'This is going to be difficult enough to edit as it is!'

'Anyway, I've seen the photos – the place is a tip. Half the windows are gone, weeds growing in the lounge, cold, damp. He'd have to be bloody desperate to go back there.'

'He's desperate. Question is: what's he up to? He's got to know we'll pick him up soon as he arranges his fifteen minutes of fame with the BBC...' Insch polished off his second pint. 'What would you do? You've only got a few days of freedom left, then you're going back to prison for the rest of your life.'

But Logan had already answered that one, back when Faulds asked the same question at the Leith house. 'What would I do?' He stood: it was time for more beer. 'Revenge.'

The answering machine was lying in wait for Logan when he finally got back to the flat, its little red light winking away, malevolent and devious. He hit the button, still feeling all bunged up and sore, even after two pints of Stella and a nip of Glen Garioch. *'YOU HAVE THREE MESSAGES. MESSAGE ONE: Laz? You awake? C'moan man, pick up . . . '* Pause. *'You're no' in. OK, tomorrow – down the beach, fireworks, half five outside the Inversnecky.'* There was a noise in the background and Colin said, *'I'm no' tellin' him to wear a jumper, I'm no' his bloody mother . . . ' Beeeeeeep*

'MESSAGE TWO: Logan, it's your mother—'

He peeled off his coat, only half listening as she rabbited on about his little brother's upcoming wedding.

'—so make sure you remember. And would it kill you to wear a kilt this time? Honestly, Barbara's son—'

Logan hit delete.

Beeeeeeep

'MESSAGE THREE: Hey you . . . it's me . . . ' Jackie, sounding drunk again. He settled onto the end of the settee and stared at the dead fireplace. *'You miss me? I'm . . . I'm probably a bit thingied . . . with the vodka . . . but I miss you, OK? Turnip Head? I miss you. I'm got a . . . a . . . '* What sounded like a burp crackled out of the answering machine's speaker. *'Oops. I'm got some time off. You wanna . . . you know . . . with sex and stuff . . . '* A garbled voice in the background said something about another round. *'Gotta go, OK? I—' Beeeeeeep 'END OF MESSAGES.'*

Logan erased the lot, did his teeth and went to bed.

17

DI Steel sat in the passenger seat, eating a bacon buttie and slurping noisily at a wax-paper cup of tea from the bakers in Newmachar, while Logan got himself outside a hot steak pie. Steel didn't bother swallowing before pointing at the dilapidated house two hundred yards away and saying, 'Mmmmghmmmf, mmmn nnn?'

'No idea. Half two, I think.'

She shrugged, and went back to chewing.

They'd parked on the outskirts of Hatton of Fintray, a tiny village on the back road from Dyce to Blackburn, so far off the beaten track it was practically invisible. Logan had manoeuvred the pool car down a wee side road – little more than a farm track – with a view through a thin stand of trees and gorse bushes to the dilapidated granite building.

One of the downstairs windows had been boarded over, but the other was an empty black hole. The roof looked as if it had eczema, shedding dark grey slates into the overgrown garden. What an estate agent would call 'a fixer-upper'.

'How the hell did he find this place?' Steel mumbled through another mouthful of buttie.

'Wiseman's sister worked for the Council, property management, probably had keys to half the abandoned buildings in Aberdeenshire.'

Logan polished off the last of his breakfast pie and started in on his coffee as Alec climbed into the back of the car.

'Morning all.' Alec pulled out his camera and fiddled with electronic things. 'Ready for a happy day of sitting about in the cold playing eye spy?'

Steel sooked tomato sauce from her fingers. 'Anyone been in there yet?'

'Not since yesterday afternoon.' Logan, pointed at the isolated halfway house. 'Insch didn't want to risk spooking Wiseman, remember?'

'So we've no idea he's even set foot in the place.' She scrunched up the paper bag her buttie had come in and tossed it over her shoulder into the back. 'Remind me again just how many man-hours we're pissing away here?'

'Three cars, two CID per car. Eight-hour shifts.'

Steel did the maths. 'A hundred and forty four man hours, every day! Jesus, no wonder Baldy Brian whinges about the overtime bill. And we've not even checked there's anyone home!' She took a swig of her tea, then stuck the steaming carton on the dashboard, fogging the windscreen. 'Come on then, get your arse in gear, we're going over there.'

'But what if Wiseman—'

'If he's here, we'll catch him. Medals and dancing girls for everyone. If not, what's the worst that can happen?'

'He comes back, spots us, does a runner, and we never see him again.'

She shrugged and picked up the car radio, putting a call out to the three unmarked cars watching the rundown building, telling them to call her on her mobile if they saw Wiseman coming.

There was a stunned pause from the other end, then: *'But we've got strict instructions from DI Insch—'*

'Aye, well now you've got strict instructions from me.' She clambered out of the car and into the blustery morning. The sky was three shades of grey, each one moving in a different direction, the trees and bushes whipping back and forth. Steel pulled out a packet of cigarettes and lit up as she marched down the lane, leaving Logan to lock up and hurry after her. Alec jogged along at the rear, filming them both.

'Are you sure we should be doing this?'

She stopped at a big, metal gate and hauled on the spring catch. 'There's more to being a police officer than sitting on your arse eating pies.' The field on the other side was stubble and mud – the crop long gone – but Steel stuck to the edge, picking her way around the soggier looking bits.

'And how come everyone thinks that cock-weasel Robertson was telling the truth when he told you about this place, eh?' she said, 'Murdering wee bastard's no' exactly— Aw shite!' She froze, standing on one leg. 'I've trod in something.' They walked the rest of the way to the small woods with Steel dragging her foot through the barley stubble like the Hunchback of Notre Dame.

They had to clamber over a barbed-wire fence to get into the stand of trees, then fight their way through the rustling mass of spiny gorse bushes to get out the other side, with Steel swearing quietly the whole way. 'Who's stupid bloody idea was this?'

'Yours.'

She scowled at him. 'You've got a lot to learn about being a sidekick, you know that, don't you?'

From here the building looked even more dilapidated than it had from the car. Plus there was the smell. As if something had died, and been left to rot.

'Jesus ...' Steel whispered, 'you thinking what I'm thinking?' She scrambled over a low stone wall and made for the front door. It was secured by a heavy padlock, the brass pitted with age and streaked with rust. Locked.

A weed-infested gravel path ran around the house, grey-brown spears of docken poking up through the tangled grass.

'Er...' Alec fidgeted with his camera, 'I'm not supposed to ... you know ... go into dangerous situations without backup.'

The inspector stared up at the vacant windows. 'What are we, haggis rissoles?'

'It's the insurance: I have to have another BBC employee to watch my back in case—'

'Fine. You can sod off back to the car. No skin off my nose if you miss us catching Wiseman, is it?'

The cameraman cursed, fiddled with his focus, then gave a determined nod.

'Aye, thought as much.'

They tried round the back. The stench of decay was even stronger: definitely rotting meat. Logan froze. 'Might be a good idea to get the IB down here. If it's a body—'

'Wimp.' Steel picked her way into the undergrowth. Following her nose. This had been a proper country garden at one point: a small orchard sat in front of a crumbling brick wall, leaves the colour of cider, fruit blackened and rotting on the yellowy grass. A greenhouse with no glass. A shed on the brink of collapse, the wood disintegrating, the contents long surrendered to mould and decay.

The stench was coming from the other side of a clump of brambles: a sheep, lying on its side, bloated and covered with flies and maggots. Logan gagged. So did Steel and Alec.

'Jesus,' she said, when they'd backed off upwind, out of the reek, 'wish I'd no' had that bacon buttie now.' She shuddered, then lit another cigarette, holding the smoke deep in her lungs, as if trying to fumigate them. 'Well, don't just stand there,' she pointed at the carcass, 'off you go and get it shifted.'

'Are you out of your—'

'You never read books, Laz? Reginald Hill? Dalziel and Pascoe? No?' She shook her head, obviously disappointed.

'Suppose you've got a deid body to get rid of – where better to stick it than under a rotting sheep? Who'd go looking underneath that?'

'Oh, come off it! That's not—'

'Sooner you do it, the sooner it's done.' She smiled at him. 'Chop, chop.'

It became something of a mantra: 'Fucking Steel and her fucking, rotting, bastarding son of a bitching fuck ... fuck...' mumbled over and over under his breath as Logan took one look at the mouldering sheep, decided there was no way in hell he was going to touch it with his bare hands and snapped on a pair of latex gloves. He looked up at Alec, filming away, face wrinkled in disgust.

'You want to put that down and give me a hand here?'

Alec shook his head. 'Fly on the wall. Remember? Not supposed to interfere. Besides...' He shifted from one foot to the other, peering into the long grass and thickets of weeds. 'What if there's rats?'

Swearing, Logan grabbed the animal's hind legs and pulled. There was a moment's resistance ... and then both back legs came off with a sickening wet noise and a roiling carpet of maggots. Logan's stomach lurched.

The inspector shouted at him from a safe distance: 'Stop sodding about! It's not going to bite you.'

Logan's mantra started up again. He fought his way through the weeds to the mouldering shed and raked through the rusting contents until he found a garden fork. It only had two of its four tines left, but it was better than nothing. He dragged it back to the sheep, took a deep breath, held it, jammed the fork under the sheep and heaved the thing over onto its back. Where it promptly burst.

He said goodbye to his pie.

'Well?' Steel shouted, when he'd finished vomiting, 'Anything?'

He scowled at her. 'No.'

'You didn't dig about where the sheep was, could be a shallow grave in there.'

Logan said 'Fuck' a lot, then poked his new-found fork in the ground. Trying to ignore the filthy yellow-brown liquid that crawled with wriggling white flecks. 'There's nothing here!'

'Ah, well. Worth a try.' Steel stuck her hands in her pockets and sauntered over to the back door. 'You coming then?'

The place was a mess: peeling wallpaper, holes in the ceiling, lath visible through crumbling plaster. The kitchen was blanketed with spiders' webs and dust, all the appliances torn out, the window boarded-up, the room shrouded in darkness. The bathroom was even worse. Everything downstairs stank of mildew and neglect.

Upstairs wasn't much better. It must have been a large farmhouse at some point, but when the council turned it into a halfway house for the mentally disturbed they'd subdivided the first floor into tiny bedrooms. Just big enough for a single bed, a bedside cabinet and a wardrobe. Most of the furniture was gone, but a couple of pieces – too nasty, cheap and knackered to be worth anything – had been left behind to rot like the sheep.

There were *some* signs of occupancy: discarded takeaway containers; empty lager tins and cider bottles; used condoms... but none of it looked recent, the debris dusty and speckled with fly shit.

Alec stuck his head into the tiny room Steel and Logan were searching. 'Through here!'

There was a room at the very back of the building, twice as big as the others. An open fireplace sat in the middle of the far wall, the hearth full of twigs and bones. An abandoned green parka sprawled on the bare floorboards. A pile of crumpled Special Brew tins in the corner. An old sleeping bag with a hole in the side – white kapok stuffing sticking out. The smell of mould.

Alec scurried round filming everything, looking pleased with himself.

'Aye, very clever,' Steel told him, 'we'd no' have found it without you. What with us going through all the rooms one at a time and all.'

There was a newspaper lying by the prolapsed sleeping bag: a copy of the *Daily Mail* with the headline 'CANNIBAL CHAOS HITS NORTH EAST HOSPITALS!' Logan snapped on a fresh pair of latex gloves and picked the thing up. 'It's yesterday's paper.' The *Aberdeen Examiner* might have got the drop on everyone with Colin Miller's story, but it was all over the place by the Saturday morning editions.

Steel stared out of the window at the overgrown back garden and its stinking sheep. 'We're screwed. This place's been under observation since what? Yesterday lunchtime? Wiseman went out in the morning, got himself a paper, couple of rowies, came back, had breakfast, and sodded off out again. If he'd been back we'd've seen him . . . ' She screwed up her face. 'How the hell could we miss him?'

'Maybe he's—'

Steel threw a finger in Logan's direction. 'Don't! OK? Don't even start. He must have spotted one of the cars on the way back here!' For a moment it looked as if she was going to kick the mound of empty beer cans all over the room. 'Bastard! We could have had him!'

18

Sunday afternoon and the phones were going non-stop: people calling in from all over the North East to say that they'd seen Wiseman, or had eaten something that was supposed to be pork or veal but was probably person. Would they get Creutzfeldt-Jakob Disease?

Logan listened for a minute to a PC trying to calm someone down on the other end of the phone. 'No,' she was saying, 'you're not going to get mad cow disease... No, sir, variant CJD is... There are only seven people in the whole of the UK with the disease at the moment, sir, so it's highly unlikely... Yes, sir, it *is* impossible to say for sure.' She slumped forward till her head was nearly resting on the desk. 'Yes, sir... Environmental Health have set up a special hotline for... Yes...' She gave him the number, hung up, and then her phone started ringing again. 'Oh, bugger off.' Click. 'Hello, Grampian Police, can I help you?'

Logan left her to it and headed back to the history room.

Rennie was already there, contemplating a copy of the *Daily Mail* and mining his nostrils for little savoury nuggets. He stopped, snapping upright and wiping his finger on the underside of the desk as soon as he realized he had company.

'Sir.' He grinned. 'Sorry. Miles away.'

'Your brain'll fall out your nose if you don't stop picking it.'

'Ahem. Yes . . . well . . . ' Rennie grabbed a pile of forms. 'I've been going over those INTERPOL results Insch wanted.'

'Anything?'

The constable shrugged. 'Depends. Kinda . . . difficult to tell, you know?' He handed over a small pile of printouts. 'Trouble is there's no real MO.'

Logan skimmed the forms. 'I would have thought abduction and butchery were pretty damn distinctive.'

'No. I mean . . . sometimes there's heaps of blood, but mostly it's just signs of a struggle and someone's missing. That could be anything, couldn't it? Doesn't have to be Wiseman. And there's hundreds more where these came from. Belgium, Israel, Romania, Kazakhstan you name it – half this crap's probably just missing persons.'

'Well,' said Logan, 'look on the bright side. Insch isn't back till Tuesday. You've still got a day and a half to finish this lot up.'

'Ha.' Rennie poked the two box files sitting beside his desk. 'Going to take a shit-load longer than that: INTERPOL's a bloody nightmare. I stuck a notice up on I-24/7 three days ago and I'm bloody swamped. Scared to open my email now . . . ' He sighed. 'And Ann Summers was out of chocolate body paint so we used golden syrup instead. Tell you, there are *still* bits of me—'

'I don't want to know.' Logan handed the INTERPOL reports back. 'Enter the lot into HOLMES, get it to look for patterns.'

'That'll take ages . . . '

'You want Insch to rip off your sticky bits? Didn't think so.' Logan hung his jacket on the back of the chair. 'Any word from Fingerprints?'

'Message on your desk.'

It looked more like an ordinance survey map than a finger-print, but according to the accompanying notes there were over sixty points of correlation between the print they'd lifted from one of the empty Special Brew tins and Ken Wiseman's right thumb. He'd definitely been at the house.

DI Steel threw the printouts back at Logan, collapsed into her chair and told him to close the door so she could have a fag. Her office was a tip, covered in stacks of paperwork and half-empty cups of tea. 'Tell you,' she said, crackling the window open and lighting up, 'twenty years ago nearly every DI kept a big bottle of duty free in their desk for moments like this. What have I got?' She went rummaging. 'Two packets of breath mints and a dirty magazine. And it's no' even mine!'

She sent a stream of smoke billowing towards the open window. 'The CC's no' exactly happy we missed Wiseman.'

'Not as if we could have done anything about it though, is it – if he sodded off before we found out about the place?'

'Aye, well, I said the same thing and he went off on one about excuses no' being good enough for the victims or their families.' She picked up the copy of *Bondage World* and flicked through it half-heartedly. Then dropped it in the bin. 'Where the hell is he?'

'We could try going through all the abandoned properties Wiseman's sister had keys for. He's obviously not worried about sleeping rough with—'

'This may come as a shock, but I did actually think of that. Wiseman's sister went missing, what: fifteen, sixteen years ago?'

'Eighteen.'

'You think anyone's going to remember what bloody houses she had keys for *eighteen years* ago?' Steel ran a hand through her devil-may-care hair. 'No wonder Inspector Fatty went loopy, this sodding case is impossible.'

Logan watched her wallow in self-pity for a minute, then asked, 'You were in Aberdeen twenty years ago, right?'

The inspector took the cigarette out of her mouth and winked at him. 'I know, hard to believe, what with me being so young and attractive looking.'

'You work the first Flesher case?'

'Nope.'

'Ever work with a DI Brooks?'

Steel laughed. 'Basher Brooks? Nut job. Always having papers served on him. Got the job done though.' She slumped a little further into her chair, cigarette dangling out of the corner of her mouth. 'Remember this one time: we were raiding a B&B in Northfield, four blokes working a protection racket, and they had this dog. Rottweiler. Big fucker with teeth like this... And it's barking and slavering and most of us are keeching our pants, but Brooks just grabs my truncheon and batters the thing's head in. And the blokes – and all four of them built like brick shite-houses, mind – take one look at Brooks, covered in dog blood and bits of skull and brains, and confess to everything.'

Her nostalgic smile faded away. 'Course, it all went tits-up a couple of years later when someone died in custody. Only so many times you can get away with prisoners falling down the stairs. Why?'

'Supposed to meet him for a pint last night with Insch and Alec. Never showed.'

'No' like Basher Brooks to miss a free drink. I remember this one time...' And she was off again, telling stories of the Detective Chief Inspector's alcoholic prowess until it was time to go home.

Logan almost made to the back door before Rennie caught up with him, shouting, 'Hoy!'

'Bloody hell ... what now?'

'Bunch of us going to see the fireworks down the beach tonight, you wanna come?' The constable had changed out of his polyester CID suit into jeans, leather jacket and lurid pink shirt, his hair jelled into random spiky tufts.

'Thought you had a whole pile of INTERPOL reports to get into HOLMES.'

Rennie grinned. 'Worked my boyish charms on a couple of lovely ladies in the support staff. They're going to start chucking them in tonight. Anyway, fireworks: I'm taking Laura – going out for a couple of pints and a boogie afterwards?'

'No way I'm spending another evening watching you crawl all over some poor peroxide—'

'No, no, no, no: she's not a bottle blonde. Collar and cuffs match, if you know what I mean.'

Logan started walking again. Rennie loped along beside him, a dopey smile on his face.

'Taking her to Spain next month. Two weeks of sun, sand, sangria, and S.E.X. She's like no one I've ever met before. I mean, you know? She's brilliant and funny and goes like a bunny! I'm giving serious thought to settling down.'

'Met her parents yet?'

'Christ no.' He stuck his hands deep in his pockets. 'So, fireworks? You up for it?'

Logan said he'd think about it.

'Hello?' Heather stood with her hands wrapped around the bars, staring out into the blackness. 'Hello? I'm thirsty . . .'

Silence.

Darkness.

'Hello?'

She felt a hand on her shoulder. *I don't think he's there.*

'But I'm *thirsty* . . .' The water had lasted longer than last time, but now it was all gone.

'*I know, Heather, I know. But it'll all be over soon.*' Duncan wrapped his arm around her shoulders, the faint light of his blood halo just strong enough that she could make out the bars. '*And then you'll be with Justin and me forever.*'

She looked at him, feeling the tears start to well up again. 'But I don't want to die . . .'

'*Shhhh . . . it's OK – everyone dies, don't they?*' He gave her a squeeze. '*Justin misses his mummy.*'

'But—'

'*Trust me, it'll all be OK. You just lie down and go to sleep.*'

Heather tried to do what she was told, but it was impossible. 'It stinks in here.'

'*Shhhh . . . sleep.*'

'What if he never comes back?'

'*It'll only hurt for a while.*'

Silence.

'Duncan, I'm scared . . .'

19

They'd arrived early to get the best spot – down on the beachfront, right up against the crowd barrier. A bitter wind whistled in off the North Sea, making everyone shudder as they waited for the fireworks to start. Colin Miller pulled out a hip flask, took a swig, then offered it to Logan: rusty nail, the mixture of whisky and Drambuie going down like alcoholic central heating.

'He's getting a bit fussy,' said Isobel, wiggling something brightly coloured in front of her son's pushchair. Sean had been OK in Pizza Hut – smearing cheese and tomato all over himself, the table, and anyone daft enough to pass within reach – but they'd been standing out here in the cold for at least half an hour. Logan was surprised the kid wasn't screaming the place down by now.

All around them people waved luminous blue lightsaber things – sparklers without the sparkle – taking photos of each other on their mobile phones.

Colin checked his watch. 'Should've started by now, but.'

The display had been set up in the lee of what looked like a Victorian concrete bus shelter, sitting below the level of the road, halfway between the Beach Ballroom and the arcades. On the other side of the barrier, people in luminous yellow jackets were fiddling with a long table of boxes and wires.

'Maybe no one remembered to bring matches with them?'

'Aye, or they've run out of milk bottles for the rockets.' Miller passed the flask over again.

Someone tapped Logan on the shoulder, and he turned to find a grinning DC Rennie. 'Don't look so surprised,' said the constable, pulling his girlfriend through the crowd behind him, 'we were speaking to McInnis: he said he'd told you this was the best spot to watch the show.' Rennie pointed at the girl beside him. 'You remember Laura?'

The natural blonde who went like a bunny gave Logan a little wave. 'Hi.'

Behind her a few more familiar faces from the station worked their way to the front, all looking as if they'd just come from the pub. Rennie wrapped his arm around the love of his life. 'And you'll *never* guess who we ran into . . . ' He pointed into the mass of lightsabers – a figure bundled up in a black padded jacket and black woolly hat was squeezing through, her face framed with dark curls, her nose and cheeks bright red. PC Jackie Watson.

She took one look at Logan and frowned. 'What happened to your face?'

He dragged on a smile. 'Didn't know you were back in town.'

'Got in half an hour ago. I phoned?'

'We—'

Swwwwwwwwwwwwwwwwwwwwwwwwwwooooooosh! And the first rocket leapt into the indigo night, exploding in a vast ball of golden sparks that fizzed and crackled.

'Why didn't you call back?'

Swwwwwwwwwwwwwwooooooooooosh! . . . BANG! More sparks.

'What?'

'I said, why didn't you—' BOOOOM! '—call back?'

'I've been out since—' CRACKKKLE!

150

The rockets were going off in a constant stream, turning the air into an iridescent rainbow of colour.

'Two months and you've not called once!'

'That's not true. You *know* that's not true!'

There was a little circle of embarrassed space forming around them. The press of bodies lessening as everyone made a point of staring at the display above, rather than the argument below.

'If you didn't want me to come home, why didn't you bloody well say so?' Jackie's face was lit for a moment in a glitter of gold, her eyes shining bright as daggers.

'Please, Jackie, let's not do this here. I—' BOOOOOM!

'It's not my fault I miscarried! It's not my fucking—' CRACKKKKKKLE!

Logan grabbed her by the arm, pulling her round so they had their backs to the clump of police officers. 'That's got nothing to do with it!'

'You think it wasn't hard for me?' She shook him loose. 'It was my fucking baby too!'

'It's not about the baby, OK? It's about you!'

She froze, and Logan ... Logan wished he could take the words back, but it was too late for that – he'd lit the blue touchpaper and now it was all going to blow up in his face. Jackie stared at him. 'You don't love me, do you?'

BOOOOOOOOOM!

'Jackie—'

'No, come on, let's hear it. Let's—' BANG! '—hear you say it.' She prodded him in the chest with a rock-hard finger. 'Have the fucking guts to say it!'

A huge rocket exploded, a circle of red and green and silver, lighting up the beach for a second. A snapshot of summer on a cold November night. The crowd ooh-ed and ahhh-ed.

A heartbeat of silence.

'I don't love you.'

Jackie slammed her fist into his face.

From up here the fireworks were beautiful – perfect spheres of fire that hung in the night sky, before fading away into darkness. Ken Wiseman took another mouthful of beer then crushed the empty can in his leather-gloved hand.

The flat was virtually empty, just a couple of cardboard boxes full of junk, a carpet that stank of dust and cats. Kitchen worktops that would never be clean again. An abandoned flat on the fifteenth floor of a tower block on Castlehill, with a panoramic view of the beach, its firework display, and the end of DCI Brooks' life.

Another flickering silver ball, then two seconds later the BOOM of its explosion.

Wiseman pulled a fresh tin of beer from the carrier bag on the kitchen worktop. 'You want a scoof?' He waggled it at the man lying on the lounge floor – hands and feet bound with black plastic cable-ties. 'No?' Wiseman smiled. 'How about one of these, then?' He took a running kick at the man's stomach, hitting him hard enough to lift the fucker off the floor, sending him rolling onto his back, groaning behind the strip of silver duct-tape.

Wiseman squatted next to him as the flat was momentarily lit by another firework. 'I should carve you up, you old fuck. Carve you into little bits.' He pulled one of his knives out and held the blade against the old man's cheek, just hard enough to break the skin. 'You'd be surprised how little difference there is between us and the animals. We all come apart the same way . . . '

Another mouthful of beer. 'Fifteen years you took from me Brooks. Fifteen fucking years in that shitehole prison with fucking rapists and paedophiles. You see this?' He pointed at the scar that ran diagonally across his face. 'They jumped me in the showers. Fuckers held me down and pulled a sharpened spoon through my face. Dragged it across the bone. Slow and deliberate.' He shuddered and drank again. 'Fucking rapists telling me *I'm* sick. Thinking they're better than me. That they've got the fucking right!'

Wiseman stood and slammed another boot into Brooks' stomach. '"Gonnae peel yer face!" "Gonnae skin yer fuckin' heid!" They would've too, guard hadn't come.'

Flash – one, one thousand – two, one thousand – BOOM! Crackle . . .

'My, my, my. Will you look at the time?' He grabbed a handful of the old man's jacket and heaved him up. 'You've got an appointment.'

The corridor outside the flat was deserted, just as Wiseman knew it would be. No one to see him drag Brooks into the stairwell and up three flights of stairs to the roof. The fire door was locked, but not alarmed. It didn't take much to kick it open.

Wind whipped across the concrete roof, and suddenly Brooks seemed to realize what was going to happen. He started struggling.

'Bit fucking late for that, don't you think?' Wiseman hauled the old man to the chest-high wall that ran round the edge. 'You remember what you said the night you arrested me? No?' He ripped the gag from Brooks' mouth, taking a big clump of moustache with it.

'Aaaaaaagh . . . God damn, fucking, bastard—'

Wiseman bounced the old git's head off the wall.

'You told me you knew people. That I wouldn't last a month in prison. That the only way I'd get out would be in a body-bag.'

'You . . .' Brooks coughed, a smear of blood on his lips. 'You sick f—'

Wiseman punched him in the stomach and the old man collapsed to the ground. 'Those going to be your last words are they?' He pulled the boning knife out again and sliced through the thin plastic strips holding Brooks' wrists together. Then did the same with the ankles.

'Ffffff . . .' The old bastard tried to get to his feet, but his legs didn't seem to be working.

'Here.' Wiseman took a handful of shirt at the back of Brooks' neck, then grabbed the old bastard's belt and hauled him up. 'Let me help you . . . '

Right over the wall and into thin air.

A huge ball of red, green and silver lit up the night sky.

For a moment the old man seemed to float, and then gravity got her claws into him. Brooks screamed: arms and legs pinwheeling as his body got smaller and smaller and smaller . . . all the way down to the concrete car park, eighteen floors below.

He hit the ground like a meat piñata, flying debris setting off car alarms.

Wiseman peered over the edge at the smear of red, lit by the flashing orange indicators of wailing motorcars. Then he went back downstairs to the flat, picked up his empty beer cans, locked the door, and headed off into the night.

20

Logan waited in the pre-dawn gloom trying not to stand in anything red. Which was easier said than done: who knew one old man could go so far? The impact zone lay in the strip of concrete between the two tower blocks. Ex-DCI Brooks covered at least a dozen feet in every direction – tarmac, pavement, wall... The cars were the worst: metallic paint pebble-dashed with shrivelled, crimson bubbles, glittering in the IB spotlights like dried-up ladybirds. Not the best accompaniment to a Monday-morning hangover.

Someone from the Environmental Health team marched over, sipping tea from a polystyrene cup, her white paper oversuit unzipped to the waist. 'You going to be much longer?'

'Don't think so.' Logan watched DI Steel mooching about on the far side of the blue-and-white POLICE tape, mobile phone clamped to her ear. 'Think you'll be able to shift all this?'

The woman shrugged. 'You should *see* some of the crap we have to deal with. She pulled a huge aerosol out of her pocket. 'Trychloroethylene: it'll bleach through pretty much anything. Don't fancy owning any of those cars, Christ knows what it's going to do to the paintwork.'

'Hoy, Lazarus!' Steel – shouting across Garry Brooks' personal Ground Zero. 'Get them going.'

'You heard the lady.' Logan skirted the taped-off scene as the Environmental Health team pulled up their hoods, strapped on their facemasks, and got to work with the trychloroethylene.

Steel lit a cigarette, watching them spraying away, the thick stench of bleach oozing out in a fine mist, caught by the morning breeze, glowing in the building's security lights. 'No' exactly my idea of fun . . . '

'How'd Insch take it?'

'How do you think?' She took a long drag. 'The guy you've looked up to for twenty-five years does a belly-flop off an eighteen-storey building. No' exactly ice-cream and balloons, is it?' A small crowd of onlookers had gathered on the outskirts of the car park. More peered out of the windows of the tower block, watching as the Environmental Health team covered everything in industrial bleach. 'He's coming in.'

Logan hadn't expected anything else. Suspended or not, Insch wouldn't trust them not to screw this up. 'Wiseman?'

'Probably.' Steel looked from the blood-splashed car park all the way up to the roof. 'That or Brooks decided to go in for a bit of freestyle plummeting.' She sucked in a lungful of smoke. 'Maybe he was wracked with guilt for screwing up the Flesher inquiry? If he'd done a proper job in the first place, they'd never have let the bastard go.'

She dragged the last gasp from her cigarette, then flicked it out into the puddle of drying blood. 'How's your vertigo?'

From the roof, eighteen floors up, the car park looked a long, long way down. The Environmental Health had finished with the spraying and were now trying to wash the remaining bleachy sludge down the nearest drain with a hose.

Steel sidled up next to Logan and peered over the wall. 'Jesus, how far you think that is?'

'Sixty, seventy feet?'

'Hmm...' She howched, and spat, watching as the glob disappeared. 'Enough time for a good long scream. You'd think someone would've noticed.'

'Fireworks. The Council had their big display—'

'Looks like Brooks wasn't the only one who had a bad one last night.' She turned and stared at Logan's bruised face. 'Twice in two days?'

Logan put a hand up to his cheek: it was still swollen, even after an evening of cold compresses and malt whisky. 'It's nothing.'

'Word is Watson lamped you one.'

'When's the post mortem?'

'Eh? Half eight, they're rushing it through 'cos he's an ex-cop. And stop changing the subject.'

Logan leant on the wall, staring out over the city as the sun rose from the watery depths of the North Sea, washing the granite buildings with gold. 'Insch and I were supposed to meet Brooks on Saturday night. He was trying to pump us for details on the Wiseman case.'

'Sounds like Basher Brooks. Silly sod could never let it— Arse...' Her phone was ringing. 'Hello? ... Aye ... Did he? ... Oh.' Her face fell. 'Aye, well, no surprise there ... No, no, it's OK. See you then.' She hung up. 'They were doing a quick check at the mortuary, making sure they'd no' left any bits of Brooks behind. Ligature marks round wrists and ankles.'

'Definitely Wiseman then.' Not suicide: murder.

The mortuary smelt like a butcher's shop, the numerous chunks of Ex-DCI Brooks arranged to make a whole, slightly flattened person, as Isobel dictated her way through the remains.

Most of the jumpers Logan had seen were from six or seven storeys high – broken bones, internal bleeding – but Brooks looked as if he'd been torn apart, then battered with a sledgehammer.

'You fancy pizza for lunch?' whispered Steel, while Isobel wrestled with the deflated football that used to be Brooks' head.

Logan grimaced.

'OK, OK, not pizza. Curry? Sushi? How about . . . ' she trailed off when she realised Isobel and the Procurator Fiscal were staring at her. Steel shrugged. 'Didn't have any breakfast.'

Isobel put Brooks' head back on the dissecting table. 'Can we all *please* remain silent while I'm dictating!'

No one said anything.

'Thank you.' She picked up the head again. 'Evidence of severe impact trauma consistent with a fall of eighty to a hundred feet—'

'There's a surprise.'

'Inspector! I'm not going to—'

The door flew open and crashed against a trolley full of sterilized implements sending them pinging and clanging to the mortuary floor: DI Insch. His white oversuit stretched nearly to bursting point. His face dark, dark red.

The PF looked up and frowned. 'Inspector, you shouldn't be—'

The fat man elbowed his way to the dissecting table. 'He was my friend!'

'That's *why* you shouldn't be here.' The Procurator Fiscal looked round for support, but everyone had developed a sudden interest in the mortuary walls.

Everyone except Isobel: 'For goodness sake! I'm trying to carry out a post mortem and if I don't get silence I'll eject the lot of you! This will be a *closed* session. Do I make myself clear?'

Insch rounded on her. 'Don't you *dare*—'

Steel laid a hand on his arm. 'Come on, David.'

'Get your bloody hands off me! I'm—'

'Let's no' burn any more bridges. Eh? Brooks wouldn't want that. Would he?'

The fat man's eyes sparked with tears. 'He was my friend.'

'I know.' She pulled him towards the door. 'Come on, you and me'll go have a cuppa. Laz'll look after him. Won't you Laz?'

Logan nodded, and the inspector let himself be led out of the sterile cutting room. For a moment everyone relaxed ... and then Isobel peeled off DCI Brooks' face.

Her head hurt. Pounding. Bang, bang, bang ... Throat dry, lips like sandpaper. 'Thirsty ...'

Duncan squatted down next to her and smiled. *'I know, but it'll only hurt for a little bit. Then you'll be OK. You'll be with us.'*

'So thirsty ...'

Heather curled up on the filthy mattress and tried not to cry. She was going to die in here, in this dark metal box. Forgotten and alone ...

'Hey,' Duncan brushed the hair from her face. *'You're not alone. You've got me, remember?'*

She kept her eyes screwed shut. 'You're not real.'

'I'm as real as you need me to be. Come on, have I ever lied to you?'

She rolled over onto her other side, turning her back on him. 'Inverness, three years ago.'

He groaned. *'I told you: it was a mistake. I was drunk. She didn't mean anything to me.'* Duncan's hand slipped down her body. *'It's always been you, you know that.'* The hand caressed her thigh. *'You were my world.'*

'I hated you so much.'

His fingers wandered north, making her breath catch. *'Let me make it up to you ...'* He kissed her neck, her throat, her breasts, her stomach, her—

There was a clang from outside and Heather froze. Light flooded the tiny prison.

He was back.

She scrabbled her clothes back into place and hurried over to the bars as the door creaked open. 'Please, I'm so thirsty.'

The Butcher placed six two-litre bottles of water on the prison floor, then stepped outside again, leaving the door open. Heather grabbed them, cracked one open and drank deep. Coughing and spluttering in her haste. Twelve litres of water!

And then the smell hit her – meaty and fragrant over the disinfectant reek coming from the chemical toilet. The Butcher was back, carrying a big plastic box. He dropped it at his feet, took a key from his apron pocket, unlocked a heavy brass padlock, and pushed open a gate in the bars.

Heather could feel her bowels clench. This was it, he was going to kill her . . .

But he didn't. He opened the box and pulled out a tray covered with slices of roast meat, boiled potatoes, green beans, Brussels sprouts, Yorkshire puddings . . . enough food to feed an army.

Heather almost wept.

All this food. All this water!

She crept forward and grabbed a slice of meat, cramming it into her mouth and chewing, washing it down with deep swigs of water.

He stood watching her.

'It's . . . very good,' she said, picking up another chunk and a handful of vegetables to go with it. Gravy dribbled down her chin as she ripped another bite out of the tender, juicy flesh. 'Mmmphnngh . . .' More water. 'Delicious, really nice.' Desperate not to sound ungrateful.

The Butcher nodded, then stepped back to the other side of the bars, closed the gate and snapped the padlock back into place. Leaving her with her feast.

Days' worth of food and drink . . .

'Are you . . . are you going away?'

He stared silently at her, then pointed at the meat.

'Please don't leave me . . .'

But he did.

160

At least DI Insch had calmed down a bit by the time Logan emerged from the post mortem. Whole bodies were bad enough, but Brooks . . . Logan shuddered. It was like some sort of horrible jigsaw puzzle.

All the chairs in the inspector's office were occupied – DI Steel in one, the Detective Chief Superintendent in charge of CID in the other. Everyone waiting for Logan's edited highlights.

'Preliminary report won't be out till the end of the day, but there's a lot of bruising to the head, stomach, thighs and chest – he'd been repeatedly beaten. Looks like Brooks was held somewhere for about forty-eight hours before he . . .' Logan tried to think of a tactful way to put it, 'before he was thrown off the roof.'

Silence.

'Sorry, sir.'

The inspector's voice was a low rumble: distant thunder getting close fast. 'Wiseman.'

'We're doing door-to-doors in the tower blocks, going through the Castlegate CCTV—'

'That's why he didn't turn up. At the pub. Wiseman had him . . .' Insch's face had gone beyond its normal angry red, into a previously undiscovered shade of trembling purple. Breath hissing out between clenched teeth. 'Get the IB round to his house. I don't care if they have to tear it apart, I want—'

The DCS placed a hand on the inspector's arm. 'David, I need you to go home. Let us handle this.'

Insch got as far as. 'Don't you—'

'Before you say it: I know. I worked with Brooks too. We'll get the bastard responsible, but you need to go home. If Professional Standards find out you've ignored your suspension they'll go ballistic.'

Insch was on his feet. 'You can't send me—'

'I can, and I am. Go home, David. Have a pint for Brooks. Come in tomorrow and we'll discuss your caseload.'

'But—'

'That's an *order*, Inspector.'

Drizzle. It drifted down from a battleship-grey sky, slowly seeping its way into everything, making the IB team miserable as they searched Ex-DCI Brooks' back garden. Logan stood at the conservatory door, watching them get wet.

On the other side of the high back wall, a development of nasty yellow-clad houses sat cheek-by-jowl with one another. Brand new and ugly in comparison to the stately granite buildings they'd been thrown up behind. McLennan Homes strikes again.

If he stood on his tiptoes, Logan could just make out pairs of uniformed officers going door-to-door in the vague hope that someone might have seen something.

A grumpy figure in a mud-smeared SOC suit trudged up to the conservatory, snapped off her latex gloves, dragged out a scabby handkerchief, and made horrible snottery noises. 'Bugger all,' she said when she'd finished. 'No hair, no fibres, no prints. We know he came over the back wall – got two good-sized indentations in the flowerbed, but nothing we can get a decent cast from. Best guess is he had plastic bags on over his shoes – that'd explain why there's no muddy footprints in the house.'

The hanky came out for another performance.

'OK, finish it up and I'll get Rennie to stick the kettle on.'

She sniffed. 'Looks like a professional job.'

'Get your team in out of the wet. We can—'

'Sir?' A panicked shout from the front of the house. 'Sergeant McRae?'

Logan knew it had been too good to last. The only surprise was that it'd taken the Insch this long... He turned and marched through the spotless conservatory; the bomb-site lounge with its overturned furniture, smashed ornaments, and bloodstains; then out into the hall, where DC

Rennie was trying to stop DI Insch from storming into the house.

'It's OK,' Logan tapped the constable on the shoulder. 'Why don't you go see to the teas?' He let Rennie squeeze past, then stepped forwards to block the entrance. 'Inspector?'

'I was out walking Lucy, and I spotted the IB van.' Insch gestured at the grubby transit parked in Brooks' drive with 'ALSO AVAILABLE IN WHITE' finger-painted in the filth. Behind him, his ancient Springer Spaniel sat on the wet grass, legs akimbo, slowly absorbing the drizzle.

'What can we do for you?'

The huge man glowered at him from the threshold. 'You can let me in for a bloody start.'

'Sorry, sir, this is an active crime scene.'

Insch rested a fat finger in the middle of Logan's chest. 'Remember I'm going to be back in charge again tomorrow, Sergeant. You might not want to go pissing me off right now. Step aside.'

'I can't do that. You *know* I can't do that.'

Insch's finger withdrew two inches, then rammed forward into Logan's chest. 'Suspended or not, I am your superior officer. And I swear to God, if you don't get out of my bloody way—'

'What, you'll punch me in the face? *Again?*' Logan looked down at the cast-iron digit, then up at the inspector. 'Sir, I know he was your friend. And I know you want to catch whoever did it. But do you think you could try fucking trusting me for five minutes and let me do my job?'

Insch actually backed off a step.

'Look, we'll be finished here soon. An hour tops. We'll have to leave someone outside till we can get the back door boarded up. But if you're a friend of the family you'll have a key. You can let yourself in.'

The inspector turned away, watching as his decrepit spaniel embarked on a vigorous ear-scratching campaign. There was a pause, then, 'I don't have a key.'

'Wait here.' Logan ducked back into the hall and picked a likely candidate from the pegboard above the telephone, then tried it in the Yale lock. Perfect fit. He held it out to Insch. 'Brooks must have given it to you a while ago, just in case he had to go away. So you could water the plants.'

The inspector stuck out a vast paw, and Logan dropped the key in it. Insch turned without a word and marched away down the garden path, taking his stinky, soggy old dog with him.

21

It was half past four before the joiner turned up to board up Brooks' back door. Logan watched him nailing the huge sheet of plywood into place, doing his best to ignore the man's rambling moan about all these Eastern Europeans coming over here and undercutting honest tradesmen like him. Then asked if Logan needed any jobs doing on the QT for cash . . . ?

Logan did one last circuit of the house, making sure the IB hadn't left anything behind, then stepped out into the rainy night and locked the front door.

A lone rocket screeched into the dark orange sky, exploding in a tiny puff of golden sparks. Not exactly spectacular.

He climbed behind the wheel of his pool car and sat there, listening to the rain tapping on the roof, looking out at Brooks' house. Maybe he should go round and tell Insch the place was all his? Not that it'd do the inspector any good – there was nothing there to link Wiseman with Brooks' death. The Butcher was too clever for that.

Logan turned the key in the ignition and set the windscreen wipers going. They'd emptied Brooks' freezer, just in case it contained any human remains, but he doubted they'd find any. The man who'd led the Flesher investigation back in 1987 hadn't been turned into meat, he'd been turned into pavement pâté.

Logan took the scenic route to Insch's house, driving through the old town centre. A clot of schoolchildren lurked in the bus shelter: some smoking cigarettes, some 'Oh-my-God'ing into mobile phones, one or two making abstract patterns in the air with hot white sparklers.

A scream.

Logan snapped upright in his seat – a young girl, no more than six years old, was being chased by a little boy in a Margaret Thatcher fright mask.

'Jesus . . . ' In his day they'd played cowboys and Indians, not serial killer and victims. He pulled out into the town square, past the weird sandstone statue of a sailor, and onto South Road.

Insch's home, 'DUNPROMPTIN', was a large granite box set back off the road, shielded by a high wall and mature trees, the leaves amber and russet, like frozen fireworks. Logan creaked the gate open and headed up the path. Another rocket exploded in the distance, this one slightly more impressive than the last anaemic attempt.

He leaned on the bell, watching the green sparkles fade away.

He counted to sixty, then tried again. A deep *ding-donggggggg* sounded somewhere inside the house. Still no answer.

Maybe they'd gone out?

So much for Insch being desperate to see round his dead friend's house. Bloody man was like mercury these days: I want this, I want that, I want something completely different. A vast, bad-tempered child.

Logan tried one last time, then headed back to the car.

'Shhhhhh . . . ' Wiseman held a finger to his lips as the last peal of the doorbell faded into silence. Then waited five minutes, just to be sure whoever it was had fucked off. Then took his hand off the bitch's mouth.

She was a good girl, didn't scream this time. Learned her lesson. She wasn't much to look at – let herself go a bit after the kids – but then, given the fat git she'd married... No accounting for taste.

He pulled out a couple of cable-ties and fastened the bitch's wrists behind her back, then wrapped another set around her ankles. Just like her darling husband and the three little girls upstairs. One big happy family.

Wiseman smiled at her. 'Now then, where were we?'

The fat bastard lay flat on his face in the middle of the carpet – spread out like a beached whale, bright red oozing from the back of his bald head.

'He ever tell you about me?'

She whimpered and shook her head.

'No? That's not polite, is it, Insch?' Wiseman heaved the fat man over onto his back and slapped a strip of duct-tape over his mouth. 'How could you not tell your lovely wife that you fucked my life over?' Wiseman sat on Insch's barrel chest, spat in his face. Then slammed a fist into it. The whale's blubber shuddered, and two dark, piggy eyes cracked open.

'The kraken awakes! Hey, Fat Boy: miss me?'

Insch struggled, breath hissing through his nose as he tried to break his bonds.

'No point, Lard Arse. Most people can't snap *one* cable tie, never mind six. You're going nowhere.' He patted Insch's chubby cheek. 'I can't believe you never told her how you beat a fucking confession out of me! Eh? How you told the court I fell...' Wiseman slammed his fist into Insch's face, 'down...' punch, 'the...' punch, 'fucking...' punch, 'stairs!'

He sat back and flexed his hand. 'See, your law-abiding, police officer husband liked beating up suspects, didn't you, Fatty?' He stood, took two steps back and slammed a foot into Insch's ribs.

The bitch whimpered. 'We ... we've got money! You can have it! Just let us go!'

Wiseman pretended to think about it for a minute. 'No.'

'But ... but they'll come looking for us! You can't—'

'Oh, shut up.' He tore off another strip of duct-tape and sealed her cakehole. 'What've I got to lose, eh? These bastards catch me they're going to screw me over. Just like last time. I've seen the papers: what is it, five, six murders? You think two more are going to make any difference?'

She mumbled something behind her gag, eyes wide, terrified.

'Shhhh ...' He dropped down in front of her, stroked her hair, cupped her podgy face in his hand; smiling as Fatty thrashed about on the floor, making angry, impotent noises. 'I've been waiting for this for ages. Believe me, there are worse things than dying. There's being banged up with fucking sickos and kiddy-fiddlers for fifteen years. There's getting raped in the showers. Now why don't you settle back and enjoy the show? It's going to be a lonnnnng night ...'

Heather sat, knees drawn up to her chest, ears straining at the darkness.

'I don't understand, what—'

'Shhh!'

Duncan pulled on his hard-done-by face. *'I was only asking.'*

'Can you hear it? I can hear it ...'

'Maybe you should eat something?'

'I can hear it breathing.'

'Heather—'

'Something's out there.' She pointed out into the darkness, where the bars were, and Duncan shuddered.

'Don't think about it.'

'You know what it is, don't you?'

'There's still plenty of pork left. Or is it veal? I can't tell.'

'Duncan – tell me!'

'Where do you think he's gone? I mean, he left enough food—'
'DUNCAN!'

When he replied it was little more than a whisper. *'It's the Dark.'*

Heather pushed herself back into the corner, praying that the line of bars would be enough to keep the Dark from breaking through. 'What ... what does it want?'

'What do you think?'

Breathing in the darkness. Watching her. Waiting.

'It wants me ...'

The morning briefing was a pretty dismal affair – DI Steel standing in for Insch who hadn't turned up that morning. Probably hungover after a night in the Redgarth, drinking to DSI Brooks' memory. So Steel was just going through the motions till he turned up: no new leads, no new victims, no sign of Wiseman. Same as yesterday and the day before.

She wrapped up the meeting with a half-hearted chorus of 'We are not at home to Mr Fuck-Up!' then let them all get back to whatever jobs Insch had given them before he'd been suspended. Which left Logan and Rennie back in the Flesher history room, clambering up the north face of Ancient Paperwork Mountain.

By half past ten Rennie was off making tea again – anything to escape all those INTERPOL reports – when Faulds reappeared. The Chief Constable dumped his suitcase by the radiator, stretched, yawned, and slouched into his seat. 'Sorry I'm so late, but I couldn't face the redeye.' He fumbled the top off a waxed cardboard cup of coffee. 'Why does everyone have to go feral on Guy Fawkes night?'

Logan looked up from the latest in a long line of crime scene reports. 'Fireworks?'

'It'll make my life a lot easier when they ban the bloody things. Seven children with first-degree burns. One little girl

169

lost most of her left hand ... mind you, she was trying to stuff a rocket up some poor dog's bum at the time: wanted to see if it would explode. What's wrong with people today?'

There was no answer to that, so Logan went back to work. But he could feel Faulds watching him.

It took the Chief Constable nearly five minutes to pop the question: 'So ... what happened to your face?'

'I'd rather not talk about it, sir.'

Faulds stared at him for a while, shrugged, then asked for an update on the case, nodding and groaning as Logan went through everything that had happened since the CC left for Birmingham on Friday.

'So basically,' said Faulds, when Logan had finished, 'I go away for three days and it all goes to rat-shit.'

'Something like that.'

The Chief Constable sniffed. 'I can't believe Wiseman threw Brooks off a roof. I mean, he was a Neanderthal and his methods were ... questionable, but he didn't deserve that.'

It was hard to imagine who did. 'We've got CCTV footage of someone helping Brooks into the tower block. He looks plastered – post mortem turned up traces of heroin in his system, Isobel only found one injection site.'

'Poor sod. At least we've got CCTV—'

'We can't make an ID. It's a council system so the resolution's terrible, and the guy's wearing a hoodie, never looks at the camera.' Logan pointed at a fresh collection of photos on the wall of death. 'We found the flat he kept Brooks in; according to council records the last tenant was a Mrs Irene Grey. She went into hospital for a cataract operation, caught MRSA. Died two months ago.'

'And?'

'Turns out her son is one Martin Grey – doing twelve years in Peterhead Prison for abduction, rape and forced imprisonment. Grabbed a sixteen-year-old boy and kept him chained and drugged for nearly a week.'

'Jesus...'

'Martin and Wiseman were in the same cell block.'

Faulds took a sip of his coffee. 'Circumstantial at best. We need prints, fibre, witnesses...'

'None of which we have. Wiseman's had years to plan all this, he's taking precautions, wearing gloves, cleaning up after himself.'

'I don't like the thought of someone bumping off retired senior police officers with impunity.' He drummed his fingers on the desk for a bit. 'So what's the plan?'

'Up in the air at the moment. Insch hasn't been in yet.'

The Chief Constable checked his watch. 'Not still suspended is he?'

'No, but Brooks' death hit him kind of hard. The DCS says we should give him a couple of days to—'

Faulds was already dialling. 'I'd better give him a call, let him know we're here if he needs to talk.' He held in silence for a moment, then left a message asking Insch to call him back. 'Not answering his mobile.'

Logan tried the inspector's home number. It rang and rang and rang and, *'You've reached the Insch residence. I'm afraid we're not able to come to the phone right now...'*

'Aren't you popular.' Wiseman listened as some policeman's voice echoed out of the answering machine. *'...can call the station as soon as you get this. Thanks.'* *Bleeeeeeep.* He hit the delete button.

'How you doing, Fat Boy? Hungry? You have to be hungry, look at the size of you!'

Insch could only scowl. Poor bastard. Ha, ha, ha.

He wasn't looking too pretty this morning: his piggy face all swollen and covered with bruises. It had taken a shit heap of duct-tape to strap the fat git to an armchair, but it was worth it just to see him wriggle. Wiseman grinned, and placed the hot frying pan down on the dining room table. The smell of

171

scorching varnish filled the air, covering the stink of two people tied to their chairs for over eighteen hours with no access to a toilet.

'Mmm . . .' Wiseman prodded the meat in the sizzling pan. 'Want some?'

Insch's eyes were like burning coals. If looks could kill, the fat bastard would be a walking doomsday device.

'Where are my manners, eh? *Ladies* first.' Wiseman grabbed the stinky bitch by the hair, pulled her head back, and gripped one end of her tape gag. 'If you shout, try to raise the alarm, warn someone, any of that shite, I'll kill you.' The tape came away with a patina of smeared lipstick. She burst into tears.

'Please. Please let us go! We won't tell anyone! You can just leave and no one will know!'

Wiseman stared for a moment, then slapped her. 'LOOK AT MY FUCKING FACE!' He hit her again. 'What am I going to do? Shave off my beard and buy a ginger wig? Think that'll work? Think people won't notice the big,' he hit her again, 'fucking scar?' Once more for luck: snapping her head round, blood and spittle dribbling down her chin.

Behind him, he could hear Insch thrashing against his bonds. 'Sit still, Fatty, or I'll give her something to cry about.' And gradually the noise stopped.

Wiseman jabbed a fork into the pan and lifted out a slice of meat. It was perfectly cooked: the skin pale and tender, the inside moist, the edges caramelised. It dripped grease on the carpet, then on the bitch's dress, then her chin. Gravy and blood mingling.

'Eat.'

'Please . . .'

'Not going to tell you again.'

She took a tentative bite. Chewed and swallowed. Wiseman glanced over his shoulder at the fat man, sitting there with a furious scowl on his bright purple face as the bitch ate the rest. 'Don't worry, plenty left for you.'

He dug another slice out of the pan and turned to Inspector Fat Wad. 'Here's the deal. You eat this, or I slit her throat.'

He ripped the duct-tape gag off.

Insch gasped and snarled and opened his mouth to shout something, but Wiseman rammed the slice of meat in. The inspector spat it out, shaking his head from side to side, swearing. Wiseman grabbed the fat bastard's ear and twisted. Then the fucker sat still.

Insch growled at him. 'I'll kill you . . .'

'Really think I won't do it? Slit her throat?' He gave the ear another twist. 'Now *eat your fucking breakfast!*'

'I'll kill—'

'OK, be like that. I gave you the chance to save her, and you blew it.' He walked over to the table and picked up the boning knife – it glittered against the bitch's throat.

She closed her eyes, gritted her teeth, and sobbed.

'Any last words?'

'Don't! I'll . . . I'll eat it!' The fat git's face was pouring with sweat. 'Just leave her alone! She didn't do anything to you, it was me. I did it. Not her . . .'

'That's better.' Wiseman laid the knife next to the frying pan and picked up the fork. He speared the slice the fat git had spat out – picking off a few stray dog hairs from where it had hit the carpet – then held it out for Insch to bite.

Insch stared at it, then at his wife, then back to the slice again. Took a deep breath. Closed his eyes. And bit. For a moment it looked as if he was going to vomit, but he chewed and swallowed instead. Shuddering as it went down.

'There's a good boy.' Wiseman smiled. 'Did you like that? Tasty and tender was it?'

'I'm . . .' He gagged.

The bitch's voice was small and trembling. 'David? What's wrong?'

'Keep it down, Fat Boy, there's more where that came from.'

Insch didn't look at her. 'Nothing's wrong. It's all going to be OK.'

'Go on, Lardy, tell your lovely wife what the Flesher does. Don't be shy.'

'Tell me what? David . . . ?'

'Tell her.'

'He killed at least a dozen people. Butchered their remains and ate them.'

The bitch's eyes went wide, then locked onto the frying pan and its tasty, meaty contents. 'Oh God . . . '

Wiseman leant down and whispered in Insch's ear. 'You haven't asked where your daughters are.'

The fat man screamed.

22

Rennie barged into the history room, skidding to a halt on the tatty green carpet tiles. 'You'll never guess what!

Logan didn't look up. 'What happened to the tea?'

'Wiseman's called the BBC again: Torry Battery, two pm! The DCS wants everyone in the briefing room, now.'

The Detective Chief Superintendent in charge of CID drew a red 'X' on the whiteboard – '... and the third set of marksmen will be here. Plainclothes officers will be in two cars parked here, and here. Another three will pose as dog walkers.' More squiggles on the board. 'Everyone else will be in unmarked police vans here ... and here.' He gave the nod, and someone clicked onto the next slide in the presentation: a grey and white outside broadcast van. 'The BBC are lending us this on the condition that one of their cameramen is present for the arrest.'

Rennie leant over and whispered at Logan, 'There's a surprise. These TV buggers—'

The DCS glared at him. 'Do you have something to add, Constable?'

Rennie froze. 'Er ... I was just saying that there's a safety issue, sir. You know, with a civilian being present.'

Logan was impressed: it was a feat of weaselry worthy of DI Steel.

The DCS nodded. 'Good point. I don't need to tell you all how dangerous Ken Wiseman is. No one is to take any chances, but I want him in a cell, not a body bag. Now, any questions?'

Logan stuck his hand up. 'He called the BBC at quarter to eleven to make an appointment for two. That's over three hours. He's got to know they'd tell us about it, why give us so much notice?'

It was Faulds who answered. 'Wiseman has a serious persecution complex. This is his chance to go down in a blaze of glory, and he gets to do it all on national television.'

The DCS cleared his throat. 'As I was saying: no one is to take any chances.' He pointed at one of the firearms officers. 'Yes, Brodie?'

'Where's DI Insch?'

'The inspector is taking some personal time. Any *other* questions?'

Back in the history room, Logan peered at Faulds over a pile of crime scene reports. 'I still say he should be there.'

The Chief Constable sighed. 'As your DCS says, Insch has been under a lot of stress lately, he just needs some time—'

'I've called his house and his mobile a dozen times, what if something's happened?'

'Like what?'

'What if Wiseman's gone after him too? Insch was part of the team that put—'

'So was I. So were a lot of people. We had about a hundred officers working the case at one point. Insch was just a constable back then, your DCS was more influential in the prosecution than Insch.' He paused. 'But if it makes you feel any better, get a patrol car to swing past.'

Logan called the Oldmeldrum station – little more than a couple of rooms bolted onto the secondary school – and listened to the phone ring ... the call was diverted to an Airwave handset that hissed and crackled, with the faint sound of yelling and mooing in the background. *'Hullo?'*

'This is DS McRae from FHQ, I need you to get a car round to DI Insch's house, South Road, number—'

'Aye, I ken where he lives. But I canna go roond there the noo. We've hid a fatal RTA – poor bugger in a Fiesta hit a coo on the road tae Turra. Some feel left the gate open: I've got coos and blood all ower the place.' Which explained the cattle noises in the background.

'How soon do you think you could—'

'God knows. Like a bloody abattoir out here.'

'Well ... do what you can, OK?' Logan hung up and fidgeted for a bit.

'You really *are* worried, aren't you?' said Faulds. 'How long would it take you from here? There and back?'

Logan checked his watch. 'If we floor it, about an hour and a half.'

'Right.' Faulds stood and grabbed his coat. 'But if we're not back before Wiseman's TV slot, I'll personally strangle you, OK?'

'Deal.'

They hurried down through the building, making for the rear podium. A small clump of cameramen loitered at the back door, smoking cigarettes and talking about focal lengths. Alec waved as Logan and Faulds pushed through the back doors.

'This is going to be so cool!' he said, following them to a pool car speckled with rust and seagull droppings. 'Can I ride with you guys? I've got a great idea for a travelling shot, all the way through Torry and up to the Battery, we—'

'Sorry, Alec.' Logan wrenched open the driver's door. 'We've got to go pick up Insch.'

'But . . . ' The cameraman looked at his watch, his colleagues, back to Logan and then at his watch again. 'But isn't he all the way out—'

'Yes, that's why we can't hang around talking to—'

'Shite . . . ' Alec clambered into the back seat. 'Come on then, let's roll!'

Logan put his foot down – the dual carriageway flashing past as they took the quick route through Bucksburn, past the airport, and out into the countryside, Bennachie looming vast and purple in the distance.

'So . . . ' Faulds watched the fields go by. 'I was talking to DI Steel this morning.' He left a pause, but Logan didn't have a clue what he was talking about.

'That's nice.'

The Chief Constable pointed at Logan's bruised face. 'She says your girlfriend beat you up.'

Gossipy old cow. 'Ex-girlfriend. And she didn't beat me up. It was an accident.' Lie. 'Do you really think Wiseman's going to be stupid enough to show up?'

'Don't change the subject.'

'There's nothing to tell, OK? We broke up. End of story.'

Alec peered through from the back. 'I dumped this girl once – law student – two weeks later she lets herself into my flat with a spare set of keys and craps in the bed. Then she covers it with the duvet and fucks off. Course, I come back steaming that night, with a quantity surveyor called Daphne. We tear each other's clothes off and jump into bed . . . Fucking horrible it was. Went everywhere.'

An embarrassed silence settled into the car.

'What? I was just saying, OK?' Alec slumped back into his seat. 'Honestly, some people would find that kinky. I used to know this guy—'

Faulds turned and stared at him. 'Better leave it there, Alec. Don't want to spoil the magic.'

In the end Wiseman had to stuff a dishtowel in the fat bastard's mouth to get him to shut up. Insch didn't look well, sat there, strapped to his armchair, face all covered with bruises and tears and snot. Trembling and furious.

Wiseman glanced at the clock – the telly people were expecting him at two – he had to get a shift on. 'Well, Fatso, I've got to go. It's been fun, but tempus fugit, and all that.' He grabbed Insch's nose and pinched the nostrils shut, watching him struggle for oxygen. He could kill him with two fingers. Just like that . . . But it would be a waste.

He let go and Insch dragged a shuddering breath in through his podgy nose. 'But before I leave,' Wiseman wiped his fingers on the fat bastard's shirt, 'have to decide what to do with you.' He picked up the boning knife and rested the point on that disgusting, huge stomach. 'I could open you up like the fat fucking piggy you are, gut you right here. Would you like that, Fat Boy?'

Insch glared at him, furious hissing noises coming from his flared nostrils.

'Thought so. But know what I'm going to do instead? I'm going to hurt you.' He slammed his fist into the bastard's face, rocking that angry scarlet head back on its huge pink neck. 'Made an appointment with the BBC – stupid bastards actually think I'm going to turn up, when I *know* the whole place will be swarming with cops.' He smiled. 'You know where I'll be while they're looking the other way, Fat Boy?'

Wiseman went upstairs and came back carrying a wriggling piglet with blonde pigtails, tied hand and foot.

The little girl took one look at her parents, and froze. He dumped her on the floor at Daddy's feet. 'Three daughters. That's one for you, one for me, and one for the pot.' Wiseman picked up the frying pan again, and poured the last of the fat and gravy over Insch's head. 'She *was* tasty, wasn't she?'

The bitch moaned and wailed behind her gag, but the fat man looked ready for murder.

'What will I do with my one? Hmm?' Bending down to stroke the piglet's hair. 'What will I do with *my* little girl?' He looked up into Insch's terrified face, then backhanded him again. 'Not that, you fucking pervert. I'm going to sell her. Get a lot of money for specialist livestock this sweet.' Wiseman winked. 'According to the paedos in Peterhead, they're easier to train if no one knows you've got them. No Social Services, no "concerned parents". You can do whatever you like.'

Insch shouted something behind the gag, thrashing back and forth, straining against the duct-tape, making the armchair creak. Wiseman picked up the girl and slung her over his shoulder. 'She's going to make some dirty old bastard very, very happy. And all because you fucked with me, Fatty. All because of you.' He turned and smiled at Insch's wife. 'You think about that next time he wants to put his dick in you.'

He could still hear them struggling as he closed and locked the front door. Throwing Brooks off the roof had been a bit of a letdown. He'd expected it to be a lot more satisfying, but it was over too quickly.

This was going to hurt that fat bastard till the day he died.

23

Logan slowed down as they reached the outskirts of Old-meldrum. 'How we doing for time?'

Faulds scowled. 'Badly.'

'Not my fault there was a tractor.' He threaded the car through the village centre, making for Insch's house. 'Anyway, if we stick the siren on all the way back we can—' There was a familiar-looking Range Rover up ahead. It only stayed in vision for a second, and then it was hidden by the curve in the road.

'What?'

'I think that was Insch . . .' Logan pulled up outside the inspector's house. Where the muck-encrusted four-by-four should have been, there was just a patch of oily gravel. 'Someone must've got through on the phone. Told him it was going down at two.'

'Are you telling me we came all this way for nothing?'

'We can still catch him.' Logan ignored the thirty limit all the way up to the T-junction. The Range Rover was just visible, driving along the A947 back towards Aberdeen. Logan followed it.

'What if it's not even his car?'

Logan accelerated, closing the gap. There were two vehicles between them and the four-by-four: a blue Audi and a tatty Daihatsu 4Trak, Logan peered past them at the car in front. 'No ... it's definitely Insch's.'

'Well, flash your lights, or something.'

Alec shuffled himself forwards. 'Jesus, that thing gets filthier every time I see it; you could grow tatties on that.'

Flashing the lights didn't seem to help so Logan leant on the horn. The driver turned, glancing back over his shoulder – only it wasn't Insch.

'Fuck!' Logan gripped the steering wheel. 'It's him!'

'What? Of course it's—'

'Wiseman! Wiseman's driving the car!'

'WHAT?'

He grabbed the car's radio handset as the Range Rover accelerated away uphill. 'He's seen us!' The road was too twisty to get past the Audi and the 4Trak. Logan fumbled on the dashboard for the siren switch, and the handset went flying: clattering down into the footwell. 'Bloody hell!' But at least the siren's wail made the slowcoaches get out of the way. Logan hammered it.

The black slab of Alec's HDV camera poked between the seats.

'Put your bloody seatbelt on!'

Over the brow of the hill. A hard right curve and the Range Rover was putting as much distance between them as possible. Round a wide bend, the four by four overtaking a JCB digger.

Logan put his foot down and followed suit, jerking them out into the opposite lane.

Faulds screamed: 'TRACTOR! TRACTOR! TRACTOR!' A huge blue and white monstrosity was coming straight at them.

Logan slammed on the brakes and screeched the car back to their own side of the road in a cloud of swearing and burning rubber. The thing trundled past and he accelerated out and round the digger.

Up ahead, Wiseman threw the Range Rover hard right, leaving the main road for a little side one. Logan followed, the pool car's back end kicking out as they slid round the corner.

A loud *CLUNK!* and a fencepost went flying.

Faulds had one hand dug into the dashboard, the other wrapped around the handle above the passenger-side door. Teeth gritted, eyes wide. 'Who the hell taught you to drive?'

'I haven't done the pursuit training course, OK? I'm doing my best!'

A hump in the road and the car left the tarmac for a second. 'Oh God!'

'Call the station! Tell them we're after Wiseman!'

Alec's voice came from the back of the car. 'This is bloody brilliant!'

Faulds released his death-grip on the dashboard and scrabbled in the footwell for the radio handset as Logan wrenched the manky Vauxhall through a succession of snaking bends. Insch's Range Rover was getting closer and closer ... they were right behind it, siren blaring, lights flashing, completely unable to get past and cut Wiseman off.

'Single-track bastards ... '

'Alpha Charlie Seven from Control, when do you—'

'This is Chief Constable Faulds, we are in pursuit of—'

A sharp bend and the pool car brushed a drystane dyke on the passenger side – a squeal of metal and a shower of sparks as Logan struggled to get them back on the road.

'—Ken Wiseman. Will you watch where you're bloody going!'

'Do you want to drive?'

'—repeat that? Wiseman? Are you serious?'

Faulds went back to the handset. 'We need back-up, now!'

And then Wiseman slammed on his brakes. Logan was fast, but not fast enough; they clipped the back bumper. The pool car's nose jerked left and buried itself in a beech hedge, sending orange leaves flying.

Faulds dropped the handset again. 'Are you trying to get us all killed?'

'What the hell was that?'

The Range Rover pulled a hard left, through an open gate and into a field of brown stubble. Logan cranked the key in the ignition. Nothing. Nothing. Nothing . . . 'Come on you *bastard*!' The engine roared into life. He reversed out of the hedge and put his foot to the floor, the tyres squealing as the car fishtailed into the field after Wiseman. But the Range Rover was built for this kind of thing, their scabrous Vauxhall wasn't. It slithered and slid, churning up the mud, snaking after the four-by-four as it rumbled straight across the field and out the gate on the other side.

'We're losing him!'

'—repeat: what is your location?'

'Come on, come on, come on!' The engine was beginning to sound like a cat in a tumble drier.

'Somewhere south of Inverurie—'

'OLDMELDRUM!' Logan fought the bucking steering wheel, barrelling them towards the exit. '*Not* Inverurie! Three miles south of Oldmeldrum, just off the A497. Side road on the right, before you get to Hatton Crook. Where there was that minibus accident last year!'

They clipped the gate on their way out – the car lurching forward as it finally got its tyres back on solid tarmac. Tree-lined road, amber leaves, no sign of the Range Rover. 'Bastard!'

Logan floored it. Hard right. Hard left. Another right and—

A horse, pirouetting and snorting in the middle of the road. Faulds yelled 'LOOK OUT!' and Logan slammed on the brakes. The manky Vauxhall skidded to a halt.

'What the hell do we do now?'

'Honk your horn!'

Logan stared at Faulds. 'That's not going to help.' He clambered out into the cold afternoon. The animal looked half demented – eyes rolling, foaming white sweat at the neck, empty saddle, bridle swinging loose. There was no sign of the rider. And then Logan got a glimpse past the bucking, rearing monster: DI Insch's Range Rover was nose-down in a ditch, rear wheels spinning. Behind it another horse shifted from hoof to hoof, looking embarrassed while its rider lay flat on her back on the grass verge.

The sound of raised voices cut through the cold afternoon.

'You stupid – fucking – inconsiderate – fucking . . . ' it was a woman, dressed in jodhpurs, sweatshirt, and riding hat, covered in mud all down one side of her body. She was beating the living crap out of Wiseman as he tried to crawl away from the crashed Range Rover. 'Inconsiderate – wanking – bastard!' Each word punctuated with another blow from her short riding crop. 'It's bad enough we've got to put up with arseholes like you roaring round the countryside.' She gave up on the whip and kicked Wiseman in the ribs instead. 'YOU COULD HAVE KILLED US!'

Logan took one look at the spinning horse, and decided discretion was the better part of not getting his head staved-in by a flying hoof. He clambered over the nearest gate and hurried through the field. The front end of the Range Rover was a mess: steam billowed out from beneath the bonnet, windscreen shattered, headlights smashed, radiator buckled around a dirty big lump of stone, taking half the barbed-wire fence with it.

'You think there's no one else on the road? You think you own – the – fucking – road?'

Logan picked his way through the debris and grabbed her before she could castrate Wiseman with her riding boots. 'Enough!'

'Did you see what this idiot—'

'Stand over there and calm down!'

'—roaring round the corner in the middle of the road!'

Logan pulled out his handcuffs and she froze.

'If you touch me, I'll scream.'

185

'Oh for God's sake: I'm a police officer. Now go see if your friend's OK.'

Wiseman was curled up on the muddy grass, clutching one arm to his chest – probably broken. His nose certainly was. The butcher's face was a spider's web of tiny cuts, little flecks of glass sticking out of his bald head. He screamed in pain as Logan forced him face down and cuffed his hands behind his back.

'Kenneth Wiseman, I'm arresting you for driving without due care and attention... And some other stuff we'll charge you with when we get you back to the bloody station. On your feet.'

It took three goes to get Wiseman upright. He might have been built like a rugby fullback, but he didn't put up a fight, just limped and swore and grimaced and cried as Logan dragged him back to the crashed Range Rover. Where the woman who'd just beaten up Scotland's most notorious serial killer was bent over her companion, holding her hand and talking softly.

'How is she?'

The rider lying spread-eagled on the grass raised a shaky thumb.

'I think her leg's broken. Lucky to be alive, that bloody idiot screaming round the corner in—'

'We'd better get her an ambulance...' Logan fumbled through his pockets with one hand – looking for his phone – as he pushed Wiseman back against the inspector's ruined car. The butcher wobbled a bit, then slid down the door panel till he was sitting on the ground looking dazed. Then threw up in his own lap.

Logan jumped back, trying to escape the rancid splatter. 'Oh you dirty f...' There was something in the Range Rover's boot, partially covered by a dog-hair-encrusted tartan blanket. A pale, white hand poked out from beneath it. 'No...'

He ran round to the back and fought with the boot release. Locked.

'Damn it!' Logan grabbed a chunk of rock from the ground and swung it at the rear windscreen.

The glass buckled, but didn't break.

Again – sending a network of cracks racing across the surface.

Again – and the lump of stone punched a grapefruit-sized hole, sending little glittering cubes of glass all over the Range Rover's huge boot. Logan stuck his hand in and fumbled for the catch to lower the tailgate, then jerked the boot lid up and clambered inside.

'Oh God ... Sophie...' Insch's youngest was lying on her side, partially covered by the tartan dog blanket, hands cable-tied behind her back, legs tied at the ankle, silver duct-tape wrapped round her head, covering her mouth. Blood caking her nose. Face pale and waxy. 'Sophie!'

Logan ripped the tape off and put his ear to her mouth. She wasn't breathing. He stuck two fingers against her throat, feeling for a pulse ... it was there, but there wasn't much of it. 'Don't you die on me, Sophie!' He flipped her over onto her back and started breathing for her.

In – out – in – out – in – out.

A voice sounded behind him: Faulds, 'What the hell do you think you're doing leaving Wiseman unsupervised out here? He ... oh shit.'

In – out – in – out.

Electronic bleeping noises – numbers being punched into a mobile phone. 'Shut up and listen! I need an ambulance and I need it now!'

In – out – in – out.

'How the hell am I supposed to know? DS McRae told you where we were, didn't he? ... Yes!'

In – out – in – out.

'...I don't care! Get someone out here now – we've a little girl who's not breathing!'

In – out – in – out.

Logan felt for a pulse again: it was getting weaker. 'She's Insch's daughter!'

'Oh God ... did you hear that? ... Yes ... yes, OK.'

In – out – in – out.

'Come on Sophie!'

24

An ambulance sat on the gravel outside Insch's house, its blue lights flickering as a pair of paramedics helped the inspector's wife into the back. As Logan marched up the drive he could hear them telling her that everything was going to be OK. She didn't look as if she believed them.

He took a deep breath, thought about chickening out and leaving this to someone else, then walked into the granite house. The place was a mess – furniture upturned, mirrors and photos smashed, little dots of blood on the oatmeal-coloured carpet. The smell of human waste fighting against a large tub of orange potpourri. Insch was in the kitchen, kneeling in front of the dog basket.

'Sir?'

'Bastard kicked her. She's fifteen, an old lady ... but she went for him.' He stroked the spaniel's coat. 'Poor old thing...'

'Sir, I need to talk to you about—'

'She's broken inside...' The inspector glanced up for a moment, puffy eyes glistening with tears in his bruised and battered face. 'The vet's on his way. And then she won't be in pain any more ... she's not...' He took a deep, shuddering breath. 'Wiseman tried to make us think we were eating one of the girls. But it was just pork. Anna and Brigit were tied up in their bedroom the whole time.'

'Sir, I'm—'

'No.' He wiped his eyes. 'Don't say it. I don't want a death message. You can't—'

'I'm sorry. The paramedics did everything they could. But Sophie ... she was so small and the crash ... it ...'

Insch bit his bottom lip, then turned silently and went back to stroking his spaniel. Shoulders trembling. Crying quietly.

Logan let himself out.

The drive back to FHQ took nearly an hour and a half as rush-hour got its claws into Aberdeen. He could have put on the pool car's siren, but Logan wasn't exactly looking forward to getting there. At least the nose-to-tail traffic put off the inevitable ...

He pushed through into the noisy incident room and everything went silent. Then the Detective Chief Superintendent started a round of applause, uniform and CID standing to join in. The DCS clapped him on the shoulder and told the room how he was a credit to the force. How they'd never have caught Wiseman if it wasn't for Logan. How everyone was proud of him.

But Logan didn't feel very proud. Not when all he could think about was that little girl lying on the tarmac, face white, lips blue. The high-pitched whine of the defibrillator as the paramedics tried to restart her heart. The look on her mother's face when he told her. Insch in tears. No, he didn't feel very proud at all.

Midnight. Two steps to the right ... lurch to the left ... bang into the thing in the hall, stuff clattering to the floor ... Logan fumbled for the light switch, missed, tried again, and finally light blossomed in the little hallway. 'Honey, I'm home.' It took three goes to get the key out of the lock. Jacket up on the hook by the door.

And stumble through to the kitchen . . .

'Oh . . . bollocks.' The place was a mess: flour and eggs all over the work surface and the floor. The bedroom was just as bad – drawers lying open, the contents spewed out over every available inch. The lounge was like a bombsite. CDs and cushions and junk mail strewn all over the carpet. Suddenly Logan felt a lot more sober.

But the TV and DVD player were still there, and so was his laptop. What sort of burglar, broke in and didn't steal anything?

The only things missing were Jackie's clothes and possessions: the industrial grey underwear; the stuffed and porcelain pigs; the hairdryer; the extensive collection of shampoos, conditioners, moisturisers, and other assorted unguents . . .

She'd come past, picked up her stuff and trashed the place. This was going to take forever to clean up.

Back in the bedroom Logan picked up one edge of the duvet and peered underneath, hoping Jackie wasn't as vindictive as Alec's ex. At least the bed was a jobbie-free zone. He sat on the mattress, looking at the devastation. Just to be on the safe side, he wasn't going to brush his teeth tonight: Jackie might not lower herself to crapping on the fitted sheet, but he wouldn't put cleaning the loo with his toothbrush past her.

'What a brilliant, fucking day.'

25

Interview Room Number Two was stiflingly hot. It stank of stale sweat, stale cigarette smoke, farts, and too much after-shave. None of which were doing Logan's hangover any favours. Plus, he was pretty certain DC Simon Rennie was responsible for the most offensive of the smells, but the constable denied everything.

Rennie shifted from one foot to the other, and Logan braced himself for the eggy onslaught.

'Will you stop bloody doing that!'

Rennie manufactured an innocent expression. 'I didn't do anything. Probably Laughing Boy here.' He pointed at the prisoner.

'Fuck you.' Ken Wiseman's voice was like razorblades and gravel. His face wasn't much better: covered in little sticking plasters, scratches and scabs; bruises spreading across his pale skin; nose squint; right arm in a fibreglass cast. Which had made getting the handcuffs on interesting.

'Ooh, hark at Oscar Wilde.' Rennie stuck two fingers up behind Wiseman's back. 'Shut up, *Kenneth*.'

'Want to make me?' The butcher raised his hands, jerking them, making the cuffs creak. 'Think these'll stop me ripping your fucking head off?'

'That's enough. Both of you.' Logan stared at the ceiling tiles. When the hell was Faulds going to get back? 'Rennie – don't goad the prisoner. Mr Wiseman, don't you think you're in enough trouble without threatening police officers?'

'And fuck you too.'

Technically the interview was suspended while Faulds was off talking to the criminal psychologist they'd drafted in, but the cameras were still rolling. Just in case Wiseman did something rash – like kill the pair of them.

'Come on Ken, why don't you make it—'

'I said, FUCK – YOU!'

Which was about as cooperative as he'd been all morning.

'Fine. Sit there and sulk.' It wasn't as if they needed a confession to put him back in prison. They'd caught him in the act: illegal imprisonment, grievous bodily harm, animal cruelty, criminal damage, abduction, causing death by reckless driving . . . That and a very good defence lawyer would get him at least another sixteen years. But it was nothing compared with what would happen if they could prove he was the Flesher. The only way he'd get out of Peterhead Prison was in a coffin. Hopefully sooner rather than later.

A murmur of conversation came from outside the interview room door – too low to make out any words – and Logan breathed a sigh of relief. About bloody time Faulds got back; with any luck he'd have brought a round of coffees with him.

The door slammed open. It wasn't Faulds: it was Insch.

Oh no.

Logan was on his feet. 'Sir, I don't think you should be—'

'You bloody animal!' The inspector's voice was a slurred growl, the smell of alcohol coming off him in waves.

Wiseman smiled and waved. 'Hey, Fat Boy.'

'Sir, come on, you have to—'

'She was four!'

'Shame, eh? I'd've got a shit-load of money selling her.'

'You're dead.' The inspector pointed a shaky finger at Rennie and Logan. 'You and you, go take a walk.'

'Sir, we can't do that.'

'Fifteen minutes. You leave me and this bastard alone for fifteen minutes.'

'Sir—'

'GET OUT!'

Rennie flinched and started sidling towards the door. Logan turned on him. 'Don't you bloody dare!' And the constable froze. 'Sir, we have a duty of care—'

'She was four years old!'

'Hurts, does it?' Wiseman struggled to his feet. 'Come on then, Fatty. You show me how much it fucking hurts.'

'Sir, you have to leave. If you lay one finger on him in custody—'

The butcher took a deep sniff, howched, then spat. A yellow-green glob spattered across Insch's cheek. And the inspector lunged.

Rennie squealed, but Logan was already moving, dropping his shoulder into the fat man's side and heaving – sending them both crashing into the side wall. They landed in a tangle of limbs, pain flaring across Logan's stomach as the inspector's elbow landed right in the middle of the scar tissue.

Then Rennie piled in, dragging the inspector up and off while Wiseman laughed and laughed and laughed.

Luck was on Logan's side for once: he actually managed to find a parking space within walking distance of the hospital entrance. He manoeuvred the pool car into it and switched off the engine. They sat there in silence.

He snuck a glance at his passenger. 'Are you sure you're OK?'

Insch didn't look up, just sat there in the passenger seat, staring at his hands. At least he'd stopped crying.

'Sir?'

The fat man curled his fingers into fists the size of sledge-hammers. But his voice was tiny: 'It's my fault.'

'You shouldn't—'

'We were convinced he had her somewhere. Brooks ... Brooks thought we could save her if we could get Wiseman to talk.' He sniffed. 'If we could *make* him tell us where Samantha Harper was. I'm not proud of what I did ... Two broken fingers. Three teeth. Black eye. Bruised ribs. Dislocated shoulder. And Wiseman still wouldn't tell us ...' A tear rolled down the inspector's cheek. 'Turned out she wasn't missing after all. She'd run off with a carpet fitter from Lanarkshire. Her husband had made the whole Flesher thing up because he didn't want anyone to know.'

Logan sat in uncomfortable silence, watching the seagulls wheeling above Aberdeen Royal Infirmary. Not wanting to believe what he was hearing.

'We were so sure it was Wiseman ...' Insch wiped the tear away, but another one welled up in its place. 'And seventeen years later, he comes back and takes my daughter. All because I,' the inspector raised a huge fist and bounced it off the dashboard, hitting it harder and harder with every word, making the plastic creak 'did – what – Brooks – wanted!' The whole car rocked as Insch hammered his massive fist down, cracking the dashboard, then dug his fingers into the hole and yanked back and forth, tearing the car apart.

'Jesus, calm down!' It was like being trapped in a wardrobe with an angry bear.

Outside, a nurse paused on her way past, then hurried off. Probably to call the police.

CRACK and a slab of black plastic came off in Insch's bleeding hands.

'CUT IT OUT!' Logan slapped him. And instantly regretted it as the inspector turned his purple, furious face in Logan's direction. He was actually foaming at the mouth, a thin trickle of blood running from one nostril.

Insch raised a massive, torn fist—

Logan closed his eyes and waited for everything to go painful...

But nothing happened.

Silence.

When Logan opened his eyes again, the inspector was slumped in the passenger seat, shuddering silently, tears running down his face.

Heather sat with her back to the metal wall, feeling its cold seeping deep into her shoulders as she started into the Dark. Duncan was right – the Dark was more than just an absence of light, it was a living, breathing thing.

When Duncan left her on her own it whispered to her. Whispered terrible, terrible things.

She pushed her hands over her ears and sang to drown it out, one of those stupid kids' songs off the telly that Justin likes ... *liked* ... so much.

Singing and crying and trying no to listen to the Dark.

Where the hell was Duncan? Abandoning her – he *knew*, he knew, he knew, he knew, he—

'Heather, come on, Honey, calm down.'

She looked up at him, standing there with his blood halo glowing red like a burning building. 'You left me!'

'I was only away for a minute.'

'You left me ...'

He squatted down next to her. *'No I didn't.'*

'You died.'

'But I'm here now.'

She squinted through the bars – just visible in the faint glow from Duncan's head. The Dark was silent again. 'It scares me ...'

'Shhhh ...' He kissed her forehead, then got up and walked over to the tinfoil parcel of sliced meat. *'You know, this is starting to smell a little funky.'*

'Don't leave me alone in the dark.'

'Probably be OK for another couple of days though. Sell-by dates are just a load of old bollocks anyway.'

'Duncan.'

'I promise, OK? I'll never leave you again.'

On the other side of the bars the Dark was silent.

Biding its time.

Knowing that sooner or later Duncan would let her down. And then Heather Inglis would belong to the Dark.

Four Days Later

26

The Identification Bureau lab looked like a school science department on the caretaker's day off. Every available surface was covered in plastic evidence bags and reports. There were more bags in the cardboard boxes stacked by the door, another mound of samples piled up by the freezer.

A little radio sat on top of the superglue cabinet, filling the air with dreadful syrupy music.

Four days since DI Insch had tried to rip Wiseman's head off in Interview Room Number Two, and the investigation was going nowhere.

Logan picked a report from the top of the pile and flicked through the results. 'Nothing at all?'

The lab technician peeled off her facemask and scowled at him – there was a perfect outline of clean skin where the mask had been, but the rest of her face was stained with a thin layer of black fingerprint powder. 'You not think I would have said if there was? That I might *actually* be professional enough to recognize a bloody clue when I found one and tell someone?'

'Who rattled your cage this morning?'

'Don't start.' She pulled an empty whisky bottle from its evidence bag and slammed it down on the vacuum table. 'There's no one else in today: I've got a whole department's work to do, hundreds of sodding samples, and now they want us to DNA-type everyone who's been reported missing for the last four months! You have any idea how much paperwork that is?' She stood and fumed silently for a moment. 'And the bloody stereo's stuck on Radio Two: I've spent the last hour and a half listening to show tunes! Sunday my arse.'

'Feel better now?'

'How come it's never like this on *CSI*? Never see them drowning in paperwork, forced to listen to Elaine Paige.' She clicked on the power and the vacuum table whined into life, sucking away the excess aluminium powder as she dusted the bottle.

Logan flipped to the last page of the report. 'So ... not even fingerprints?'

'Which part of "nothing" are you having difficulty with? Believe it or not, some criminals actually wear gloves these days.'

Something from *Kiss Me Kate* warbled to a close and the news came on: '*The headlines at four thirty: Oil-workers strike in cannibal-meat protests; Government minister apologizes for affair; Interest rates set to rise; and memorial service for Inspector's daughter—* '

'We did get some fibres, but unless you get me something to match them to, they're bugger all use.'

'*—four-year-old Sophie Insch was killed on Tuesday during a high-speed pursuit by Grampian Police to capture Kenneth Wiseman. Mourners gathered today at Oldmeldrum Episcopal Church to pay tribute—* '

It had been one of the worst mornings of Logan's life: picking Insch up from his house, driving him to the church, sitting with him and his two remaining daughters while the vicar read the eulogy. Holding the girls' hands as their father cried. Their mother didn't even make it out of hospital for the service. The wake at the Redgarth afterwards ... then back to the house for tea and sympathy. And all the time Logan *knew* it was his fault.

He'd been the one driving the pursuit car, he'd forced Wiseman to crash.

'...scumbags, eh?'

'Mmm? Oh ... probably.' No idea what she was talking
about.

'I mean, look at all this!' She pointed at the mound of bagged
hairbrushes and clothing. 'I have to scrape DNA samples off
dirty underwear! How screwed up is that? And you know how
many bits of meat we've actually managed to ID? One. And
before you get all excited, don't. The chunk they found in the
Leiths' freezer belonged to Valerie Leith. Bastard butchered
her and left a slab of her thigh behind.'

'—strike action on the North Sea oil platforms supplied with meat
by Thompson's Cash and Carry in Aberdeen. The workers are
demanding immediate medical evacuation back to the mainland for
tests to be carried out. One of the catering companies involved, spoke to
our reporter—'

'And how the hell am I supposed to DNA-test every missing
person? You have any idea how many get reported in Grampian every year? Fucking *thousands*!'

Logan let her rant for a bit, while he listened to the rest of
the news. Then the radio announced it was time for *Pick of the
Pops*. The IB technician said, 'No you bloody don't!' grabbed it
off the top of the superglue cabinet and stuffed it in the freezer,
slamming the door on the jangly theme tune. 'Elaine Paige is
bad enough; I am *not* listening to Dale Sodding Winton!'

'How's he taking it?' Faulds stuck a mug of milky coffee down
in front of Logan. The canteen was quiet, just the two of them
and the old man behind the counter.

'Not great. His house's been trashed, his dog's been put to
sleep, he's got two traumatized kids, his wife's in hospital with
a breakdown, and his daughter's dead...' Logan stared into
the depths of his mug. 'Usually he just gets angry about stuff;
don't think I've ever seen him depressed before.'

203

'There's been an accident with that interview tape, by the way. Seems the whole ... ahem, "episode", was accidentally recorded over. Audio *and* video.'

Logan nodded. At least there'd be no evidence that Insch tried to assault a prisoner in custody. 'Thanks.'

'Bloody interview's going nowhere anyway. Wiseman won't even cop to the things we've got him red-handed for – it's like talking to a brick wall.' Faulds emptied a couple of sugar packets into his latte. 'I'm going to get the psychologist to talk to him. See if he can loosen the mortar a bit ... '

'Always works on the telly.'

'I really wanted a confession before I had to go home, but there's no chance of that now.' He took a sip of his coffee, then added another sugar. 'Got to get back to Birmingham tonight. Curse of the Chief Constable: they like to think they can manage on their own, but the whole place turns into *Lord of the Flies* if I'm away for more than a week.'

'You going to come back up for the trial?'

'Probably: couple of days, here and there. Depends what I've got on. But I'll make the sentencing. Hell or high water I'm going to see that bastard put away for the rest of his life.'

'Wait, wait, this is the best bit ... ' Rennie pointed the remote control at the little telly in the CID office, cranking the sound up as Logan wandered in. There was a small knot of plainclothes officers listening to Chief Constable Faulds' voice booming out of the speakers, sounding terrified: *'TRACTOR! TRACTOR! TRACTOR!'* The picture lurched as the car braked hard and screeched back in behind a canary-yellow digger.

'Don't you lot have any work to do?'

Rennie grinned at him. 'Just doing a little teambuilding. Very impressive driving, by the way. I especially liked the way you tried to go through the hedge.'

'Who the hell taught you to drive?' Everyone laughed.

But Logan really wasn't in the mood. 'You do know a little girl died during that, don't you, Constable? Insch's daughter. The one we had a bloody service for this morning!'

The laughter stopped.

'She's lying there in the boot, bound and gagged, on her way to be sold to some paedophile. You still think it's fucking funny?' Logan snatched the remote out of Rennie's hand and hit the eject button. Everyone suddenly seemed to remember they had something important to do. Elsewhere.

Only Rennie remained, shuffling his feet. 'Sorry sir. I wasn't meaning to ... you know.' He pointed at the TV. 'Alec made it up. It's kind of a blooper reel. Now that we've caught Wiseman. You know: highlights of the case.' He coughed. 'They've even got that bit in it where DI McFarlane trips over and ... breaks his wrist ... it ... they put a funny soundtrack on it ...' He pulled the DVD from the machine and handed it to Logan. 'Sorry, sir.'

'Thought you were supposed to be dealing with those INTERPOL files.'

'DI Steel said it was a waste of time and I had to try identifying the other victims instead. So I'm trolling through the misper lists looking for fatties ... I mean larger men and women who fit the victim profile. Then getting stuff to DNA-sample. See if they match any of the chunks we found.'

'Yeah, I heard.' Logan turned the disk over – Alec had even made a cheesy label for the thing: 'GRANITE CITY 999: LICENSED TO LAUGH'

'Trouble is, half the buggers aren't even missing any more. Three thousand misper reports last year, and does anyone bother to let us know when their nearest and dearest turn up safe and sound? Do they hell. What are we, psychic?'

'Poor old Simon Rennie. Boo-hoo.'

'Yeah, well ... Word is we're going get a case review.'

Logan groaned. 'When?'

'No idea. Soon.'

'Who?'

'Strathclyde.'

'I see . . .' Strathclyde Police – where Jackie was. He'd not heard from her since she'd trashed the flat. He should take a leaf out of those home security lectures they kept having to give and get the locks changed, just in case she decided to come back and 'redecorate' again.

'—tonight?'

He looked up to find Rennie staring at him. 'What?'

'You know, in the old days at least you used to pretend you were listening. Do – you – want – to – go – out – tonight? Bowling and beer. I can ask Laura to bring along a friend if you like? You know, now that you and Jackie . . . well, you know.'

'Thanks,' Logan dropped the *Granite City 999* DVD in the bin. 'But I really don't feel—'

Rennie backed away. 'Hey, just think about it, OK? No need to be miserable all your life.'

'Shhhhhhh, shhhhhh . . . ' A cool hand on her hot forehead. *'You're burning up. '*

Heather shivered. 'Cold . . . '

Duncan frowned. *'You don't look well—'*

Their dark metal prison stank: the acrid tang of vomit and the cloying reek of diarrhoea.

'Thirsty . . . '

'Sorry, Honey, there's no water left.'

'But I'm thirsty . . . oh God . . . ' She scrabbled into the corner and fumbled with the chemical toilet's lid, grabbing the seat and retching. It was like being punched in the stomach time and time again, but all that came out was a bitter trickle of foul-tasting bile. 'Oh God . . . '

'Shhhh . . . it'll be OK.' Duncan helped her back to the mattress. *'How you feeling?'*

'I just want . . . I just want to die . . . ' Everything hurt. Her throat ached, mouth dry, lips cracked, pounding headache, cramps – all signs of acute dehydration. She'd seen a programme about it on the Discovery Channel.

'You're not well.' He peeled a strand of hair from her clammy forehead. 'You need to rest.'

'So tired . . .'

'That's because you're dying.'

'I want . . . to go . . . home.'

'I know, I know' He leaned forwards and kissed her on the forehead. 'You'll be with us soon, and it'll all be OK. Just you, me and Justin. No more darkness.'

Heather nodded, it hurt less than trying to talk.

'It'll all be over soon.'

27

Logan wasn't really in the mood for getting pished, but he made a brave stab at it anyway. Four hours sat in the cramped viewing room with DI Steel – watching Faulds and his criminal psychologist trying to get something useful out of Ken Wiseman – meant that Logan was more than ready to go bowling with Rennie and a couple of people from work. There were only so many times you could watch a murdering scumbag tell a Chief Constable to go fuck himself with a cheese grater.

By the time Rennie's girlfriend, Laura, turned up at the bowling alley, they were all on their fourth pints. Logan wasn't sure if he was disappointed or relieved that she hadn't brought the promised friend with her.

More beer, then tequila, then chips. Then Logan called it a night, walking home to the flat alone, feeling drunk and more than a little sorry for himself.

The flat wasn't the same without Jackie's crap lying all over the place: the strange little porcelain things, the dozens of unidentifiable potions in the bathroom, the little tangles of hair on the carpet by the mirror in the bedroom. Cold feet beneath the duvet...

Jammy bastard Rennie with his nice perky new girlfriend.

Logan collapsed into bed, sprawled out like a half-cut starfish, and stared up into the darkness. They'd caught the Flesher – everything should have been hunky dory. But it wasn't.

Eventually he drifted off to sleep, his dreams full of little dead girls and their grieving fathers.

Bright light. Hazy, painful ... but that was nothing new. Everything hurt. Heather rolled over onto her side and squinted at the open door.

He was back!

She scrambled to her knees, fell over, crawled to the bars. 'P...' Just enough water left in her body for a few burning tears.

HE WAS BACK!

The Butcher dragged someone new into the prison, dumped them on the other side of the bars, then turned and stared at Heather.

'P...' She choked. Tried again. 'Please...'

He pulled a bottle of water from his apron and handed it through the bars. Heather grabbed his leg, pulling him off balance, hauling him forwards till he was hard against the metal. Then she wrapped her arm around his leg, croaking, 'Don't ... ever ... leave me again...'

She fumbled the lid off the bottled water and drank, spluttered, brought most of it back up. Sobbing. 'Don't leave me! Don't leave me!'

The Butcher froze, then reached down and stroked her matted, greasy hair.

Everything would be OK now.

He was back.

Memorial... Inspector's Daughter

A service will be held later today for Sophie Insch (4) who died during a high-speed pursuit of Ken Wiseman last week. Sophie was allegedly abducted by Wiseman following an incident in the Insch family home, where members of the family were tied up and tortured.

Grampian Police are expecting a considerable crowd to gather this afternoon, even though the family have requested a quiet memorial service to help them mourn the passing of their daughter.

"It's inevitable that something of this nature will attract members of the public," said Cannon Philip Forres. "At times of grief a community comes together to mark the passing of a life, especially one so precious and young as Sophie. But we have to remember that this is an intensely painful and personal time for the family and respect their wishes."

"We will be holding a candlelight vigil on Sunday for those wishing to pay their respects."

"It is a small con[...] to us all, that with the arrest of Ken Wis[...]"

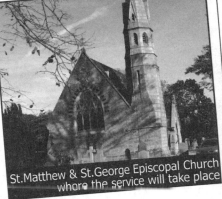
St.Matthew & St.George Episcopal Church where the service will take place

Flesher's last ever victim."

The service is by invitation only and the family have asked that no flowers be sent. Instead donations can be made to the Diced Cap Charitable Trust: www.dicedcap.org/

---

gripping the North Sea [...]man remains turning up in [...]supermarkets, Grampian [...]oming under increasing [...]lve the Flesher ca[...] [...]ve esc[...]

arreste[...]
parties [...]
discuss[...]
wrong. [...]
MSP R[...]

Aberdeen Trades Set to Fight Back

ABERDEEN'S seven incorporated trades hit back last night at criticism that they are in any way responsible for the current spate of killings in the city.

"It's ridiculous," said Ewan Morton, Boxmaster with the Fleshers' Incorporation, "it's like someone leaving a copy of the Bible behind when they kill someone and every Christian being stigmatised because of that."

The Fleshers (butchers), Weavers (textile workers), Hammermen (gold and silversmiths), Shoemakers (cobblers), Wrights and Coopers (joiners), Tailors, and Bakers joined forces to present the message that the seven incorporated trades are an integral part of Aberdeen life, and have been for generations.

"The trades have a rich history that goes right back to the time of

Trinity Hall: where the Fleshers meet

were in a trade organisation."

"We can't stress strongly enough how sickened we all are at what's been happening, but it's really not the trades' fault."

Vandalism

The police have been called to Trinity Hall – where the trades meet – over a dozen times since the discovery of human remains in an offshore container at Aberdeen Harbour the night before Halloween.

"We've had windows smashed and graffiti on the walls. People don't seem to realise that the Hall

---

SHE[...]

[...]an Arrested Af[...]

VE

[...]ner.com

SWEET
[...]ampian
as they
d Ken
se it came
e officer's

Sophie Insch
he boot of her
[...]er – stolen by
his getaway.
ws raced to the
nable to save the
father, Detective
Insch, was leading
eman.
is believed to have
e Insch household
inspector and his

Ken Wiseman, th[...]

cameraman was also
the *Examiner* unde[...]
entire car chase v[...]
film as part of t[...]
upcoming do[...]
Grampian Polic[...]
999.

Wiseman's a[...]
[...]d the horrifi[...]

SMOAK WITH BLOOD

28

'Sodding cock-monkeys . . . ' DI Steel puffed out her cheeks and blew. 'What time is it?'

Logan peeled back the cuff of his SOC oversuit and checked. 'Nearly half seven.' Monday morning hadn't started well – three hours they'd been at it, and the sun was still nowhere to be seen.

The inspector groaned. 'It's going to be a long bloody day.' She stepped back to let an IB technician carrying a plastic evidence box squeeze past. 'What the hell is that?'

'Everything from the freezer.' The man said, holding it up for inspection.

Steel went for a quick rummage. 'Peas, sweetcorn, fish fingers . . . ' She pulled out a solid brown lump of something wrapped in clingfilm and waved it at Logan. 'That look like goulash, sausage casserole, or curry to you?'

'Could be mince?'

She chucked it back in the box and picked up a chunk of something pinky-red. 'Ahoy-hoy, this looks promising. Human remains?'

Logan shrugged – it all looked like meat to him.

'Go on then,' she told the guy holding the box, 'don't just stand there, get it tested.'

The technician said, 'Yes ma'am,' but Logan could hear him muttering 'silly old cow . . .' under his breath as he carried it out to the IB van.

Steel fidgeted about in her pockets. 'Got a bad feeling about this, Laz – something in me water. Like bloody cystitis.' She wandered through to the lounge and watched the white-suited figures picking their way through the contents with tiny hoovers and fingerprint powder. 'Only thing stopping the press buggering us with a cactus is that everyone knows Wiseman's guilty.' She shifted from foot to foot. 'He *is* guilty, isn't he?'

'Faulds says they thought Wiseman had an accomplice twenty years ago. Maybe this is him working on his own?'

Steel scowled at him. 'Thought you bloody caught the accomplice – what's-his-face, the brother-in-law?'

'Yeah, well . . . .' Cough. 'Maybe it wasn't him.'

'Gee, you *think*?' The inspector turned on her heel and stomped upstairs, her SOC suit making zwip-zwop noises as she climbed. Logan followed her up, across the landing and into the master bedroom, where she cracked open the window and lit a cigarette. Outside, in the back garden, two uniformed officers in the ubiquitous white paper oversuits were rooting through the bushes and shed, the grass twinkling with early frost in the half light.

'Hairy bastarding arseholes.' Steel flicked a few grey flakes of dove-grey ash out into the cold morning. 'How the hell am I supposed to solve this one?'

'There's a press conference at half eleven. Do you—'

'I mean it's no' as if them other bastards managed, and they tried for *years*!' She ran a hand across her face, pulling it all out of shape. 'You know I had to phone the Chief Constable at half three this morning and tell him we'd screwed up on this one? "Wiseman's no' the Flesher after all, terribly sorry old bean." Went down like Mother Teresa in a brothel . . .'

Logan let her moan while he picked through one of the bedside cabinets. One drawer for socks, one drawer for

216

underpants, one drawer for the assorted junk every man collected: handkerchiefs, playing cards, bookmarks, a little wind-up plastic nun that was probably supposed to walk, but just made obscene grinding motions instead. There was a photo next to the bedside light – Tom and Hazel Stephen, the Flesher's latest victims. They were at some sort of formal event, him in a suit and tie, her spilling out of a low-cut black cocktail dress. They looked happy.

'—creek without a paddle. Why the hell did those bastards no' finish the damn case properly twenty years ago? How come it's my fault all of a sudden?' Steel sank down on the edge of the double bed and sagged. 'And that wee bugger Alec's been following me about for days. Everywhere I go – there's his bastarding camera. Can't even take a crap without the BBC filming it.'

She pinged an inch of ash onto the oatmeal-coloured carpet and ground it in with her blue plastic bootie. 'Couple more days of this and I'm going to end up like Insch.'

Steel collapsed back on the bed, hands clamped over her face, cigarette poking out of her mouth, spiralling smoke towards the ceiling. 'Come on then – one more time.'

Logan stuck the photo back where he'd got it. 'Do we have to?'

'Yes.'

'Fine ... Next-door neighbour calls 999 at one fifteen and complains about the Stephens' dog barking. Calls back at two when the dog stops – says she was about to go round and give them a piece of her tiny mind when she looks out her window and sees someone dressed in a butcher's apron and Margaret Thatcher fright mask, loading plastic bags into the boot of the Stephens' car.'

Steel was silent – and Logan was beginning to think she'd fallen asleep, when she said, 'And?'

'And nothing.'

'How did he get here? He left in the Stephens' car, but how did he get here in the first place? If the bastard hopped on the number fifteen bus, dressed in his blood-soaked apron, I think someone would've noticed, don't you?'

'I'll get someone to run the number plates on every parked car within, what, three streets?'

'Four.' She pulled the fag from her mouth and coughed. 'Not that it'll do us any sodding good. He'll have picked it up by now. Get a lookout request on the Stephens' car.'

'Already done.' He wandered over to the other side of the bed. Hazel Stephen's bedside cabinet held the clock radio and a stack of romance paperbacks and *How To* diet books.

'Right . . .' Steel hauled herself off the bed and stretched. 'Hold the fort for five minutes, I'm off for a wee.'

Logan pulled the bottom drawer out: pop socks and tights. Middle drawer: pants, thongs and huge knickers. Top drawer: bras, a pair of reading glasses, and a newsletter from Weight Watchers.

He picked it up and flicked through, looking at all the miserable-before and happy-ever-after pictures. How did Rennie put it: *'So Wiseman's a chubby chaser then.'* Logan dug out his mobile phone and called Control, wanting to know if Heather Inglis had been going to Weight Watchers too. She had. 'What about Valerie Leith?'

There was a pause and some clacking keyboard noises. *'No idea. I can put you through to the FLO though?'*

Another pause, bleeping, and then, *'Aye? I mean, PC Munro?'*

Logan asked the same question.

'Don't think so, but—'

'Well, can you ask the husband?'

'I wish. Bugger's gone into Witness Protection. You know what they're like: law unto them-bloody-selves. Aye, unless they want something then it's all "we're on the same team, aren't we?" Tell you—'

'What about the timeline? Any sign of her going to meet-ings?'

'Eh? Oh, no. None of her friends mentioned it. Nothing in her diary either.'

'Can you speak to the Witness Protection lot and get them to ask?'

'Aye, but don't hold your breath.'

Alec sloped into the bedroom, HDV camera dangling from his hand, and slumped against the windowsill. 'No offence, but this isn't making good television.' He looked around. 'Where's Her Royal Grumpiness?'

'Gone for a pee. They finished downstairs?'

'It's another crime scene soaked in blood, but there's noth-ing happening – no narrative drive. At this rate half the bloody programme's going to be shots of white oversuits searching stuff.'

'Sorry if our murder enquiry's boring you, Alec.'

The cameraman shrugged. 'Not your fault. But we need—'

'Oh for God's sake!' Steel appeared at the bedroom door, staring down at the oatmeal-coloured carpet and the new set of sticky red footprints. 'Alec!' The trail ended at the camera-man's blue booties.

'Oops . . . It was kinda all over the kitchen . . .'

'And now it's all over the bloody house!'

'Sorry.'

'Do you have any idea—'

Logan stopped her before she could get going. 'Found a possible lead: Heather Inglis and Hazel Stephen both went to Weight Watchers.'

'Valerie Leith?'

'Can't tell yet, waiting for Witness Protection to get back to us.'

'Aye, and we'll all be drawing our old-age-pensions by then. If she's in Weight Watchers there'll be evidence up at the crime scene. Low-fat Sellotape, membership forms, before-and-after

219

trousers, that kind of thing.' Steel undid the zip on her SOC outfit. 'Well, come on then – romper suits off, we've got a house to ransack.'

'It's ... it's important not to panic ...' The new person's voice came through from the other side of the bars, where Duncan died. Where the Dark was the strongest. 'You hear me? We have to stay calm ...'

At least he'd stopped screaming.

Heather picked another escalope from the tinfoil parcel, biting through the herb crust. Very tasty.

'He's a bit of a whinge, isn't he?'

'Leave him alone, he's just scared.'

She could hear Mr New scrabbling forwards in the darkness, grabbing hold of the bars. 'Who are you talking to? Why won't you tell me who you're talking to? What's happening? What's—'

Heather cut off the rising tide of panic before he drowned them both. 'I'm talking to my husband.'

'Is he ... hello? Why don't—'

'He won't talk to you. Because he's dead.'

'Oh Jesus ... I'm locked up with a lunatic.'

Heather nodded, even though the new man couldn't see her. 'I've gone mad.'

There was a long pause ... and then Mr New said, 'What's your name?'

Heather chewed, swallowed, then told him.

'You're Heather Inglis? *The* Heather Inglis? I read about you ... oh Jesus ...' He started to cry. 'Oh fucking Jesus ... it ... it was *him*, wasn't it? The Flesher ... oh Jesus Fucking Christ ...'

'Who's the—'

'I didn't see him! I was ... from the back garden and ... oh God, Hazel ... What happened to Hazel? Where is she? WHERE'S MY WIFE? HAZEL?' He was screaming again. 'HAZEL?'

'*Well, this is going to get old really fast.*' Duncan plonked himself down on the mattress and sniffed at the tinfoil parcel in Heather's hands. '*That smells nice.*'

'You want some?'

'HAZEL!'

'*Can't: dead remember?*'

'HAZEL!' The screams gave way to sobbing. 'Hazel...'

Heather took pity on him. 'Are you hungry, Mr New? Do you want something to eat?' She held one of the escalopes out between the bars. 'It's good.'

'Hazel...'

'You need to keep your strength up.'

'*Heather, I don't think you should get too attached to this guy.*'

The sobbing went on for a while, but eventually Mr New accepted a drink of water and one of the escalopes. She could hear him sniffing it, then the crunch as he bit through the crust, mumbling, 'What is it?' as he chewed.

'Veal, I think ... or pork. Difficult to tell in the dark. Maybe—'

Mr New was spitting, gagging, retching.

'Are you OK?'

'Aaaaaaaaagh, Jesus...' A wet splattering noise as he vomited onto the cold metal floor – the stomach-churning reek filled the stale air.

'It's not *that* bad.'

He was crying again. 'It's people! Oh Jesus... Don't you get it? It was on the news: the Flesher kills people and cuts them up for meat! We're eating people...'

Duncan nodded. '*He's right, you know.*'

Heather felt her stomach lurch. 'But I've been eating it for ages...'

'*You didn't have a choice, though, did you? It was that or starve.*'

Heather stared at Duncan, remembering what the Butcher – the Flesher – did to him. 'It was you, wasn't it? All this time ... it was you.'

He nodded.

'Oh Duncan.'

Her dead husband smiled. *'Hey, at least I was tasty.'* He pointed at the tinfoil parcel in her hands. *'Don't let it go to waste.'*

'But it's people . . . '

'It's just meat, Honey. In the end we're all just meat.'

Heather picked up another slice from the parcel . . . 'I can't.'

'Yes you can.'

Duncan was right.

29

Alec fired up his camera, pointing it through the windscreen at the darkened house. 'We looking for anything in particular?'

Logan waited for Steel to say something, but she was already clambering out of the car, a freshly lit cigarette between her teeth. Blue-and-white POLICE tape flapped in the wind, a wriggling snake of it caught in the bramble bushes that grew along the drystane dyke opposite the Leiths' converted steading. Other than that, there was no sign that this place had witnessed a sudden, violent death.

He dug the key out of his pocket – courtesy of a brief stop past FHQ – unlocked the door and flicked on the lights. A high-pitched *bleep, bleep, bleep* came from a small plastic box on the wall, lights flashing, showing an intruder in 'Zone One'. The keypad was in the cupboard under the stairs and Logan punched in the code he'd got from the FLO. 'One, nine, nine, five . . .' the year the Leiths got married. Alarm disarmed.

The Environmental Health team had pretty much wrecked the place getting rid of anything contaminated with body fluids. They'd cut large chunks out of the carpet, removing it and the underlay beneath, exposing pale patches of bleached chipboard. The smell of chlorine in the kitchen was almost overpowering, but the blood was gone. God knew how many canisters of trychloroethylene they'd had to use to get rid of it all, but the walls were blotchy where the super-strength bleach had eaten away the colour. Logan threw the kitchen window open, then did the same with the back door, trying to get rid of the swimming pool stink.

And then he went through the kitchen units, looking for anything from Weight Watchers that might suggest Valerie Leith had been a member. There were a couple of cartons of Slim Fast in the cupboards, a packet of Ryvita, but no official products.

Steel was in the back garden, fag in one hand, mobile phone clamped to her ear with the other. She shouted in through the open window, 'Found anything?' And when Logan told her no, went back to her phone call. 'I'm not saying that, Susan, I was just ... but ...'

So Logan searched the lounge, then the dining room, bedrooms, bathroom, with Alec trailing along behind him. 'You going to tell me what we're looking for then?'

'The Flesher's victims aren't just picked at random: he has a selection criteria. If we can figure out how he finds them, we've got a much better chance of catching the bastard. And I thought ...' They'd ended up back in the kitchen and Logan still hadn't found anything. 'I thought I had a connection, but Valerie Leith never went to Weight Watchers. Close, but no low-fat Chicken Kiev.'

Alec shrugged. 'Shame – that would have looked good on telly: lone-wolf cop makes connection that breaks the case.'

'Always thought of myself as team player.'

'Yeah, well, the public likes lone wolves better. More romantic.'

Logan pulled the window closed, then did the same with the back door. Stopping with his fingers resting on the handle, looking back at the bleach-stained kitchen. All the way up the walls. Not just all over the floor.

A slow grin spread across Logan's face: he finally knew what had been bugging him about the Leith crime scene.

30

DI Steel leaned back against the working surface and ground her cigarette out in the sink. 'It doesn't prove anything.'

'Look.' Logan pointed at the bleach marks above the tiled splashback. 'There was blood all the way up the walls. Four streaks.' He wrapped his hand around an imaginary knife, raised it high, then stabbed the inspector four times. 'Each time the knife comes out it sprays blood in an arc up the walls.'

'Aye, it was in the SOC report.' She shook her head. 'Jesus ... I do read these things you know!'

'None of the other crime scenes have that kind of stabbing-blood-pattern.'

'So she fought back, it's—'

'Alec, you got the footage you shot this morning at the Stephens'? I need to see the kitchen.'

Alec went through his pockets, pulling out HDV tapes and reading the labels. He found what he was looking for, swapped out the one in the camera and fiddled with the buttons.

'I don't see what this has to do with—'

'Got it.' Alec flipped the camera's little screen around and pressed play.

'See?' Logan pointed at the picture, 'There's blood all over the floor, none on the walls or ceiling. I've been through every crime scene photo since 1985 and when he kills them onsite it's always the same – floor soaked, blood splashed to about knee high, fine spray on the units. No marks up the walls.'

'Oh come off it. Leith *saw* the bloody Flesher!'

'Yeah, and lived to tell the tale. This guy has enough time to turn the kitchen into a butcher's shop as he hacks up Valerie Leith, but doesn't get round to killing the husband? Does that sound like the Flesher to you?'

Steel sucked a breath in between her teeth, face creased into an unhappy grimace. 'But the husband *saw* him!'

Logan held up the copy of *Smoak With Blood* he'd found in the Leiths' bedroom. 'It's all in here. The MO, the costume, the fact he leaves bits of meat behind. Best selling book in Aberdeen since we raided that butcher's shop. You got any idea how many Margaret Thatcher fright masks were bought last week? Hundreds.'

'Stop. Back the What-the-Fuck bus up right now. You are *no'* making this bastarding case any more complicated than it already is. Understand?'

'Plus I called the lab – they did a rush job on that slab of meat we found at the Stephen house this morning. It was a bit of Duncan Inglis. If the Flesher's still got slices of him knocking around, how come Valerie Leith ends up in her own freezer?'

The inspector took another look around the kitchen: the bleached-out walls and ceiling. 'Oh bloody hell . . . Fine. OK. You win, get another search team up here – half a dozen uniforms, couple of dogs, and the IB – we'll go through the place from scratch, but if this is all a sodding waste of time *you* can tell the ACC why we pissed away a dozen man-days.'

'Heather? Heather, are you awake?'

Darkness. Stench. Cold.

She groaned and slapped both hands over her eyes.

'Heather?'

'Go back to sleep, Mr New.'

'Don't call me that – my name's Tom, I told you three times already.' Pause. 'It *stinks* in here ...'

'Well, whose fault is that?'

'I'm thirsty.'

She let her hands fall away and stared up into the void. Mr New was always bloody thirsty.

'Is there anything to drink on that side?'

Heather felt the water bottle, lying next to her on the smelly mattress. 'He'll be back soon.'

A shuffling sound, then Mr New was whispering to her through the bars. 'We have to get out of here.'

'The Dark won't let us.'

'We have to try! What have you got on that side? Anything we can use as a weapon?'

'You can't—'

'I'M NOT DYING IN HERE!' He hammered on the bars, making them boom and rattle. 'I'm not ...'

Later.

She could hear him feeling his way around on the other side of their cold, dark prison. 'It's a container ...' he said at last. 'Like the ones they send offshore. It has to be. I can feel the locking bar on the door ...'

He fumbled with something, grunted, swore, then tried again. 'Fuck, fuck, fuck, fuck!' More fumbling, then what sounded like a man's belt being unfastened and removed. 'Go on you bastard ...' Clicking noises, and then a rusty creak. 'Come on, come on ...' Another creak. 'Yes, yes, come on ...' CLANG. More swearing.

And then a loud metallic groan. 'You fucking beauty!'

A thin shaft of light streaked into the darkness. Heather could just make out Mr New's face – he was grinning.

Duncan placed a hand on Heather's shoulder. *'This isn't a good idea.'*

She grabbed the bars. 'Get me out! Don't you dare leave me in here!'

Mr New looked back at her. 'It's padlocked, OK? The bars are padlocked. I'll get help. I'll bring them back.'

'Seriously: this is a really, really bad idea!'

'Don't leave me!'

'I'll be back...' He put one hand against the door and pushed. Outside, there was nothing but a dirt-walled corridor lit by a flickering fluorescent tube. And for the first time, Heather got a look at her cellmate: he wasn't a tall man, but he looked ... *friendly*, with his bald head and little white beard. He stepped over the threshold. 'I promise. I'll be back.'

And Mr New was gone.

Duncan wrapped his arm around her and pulled her close. *'Shhhh. It's OK. He'll be back soon. You'll see. He'll be back soon, then everything will be all night again.'*

The sunlight was already beginning to go as the search team worked its way across the large back garden. 'You know what, Sherlock,' said Steel, cigarette firmly clamped between her lips, smoke curling away into the pale blue sky, 'this wasn't one of your better ideas.'

Logan leant on the decking rail and watched one of the dog handlers trying to persuade his Alsatian not to crap in the flower beds. 'There's got to be *something* here.'

'I'm giving this ten more minutes then we're sodding off back to the station.' Steel flicked her cigarette butt away to join the little pile she'd made in the last couple of hours. 'But first – you can go put the kettle on.'

Logan opened the patio doors and they stepped back into the kitchen, just as one of the IB techs was shovelling a dessert spoon of ice-cream into his gob. He froze as he caught sight of them. 'Whad?' mouth full, 'Id was onry goig to wasde...'

Steel snatched the spoon from his hands. 'This is *supposed* to be a crime scene!'

The tech swallowed, blushed and stuck the carton back on the work surface. 'I was only—'

'Don't give me that bollocks.' She pointed back towards the rest of the house. 'Now get out there and find me some forensics: you're supposed to be a bloody professional, for God's sake!' She waited until the kitchen door closed behind the tech's embarrassed backside before asking Logan, 'Well – what is it?'

'Mackie's, vanilla.'

'Ooh, cool. Get us a clean spoon, eh?'

Logan rummaged one out of the kitchen drawer and passed it over.

'Ta ... You heard from Insch?'

'Wife gets out of hospital today. She wasn't well enough for the memorial service.'

Steel was silent for a long time. 'Poor sods.' She dug her spoon into the tub and extracted a heap of vanilla. 'We're up to about two hundred pound in the kitty, going to get one of those benches in Duthie Park. Somewhere nice, you know: with a view of the ducks or something? In memory of Sophie Insch, 2003 to 2007. Sorely missed. That kind of thing.'

'He'd like that.'

'Aye, well...' The ice-cream disappeared. 'Best present we can give Insch is to put that cock-weasel Wiseman away for the rest of his sodding life.' She stood there with a thoughtful look on her face, as if she was on the verge of some portentous announcement. 'See if you can find some chocolate syrup.'

Duncan was right, Mr New did come back: unconscious and thrown over the Flesher's shoulder like a side of meat. He was dumped on the metal floor in a puddle of his own vomit.

The Flesher stared down at Mr New for a minute, then turned and left the room, slamming the door behind him. Leaving Heather in darkness again.

She shuffled forwards. 'Mr New?'

'See: told you it was a bad idea.'

'Mr New, are you dead?'

She strained her ears, just able to make out a wet breathing sound. But she couldn't tell if it was Mr New, or the Dark. Heather waved Duncan over. 'Is he dead?'

'Not yet. Soon.'

She unfastened the top of her water bottle and reached through the bars, groping her way along the rusty floor with her fingers: metal, metal, cold sick – 'Urgh' – metal, hair. She dragged his face round, and poured water over it.

Coughing. Spluttering. Groaning. And then tears. 'Oh Jesus ... '

She heard him struggle to his knees, breathing in painful hisses. Then there was a clang as he fell back against the bars. He stank of puke and fear and blood.

'He's ... ' Mr New spat. 'Ow ... It's like a rabbit warren out there ... underground ... dirt ... I found her. I found Hazel ... ' He was sobbing now, the words getting harder and harder to make out. 'He's got a butchery with ... with bits of ... She was my wife ... '

BANG – something thumped into the bars. 'SHE WAS MY WIFE!' Then Mr New's sour breath washed across Heather's face. 'He's going to kill us. I've seen it – bits of body hanging from hooks in the ceiling. I won't be a victim. I won't!' He was whispering now, as if that would make any difference to the Dark. 'When he comes back, I'll pretend to be dead and ... and then you start screaming, and he goes over to see what's wrong and I ... I'll ram his head into the bars. Keep doing it till the bastard's dead. You grab his hands! You grab his hands and pull, so he can't get away!'

'I don't—'

'You have to! You have to or we'll both die in this shit-hole! Is that what you want?'

Duncan stood behind him, staring at the closed door. *'Maybe he's got a point? If you don't do it, you'll end up dead like me.'*

'But I can't—'

'Yes you can!'

Heather shook her head. 'I can't.'

'We have to work together, Heather. We have to, or we'll die in here.' Mr New took a deep breath. 'He comes in, you scream, I charge. It'll all be over in a couple of minutes and we'll be free. OK? We'll be free . . . '

'Well,' said Steel, watching as the IB packed their kit back into the filthy Transit van, 'that was a waste of time and money.' It was cold and dark outside, just a sliver of moon poking out between the clouds as everyone locked up and got ready to go home.

The lead tech peeled off his SOC suit. 'Nothing left to find – the whole place's been bleached to buggery and back, half the carpet's missing, any evidence is so compromised it's not funny.'

Steel turned and poked Logan in the shoulder. 'Well, Poirot, you figured out how you're going to explain this one to the ACC?'

'But it's a copycat, it *has* to be.'

'Blah, blah, blah.'

A loud bleeping noise came from inside the house, closely followed by the wailing alarm and a uniformed PC's head. 'It's not working properly!'

Logan rolled his eyes. 'Did you enter the alarm code?'

'Course I entered the alarm code:1993.'

'Five. One, nine, nine, *five*.'

The PC disappeared back into the house muttering, 'Bloody handwriting's appalling . . . '

Logan turned back to the IB team-leader. 'Is there anything we didn't search?'

'House, garden, garage, cars – we did the lot.'

'Come on, Laz,' said Steel, 'give it up, eh?'

He pulled out the last search report again, flipping through to the photocopied map at the back – reading by the glow of the Transit van's headlights. They'd gone over every inch of the property, twice, and still not turned up anything. Logan took one last look around him: house, front garden, flash cars, road, field, other field, garage, and back to the house again. The nearest neighbours were a faint yellow flicker through trees. Miles from anywhere.

'You think they're on mains water?'

Steel shrugged. 'Probably.'

'What about sewage?' Clutching at straws.

'How the hell would . . .' She drifted to a halt and stared at him. 'Oh, you're *kidding* . . . Tell me you're kidding!'

'It'd have to be downhill from the house, but close enough to the road so the tanker can get in and drain it.' He started walking round the garden, Steel hot on his heels.

'If you think I'm rummaging through someone else's jobbies in my good work suit, you've got another think coming!'

There was no sign of a septic tank cover anywhere in the front garden. 'OK, the road runs downhill to the right. We just have to see if we can find one there.'

'I'm warning you, Sergeant, if I get shite on my suit—'

But he was already out of the front gate, wandering down the road in the dark, probing the field next to the house with a torch. Mud, grass, mud, sheep . . . He switched his attention to the grass verge: more mud, patch of dead nettles, brambles, a roadkill rabbit, yet more mud. A rectangular shape poked out between tufts of grass. Logan squatted down and rapped on it with his knuckles. Solid.

He ran the torch round the edges of the slab. It was over-grown with grass and weeds, bedded in with a thick layer of mud.

Steel stood beside him, staring down at the septic tank lid. 'There you go: no bugger's moved that for ages. No need to go guddling about in crap after all. Oh dear, what a shame.' She consoled herself with one last cigarette. 'Time to call this little disaster to a halt and bugger off to the pub.'

'Yeah, I suppose you're right.' He stood, torch grazing across the lid one last time. There was a faint glimmer of something white … Logan bent down and peered at it – a scrape in the side of the concrete, pale cream in the torch's yellow glow. It was the only thing not clarted in mud.

'Come on then, I'm parched.'

He took a handful of grass and pulled – it came away from the lid in a slab of spiky green, like a punk toupee. 'It's been peeled off and slapped back on again, so no one would know. Look.'

Steel did. 'So, maybe they had it emptied recently, and …' She stood there, smoking furiously. 'Ah bugger it, we're going to have to search the bloody thing, aren't we?'

'Yup.'

Mr New's voice was a painful whisper in the darkness: 'That's him! Are you ready?'

Heather shrank back against the wall. 'I don't feel well …'

A rattle and clunk from the door to the prison.

'It's our only chance!' And then Mr New was silent as a shaft of light rushed across the rusty floor. He was lying on his side, arms and legs arranged as if he were still unconscious. As if he weren't dangerous.

Enter the Flesher, carrying a bucket of soapy water; the smell of pine disinfectant cutting through the bitter reek of Mr New's vomit. One step, two steps, three steps …

She glanced at Mr New who was mouthing, 'Now. Scream now!' at her.

Heather moaned. Clutched her stomach.

Mr New glared at her, forming words without sound: 'Please!'

She screamed.

The Flesher ran to her, water and foam slopping out of the bucket. Mr New lurched to his feet and charged, lips curled back in a snarl, exposing missing teeth and bloody gums, his face covered in bruises. He slammed into the Flesher's back and they both crashed into the bars. The metal room reverberated with the sound of flesh and bone against metal.

The bucket hit the rusty floor and bounced, end over end, the contents spraying out.

Mr New reeled backwards, and charged again. BOOOOM! The Flesher staggered. Mr New grabbed the back of the rubber Mrs Thatcher mask and rammed the Flesher's head into the bars.

'Grab his hands! Grab the fucker's hands!'

Duncan was right behind her. *'Don't do it, Heather.'*

'I...'

'GRAB HIS HANDS!'

'He can't beat him. No one can beat him.'

Mr New smashed the Flesher's head off the bars again. 'GRAB HIS FUCKING HANDS!'

The Flesher looked up, hollow eyes latching onto Heather's. He was the Dark and he knew. This was a test.

'No.'

'HEATHER: GRAB HIS FUCKING HANDS!'

'I can't...'

'Don't get involved.'

The Flesher turned and grabbed a handful of Mr New's shirt. Then buried a fist in his face.

Mr New staggered, slipped in the puddle of vomit, and fell back against the wall. BOOOM... He lay there, groaning, and the Flesher kicked him in the head. Mr New's skull clattered off the metal wall. A spray of blood burst from his lips, spattering down onto the rusty floor.

'No one can beat Him. He's eternal.'

The Flesher lurched back a couple of steps, and kicked Mr New again. Then grabbed him by the throat, dragged him upright, and slammed him against the bars. Mr New's arms hung lip at his sides, and then his knees gave way. He slid sideways down the bars, his head bouncing off the floor.

Two minutes later the Flesher was hauling the tin bath into the prison – Heather nearly wet herself. She scrambled back into the far corner, biting her lip, trying not to cry, trying not to draw attention to herself. She'd been good, she'd been good, she'd been good . . .

Mr New groaned and tried to get up, arms and legs trembling with the effort. He didn't even make it to his knees: the Flesher reached into the tin bath and pulled out a small plastic rectangle – no bigger than a TV remote control – and clicked a switch. Lightning crackled between the two electrical contacts at the end. *Click-click-click-click-click* . . .

He rammed the tazer into the small of Mr New's back and the man convulsed – one leg sending the tin bath flying, spilling its contents all over the floor: chains, the wire rod, the lightsaber, knives . . . one skittered up against the bars.

And then Mr New was still, lying on the floor groaning – all the fight electrocuted out of him – crying and twitching as the chains were fastened around his ankles.

The Flesher winched him up into the air, cut away his clothes, grabbed his face in one hand. And brought the lightsaber down on the crown of Mr New's shiny head.

CRACK.

Mr New didn't stop twitching until the bright blue rod was rammed into the hole in his skull.

Two quick cuts – clean and deep – and dark red flooded into the tin bath. Mr New's body hung still and silent and pale.

His head came off with a single pass of the blade, sliced from back to front, then tossed unceremoniously onto the floor. It lay on its side, staring open-mouthed at Heather as she cowered in the corner.

The skinning was horrific and fast. The Flesher peeled him with swift, economical movements, then opened him up from stem to stern. The bulging white sack of Mr New's innards came free in one slithery lump . . . His body was a hollow shell in less than five minutes.

Then came the axe: hacking down along the spine, splitting the body in half lengthways. With nothing left to hold the two pieces together they swung outwards on the chains around each leg, clanging into the metal wall on one side and the bars on the other.

And just like that, Mr New was a carcass. Nothing more than meat. Just the hands and feet to show that this was once a human being. And his head, staring accusingly up from the floor.

'Do we really have to do this?' The IB technician held the crowbar tight against his chest, eying the septic tank's lid as if it were the trapdoor to hell.

'Aye, DS McRae's got a thing for other people's jobbies, don't you Laz?' Steel took a deep draw on her cigarette and pointed at the concrete slab. 'Just make sure you don't sod up them scrape marks.'

They'd reversed the IB's van down the lane, the little diesel generator in the back chugging away, powering a pair of halogen spotlights. The technician adjusted his breathing mask and tightened his grip on the crowbar.

Steel pointed at the septic tank cover. 'Some time today would be nice.'

'OK, OK, Jesus . . . ' He slid the end of the crowbar between the lid and the base – his SOC suit glaring in the harsh lights – and heaved. There was a grinding noise as the concrete slab shifted— 'Ah, *Jesus!*' He dropped the crowbar and backed off, waving a hand in front of his face.

'Oh for God's sake, Frank.' Steel took the fag out of her mouth, 'don't be such a . . . fucking hell!' She stuck the cig- arette back, puffing, surrounding herself in a little protective cloud of smoke.

A rancid, cloying reek filled the small lane: raw sewage, like a hundred dirty pub toilets all at once. Logan clamped a hand over his mouth and retreated upwind, to the other side of the road.

Frank edged forward, put one blue, plastic overbootie against the concrete slab and pushed till it was fully open.

Logan had expected the smell to drop off when the lid was removed – that the air would get in and disperse the worst of it – but it just got worse.

Frank peered into the foetid darkness. 'I am *not* going down there.'

Steel inched forwards. 'Well, at least poke about with a stick, or something.'

'Might not even be anything in there...'

'We're no' going to find out, standing round like a bunch of idiots, are we?'

'Don't see you volunteering.'

'Bloody right you don't. No' my job, Sunshine.'

He said something very rude under his breath, then grabbed a full-face splash guard and a pair of thick, black rubber gloves. Someone handed him a long pole with a hook on the end, and Frank went fishing in the Leith's septic tank. The swearing was bad, but the smell was worse as he swirled his pole through the reeking muck.

And then he froze. 'Found something...'

Steel didn't look impressed as whatever it was rose slowly from the stinking depths. 'Tenner says it's another mouldy sheep. They chuck them in to get the bacteria going when ... oh bollocks.'

It was a naked human forearm, complete with hand, covered in brown and grey sludge.

31

'Deceased is female, mid thirties. Approximately fifteen stone.'
Dr Isobel McAllister picked her way around the post mortem
table, voice raised over the howl of the extractor fan.

'You know what,' said DI Steel, tugging at the crotch of her
white SOC coveralls, 'I'm sick of wearing these bloody things.
Who the hell were they designed to fit? Quasimodo? It's
bunching right up my—'

Isobel glared. 'Can we *please* have quiet for once!' Then went
back to her external examination. Valerie Leith was laid out on
the shiny cutting table like a broken Barbie doll: forearms,
biceps, head, torso, thighs, legs, all separate. Still covered in a
thin grey-brown film of stinking gloop.

'Can you no' hurry up and wash the damn bits off?'

'If you *will* insist on dragging me in here in the evening to
perform a post mortem, the least you can do is not interrupt
while I'm doing it.'

Steel puffed out her cheeks, readjusted the breathing mask
over her face, and hauled at the crotch of her suit again. She
lasted a whole two minutes before leaning over and whispering to Logan, 'You're a bloody jinx, do you know that? Anyone
else finds a body it's usually pretty fresh. You: it's half rotten
and marinated in shite.'

'It's not my fault – it was just a hunch, OK?'

'Blind bloody luck, more like.'

'A considerable portion of flesh has been excised from the left thigh. Edges of the wound are deteriorated after prolonged immersion in sewage—'

'I said there was something funny about the Leith crime scene.'

Steel scowled at him. 'What d'you want, a parade?'

'—dismemberment was caused by a knife: single-sided blade, approximately eight inches long—'

'I'm only saying.'

'You have any idea how much trouble this is going to cause?'

'—angle of incisions implies a right-handed suspect—'

'What happened to "good job, Logan, you're a credit to the force"?'

'Oh don't be such a drama queen, we —'

'Inspector, I will not tell you again! This is a post mortem, not a playground.'

Steel actually blushed. 'Sorry, Doc.' And then, when no one was looking, she punched Logan in the arm. 'That was your fault!'

The mortuary clock read eight fifteen before Isobel finally told her assistant to wash off the remains. Eight fifteen and Logan had been on duty since four in the morning. That was ... he was too tired to work out how long.

Isobel's assistant started with the head. Dirty water gurgled down the cutting table drain, and as Valerie Leith's face slowly appeared from its coating of foul-smelling slime, Logan's spirits sank. With the other victims it'd been easy to maintain a sense of detachment. They were just hunks of meat. But this was different, this finally looked like a human being. Valerie Leith: thirty-five, skin all puckered and discoloured, brown hair straggly round her face as Isobel's assistant rinsed the sewage away.

And somehow Logan didn't feel as pleased with himself as he had.

Aberdeen was a sparkling blanket – yellow and white street-lights shining in the deep blue November night outside DCS Bain's office window. The head of CID stood with his back to the room, staring out at the view. Taxis drifted by on the streets below; drunken clots of Aberdonians lurched for the nearest club, chip shop or taxi rank; the sound of sirens in the distance. Nearly midnight.

'Why the hell wasn't that septic tank searched the first time round?'

'Why would they?' Steel didn't bother covering her mouth, just let go a jaw-cracking yawn, followed by a little burp. 'God ... no reason to think this was anything other than what it looked like.'

'Insch should have—'

'Yeah, well, he didn't. And if it was me, I wouldn't have either. And neither would you, Bill.'

The DCS turned and stared at Logan. 'But you did, Sergeant?'

'It was just a hunch ...'

Steel clapped him on the shoulder. 'Don't be so modest! Tell you, Bill, he—'

The DCS cut her off. 'The question is: what are we going to tell the media? How's it going to look when they find out her body lay undiscovered, less than thirty feet from her house for a fortnight? DI Insch—'

'Don't start, Bill, OK? Been a long day and I can't be arsed fighting with you.' Steel stretched out in her chair, making creaking noises. 'Doesn't matter what we tell the press: they'll just make up their own shite anyway.'

'You're not seeing the big picture here, Inspector. We told the world and his bloody dog that Wiseman killed Valerie Leith, didn't we? And if that's not bad enough, it looks like the same person killed the Inglises *and* Tom and Hazel Stephen. Where was Wiseman at the time? Craiginches!' The DCS sat back behind his desk. 'So now we've got *two* psychopaths out there, butchering their way through the populace, and our only suspect is looking less and less guilty every day!'

'Actually,' Logan dug in his jacket pocket, pulled out the dog-eared copy of *Smoak With Blood* Steel had given him, and dumped it on the desk, 'We do have another suspect.'

'What,' the DCS examined the cover, 'Jamie McLaughlin?'

'No, William Leith. I found a copy of that in the master bedroom.'

Steel made a sound like a drowning elephant. 'You remembering he nearly got his head chopped off?'

'They have an alarm system at the croft, but somehow the killer managed to break in without setting it off. Then he dismembers Valerie Leith and dumps her in their septic tank. How did he know where it was? I'll bet if we search the garage again we'll find a crowbar or something that matches the grooves in that septic tank lid.'

'But Leith's head—'

'Wouldn't be the first time someone's injured themselves to shift the blame, would it?'

The DCS swore, grabbed his phone and started dialling. 'Yeah, Pete, it's me. I want William Leith brought in ... No, no I don't. I want him here *now* ... Well, I don't care, do I? Just sort it!' He hung up, steepled his fingers, brooded for a minute, then asked Logan, 'You still friends with that journalist scumbag?'

AMINER.COM

SHORE DISP

MERGENCY MEDICALS, DANGER MONEY, AND VEGETARIA

ESHER VICT
LED BY HUS

Shocks Community ▣ William Le

NO MO
MEAT!

WILDCAT STRIKES
broke out on a number of offshore installations yesterday as talks to resolve the 'cannibal crisis' broke down yet again.

"They just don't get it," said Mark Kennedy, a roughneck on the Kittywake Delta, "we're trapped out here eating God knows what, day in day out. What happens if everyone in the oil industry comes down with CJD? How are the oil companies going to make money then?"

CapreSana, the offshore catering company who operate the Kittywake Delta canteen, said were doing all they could provide the men with alternative meals, but it... **More on page 4**

EXCLUSIVE
By Colin Miller
C.Miller@Aberdeen-Examiner.com

IT MUST have seemed like the perfect crime: but William Leith's dreams of getting away with murder came to a crashing halt in the early hours of this morning when Grampian Police charged him with killing his wife Valerie (35).

In sec...

the alleged witness protection programme, enjoying four-star food, wine and round the clock medical care in a police safe-house in Aviemore.

Friend of the family Amy Hall said, "Val was a lovely, loving person. She had a great personality and didn't deserve to die. I hope they lock William up and throw away the key."

In an effort t...

FLESHER IN PRISON
BUT THE KILLING GOES ON!

By Russel D McLean

Tragedy strikes a stunned Aberdeen again.

In a sickening twist it now looks like Ken Wiseman, arrested on Tuesday after a high-speed car chase that cost Detective Inspector David Insch (42) his daughter's life, was not the only one preying on the Granite City's citizens.

Last night Agnes Broach was awakened by screams coming from her next door neighbour's house. "It was horrible, like the wailing of the damned!"

Terrifying

"I've known Tom and Hazel Stephen for years. They were a lovely couple. It's terrifying to think that they're gone."

Mrs Broach (65) – a widow with a disabled son – bravely went next door to see if she could help and found the kitchen awash with blood. "It was kitchen awash with blood. "like something out" she said, "like something out

at his local club. His wife Hazel (47) played indoor and outdoor bowls for the Old Rayne league team.

Copycat or Partner?

Police had hoped that with Flesher's

Could th
killer ha
a partne
in crim

Police appeal for inforn

If you have any information Ken Wiseman or any of his as Grampian Police want to hear All calls treated as confidentia

Call now on: 0800 99

that Wiseman was not working alone. But noted Criminal Psychologist Bushel

killed by the

IVES of A
appealed today.

ear-old truck driv nearly two years ago harity run to deli

32

'All hail the conquering hero!' DI Steel was sitting in Logan's chair, feet up on his desk, a copy of that morning's *Aberdeen Examiner* open on her lap. 'Where the hell you been? I came in *hours* ago.'

'Really?' Logan stuck the brown plastic tray from the canteen down in front of her. 'Because Big Gary says you didn't get in till eleven. It's only quarter past.'

Steel grinned, 'Aye, aye: make with the bacon buttie, hero boy.'

He handed over a tinfoil package and sat back against the room's only radiator. 'I didn't write the bloody thing, OK?'

Steel unwrapped her buttie and tore a huge bite out of it. 'Chief Constable Baldy Brian wants to congratulate us personally for catching Leith. Of course, I put it all down to my inspirational leadership and—'

'You've got tomato sauce on your blouse.'

The inspector peered down at her chest. 'Aw no' *again!*'

'Anyway,' Logan picked up his coffee and went to peel the Leith crime scene photos from the death board, 'not as if makes any difference, is it? Doesn't get us any closer to catching the Flesher.'

'Are you mental?'

'Well, it doesn't, does it? He's still out there—'

'God, no' again . . . Fine, be miserable. Your glass might be half empty, but mine runneth over. No' had a pat on the back from Baldy Brian for ages.' She took another massive bite, chewing happily. 'Mmmmph, mmm, mph-mmmm?'

'Yeah, I suppose. But not till Insch comes back.' He slipped the crime scene photos back in the Leith file, then stuck the whole thing in his out-tray. 'If there's nothing urgent on, I thought I'd go home and—'

'Oh no you don't! You heard the DCS last night: if Wiseman's slipping out the frame we need to find someone else to pin all this shite on. You and me are going through that 1987 case file with a nit comb.'

'You're kidding – we pulled a twenty-hour shift yesterday!'

'Aye, well feel free to whinge to your Federation Rep about it. And have one for me while you're there.' She polished off the last of her bacon buttie, scrunched up the tinfoil and lobbed it at the bin. Not even close.

'We've already been over the historical stuff, and—'

'And now we're doing it again. OK?' She sooked something out from between her teeth and chewed. 'Don't be such a work-shy bastard. Our pat on the back's not till after lunch: plenty of time to get cracking.' She pulled out her cigarettes and stood. 'Let me know how you get on. I'll be in a . . . meeting. Yeah – anyone asks I'm in a meeting.'

Logan stifled a yawn, took another mouthful of coffee, and crawled back inside the McLaughlin case file. He hadn't been entirely honest with DI Steel – he'd not really read the whole thing before. Not all of it. He'd just skimmed the day-to-day stuff on his way to the post mortem and crime scene reports. Going through it from start to finish was something of a revelation.

Once Detective Chief Inspector Brooks – this was 1987, before he'd got the promotion to DSI – had Ken Wiseman in his sights, he never looked at anyone else. As far as Brooks was concerned, Wiseman was guilty.

It was the car boot full of blood that had done it. Brooks kept coming back to it in the transcripts, time and time again.

DCI Brooks: Stop messing us about Ken, we know you did it.

Wiseman: I told you! It was a Roe Deer, OK? Found it at the side of the road.

DCI Brooks: Do you seriously expect me to believe—

Wiseman: It was still twitching. I took it home and butchered it.

DCI Brooks: They found human blood in there too, you idiot.

Wiseman: Mine. It was mine. Bloody deer kicked out when I hefted it into the boot, didn't it? Got me right in the face. Bled all over the place.

Logan flicked through to the forensic reports. According to the lab, the samples were too degraded for a positive identification, the DNA test inconclusive.

They'd tried again in ninety-five, fighting Wiseman's appeal. DNA testing had come on a bit since 1990, but the only human blood they could extract from the evidence shared so many markers with Wiseman's own that even an idiot defence lawyer could have poked holes in the prosecution case. So good old Detective Chief Inspector Brooks had tried to suppress the evidence.

The defence managed to get hold of it anyway and that was it – case dismissed.

Wiseman's original confession was given pride of place at the very back of the file, in its own clear plastic evidence pouch, obviously typed by someone with more fingers than brain cells:

I did it. I did it and I am sorry. I did not mean to hurt her, but I did. Their was a lot of blood. Afterwards I did not know what to do, so I proceeded to dispose of the body by ~~dismembering~~ cutting it up and getting rid of the parts. I do not remember ware I burried them. I had been drinking.

There was another page and a half – a tortured mass of bad typing, poor spelling and twisted lies, and then, at the end, a shaky signature. As if the writer's hand had just been slammed in a drawer. There was a second version of the confession, all neatly typed by someone who could spell. Wiseman's signature wasn't any better on that one.

Logan pushed the file away, wondering how the hell someone like Brooks had ever made it to the rank of Detective Superintendent; the bastard was little more than a criminal himself. And Insch had helped him. Mr Everything-Has-To-Be-Done-By-The-Book had beaten a suspect in custody and forced him to sign a confession. No wonder Wiseman went after him . . .

Lunch was a baked potato in the canteen, eaten one-handed as he re-read the SOC report on the derelict butcher's shop where Ian and Sharon McLaughlin's remains had been found. He stuck the report back in the folder and pulled out Faulds' tatty copy of *Smoak With Blood*, flicking through till he got to the chapter on the same scene.

> When God makes man, he does so from the simplest of materials. Our bodies, our minds, the blood that courses through our veins, are no different from those of the animals we slaughter for food. A pig, a cow, a human being: after the butcher's tender ministrations it's all just meat. *We* are all just meat.
>
> It was an anonymous tip-off that led police to the disused butcher's shop on Palmerston Road, within spitting distance of the railway station; the rumble of passing freight trains making the ground shudder beneath their feet as they picked through the debris-strewn interior. Rats scuttled through the piles of broken plaster and crumbling furniture. The floor and walls

spattered where pigeons had passed judgement on a shop closed for eighteen years and turned into a storage shed.

Today, the sign outside says 'Property Management', but in January 1988 it was the final resting place for my parents. Or would have been, if not for that anonymous phone call in the dead of night.

Logan flicked through the file – finding reference to a call made from a public phone box in Torry. The note said it was a woman's voice: drunk and scared. They thought it was probably a working girl, looking for somewhere to take a punter. Or maybe one of the city's growing homeless population, looking for a place to drink themselves to sleep. Brooks put out the usual appeals, but no one came forward.

The fridges at the back of the shop had been cleared of their contents, the detritus piled up in the serving area. In here the walls were smeared with filth, mildew reaching out of the corners: a permanent shadow that not even the pathologist's spotlights could banish. My parents hung from hooks in the ceiling.

That sounds more dramatic than it actually was. Although the smell was appalling (the power being long gone, and the fridges at ambient temperature) there was little to show that the cuts of meat hanging there had once been someone's mother and father. My mother and father. Now just meat.

And on those filthy walls were written the words that would forever be emblazoned upon my soul. A message from the man who would become known as 'the Flesher'.

"From ancient times, our origins we draw,
When priests were cons'crate to keep God's law,
When sacerdotal sacrifice and feasts,
Made alters smoak with blood of slaughter'd beasts..."
A message written in blood. The blood of my parents.

After a period of sober reflection involving jam sponge and custard, Logan grabbed a cup of tea and went back to the history room. The file said Brooks traced the quotation scrawled on the butcher's shop wall to Trinity Hall – home of the Seven Incorporated Trades – a 1960s concrete box of a building with delusions of grandeur, on Holburn Street, not far from McFarlane's . . .

'Smoak with blood' – a line from a painting belonging to the butchers' trade incorporation, AKA: 'the Fleshers' And that was how he got his name.

Logan's tea was stone cold by the time he'd finished reading all the interview transcripts: Brooks had hauled in every butcher in the city, whether they were members or not. That was when the fixation with Wiseman started.

'Wakey, wakey.' DI Steel meandered into the room, bringing a waft of stale cigarette with her. 'Half two: ready to be told what a clever little boy you are?'

Logan looked up from Wiseman's first ever brush with the police. 'Give me a minute, I— hey!'

Steel snatched the transcript from his hand. 'Let's see what's so important . . . ' her lips moving as she read. 'Jesus,' she turned it over in her hands, peering at the biro notes scribbled on the back, 'Basher Brooks strikes again. You see these? "He's obviously hiding something.", "Shifty.", "Evasive.", "Reeks of guilt . . . " Talk about keeping an open mind.' She stuck it back on Logan's desk. 'Anyway, come on: arse in gear. Pat on the back time.'

30 minutes later

'Bastarding cock-weasel son-of-a-bitch!' Steel hurled herself into Logan's seat. 'Can you believe this shite? Fucking bastard!' She stood, swore some more, kicked the filing cabinet, called Chief Constable Brian Anderson a 'Sheep-shagging prick.' And collapsed back into the chair again.

'Well,' said Logan, picking his words carefully, 'it could be worse . . . '

'How? How could it possibly be worse?'

'Could've been DCI Finnie.'

'That ... *cock*?' She scrubbed her hands across her face. 'How could they say I'm not pro-active enough? How? How much more pro-fucking-active could I be? Did we not just catch Leith?'

Logan settled himself in behind the other desk, bracing himself for the oncoming rant. Ten minutes later she was still at it.

'Course you know what this is really about, don't you? Can't have a lowly *woman* heading up a high-profile case like this. *Nooooo*. That needs a baldy-headed bastard, doesn't it?' She put on a broad Banff and Buchan accent for, '"I think it'd be mare appropriate fer DCS Bain tae tak a mare active roll..." Wankers didn't take the damn thing off Insch, did they?' Steel sat and seethed in silence for a while, then pulled out her cigarettes, turning the pack over and over in her hands. 'Do us a favour, eh? Go see how the fat git's doing.'

'What, now?'

'No, no' now: tonight. I know he's been a tosspot lately, and he smacked you in the face ... but ... well ... take him a bag of jelly babies or something.'

'I can't, I've got something on tonight.' Which was a lie. Logan just couldn't face dealing with Insch's grief on top of all the guilt. Not yet.

'Insch is one of us, Laz, we've got no right abandoning him. No' with his wee girl dead like that.'

'But if I hadn't chased Wiseman—'

'You've always been Inschy's favourite. He needs someone to talk to, and you're it. Besides, what's the worst that can happen? He shouts at you a bit? Least it'll make him feel better. You no' think we owe him that?'

Logan swore. But the inspector was right: he owed Insch that much. 'OK, OK, I'll go see him.'

251

'Good lad.' Steel hauled herself out of the chair and headed for the door, calling over her shoulder, 'But for God's sake don't tell him I sent you! Got my reputation as a hardnosed bitch to think about.'

Half four and Steel still wasn't back. Logan sat with a fresh cup of tea and the old Media Office file on Ian and Sharon McLaughlin – all the press releases, the follow-up articles culled from the newspapers, speeches written for whoever was Chief Constable at the time. One of the newspaper clippings included a photo of Ex-DSI Brooks outside the Sheriff Court, a thin and hirsute DC David Insch standing off to one side. 'SUSPECT REMANDED IN CUSTODY'

He laid the article out on the desk and sat back, staring at the death board. How many of them died because Brooks couldn't get over his Wiseman-focussed monomania?

Logan called Colin Miller and asked for a favour.

'What, again? You still owe me lunch from last time. '

'Do this one and we'll call it dinner – takeaway Thai?'

'I'm listening . . . '

'Need you to go through the paper's archives. Missing persons, housebreakings, outbreaks of food poisoning, CJD . . . that kind of thing. 1987 to 1990.'

There was silence on the other end.

'You gonnae tell me what this is all about? '

'Nope.'

'You expect me to go huntin' through three years worth of pish, and you're no' gonnae tell me anythin'?'

'Look we—'

'Exclusive. I get the scoop on whatever it is, or I'm no' liftin' a finger.'

'I'm just trying to put the original investigation into context.'

'No exclusive, no deal.'

Logan said he'd see what he could do. 'It's up to the inspector.'

'Which one: Fatty or Wrinkly?'

'Steel. Insch is on compassionate leave. His daughter—'

'Fuck – sorry, man, I forgot. Look, I'll do what I can, but I've got to go interview some scientist at the Rowett this afternoon. "Hepatitis C in the food chain: how safe is your dinner?" kind of thing.'

Just what they needed, the papers stirring up more panic.

'Tell you what: the Howff, eight o'clock, buy us a pint and we'll talk about that exclusive.'

'OK, we . . .' Logan closed his eyes and swore quietly. 'I can't tonight, I've got a thing. Tomorrow?'

'Fine, but you're buying.'

'Deal.' Logan hung up and went back to the McLaughlin case file – putting off the inevitable, until guilt and hunger got the better of him. Like it or not, he had to go see the parents of the little girl he'd got killed.

Logan pulled the CID pool car up to the kerb and killed the engine. Then sat there, looking out at the night-shrouded countryside. Psyching himself up. Two deep breaths. Count to ten.

Count to ten again.

'Come on . . .' Logan grabbed the plastic bag from the passenger seat.

There were no lights on at the front of the house, but a dented Renault Clio with 'I'M DRIVING COURTESY OF TAM'S TURRIFF MOTORS!' emblazoned down the side, was parked in the drive where the inspector's Range Rover usually sat. Logan tried the bell.

Brrrrrrrrrrrrrrrrrrrrrrrrrrrrrrrrrrrrringgggggggggggg . . .

It was cold out here. The faint yellow glow of streetlights filtered through the trees, making the autumn leaves shine like reptile skin. A gust of wind sent a couple swirling to their death, adding to the greasy slick that littered the front garden.

He pressed the bell again.

One more time, then he was going to give up and go home.

Brrrrrrrrrrrrrrrrrrrrrrrrrrrrrrrrrrrringgggggggggggg . . .

A light blossomed above the door.

'Inspector?'

Clunk, jingle, and the door drifted open a crack. Then came the sound of someone shuffling off back into the house.

'Inspector? Hello?' Logan put one hand on the wood and pushed. The hallway was in darkness, but down at the far end he could just make out Insch's rounded bulk as he placed a foot on the stairs and began to climb.

Logan stepped inside and closed the door behind him. 'Are you OK?'

Insch just kept on climbing, the stairs creaking as he disappeared from view.

'Oh God . . . ' Logan peered into the lounge: it was a disaster area. The settee and armchairs upturned, stuffing ripped out, wooden frames buckled, coffee table a heap of twisted metal and broken glass. The dining room was just as bad: chairs broken, table on its side – a perfect circle of scorched varnish just visible in the gloom.

Insch must have run out of steam by the time he'd reached the kitchen. Logan backed out into the hall and crept up the stairs.

He found the inspector sitting on the floor in the corner of a small bedroom, surrounded by stuffed animals. The faint orange glow of a plug-in nightlight glittered back from dozens of black plastic eyes. A hand-painted sign on the door said, 'SOPHIE'S SECRET PALACE ~ BEWARE OF THE DRAGON!!!'

Logan stopped at the threshold. 'How's Miriam?'

Insch sniffed, wiped his nose on the back of his hand, then picked up a fluffy unicorn. His voice was small and ragged: 'She was going to be a doctor. Or a ballerina. Or an astronaut. Depended on what day it was . . . ' He hadn't showered or shaved in a couple of days; his jowls covered in dark-blue stubble, heavy black bags under his eyes, clothes rumpled and stained. The smell of stale alcohol oozed out of him.

Logan picked his way through the furry minefield of bears and dinosaurs and pigs and dragons, then sank down with his back to the unmade bed. 'Everyone at the station's asking for you. They're getting up a collection. Going to get a park bench dedicated to Sophie.' It had sounded so appropriate when Steel had told him about it yesterday, now it just sounded hollow and crass. '. . . I'm sorry.'

'She left me. Miriam. She got out the hospital, took the girls and went to her mother's.' Another sniff. 'Said she couldn't bear to look at me anymore. That it was my fault.'

'Sir, I—'

'Wiseman was after me, and they paid for it.' He wrapped his huge arms around the little unicorn, buried his face in its fur.

Logan closed his eyes and stepped off the cliff: 'I wasn't your fault, it was mine. If I hadn't chased Wiseman—'

'He was going to sell her to a paedophile. Right now, she'd be . . .' The huge man shuddered. When he looked up his eyes sparkled with tears. 'How do you explain to a child's mother that her little girl's better off dead?'

'I'm so sorry . . .' Logan pulled open the carrier bag, and dragged out four tins of Guinness. 'Got them at that wee supermarket in Newmacher. Still cold.' He held one out.

Insch took the tin, clicked the ring pull and drank deep.

'Here,' Logan went back into the bag for a family-sized packet of jelly babies and a box of Terry's All Gold, 'The chocolates were for Miriam.'

The inspector stared at the bag of little pink, red, green, purple, and yellow figures. 'I can't eat those. Borderline diabetic as it is . . .' Then he snatched the bag from Logan's hand and tore it open, stuffing baby after baby into his mouth. Chewing on automatic. Washing them down with more Guinness.

Logan pulled the tab on his own tin and raised it. 'It's going to be OK.'

'No.' Insch shook his head, clutching the little furry unicorn to his chest. 'No it's not. It's never going to be OK again.'

The kitchen light seemed harsh and artificial after the soft glow of Sophie's bedroom. They sat at the kitchen table, Insch hunched over a glass of whisky and a mug of sweet, milky coffee, the steam curling up around his bald head. Logan slid the opened box of All Gold back across the tabletop.

Insch didn't look up. 'Has he confessed?'

'Denying everything: says I beat him up. You imagine that? He'd have me for sodding breakfast. Besides Alec got the whole thing on camera.'

Insch took a Caramel Nectar and stuck it in his mouth, followed by a sip of whisky. 'Did he ... is Sophie on it?'

Logan didn't want to answer that one, but he didn't see that he had any choice. 'Yes.'

The inspector nodded. And helped himself to another chocolate. 'I want you to do something for me.' His voice was a dark rumble, colder than the November night howling against the kitchen window. 'I want you to go to Craiginches and you tell Wiseman that I'm sorry.'

Logan nearly choked. 'Did you say—'

'I should never have assaulted him. I was a policeman, he was a prisoner, I had no right.' Insch downed half his whisky in one go. 'I looked up to Brooks. He was everything I wanted to be: he got the job done. Put people behind bars. He bent the rules, but it ... it took me a long time to realize he was wrong. The ends didn't justify pounding the crap out of suspects. Made us no better than they were.' The last of the whisky disappeared. 'You'll tell him?'

'Are you sure?'

The inspector held the cut crystal glass in his huge hand, twisting it so that little diamonds of light sparkled on the tabletop. 'And then you tell that piece of shit I'm going to be waiting for him.'

'Sir, you can't *do* that. He's—'

'I don't care how long it takes: I'm going to rip his balls off with my bare hands and feed them to him.'

'But—'

'No bastard is ever going to find his body.'

'It's *over.* Even if we can't pin the Flesher killings on him, after what he did to you and Miriam and Sophie, they'll never let him out. He's going to die in Peterhead Prison.'

Insch looked up, his eyes dangerous and black. 'I know. And I'm going to be there when he does, with my hands round his throat.'

33

Thursday morning lashed against the tiny window of the Flesher history room, the wind and rain playing counterpart to the ping and groan of the solitary anaemic radiator. Logan stuck his finger in his ear and tried again, shouting into the phone: 'No, not McKay, *McRae*: Mike, Charlie, Romeo, Alpha, Echo.'

Static. A high-pitched buzzing noise.

'Is this Detective Superintendent Danby? Hello? You left a message about the Flesher's Newcastle victims?'

More buzzing, and then: '...*know what I'm sayin'?*' The DSI's voice was like a Geordie foghorn.

'Sorry, I can barely hear you.'

'*Look, I went through the files, right? There's nothin' in there about them bein' in Weight Watchers.*'

DI Steel slouched into the room, but Logan got his hand up before she could open her mouth. 'I know,' he said, 'I've got a copy of the investigation reports here. But did anybody ask the families? I mean, if there wasn't any reason—'

'*So what are you expectin' me to do? Go round and ask the poor bastards' relatives if they were tryin' to lose weight? It was nearly twenty years ago: know what I mean?*'

'Look, I wouldn't ask, but we've got some victims here who *were* members and—'

'And you think this is how he finds them.'

'Well—'

'I'll stick a couple of woodentops on it, OK? Can't say fairer than that, know what I mean?'

'Thank you, sir. I appreciate it.'

'You can thank us by catching the bastard.'

Steel waited for Logan to hang up, then plonked herself on the corner of his desk and peered at his notes. 'Oh for God's sake: you were supposed to chase up this Weight Watchers thing *days* ago. What the hell have you been doing?'

'I did. That was Newcastle getting back to me. And how come you're so bloody cheery this morning?'

She scowled at him. 'Don't start, I'm no' in the mood. Where's Defective Constable Rennie?'

'Bain's got him going through more of those INTERPOL reports.'

'Yeah, like that's going to help.' She stuck her hands into her armpits and turned to face the death board, in all its blood-stained glory. 'Susan proposed last night.'

'Congratulations?'

''Cos I don't have enough to worry about. Last year it was all, "Let's get a cat!" now it's, "Let's get married!" You know what's next, don't you? Bloody babies.' She shuddered. 'Creepy little bastards . . .'

The inspector started rummaging through the paperwork on Logan's desk. 'So come on then: how is he? Insch.'

Hunched up and crying at the kitchen table. Planning revenge. Depressed. Dangerous. Destructive. Drinking away his pain. Grieving . . . 'He's OK.'

Steel nodded. 'Thought so. Hard as nails is our Inschy.' She stopped at the plastic wallet containing Wiseman's second – better typed – confession and skimmed through it. 'This is appalling . . .'

'Got a call from Craiginches – Ken Wiseman beat the living hell out of Richard Davidson last night. Thought I should go

259

up, have a word. Maybe ask him about that,' He pointed at the confession.

'What, Wiseman won't speak to Faulds, or Bain, or me, or that Liverpudlian psychologist toss-pot, but police hero DS Logan McRae'll get him to talk?'

'I only meant—'

'Ah, like I care.' She dropped the confession back on Logan's desk. 'It's the mighty DCS Bain's investigation now. You can do whatever you like, I'm off for a fag.' She stood. 'I'd say take Alec with you, but he's got his camera glued to His Holiness DCS Bain's arse.' Putting on a whiny voice for: 'Oh Detective Chief Superintendent, you're so big and clever!'

Probably just as well – Logan didn't really want a BBC film crew there while he passed on Insch's message.

'But don't forget we've got that bloody case peer-review with Strathclyde at half twelve.'

'But I'm not—'

'If I have to be there so do you. And you're no' wriggling out of it, so don't even try. Half twelve: if you're late I'm going to ... do something nasty to you. Can't be arsed thinking what at the moment, but it won't be pleasant.'

Wiseman coughed, then spat whatever he'd brought up onto the scuffed linoleum floor. The interview room wasn't exactly straight out of *Better Homes And Prisons* magazine, but the glob of glistening phlegm didn't help. The butcher's face was a mass of bruises, elastoplasts, little white butterfly stitches, and scabs.

Logan took another sip of what passed for coffee from the vending machine in reception. 'Little birdy tells me you and Richard Davidson had a falling out.'

Wiseman shrugged. 'Some people are born stupid.'

'You put him in hospital: broken leg, cracked ribs, concussion—'

'Little shit came at me, crying about his mummy.'

'Not think you're in enough trouble, Ken?'

'What are they going to do: arrest me?'

Fair point.

'I've got a message for you. From DI Insch.'

'Let me guess: he's going to kill me? Only way I'm getting out of Peterhead Prison's in a body-bag?' Wiseman snorted. 'Heard it all before. His mate Brooks said the same thing. Look what happened to him.'

Silence.

'He says he's sorry.'

The ex-butcher frowned, sat back in his seat and pursed his lips, looked down at the handcuffs holding his left wrist to the plaster cast on his right, then up at the camera bolted to the wall. 'What for?'

But there was no way Logan was going on record saying Insch assaulted a prisoner, even if it was seventeen years ago. 'I want to talk to you about your confession.'

'Thought that's what we *were* talking about.'

Logan pulled the plastic envelope from his pocket and placed it on the desk. '"I did it. I did it and I am sorry. I did not mean to hurt her, but I did. There was a lot of blood—"'

'I know what it says.'

'"Afterwards I did not know what to do, so I disposed of the body by cutting it up—"'

Wiseman lurched forwards, banging his grubby fibreglass cast on the scarred tabletop. 'I said I know what it fucking says!'

Logan smiled. He'd just been using the confession and Richard Davidson's assault as an excuse to pass on Insch's message, but somehow he'd managed to hit a raw nerve. The butcher was so blasé about everything else . . . 'Who was she?'

'She wasn't anyone. I made it up. It's what they wanted to hear. They said they'd—'

'Remember Angus Robertson? The Mastrick Monster?'

'I don't have to sit here and listen to this.'

Logan pointed at the interview room, the camera, the officer standing by the door. 'Prison, remember: not a social club.

261

Robertson said your cells were next to each other. That late at night you'd tell him about the woman you dismembered and the guy you beat to death in the showers.'

'You going to take Roberson's word for it? Lying little bastard killed fifteen women—'

'Who was she?'

'Fuck you.'

'Your car boot was full of blood.'

'And you're full of shite.'

Another sip of horrible coffee. 'Why did you run, Ken?'

'You deaf? I said...' It seemed to take him a moment to catch up with the change of subject. 'What was I supposed to do? Sit around and wait for that fat wanker to stitch me up again? Like last time?'

'Someone's still out there killing people.'

'My heart bleeds.'

'Who was she? The woman?'

'Fuck. You.'

Logan tossed his plastic cup of plastic coffee in the bin, a little geyser of milky brown erupting as it hit the bottom. 'Fine. Lie all you want, but I'm going to find out.'

Wiseman burst out laughing. 'Oh, big scary policeman!'

'Get him out of here.'

Logan made it back to FHQ just in time see a line of Grampian's finest disappearing into the boardroom. DI Steel, loitered at the back, scowling at him. 'What did I bloody tell you?'

'Traffic was awful, OK?'

She grabbed his arm, speaking in a sharp, smoky whisper, 'Listen up: you follow my lead in there – no volunteering information, no verbal diarrhoea, no pointing bloody fingers. We present a united front to these Weegie bastards. Understand?'

A voice from inside: 'Inspector? We're ready to start.'

'Just a minute.' And back to whispering again, 'Everything was done by the book.'

'Thought this was supposed to be a review to help us identify new ways to tackle the case.'

'Oh don't be so sodding naïve. What do you think they'll do to Insch if they think he cocked this one up? Give him a pat on his fat arse and a big bag of sweeties?'

That voice again: 'Inspector?'

'Remember – everything done by the book.' She turned and pulled Logan into the boardroom. 'Sorry, sir, DS McRae was having difficulty tying his shoelaces and I had to supervise.'

DCS Bain waved them towards a pair of empty seats. 'When you're quite ready.'

Logan settled in beside Steel, and ... oh ... *fuck* was the only word that sprung to mind. The Strathclyde contingent were at the head of the boardroom table. The DCI they'd sent up to run the case review sat in the middle – red hair, sharp suit, statuesque in a mid-forties kind of way; to her left was a bearded sergeant with a face full of acne scars; and on her right, taking notes, was PC Jackie Watson. Fuck, fuck, and thrice more: fuck.

'Will you sit down? Making me feel sick, pacing about...' Steel was onto her second stick of nicotine gum, chewing with her mouth open as Logan marched up and down the history room. Pretending to read a witness statement from January 1988.

'Why did it have to be her?'

'Why do you think? She's got a foot in both camps, she knows all our dirty little secrets and— look either you sit your arse down or I'll twat you one.'

'Didn't look at me the whole meeting, as if I was a bloody stranger.'

'Hell hath no fury like a Ball-Breaker scorned.' Steel puffed out her cheeks and tried to blow a bubble with her gum. No luck. 'What time is it?'

'Twenty to five.'

'Time for one last cuppa before we hit the pub then. Get them in, eh?'

Logan started collecting the mounds of dirty mugs. 'Can't tonight, I've got a prior appointment.'

'Oh aye? Hot date? Randy Rachael from the PF's office sniffing around again, is she? Or have you got yourself an eighteen-year-old nymphomaniac like Rennie? Trying to make Watson jealous, are we?'

He wasn't rising to that. 'Faulds kept saying we should go see Trinity Hall, speak to someone in the Flesher's Incorporation about the original investigation. I got an appointment with their Boxmaster.'

'What is he, a superhero? Boxmaster and Carton Boy, saving the world from the evil forces of plastic packaging?'

'Sort of a cross between deputy club president and accountant, I think.'

'And this can't wait till tomorrow?'

'Only time the guy could make it. You want tea or coffee?'

'Surprise me.'

When Logan got back from the canteen, Alec was slumped in one of the visitor chairs, moaning about DCS Bain. 'You know where I spent all day? Bored off my tits filming meetings. Yesterday too.'

Logan handed the inspector's coffee over.

'Ooh, ta.' Steel took a slurp. 'That's what you get for following Bain about, isn't it? Should have stuck with the A-team, you disloyal bastard.' She swept a hand through her startled-terrier hair. 'We're much prettier too.'

Alec just sagged deeper into his chair. 'You guys aren't up to anything exciting are you?'

The inspector nodded. 'Fifteen minutes I'm off to the pub.' She pointed at Logan. 'Laughing Boy here's going to Trinity Hall because he's got no mates.'

And at that the cameraman perked up. 'Cool! Can I come?'

Logan shrugged. 'It—'

'Hold on a minute . . . ' Steel put her coffee down and squinted at him. 'You planning on solving anything while you're there?'

'Doubt it,' he picked up the list of trade members interviewed in 1990 and stuck it under his arm, 'half these guys were in their late fifties when Brooks spoke to them seventeen years ago. Most of them'll be making sausages in that great butcher's shop in the sky by now.'

'Aye, well,' Steel grabbed her coat. 'I'm no' taking any chances. If Alec's going, so am I.'

The little old man who met them at the side door to Trinity Hall was all smiles, cardigan and wrinkled suit. 'I've always wanted to help out in a murder enquiry,' he said, ushering them in to a tiny stairwell. 'I love *The Bill*, *Frost*, *Midsomer Murders*, *CSI*, *Wire in the Blood*, only that's not really a police show, is it? More one of those psychological things. I met someone from *Taggart* once.' He stopped with one hand on the institution-green double doors. 'Now, would you like the tuppence ha'penny tour, or the full Trinity Hall experience?'

Logan pulled on a smile. 'How about we just make it about the Fleshers, sir?'

'Perfect! Oh and call me Ewan, "sir" makes me sound like an old man!' He winked, laughed, coughed for a bit – ending in a thin, rattling wheeze – then opened the double doors, revealing a long, dim corridor lined with ancient, grimy-looking paintings. Low-wattage spots cast tiny pools of light on the pictures and dark-blue carpet. 'Trinity Hall has to be one of the best-kept secrets in Aberdeen: did you know we have a portrait of King William the Lion here? One of the oldest paintings in the place, been in the trades' possession for *centuries*. Absolutely priceless, can't even get it insured. We've got swords from the Battle of Harlaw in 1411. You see, the Seven Incorporated Trades have always been an integral part of the city. Did you know that for hundreds of years . . . '

Logan let him chunter on about the Weavers, Wrights and Coopers, Shoemakers, Hammermen, Tailors, Bakers, and Fleshers, as they wandered past darkened meeting rooms. Steel slouched along at the back, making popping noises with her nicotine gum.

Strange, old-fashioned paintings in ornate golden frames hung on one side of the corridor, their paint blackened by the passage of time. Each had a coat of arms on it, some decoration, and a wodge of text, nearly indecipherable in the low light. On the other side it was all portraits, sour-faced old men in various disapproving poses.

'Bloody hell,' said Steel, interrupting an involved anecdote about the first Flesh House being built in 1631 to stop people slaughtering animals in the streets, 'who ordered the ugly blokes with a side order of extra ugly?' She pointed at one of the portraits. 'My cat's arse is prettier than that.'

'Ah ... yes...' The old man glanced at Alec's camera. 'Actually, that's—'

'Jesus! This one looks like a wart with a moustache!'

'And, er ... this,' said call-me-Ewan, changing the subject, 'is the Fleshers' coat of arms.'

The painting was about the same size as Logan's kitchen table. A red shield – with three knives, an axe, and one of the little Aberdeen castles on it – sat in the middle, a severed ram's head on the left, a bull's on the right. Beneath each head was a passage of flowery script, ancient varnish making the words crackle.

Steel squinted at the text: '"When sacerdotal sacrifice and feasts, made altars smoak with blood of slaughtered beasts ... "'

The old man sighed. 'You have to understand that the Fleshers date back to a time when Aberdeen was in her infancy – all the trades do. If you look in our books, you'll see the same family names year after year, century after century. Generations of butchers all dedicated to supporting their trade and the community.' He ticked the points off on his fingers: 'Alms to the poor, funding public works, providing social care long before the NHS was even dreamt of. What's happening now has nothing to do with the trade. We shouldn't be stigmatized just because some ... because someone hijacked the words from this painting.'

'It's OK,' said Steel, 'you can call him a cock-sucking arse-weasel I won't faint.' Wink. 'So come on then, how many people had access to this twenty years ago?'

'This painting's over a hundred and seventy-eight years old, Inspector. We have open days a couple of times a year: show members of the public around the hall, explain things to them, give them a bit of the history of the things we have here.'

'So you're saying it could have—'

'And each trade has a big annual dinner dance. The members invite their friends and family, clients sometimes.' He stared at the paintings. 'We've had to cancel ours. No one wants to accept an invitation from the Fleshers with all these horrible things going on ... '

Which wasn't surprising. Logan pulled out his list of names from 1990. 'You weren't interviewed during the original investigation?'

'No, my uncle died in seventy-four – I went back to Cupar for six months to help get everything in order, stayed for nineteen years. Didn't come up again till ninety-three.' He smiled. 'Missed all the excitement.'

'Do you recognize any of these names?'

Ewan produced a pair of half-moon glasses and polished them on the hem of his cardigan. Even then he had to hold the list at arm's length, going through the names one by one. 'Oh aye, he's still here ... so's he ... poor Charles took pancreatic cancer ... this one's moved to Australia to be with his grandkids ... no idea – before my time ... pneumonia ... Alzheimer's ... you know, I haven't seen Peter for ages. Think

267

he's in a nursing home now . . . ' and on it went. Ewan seemed to sag as he got to the end of the list. 'Sorry. Seeing them all written down like this . . . death gets us all in the end . . . '

He took off his glasses and started down the corridor again. 'Would you like to see the Dead Man's Gallery?'

It was more like a passageway than a gallery – a long, thin space next to the main hall, lined with huge gilt frames containing dozens of little black and white photographs. 'When I first joined,' said Ewan, pointing at old-fashioned pictures of stiff, formal men with wild Victorian facial hail, 'I'd show guests round here and we'd laugh at all the beardie-wierdies. Look at this one,' it was a young man with huge sideburns and mutton chops that reached well past the collar of his starched shirt, 'like something out of *Abbot and Costello Meet the Wolf Man*, isn't he? It's not till you start seeing the faces of people you know in here that it really hits you: these were men. They had hopes and dreams, just like you and me. Families who loved them. Wives and children who mourned . . . '

He led them down to another huge frame, this one with a tiny plaster coat of arms at the top: red background, curved knives. The frame was only half full and some of the photos were even in colour, fading away to that strange seventies orange tone. Wide lapels, brown suits, and more sideburns.

'And these,' said Ewan, 'are our recently deceased members. There's Charles, I was telling you about him. Simon, Craig, Thomas . . . This is John: he was in the second wave on D-Day. And that's my old mentor Edward. Lovely man; orphan, grew up in a children's home, came from nothing and ended up with three butcher's shops and a house in Rubislaw Den. Couldn't have kids of his own so they adopted a little girl from a broken home.' He pointed at a man with a ludicrous comb-over. 'Robert there took in a wee boy with polio. Jane and I had two girls of our own, but I never forgot Edward's example. So we adopted our youngest, Ben. Abandoned on the steps of St Nicholas church the day after he was born. How could someone just throw away a life like that? Madness . . . ' Ewan stared at the photos in silence for a moment. Then went through them one by one: 'Cancer, cancer, heart attack, pneumonia, cancer, Thomas had a stroke two weeks after his wife died; Edward and Sheila went in a car crash. Robert took an aneurism on Union Street.'

He tapped the glass. 'One day I'll be in there. And people will come in and laugh at my photo. I'll be dead, but I'll always be part of something. That's important, isn't it? Not to disappear into nothing . . . '

'*Pierdolona kurwa* fuck.' Andrzej Jaskólski jabbed at the start button again. 'Work *jebany* piece of shit!' he kicked the metal wall, but the mill still wouldn't start. Typical: the boilers go down for two days and now the *pierdolone* bone mill was broken too. 'Go to UK,' said his wife, 'earn lots of money, come back and set up own clinic in Warsaw. Be rich man.' *Kurwa mać*. Degree in Orthopaedic Therapy and he ends up working in stinking rendering plan in stinking abattoir in stinking arse end of nowhere Scottish backwater.

Another kick. 'Start, dirty bitch fuck!'

One more kick and the machine rumbled into life, the huge steel teeth at the bottom of the trough grinding through bones and off-cuts and fat.

Only no chopped up bones fell into the next hopper.

Ja pierdole!

He grabbed the long wooden pole that leant against the wall – still not laughing at the *kurwo* foreman's joke – and jabbed at the mass of bones.

Poke, jab, poke. A sudden *clunk*, and the pile slumped. Grinding noise. Bone and gristle fragments chugged into the next hopper, ready to be torn up into even smaller pieces.

Andrzej Jaskólski turned to put the pole back where he'd got it. Tonight he'd go into town with other Polish workers from abattoir. Drink. Maybe dance. Maybe find nice woman with own flat and not go back to *jebanego* bed and breakfast with no hot water and stains on ceiling and bed made of concrete.

He froze, one hand on the pole, then turned back to the sinking mass of cattle bones. Sweat breaking out on his forehead. Hoping his eyes were playing tricks on him ...

They weren't.

'O kurwa jebana mać ...'

34

Logan had never seen an abattoir before. He'd been expecting a wooden building with blood-smeared concrete and wailing cattle, but from the outside, Alaba Farm Fresh Meats looked more like a warehouse. A big, breezeblock building with a green metal roof and a two-storey block of offices, all hidden behind a thick, twelve-foot-high leylandii hedge. From the street you'd have no idea what was going on inside – if it wasn't for the smell.

The company sign tried to make everything look jolly and approachable: 'FARM TO PLATE, SCOTCH MEAT IS GREAT!' and a happy cartoon pig, wearing a butcher's outfit and holding a cleaver.

Logan marched past the thing, across the car park, and up to the security bunker. An articulated lorry was stopped at the barricade, its headlights glowing in the thin, cold drizzle, sheep staring out from the four-storey trailer as the driver argued with one of the guards.

'What the hell am I supposed to do with all these bloody sheep?'

'It's no' ma fault, is it? Police say naebiddy gets in or oot till they've finished.'

Logan hurried inside. Security monitors dominated one wall, showing white oversuited figures picking their way through the abattoir and its outbuildings. Three uniformed PCs sat going through the old tapes, wreathed in the comforting steam of hot coffee. Logan helped himself to a mug, then stood with his backside against the radiator, watching them work. 'Anything?'

One of the PCs shrugged. 'Not yet.'

When his bum had defrosted, Logan topped up his coffee, poured one for Steel, and headed out into the abattoir grounds.

Everything was going on round the back, the harsh white glare of the IB's spotlights cutting through the cold November night.

He struggled into yet another SOC oversuit and followed a line of blue-and-white POLICE tape into a three-storey, enclosed metal structure. The smell was much worse here: raw meat and roasting animal fat, like a lamb chop left under the grill for too long. The air felt . . . *greasy* with a sour edge to it that made his stomach churn.

Steel was at the top of the stairs, hands jammed deep into her pockets, her face creased in disgust. 'What took you so long?'

'You're welcome.' He handed over the extra mug of coffee.

'This got sugar in it?'

'What do you think?' Logan stepped round the inspector, peering over the guard rail at a mass of bones, hooves and offal. There were two IB technicians in there, passing chunks out to a third who carried them over to a collapsible table, where Isobel scrutinized them.

'Bloody stinks in here . . . ' Steel wrapped her hands around her mug. 'Come on then, door-to-doors?'

Logan pointed towards the back wall of the bone mill. 'All the houses on that side are derelict – apparently no one wants buy a three-bedroom semi downwind of an abattoir.'

'There's a surprise.'

'Uniform are going through the rest. Nothing so far.'

'Yeah, well, the pretty and talented DCS Bain is interviewing the workforce as we speak. So that'll be a bloody disaster.' The inspector sipped her coffee, and grimaced. 'This taste funny to you?'

'It was fine in the security bunker...' but Steel was right, out here it had developed an unpleasant flavour of rancid lard.

'Right,' she leant on the guard rail, watching as Isobel chucked a long bone into a wheelbarrow and waved for the next sample, 'half six – the abattoir's running double shifts to catch up, 'cos they've had an equipment failure – and some poor sod's clearing out the bone cruncher. Turns out he's an orthopaedic thingy back in Poland, so when he sees a human thighbone poking out of the pile he hits the emergency stop and refuses to budge till they call the police.' She shook her head. 'Weird, eh? Guy goes to medical school and ends up over here, 'cos he can make more money working in an abattoir shovelling bones than he can doctoring back home.'

'You question him?'

Steel turned. 'No, I took his word for it when he said he'd no' hacked anyone up. Looked like an honest bloke...' she slapped Logan on the arm. 'Course I bloody questioned him.'

Isobel straightened up from her table and passed a triangle of bone to her assistant. 'Scapula.' It went into a blue plastic evidence box.

Steel pointed at the growing pile of human remains. 'It's Tom Stephen, they found his head ... you want to see?'

'Excuse me?' A man in white Wellington boots, baggy plastic trousers, overcoat, hairnet and hardhat had appeared on the walkway behind them. 'Do you think this is going to be finished tonight? Only we've got a backlog—'

'How'd you get up here?'

He pointed over his shoulder. 'Access door from the Den of Dung – where we rinse out the intestines and stomachs...' He dropped his voice to a whisper, 'Look, can't you just empty this lot out and take it with you?'

273

'Excuse me a moment, sir,' Steel leant on the guardrail and shouted down at someone on the ground. 'I told you to seal the bloody entrances! That means *all* the entrances, no' just the ones you can be arsed with!'

She turned back to the gentleman. 'Sorry about that. Now if you don't mind: this'll go a lot faster if you let us get on with out jobs.'

'But—'

'This is the way it works. We have to go through each and every chunk of crap in that hopper. Then we're going to examine every bit of meat in the place. And until we've done that, you're no' hacking up anything else. Comprende?'

'But I've got orders to fulfil! We have to—'

'Oh, is this no' a good time for you? You should have said! Tell you what, why don't we just forget all about the human remains we found in your rendering plant—'

'Protein processing. We don't call it "rendering" anymore, on account of—'

'I don't care! You're shut down till I tell you different!' And with that she stomped off. It would have been an impressive exit, if she hadn't stopped halfway down the stairs to haul her SOC oversuit out from the crack of her backside.

The man in the white outfit watched her go. 'But we've got a backlog ...'

Logan patted him on the shoulder. 'I'm afraid she's right: we can't risk any more human meat getting into the food chain.' He looked up at the company name, written along the side of the abattoir building in three-foot-high lettering. 'It's an unusual way to spell Alba.'

'The MD's idea: he got fed up having to explain how to pronounce it all the time.'

'Look on the bright side, it ... ' Logan stopped and frowned. 'Do you supply wholesalers? Butchers, cash and carrys, things like that?'

'Couple of supermarket chains too. We're very proud of our traditional—'

He was starting to get a very bad feeling about this. 'I'm going to need a list of your customers.'

DI Steel was slumped in one of the boardroom chairs, hands over her face, listening as Logan told her the bad news. Again. He waited for her to go off on one, rant and swear, try to pin the blame on someone else. But instead she let her head fall back, stared at the ceiling, and said, 'Oh ... sodding hell.'

The boardroom was lined with posters of steaks, roasts, things on skewers, mince, chops, and those charts telling you which cut comes from which part of which animal. Like a preschool puzzle in meat.

She scrubbed her hands across her face, sighed, then asked Logan if he was sure.

'Positive. The abattoir supplies Thompson's Cash and Carry, and McFarlane's butcher shop.'

'Oh, we are *so* screwed!'

Midnight. Logan stopped on the damp concrete walkway and yawned, caught in the glare of a security spotlight. Drizzle made his SOC suit shine. The bone mill had been cleared out, the abattoir's butchery and packaging areas searched and sealed off, and all the senior officers had buggered off to their beds. Bastards.

Logan stretched, groaned, and yawned again. Three disembodied sheep heads lay on the ground beside an empty skip, their creamy wool tinged with dark red. He knew how they felt.

The shed where they aged the beef and lamb stood off to one side – a large refrigerated building full of vacuum-packed meat and shivering police officers. They'd been at it for four hours, and still didn't know if they'd found anything or not.

'Like pulling teeth.' The Police Search Advisor in charge of the shed team cupped his latex-gloved hands and blew into them. 'I mean, look at it . . . ' he indicated the rows of shelving, the green trays full of meat – dark purple in the fluorescent lighting – the black plastic latticework of the big storage bins. 'There's tons of the bloody stuff in here and it all looks the same to me.'

It was Thompson's Cash and Carry all over again, only on a *much* larger scale.

The POLSA turned and nodded at Doc Fraser. The old pathologist was huddled in a vast tartan blanket, examining shiny packages of dark meat. 'Poor sod's pushing sixty: should be sat on his backside drinking cocoa and fantasising about Doris Day in a bath full of jam, not buggering about in a bloody big fridge.'

'You better tell everyone to take a break in . . . ' Logan checked his watch. 'What, twenty minutes? Don't want them keeling over with hypothermia.'

'Any chance of a cuppa, or something?'

'They're opening the abattoir canteen for us – do everyone a hot meal, something with chips. It's—'

'Ah, no offence, like, but they sell human meat here. I'm no' eating *anything*.'

Logan had to admit that he had a point.

The second search team were working their way through the skin shed – four constables in grimy SOC suits – smeared with dirty-pink salt and globbets of fat – peeling the cattle skins from their piles one at a time, making sure nothing looked as if it belonged on a human body.

Logan got an update from the officer in charge, commiserated with him about the stink, then got out of there as quickly as possible. But the skin shed was Santa's Grotto compared to the protein processing plant.

It was a dark, low-ceilinged room, just off the bone mill, oppressively hot and humid. Logan gagged: the smell of greasy, rendering fat was nearly overpowering. For some bizarre reason a small, wooden garden shed sat against one wall, the windows fogged over with condensation and a film of tallow.

Filthy pipes snaked through the air, leading in and out of three large black ovens that wouldn't have looked out of place in a horror movie. Team three were working their way through a trio of centrifuges, picking tiny chunks out of a hessian-wrapped disk the size of a tractor wheel.

He'd been there less than thirty seconds, but Logan was already starting to sweat. 'How you getting on?'

The female officer pulled off her facemask, pushed a limp strand of hair from her shiny face, and said, 'Bloody dreadful, sir. Ovens've been off since about seven and it's still baking in here. And this,' she held up a handful of little lumps, 'could be anything! Look at it! Bones, hooves, heads, blood, fat, it all gets passed through two sodding big sets of metal teeth till it's no bigger than the tip of your thumb. Then it gets stuffed in those boilers and cooked to death. It's just rubble!'

She tossed her handful of animal-gravel into a big metal sieve. '*And* we're dying of thirst.'

Logan looked at the centrifuges and their unidentifiable grey loads. 'How much more you got to do?'

'Heaps.'

'OK, go get a cup of tea and—'

'Holy shit!' It was one of the male officers, he had something clamped between his thumb and forefinger, twisting whatever it was, so it glittered in the gloom. Everyone hurried round, peering at the tiny lump in his hand. He dropped it into Logan's open, latex-gloved palm. It was a gold tooth.

Ten minutes later someone found another one – the crown for a rear molar. And that seemed to get their eye in. In twenty minutes they turned up half a dozen little lumps of grey-black metal: fillings, some still attached to their teeth.

Whoever the Flesher really was, he'd discovered a nearly perfect way to dispose of a body. After the bone mill, the ovens and the centrifuges, whatever solids were left went into another hopper to be ground into powder and sold to pet food manufacturers. God knew how many victims' remains had gone through people's dogs and cats, but Logan got the nasty feeling Thomas Stephen was just the tip of the iceberg.

Warm. Heather rolled over onto her side, smiling in the darkness. She bunched the duvet round her body, enjoying the feeling of fresh pyjamas on her clean skin. The soft swell of the pillow beneath her head.

'It's not that surprising, when you think about it,' said Mr New. He'd calmed down a lot – death seemed to agree with him.

Duncan sighed. *'She's trying to sleep.'*

'Stockholm syndrome they call it. She's been here for so long, dependent on the Flesher for everything: food, water, survival. She identifies with him. Not to mention the physical and mental strain she's been under.'

'She's not mental!'

Mr New laughed. *'Duncan: we're dead, remember? We're figments of her imagination and we're arguing about whether or not she's off her rocker. I think it's pretty much a moot point, don't you?'*

'I . . . Yeah, you're probably right.'

Heather felt the weight of a body settle next to her in bed.

'And don't forget the knife,' said Duncan.

'Yeah,' Mr New sat on the opposite side of the mattress, the pair of them trapping her beneath the duvet, *'you've got the knife now.'*

Even with her eyes closed she could see it shining pale blue in the darkness, tucked down the side of her cosy new bed. She had the knife – the one that had clattered against the bars when Mr New kicked the Flesher's tin bath over. The knife was long and sharp and glowed like death.

'You could kill Him.'

'He's too big, Mr New. You can't kill Him. He's the Dark. He's always been.'

Duncan patted her on the shoulder. *'Don't be such a flid, Heather: a person can't be the Dark. The Dark's a thing in its own right. The Flesher's just a man but the Dark ... the Dark is eternal.'*

Heather tried to get comfortable. 'Can you move over a bit?'

'Are you happy?'

'Duncan, don't be like—'

'I'm not being anything.' He pulled back the duvet so she could see his face. *'I'm asking a question: are you happy?'*

She thought of Him, standing there in His butcher's outfit, breathing hard as he scrubbed away at the blood-smeared, rusty floor. The scent of Jeyes Fluid gradually replacing the stench of Mr New's death and her food poisoning. 'I couldn't do it.'

Duncan bent down and kissed her on the top of the head. *'I know, Honey, I know. But you could have been free.'*

35

Ten am and Logan was buzzing from the three large espressos he'd downed in the canteen, trying to make sure he'd stay awake for Thomas Stephen's post mortem. Doctor Isobel McAllister presiding. In attendance: DI Steel, DCS Bain, the Assistant Chief Constable, the Procurator Fiscal, a queasy-looking PC, an IB photographer, and old Doc Fraser with his hairy ears corroborating. Full house.

Isobel had 'rebuilt' Thomas Stephen on the larger of the two cutting tables, his meatless bones all arranged in the right order, the innards tucked in beneath the two halves of his ribcage. And right at the very top: the bruised and battered head. In all the years he'd been attending these things, it was probably the most surreal sight Logan had ever seen. A skeleton man with glistening innards and a human head.

DI Steel wrinkled her nose. 'What the hell is that smell?'

Logan scowled at her. 'I showered, OK? Twice last night and three times this morning. It's that bloody protein processing plant, the grease sinks into your skin like fake tan.' Every time he blew his nose, the smell of rendering fat came flooding back, that and the mortuary's acrid formalin reek was making him queasy ... or maybe it was all the coffee?

Or maybe it was Isobel, picking over Thomas Stephen's severed head – her fingers working their way across the swollen face, as if trying to memorize his features by touch alone. He was bald on top, with a fringe of grey hair round the edges, a small white goatee beard sitting beneath a newly broken nose – his skin covered with bruises and scrapes. Isobel placed the head on the cutting table and peered at the very top. 'There's a hole here ... some sort of wadding's been forced into the wound...' She pulled out a clot of dark red fabric. 'Circular puncture wound in the crown of the skull. Flesh isn't torn around the hole; bone isn't striated, so it probably wasn't a drill. Something solid moving vertically at high speed. Looks like a close-range bullet hole, but there are no burn marks...' She flipped the head upside-down, peering at the neck stump, while a thin, pink-brown slime dripped from the not-bullet-hole. 'That's odd ... Brian,' holding a hand out to her assist-ant, 'I need the bone saw.'

Logan tried not to think about the next bit.

When it was all over, and her assistant was rinsing the sticky sludge off the dissecting table, Isobel gave them the edited highlights. 'The hole in Thomas Stephen's head was caused by a rod extending four and three-quarter inches into his brain. It punched through the skull – embedding bone fragments in the surrounding tissue – tore through the edge of the left cerebral hemisphere, caused extensive damage to the cerebellum, and pretty much obliterated the brain stem. The exit wound where the skull meets the spine is much smaller than the entrance.'

'Something pointy?' For once Steel didn't look as if she was taking the piss. 'Maybe an ice pick?'

'No... The killer withdrew whatever he'd used to punch through the skull, then threaded something else into the entry wound.' She picked up a marker pen and drew a small diagram on the mortuary whiteboard. 'The vertebrae were split verti-cally more or less in the middle – probably with an axe – but

281

the damage to the upper spinal chord is uniform. Whatever it was, it was forced down, *inside the spine*, to the fifth cervical vertebrae. Effectively destroying the brainstem and stripping the nerve branches.'

Someone swore, and Logan didn't blame them.

'Death would have been nearly instantaneous. No motor functions: no breathing and no heartbeat.'

Doc Fraser nodded. 'Pithing cane.'

Isobel stuck the cap back on her pen. 'I beg your pardon?'

'Pithing cane. What they used before BSE came along and made it illegal.' Doc Fraser made a gun of his hand, placing the barrel-finger in the middle of Logan's forehead. Then pulled the trigger. 'Bolt gun shoots a metal rod through the skull of your cow, pig, sheep, or Detective Sergeant, only death's not instantaneous. Sometimes they're just stunned. And even if they *are* stone dead you can still get muscle spasms – no one wants kicked by half a tonne of dead bullock. So you take a flexible metal rod and shove it in the hole, through the brainstem and down into the spine. Jiggle it about a bit. Then you slit the animal's throat.' He shrugged. 'I grew up on a farm.'

Isobel bristled slightly. 'I see. Well, that would be consistent with my—'

The Assistant Chief Constable cut her off. 'So we need to start looking at what, vets and farmers?'

'Nah,' the old pathologist ferreted about in his ear for something. 'A vet wouldn't be able to bone out the body like that. You're looking at abattoirs. A lot have gone electrical, but some still use bolt guns.'

Steel grinned. 'And there's us found the body in a slaughterhouse. Who'da thunk it, eh?'

You couldn't say that DI Steel didn't learn from other people's mistakes. As soon as Logan found out who Alaba Farm Fresh Meats were supplying, she was straight on the phone to the

282

Environmental Health. She was *not* going to be beaten with the same shitty stick as Insch.

Her office was a tip, so they convened in the history room, pointing at things on the whiteboard and generally getting in Logan's way. They'd made a big list of every butcher's shop, supermarket, delicatessen, baker's, corner shop and cash and carry in the city and were working through them one at a time, confiscating anything that might have come from the abattoir.

The man from the Environmental Health Department took off his glasses and rubbed at the black bags under his eyes. 'We're going to need more police backup. I've had four inspectors assaulted since seven o'clock this morning.'

The DCS shook his bald head. 'Can't do it. We're stretched as it is.'

'Then you have to get officers in from Dundee, Glasgow, Inverness – I don't care. My people are getting verbally and physically abused! And it's not just the shopkeepers – one of my men got his nose broken by a pensioner's handbag when he wouldn't let her leave the shop with half a dozen pork chops. We need more police officers.'

Logan tried to ignore them, concentrate on the transcripts of yesterday's abattoir interviews, but it was impossible.

Finally the argument ended and they went back to the list, marking the outlets at serious risk of selling contaminated meat and meat products.

Steel swore. 'I bought a big steak and kidney pie from there last week.' She poked the whiteboard with a nicotine-stained finger. 'Must've been OK though: I'm no' feeling all Hannibal Lectery.'

The Environmental Health Officer scowled at her. 'It's not funny. Until you identify all the victims we've no idea what sort of diseases they were carrying.'

That wiped the smile off her face. 'Diseases?'

'If he's used a pithing cane there's a risk of variant CJD. Then there's HIV. And Hepatitis C doesn't die unless you cook it at one hundred and sixty degrees, for about three-quarters of an hour. How long did you give your pie?'

'I . . .' Cough. 'I don't know, do I? Stuck it in the oven and opened a bottle of wine . . .'

He looked at her. 'There's going to be a lot of people wanting blood tests. We'll have to draft in extra health staff to cope with demand.'

Steel didn't say much for the rest of the meeting, just fidgeted nervously till everyone was gone. Muttering to herself, 'I can't have diseases: I'm getting married!'

...UGHTERHOUSE

...an Remains Found in Abattoir 🔪 Is Our Food Really Safe?

...ski came to Aberdeen six ...s ago hoping for a better life ...imself and his family. A ...d orthopaedic specialist, he ...d a human femur in the ...ir's 'bone mill'.

...recognised it straight away," he said, speaking exclusively to the *Aberdeen Examiner*, "I've never seen anything so horrible. It wa...like a horror film."

Jaskólski immediately stoppe... the bone mill – where t... abattoir's off-cuts are ground in... small pieces for pet food – a... called the police.

skeleton – stripped of meat – along with the victim's head.

Police immediately shut the abattoir and confiscated every carcass and joint of meat on the ...

Alaba Farm...

FACTORY SHOP →
100 YARDS ON LEFT

ALL VISITORS MUST
REVERSE PARK

ALL VISITORS MUST REPORT
TO SECURITY

5

...laba Farm Fresh Meats – at the centre of cannib...

MISSING
Man's Family Fears for Safety

By James Oswald

TRACY DUNBAR spoke last night of her fear that her brother John (35) – missing since September – intended to do himself harm.

"It's not like him to just go off without his medication," she said, "he was usually very good about that kind of thing. He has high blood-pressure and knows not to exert himself."

John Dunbar went missing in Inverness after a night out with some friends. They were on the way back from a restaurant when John complained he was being watched.

Excuse to disappear

"I think he was paranoid a lot of the time," said one friend, "for about a week before he went missing, though, it became really obvious. He kept saying someone was messing with the post. He kept saying spying on him.

INTERE...
PORK OR W...

SALES of meat have ... nearly zero in the city o... Instead a sudden wave o... panic buying has seen ... shelves stripped of... sweetcom and Brussels s... BBC 2's *Saturday,*... reputedly doing a speci... Express' episode this ... those suddenly findin... with no option, but to g...

HOW DO YOU KNOW ... eaten human flesh? Well, ex... the safest way to avoid any a... you *have* to eat meat, then y... to know what people actual... like to avoid it.

New York Times co... William Buehler Seabrook fou... in 1930 when he ma...

Cannibal Chaos

IT'S not every day that you find out you've been eating other human beings, but in Aberdeen that's...

bringing the health service to a complete standstill. The problem is that no...

MCHANDWICH

Stuart

...ce in the Flesher ...ation last night, ...lice were called to ...arm Fresh Meats – ...utskirts of Turriff

...ealth

...TITIS C is probably ...ost virulent problem ... the residents of ...een – the virus may ...resent in the Flesher's ...ms. And if that's the ..., it's now in the food ...n.

... how do you make sure ...'t you're eating isn't ...t to give you some ...rific disease? ... best bet is to make ...re you cook everything at ...0° for at least 45 ...nutes. This makes steak

...no-no. ...n fact, just about the ...hing you can safely meat

36

Saturday evening was a tin of beer, a soak in the tub, and then a prolonged period of standing in front of the open fridge, wondering if any of the contents were safe to eat. Just in case, Logan made broccoli cheese and chips. He ate it slumped in front of the telly, flicking idly through the channels: crap, crap, reality TV, crap, Simpsons repeat, crap, crap, more reality TV, crap . . .

'—scenes outside the Sheriff Court yesterday as Andrew McFarlane was released on bail.' The picture jumped to a shot of Wiseman's brother-in-law clambering into the back of a big black Mercedes with tinted windows, caught in the strobe-light of two dozen press cameras.

Logan yawned and sagged even further down the sofa.

'—the following statement.'

A podgy-faced lawyer appeared. 'My client, Mr McFarlane, has always protested his innocence, and the discovery of human remains at Alaba Farm Fresh Meats yesterday was proof of that. Mr McFarlane's butcher shop was supplied by that abattoir, and they are the ones responsible for human meat entering the food chain, not my client. Thankfully the Sheriff recognised that fact this morning.'

Logan got himself another beer, returning just in time to watch the tail-end of the press conference, and the Chief

Constable trying to assure everyone that Grampian Police *could* actually find its arse with both hands, no matter what some of the tabloid papers were saying.

Then it was the weather, and after that some God-awful, *'I'm a celebrity'* –style garbage. Logan switched the TV off, went to bed, and slept like a corpse.

'Well?' DI Steel stood with her back to the death board and its disturbing new photo of Tom Stephen's semi-skeletal remains. 'Any joy?'

Logan picked up the next interview transcript in line. 'How come this is now *my* job?'

'Because you're Auntie Roberta's special little soldier. Besides, you got any idea how much this enquiry is costing? Need to economise, so you're multitasking.' The inspector made an exploratory foray into the world of the underwire, peering down at her own cleavage. 'Why can no bugger make a decent bra that fits?'

'I'm supposed to be going through the 1987 case files. How can I do that *and* everything else at the same time?'

She hauled at her underwear. 'I mean they're either all lace and bugger-all support, or they look like my granny's surgical truss.'

'Can we *not* discuss your bra for a change?'

'Still not getting any, eh? Thought that Procurator Fiscal Depute was after your truncheon d'amour?'

'Why am I the only person with any work to do?' He tried to ignore her, focus on the transcripts, but she wouldn't go away.

'So come on then: teeth?'

Logan tried not to sigh, he really did. Then he dug out the relevant paperwork from the ever-expanding mound on his desk. 'Two incisors, three pre-molars, nine molars. They checked against the known victims' dental records – they're probably Hazel Stephen's.'

'Probably? What bloody use is—'

'They've been bashed about and boiled to death. "Probably" is as good as we're going to get.'

Steel blew a wet raspberry. 'Lazy bastards hedging their bets, more like. Next: Polish workers, dead body? Connections?'

'Nothing back from the Polish police yet so we don't know about priors, but most of them only came over to Scotland six months ago. They can't have taken part in the 1987 killings.'

'But . . . ?' Looking hopeful.

'There is no "but". Wiseman's never been to Poland, he doesn't speak Polish, and according to Alaba's security logs he's never been to the abattoir either.'

'Bugger.'

Logan turned his head to the death board, looking at the aftermath of pain and suffering. 'It's beginning to look like Wiseman isn't the Flesher. Not now, not twenty years ago: it was all a figment of Brooks' imagination.'

Steel slapped him on the shoulder. 'For God's sake don't let Insch hear you say that.' She was peering into her cleavage again. 'Silly sod's come in today and he's in enough of a grump as it is . . . Do these look droopy to you?'

She wasn't kidding about Insch's mood – by the time Logan bumped into the inspector, he looked as if someone had stuffed a hand grenade up his bum and pulled the pin. The explosion was imminent. Fire in the hole.

Logan paused in the doorway of the muster room; maybe he could just sneak out again without the fat man noticing—

'And where do you think *you're* going?'

Bugger.

Logan forced a smile. 'Sir, I heard you were in, did—'

'Apparently I demonstrated severe lapses in judgement.' Insch scrawled another item on the muster room whiteboard. 'I had my meeting with Professional Standards. Severe – lapses – in – judgement.' The pen creaked and squeaked as he

289

mashed the words out with his huge fist. 'Should've called the Environmental Health; should have recognized the risk of infection from eating human flesh; should have searched that bloody septic tank; should have figured out that McFarlane's butcher's and that cash and carry got their meat from the same – bloody – place.'

He rammed the cap back on the pen and stood there: trembling, purple-faced. 'Tried to make me go home: "Compassionate leave's there for a reason, *Inspector.*" "We're concerned about your wellbeing, *Inspector.*" "You've been under a lot of pressure." "You've suffered a terrible loss . . ." Like I don't already bloody know that! What am I supposed to do? Go home to an empty house? They wouldn't even let us bury her!' Insch hurled the pen down on the desktop. It bounced, sending a small stack of crime reports fluttering to the floor.

'How . . .' Logan looked away. 'How are the girls holding up?'

'How would I fucking know? Miriam won't let me see them.'

'I'm sorry.' It didn't seem like enough.

The inspector ground his teeth for a moment, breath hissing in and out of his nose as he slowly returned to a more normal shade of pink. 'With everyone running round like headless chickens trying to catch the Flesher, the crime statistics are going through the roof. Muggings, rapes, assaults, shoplifting, vandalism, extortion . . . The whole city's going to hell.' He sniffed. '*Someone* has to hold the fort. You'd think that'd be obvious to anyone with half a brain, but I had to argue for two bloody hours till I got them to see sense.'

'They let you come back to *work*?'

Insch bent to pick up the pen from the floor at his feet; his knees popped like gunshots on the way down. When he came up again it was with a grunt. 'Just because I'm dealing with all this shite, doesn't mean you're off the hook: anything happens with Wiseman I want to know about it. Understand?'

'I gave him your message.'

'Do – you – understand?'

Logan nodded.

'Good. Now get out there and find me some bloody evidence.'

37

'Hello?' A voice in the darkness. Small and hesitant.

Heather rolled over onto her side. 'Duncan?'

'What?' Definitely not Duncan or Mr New. She was hearing things again.

She sat up, peering into the Dark. Trying to pick out a shape to go with the voice coming from the other side of the bars. 'Are you real?'

A pause.

'Am I real?' It was a woman.

'Or are you dead like the others?'

Silence.

And then the voice said. 'I'm cold.'

Heather gripped the duvet closer around herself.

'Heather,' Mr New stepped through the bars, *'share, it's only fair.'*

'But what if she dies?'

'Dies?' The new voice tried again: 'What if who dies?'

'Heather . . .'

Sigh. 'I've got a duvet.' Heather clambered out of bed and dragged the mattress over to the bars, then poked half the duvet through a gap between two of them. 'Happy now?'

She'd been talking to Mr New, but it was the woman who answered. 'Thank you.' A scuffing sound, then Heather heard her settle back against the bars. There was a tug as the new girl wrapped the other half of the duvet around herself.

A long pause.

'My name's Kelley ... Kelley Souter.' A shaky hand was extended between the bars, brushing Heather's shoulder.

'Heather Inglis.'

'I ... I read about you in the papers.'

Silence.

The new girl, Kelley, said, 'You have a little boy.'

'Justin. He's ... he was three ...' She bit her lip to hold back the tears.

'I had a little boy too. They took him away from me in the hospital ... said I was too young.' And so it all came out: how she was only thirteen, but it didn't matter because her boyfriend promised to stand by her. How he was nearly twenty years older than her. How one day he just vanished, never to be heard from again ...

Heather listened quietly, then told Kelley about how Justin was born four and a half weeks early. 'He was so small, like a tiny doll, all purple and red ... They let me hold him for a minute before he went into the incubator. Lying there with all those tubes and wires ...' She wiped her nose on the back of her hand. 'Mother told me he'd never survive and I shouldn't get too attached. That it was probably Duncan's fault because he smoked pot.'

'*What a bitch!*' Duncan paced back and forth, the blood light pulsing from the hole in his head. '*Why didn't you tell me?*'

'But Justin showed her – grew up into a big strong boy ... I miss him so much.'

Kelley's hand wriggled through the gap again, taking hold of Heather's. 'I'm glad you're here.'

Two living people, in the kingdom of the Dark.

'*You shouldn't get too friendly with her,*' said Duncan, still pacing. '*She'll die, and then you'll have to eat her, and you'll feel guilty about it.*'

'Go away, Duncan.'

'*I'm just saying, OK? It's for your own good.*'

'Who are you talking to?'

Heather didn't really want to go through it all again. 'My husband. He's dead. And a selfish arsehole.'

The grip on her hand tightened: 'You can speak to the dead?'

'*Thanks. That's very nice. Selfish arsehole. Jesus, Heather, after everything I've done for you!*'

'Piss off, Duncan. I'm not in the mood.'

'*Look – you know I'm right. She's going to end up on a plate.*'

'I ... I wish I could talk to the dead. I'd tell my mum and dad how much I loved them.' Kelley's voice broke. 'It was my twelfth birthday ... The lorry was on the wrong side of the road and ... The firemen couldn't ... They had to cut us out. Mum and dad were ...' She shuddered into silence.

Heather sniffed back a tear. 'I lost my dad when I was fifteen. He jumped off Union Bridge. I hated my mother for that ... hated her. All those years.'

Kelly gripped her hand so tight it hurt. 'I wanted them to love me so much ...'

Heather sat in the darkness, head back against the bars, holding onto Kelley's hand. Knowing that everything was going to be all right, because the Flesher would be back soon with his tin bath. And make Kelley's pain go away.

38

'Come on, come on, come on . . .' Logan willed the lift doors to open, wishing he'd taken the stairs instead. *Ping*: out, right, and through the double doors, barrelling down the corridor towards Detective Chief Superintendent Bain's office. Glad to be the bearer of good news for a change.

The door was shut, but the sound of raised voices filtered through.

DI Steel: 'What the hell were you thinking?'

DCS Bain: 'Oh come on, what was I supposed to do? His wife's left him and taken the kids, he needs something to focus on.'

Logan changed his mind about knocking and loitered with intent to eavesdrop instead.

'He's grieving. He's no' thinking straight. He's bloody dangerous!'

'He begged, OK? He begged me to let him come back to work and—'

'He shouldn't be here! And I'm no' just saying that to be a bitch – he needs time. You push him and he'll bloody break.'

'It's light duties *only*. Admin, organizing the backlog. I've told him to stay away from the Flesher investigation *and* Wiseman. It's—'

'How could you be so stupid? You really think—'

'INSPECTOR! That's enough. You're—'

Logan knocked on the door before the DCS could say something Steel would regret. There was a terse silence, and then: 'Enter.'

When Logan opened the door, the two of them were standing nose-to-nose, scowling at each other.

The DCS barely glanced at him. 'This better be important, Sergeant.'

'We've got a result off the CCTV footage.'

'What, you mean the abattoir?'

Steel looked at her superior officer as if he were an idiot. 'No, Storybook Glen. Of course he means the abattoir!' She turned and marched from the room, pausing only to grab Logan by the sleeve. 'About time too.'

Five minutes later they were all in the main incident room, clustered round a scabby old television someone had wheeled in on a trolley. DCS Bain told Rennie to hit pause then tapped the screen: it was night, and a man in a thick padded jacket and dark woollen hat was caught halfway between the protein processing area and the shed where they kept the salted hides. He had a heavy-looking holdall slung over his shoulder.

DI Steel peered at the timestamp flickering away in the corner. 'When was this?'

Rennie checked something on a clipboard. 'Friday night. Twenty-eight minutes past eleven: when the security guards usually have their fly cup – official tea break's not till midnight, but they slip one in when no one's looking. It's about thirty-six hours after the pathologist reckons Tom Stephen was killed.' He pressed play again, and the figure hurried past the skin sheds; one frame every two seconds, like cheap Canadian animation, then disappeared through the fence and into the leylandii hedge.

'Bloody hell . . .' Steel slapped Rennie on the shoulder. 'How come no one noticed this sooner?'

'Ow!'

Bain told him to stop whining and get onto Photographic: 'I want that man's face blown up and enhanced. Tell them nothing else takes precedence, understand?'

The constable snapped off a salute and stabbed the video's eject button.

'Next, I want everyone to go back through the list of abattoir workers: find me a face that fits.' He smiled. 'We've finally got him.'

Logan stood outside on the rear podium, trying to get through to Chief Constable Faulds on his mobile. It rang through to an anonymous electronic answering service. He declined to leave a message and tried the number Faulds had given him for Lloyd House – Birmingham's version of Force Headquarters instead.

'West Midlands Police, how can I help you?'

He asked to be put through, ending up in Hold Music Hell with a panpipe rendition of *In the Air Tonight*. Before finally getting through to a human being who told him Faulds was taking a couple of personal days, but he'd be back on Wednesday. Would Logan like to leave a message?

'Yeah, tell him we've got a suspect: Marek Kowalczyk, works at the abattoir where we found the body parts.'

Alec appeared through the back door, grinning from ear to ear, a bulky stab-proof vest on under his parka. 'This'll make a kick-ass finale to the programme!'

Logan thanked the sergeant on the other end of the phone and hung up. 'You do know this is probably going to be hours of sitting in a car waiting for nothing to happen, don't you?'

'Ah, where's your sense of adventure? This is going to be great!'

Which just went to show how much *he* knew.

39

Garioch View Guesthouse, Turriff – Sunday 19:54
The bed and breakfast was a crumbling building not too far from
the centre of Turriff. God knew why they'd called it 'Garioch
View', the only thing visible from the pokey rooms was a bus
stop on other side of the road and a swathe of grimy red
sandstone houses. According to the landlady, Marek Kowalczyk
was out, but he'd be back later – probably half-cut – so they
parked the CID pool car two doors away under a streetlight,
where they'd have a good view of the entrance. Logan wound
the car window down, letting in the cool night air.

DI Steel shivered in the passenger seat. 'You trying to give us
all hypothermia? Shut the bloody window.'

'Put your shoes back on then.'

'No.'

'Smells like mouldy gorgonzola in here.'

'Cheeky bastard. Anyway, Alec's no' complaining, are you
Alec?'

The cameraman leant over from the back seat. 'No, but that
sod Paul gave me his cold, didn't he?' Blowing his nose for
dramatic effect.

'See: Alec's got pneumonia and you won't shut the window.
You *trying* to kill him?'

'Fine. OK. Whatever.' Logan wound the window back up. 'Jesus . . .'

Garioch View Guesthouse, Turriff – Sunday 20:13
Still no sign of Kowalczyk. DI Steel yawned, stretched, then said, 'What's green and smells of pork?'

Logan didn't look up from the copy of yesterday's *Evening Express* he'd found on the back seat. 'No idea.'

She grinned at him. 'Kermit's willy! Pause for laughter. Nothing. 'Miserable sods.' She rubbed at the small of her back. 'Why can't we go wait for him in the B&B?'

'Because the DCS and Rennie are in there. You really want to spend the whole evening listening to Rennie banging on about how much he loves his girlfriend?'

'Good point.'

Garioch View Guesthouse, Turriff – Sunday 20:31
'No, but don't you think it's a bit weird?' said Alec, offering round a packet of Lockets, 'I mean Kermit's a frog right? He doesn't have a penis, so how's he supposed to get it on with Miss Piggy? What's he going to do: wait for her to lay her eggs, then squirt his sperm all over them? Not exactly a fulfilling sex life, is it?'

Steel turned to look at him. 'Pigs don't lay eggs. Chickens do.'

Logan pointed off down the street at someone stomping their way home in the dark. 'There! Is that him?'

The inspector dragged her binoculars out of the glove compartment . . . 'No.'

'Damn.' Logan went back to his crossword.

Garioch View Guesthouse, Turriff – Sunday 21:04
'So how come,' said Logan keeping one eye on the deserted street, 'in *A Muppet Christmas Carol*, Kermit and Miss Piggy—'

299

Steel: 'You mean Mrs The Frog, they were married in that one.'

'How come they had two piglet daughters and one little frog boy?'

Alec: 'Maybe they adopted.'

Steel: 'She was screwing around behind Kermit's back. Can't say I blame her: he's no' got a penis, remember?'

Alec: 'Artificial insemination. My cousin Peter and his wife had that.'

'Ah,' Logan boinked a finger off the steering wheel, 'then why didn't they have some sort of freakish half-pig-half-frog hybrid child?'

There was a thoughtful pause. 'Maybe that's why Tiny Tim was dying: he wasn't genetically viable.'

Garioch View Guesthouse, Turriff – Sunday 21:17
'Christ I'm *bored!*' Steel slumped back in her seat and put her hands over her face, muffling a scream. 'Aaaaaaaaaaargh!'

Logan checked the dashboard clock: they'd been here nearly three hours. 'He's got to come home some time – all his stuff's still in his room.'

'Aye, well I've had enough. I'm no' spending all night with you and Captain Sniffles here, talking about the reproductive habits of fucking Muppets!'

Alec stuck his head between the two front seats. 'But this is going to be the final showdown! Grampian Police catch the Flesher! You want to be here for that, don't you?'

'What I want is a huge glass of Chardonnay, a jar of marmalade, and Keira Knightley in a thong. How about you, Laz?'

'Shhh!' Logan dug about in his jacket pocket, looking for the photo they'd got from the abattoir's personnel files.

'Don't you bloody shoosh me. I'm no' the one banging on about Kermit the Frog's sex life.'

'I think it's him!'

The figure weaving along the road towards them paused for a moment to swig from a litre bottle of supermarket vodka. Thick moustache, little round glasses, cleft chin. 'It's Kowalczyk.'

'Right.' Steel hauled her shoes back on. 'Here's what we do: when he gets level with the car, we jump him.'

'We're supposed to let him go into the B&B, and take him there, remember? Rennie and Bain—'

'What the hell's wrong with you?' She smacked Logan on the shoulder. 'Carpe fucking diem!'

'What if he does a runner?'

Steel chewed on the inside of her cheek. Kowalczyk was getting closer. 'If we lose him, we're up shite creek without a snorkel . . .' She scowled. 'OK, OK, we'll stick to the plan. You happy?'

Kowalczyk took one more swig, threw his arms wide, and started singing. *'Sto lat, sto lat, niech żyje, żyje nam!'* He lurched into a little dance. *'Sto lat, sto lat, niech żyje, żyje nam!'*

Steel pulled out her mobile and started dialling. 'Come on, come on . . . Yeah, Bill, it's Koalasick— I don't care if that's not how you bloody pronounce it: he's outside. Heading up the drive . . . now.'

He was really getting in to the swing of things, bellowing out, *'Jeszcze raz, jeszcze raz, niech żyje, żyje nam! '* He nearly collapsed into a knot of scabby rosebushes, then gave it laldy for the finale: *'NIECH ŻYJE NAM!'*

Fumble for key . . . two . . . three . . . four . . . key in the lock. Stagger inside. Steel was back on the phone again, 'He's in. We're on our way.' She clambered out into the cold night and marched across the road, Alec trailing along behind her, filming everything.

Logan was just locking the car when a loud crash sounded inside the B&B . . . then a television smashed through the lounge window in a shower of glittering glass.

Someone shouted, 'Come back here!'

'*Odpierdol sie!*' Marek Kowalczyk followed the television set, leaping out through the shattered window, landing in the rosebushes. '*Kurwa!*' Then he was scrabbling out the other side and away, sprinting back down the street, arms and legs pumping like mad.

Logan leapt back in the car, cranked the key, and roared out onto the street. 'Shit!' He slammed on the brakes and the Vauxhall screeched to a halt again, two feet short of flattening DI Steel as she ran out into the middle of the road, waving her arms. She wrenched open the passenger door and threw herself inside.

'Don't just sit there! Get after the bastard!'

Logan put his foot down.

They were just in time to see Kowalczyk take a left onto Main Street. The pool car skittered into the turn, leaving a screech of tyres behind. Logan slapped the siren button, and the distinctive *Weeeeeeeeeeeooooooow* blared out, blue lights flashing behind the front grille.

Kowalczyk glanced back over his shoulder and put on a fresh burst of speed.

Which was why he didn't see the Volkswagen Golf coming the other way.

Marek Kowalczyk had time for one last '*Kurwa!*' before it hit him.

A screech of brakes. The *THUMP* of flesh meeting metal clearly audible over the pounding music. Pinwheeling limbs. The wet crunch of a body slamming down onto the tarmac.

And then someone screamed.

40

A muffled scream. The sound of a body hammering against metal. Heather sat up, groggy, blinking in the darkness.

Boom, boom, boom. 'Help me! I don't want to die!' A woman's voice, muffled, coming from somewhere outside the prison.

'Kelley?'

'How can it be Kelley? She's asleep.' Duncan was right – Kelley's breathing came soft and rhythmic from the other side of the bars.

'Kelley! Wake up! Can you hear that?'

Boom, boom, boom. 'HELP ME!'

'Mmmph?'

'There's someone out there!' Heather stood and felt her way into the darkness. 'Hello?'

'HELP ME!' Boom, boom, boom.

She put her ear against the prison's metal wall.

Boom, boom, boom.

'Hello?'

'Heather?' Kelley yawned, shifting in the dark. 'Heather? What's going on?'

'There's someone out there . . . Hello?' She banged her palm against the wall.

'Help me! He killed my little sister! He killed Sandra! HELP ME!'

'We can't, we're locked in!'

'I DON'T WANT TO DIE!' More screaming, then crying. And eventually silence.

Heather backed away from the wall – her foot caught on the edge of the mattress and she stumbled backwards, arms flailing out for balance as she fell. BANG: the back of her head bounced off the bars.

Muffled noises.

'Heather?'

'Honey, are you all right?'

'Heather?'

And the Dark took her.

Rennie stifled a yawn. Stretched. Shivered. Then had a bit of a scratch at his trousers. 'God I'm knackered . . . You see the papers this morning?'

Logan looked up from the chest of drawers that lurked in the corner of the little room. 'Did you check under the mattress?' The Turrabrae Guesthouse was the most depressing B&B he'd ever been in: the walls were covered with cheap woodchip wallpaper; water stains on the ceiling; threadbare brown and orange carpet that was probably fashionable back in the seventies and hadn't been changed since; a single bed that wouldn't have looked out of place in a medieval torture chamber.

So far this morning they'd visited two of the three abattoir workers who'd provided Marek Kowalczyk with an alibi for the night Tom and Hazel Stephen were snatched. And Turrabrae Guesthouse was easily the worse. Piotr Nowak – alibi number three – wasn't exactly living in the lap of luxury.

Rennie sniffed. 'You ever thought about getting married?'

Logan pulled out the bottom drawer and carefully picked through the pile of paired-off socks. 'You're not my type.'

'I've been thinking about it a lot. You know, with Laura?'

'Mattress!'

'Eh? Oh, aye . . .' The sound of rummaging. 'Course it wouldn't be for a while yet. Have to save up for a house.'

The sock drawer contained nothing but socks. Logan gave the whole thing one last tug – pulling it out of the unit and onto the swirly brown carpet – then peered into the hole. Two magazines, both explicit, but nothing illegal.

He stuck the magazines back where they'd come from and replaced the drawer, then stood at the little window, looking out at the dismal day in all its grey glory. Twenty to eleven on a cold November morning and it was probably warmer outside than in here. He could see DI Steel standing half-way down the garden path, smoking cigarettes and fiddling with her underwear. Logan let the curtain fall back. 'You come all the way from Poland looking for a better life and what do you get? A manky box-room in a crappy little B&B and a job shovelling sheep heads into a skip.'

'Give us a hand . . .' Rennie was fighting with the saggy mattress, its stripy fabric stained and fraying round the edges. Logan helped him raise it all the way up, where gravity promptly folded it in half. Swearing, Rennie struggled it to the floor beside the single bed.

It was a divan and the base unit looked just as bad as the fusty mattress.

Logan's phone made strangled metal chicken noises – Control calling to say they couldn't get through to DI Steel, but Logan was to tell her the Polish police had just faxed over details on Kowalczyk and the three abattoir workers who'd alibied him. Only Piotr Nowack had prior, and it wasn't for cannibalism – he was part of a gang who broke into industrial estates and stole anything not nailed down.

Logan hung up as Rennie wrestled the saggy mattress back where came from, grumbling about bedbugs and pee stains.

'Not so fast.'

A pained look slid onto the constable's face. 'What?'

'You didn't check the base unit.'

'Oh bloody hell . . .' Rennie heaved the mattress back onto the floor again.

It took both of them to heave the wooden-framed base up onto its side, and when they did they discovered an Aladdin's cave. Assuming Aladdin had fallen on hard times, and instead of gold, jewels and coins he'd taken to hoarding pens, Post-its, staplers, telephones and four-hole punches. The divan was stuffed with office supplies, some still bearing little 'PROPERTY OF ALABA MEATS LTD.' stickers. There were even a couple of fax machines and a laptop.

And right at the back: a holdall that looked eerily familiar.

Rennie picked up a packet of Blu Tack. 'Not exactly the great train robbery, is it?'

Logan slipped on a second pair of latex gloves and pulled the holdall from the pile of pilfered stationary. It was identical to the one Marek Kowalczyk was carrying on the abattoir's CCTV tape, only it wasn't full of blood and meat, it was full of whiteboard markers and DL envelopes.

'Oh . . . bugger.'

41

Logan stood on the B&B's top step, listening to DI Steel swearing a blue streak. 'You sure?' she said, when the well of profanity had finally run dry, 'Post-it notes?'

'Loads of them. Envelopes, paperclips, ring-binders, you name it.'

More swearing. 'The DCS's going to kill me . . .' She took an angry drag on her cigarette. 'He thinks we caught the Flesher, not some silly bugger raiding the stationery cupboard.'

'Nowak didn't say anything when you spoke to him?'

'Course he bloody didn't. Just kept bleating for a lawyer.' Puff, puff, puff. 'Look, you're absolutely positive? No wee chunks of meat in there at all?'

'Not a sausage. Looks like Nowak was trying the same scam he ran back home, probably got Kowalczyk, Wiśniewski, and Laszenyk to do the actual stealing. I've told Rennie to go round the local pubs, see if anyone remembers being offered a dodgy fax machine and a load of yellow highlighers.'

'Sodding hell.' Steel was quiet for a moment. 'Can you no' concentrate on solving the main crime for once? We almost had the bastard!' She hurled her cigarette butt to the path and ground it out with her boot.

'It wasn't him though, was it?'

'If you don't stop rubbing it in, I'm going to introduce the point of my boot to the hole in your arse.'

'You're welcome.'

DI Steel was right: DSC Bain wasn't happy to hear the news. 'GRAMPIAN POLICE CATCH ABATTOIR KILLER' had turned into 'MAN FLATTENED BY VOLKSWAGEN GOLF FOR NICKED POST-IT NOTES'. Or it would do as soon as the papers found out Marek Kowalczyk wasn't the Flesher after all.

Logan sloped off before anyone found a way to make this all his fault, and went to the canteen for lunch. After all, it was Monday and that could only mean one thing: lasagne and chips, lasagne and chips, lasagne and ... fuck.

He turned from the serving counter, tray in hand, to see DI Insch sitting at a table by the window with Jackie. If that wasn't bad enough, the inspector was staring straight at him. And now Jackie was staring at him too.

The fat man pushed the chair on the other side of the table out with his foot.

Damn ... Logan took his lunch over and sat, trying to act casual as he helped himself to the vinegar. 'Sir, Jackie.'

She didn't even pretend to be on first-name terms anymore: 'Sergeant.'

There was an awkward silence.

Logan started in on his lasagne. All he had to do was eat fast and get out of here. Why the hell did Insch have to—

'Soon as you've finished,' said the inspector, scooping the last remnants of custard out of a bowl, 'you can get us a pool car. You and I are going to see Andrew McFarlane.'

And there went Logan's appetite. 'Sorry sir, the DCS gave strict—'

'I'm not supposed to interfere in the Flesher case? You'll be happy to know, Sergeant, that we're going to talk to Mr McFarlane about a spate of recent vandalism. Which *does* fall under my remit.'

Logan looked at Jackie, hoping for some support, but all he got back was a stony silence.

He tried again. 'Sir, don't you think—'

'No I don't. Now eat your bloody lasagne.'

'So,' said Logan, looking up at the butcher's shop, 'you were having lunch with Jackie...?' The shop windows were boarded up: huge sheets of plywood, peppered with nightclub flyers and a patina of graffiti: 'Cannibal Bastard!' 'Murderer' 'Scum' and for some reason: 'English Out'

Insch unwrapped a chocolate éclair, stuffing the sweetie in his mouth, and the wrapper in his pocket. He pointed at the blue door next to the butcher's shop. 'You know the drill.'

There was an intercom with McFarlane's name printed on a plastic slip. Logan pressed the button. No reply. So he did it again, and twice more for luck. A scared voice crackled out of the speaker. *'Go away! I'm calling the police!'*

'This *is* the police, Mr McFarlane. It's DS McRae: we met at the prison? We're here to talk to you about the vandalism.'

'Oh...'

A low grinding buzz sounded and Logan pushed the door open. They went through a short hallway and up a brightly painted flight of stairs.

McFarlane was waiting for them at the top. He didn't look much better than the last time Logan had seen him. Yes the bruises were fading, but the butcher had a caved-in look, as if all the stuffing had been knocked out of him, leaving behind an empty shell with a broken nose and missing teeth.

They followed him through into the lounge.

McFarlane's flat wasn't quite what Logan had been expecting. Lone alcoholic living above a shop: it should have been all discarded takeaway containers, empty bottles, peeling wallpaper, and dismal country music on the stereo. Instead it was painted in shades of off-white, spotlessly tidy, watercolour landscapes on the walls, and what sounded suspiciously like *Carmen* coming out of the speakers.

A line of framed photographs sat on the mantelpiece: McFarlane, McFarlane and a younger woman, the same woman in a graduation cap and gown, the two of them getting married. She'd walked out on him eighteen years ago, and he still had her photos up. That was devotion for you.

The butcher sank into a leather armchair within easy reach of a litre bottle of vodka. He poured himself a juddering tumbler-full. 'I'd offer, but you're both on duty.'

'Not to worry, sir,' Insch stood in the middle of the room, hands in his pockets as he surveyed the photos, the pot plants and the paintings. 'You have a lovely home.'

The butcher shrugged and drained half his glass in one go.

'So . . .' Insch smiled at him. 'Still expect us to believe you had nothing to do with the bits of dead people in your shop?'

McFarlane ground his eyes with the heels of his hands. 'Thought you were here about my vandalism.'

'Just between you and me, sir, I think the two things *might* just be connected.'

'They're here every night. Throwing things. You should see the state of the shop . . . it was like a bombsite when I got out of . . . when I got home.'

'And did you speak to Wiseman when you were inside?'

'I never did anything, and my life's ruined.' Another slug of vodka. 'Who's going to buy meat from my shop now? After all this? *Years* I spent building the business—'

'I'm sure everyone's sorry for your loss. I know *I* am. With my daughter lying dead in the fucking morgue!'

McFarlane worked another large measure of vodka into his glass, then into himself. 'That's not my fault – I didn't *do* anything.'

'She was FOUR!'

'Sir, I think we should—'

310

Insch towered over the hollowed-out butcher. 'She was four and that *bastard* killed her!'

'I...' McFarlane shuddered, then looked up into the inspector's furious purple face. 'Do you know what it's like to have a killer in your family? Do you? To live with the hate and the lies and the shame? When it's none of your bloody fault?'

'I ought to tear your—'

Logan put a hand on the inspector's arm. 'He wasn't there. He was in prison when Wiseman killed Sophie.'

'He—'

'Why don't you wait for me in the car, sir? I'll finish up in here.'

Insch didn't move.

'Please.'

For a moment it looked as if Insch was about to turn the butcher into fourteen stone of alcoholic mince, but in the end he turned on his heel and stormed out.

The butcher poured himself another shaky drink, the bottle clinking round the mouth of the glass. 'I didn't...'

'I'm sorry, sir. He's had a lot on his mind.'

'It was *never* me...' The vodka disappeared.

Logan picked up the wedding photograph from the mantelpiece: it was McFarlane and Wiseman's sister – Logan couldn't remember her name – on the steps of King's College Chapel. Him in a kilt, her in a huge white dress. 'Do you ever hear from her? Your wife?'

McFarlane stared down at the carpet for a beat. 'No.' He picked up the bottle, then put it down again. 'Eighteen years. Eighteen bloody years...' His saggy pink eyes were beginning to fill with tears.

Logan put the wedding photo back with the others. Eighteen years – he was willing to bet that was when the butcher climbed into a bottle and forgot the way out. 'Well, sir, if you can think of anything—'

'It's not easy losing someone you love.' This time the bottle made it all the way to the glass. 'I've lost everything. Every last bloody thing.' His voice was starting to slur round the edges. 'My whole life is buggered. All because of … because of Ken Wiseman.' The vodka went down in one. 'But he's family, isn't he? He's family so I had to give him a job. And now look at me: no wife, no business, no friends, prison. What am I going to do? Eh?' He scrubbed a trembling hand across his face, trying to wipe away the tears. 'What am I going to do?'

McFarlane lurched to his feet, grabbed the bottle, and headed for the door. 'Come see…' He stomped down the stairs, but instead of going out onto the street, the butcher led Logan round to a small internal door. 'Come see…'

He hit-or-missed a key into the lock and then they were through into the shop. Darkness. The butcher fumbled with a switch and the lights flickered on. The place didn't look anything like it had the last time Logan was here: with the plywood over the windows, it had all the charm of an open grave. Both chiller cabinets had been torn from the wall, then hurled to the floor. The display case was a study in fractured glass. A red fire extinguisher poked out of the deli counter's ruptured sneeze-guard. Gouts of dark red paint covered the walls like arterial blood.

'Twenty years.' McFarlane swigged straight from the bottle. 'Twenty years I've been building this business … and now look at it.' He threw his arms wide, shouting at the top of his voice, 'COME BUY YOUR MEAT FROM THE CANNIBAL BUTCHER!'

The next mouthful finished the vodka. He peered through the empty bottle, twisting it round and round – as if trying to get his old life to come back into focus – then hurled it at the wall above the ruptured till. An explosion of glass.

McFarlane stood in the centre of his ruined life and cried.

42

DI Insch was back in the passenger seat of Logan's pool car, the tips of two fingers pressed against the side of his throat. Teeth gritted. Face still purple. Eyes screwed shut. There was no way Logan was getting in there with him till the inspector calmed down, so he wandered down the road to a little newsagents' and spent a couple of minutes browsing the magazines, then the selection of sweeties – buying a big bag of jelly babies and another of fizzy cola bottles. And a lottery ticket, just in case. Was it ethical to still use Jackie's birthday as two of the numbers?

By the time he got back to the car, Insch seemed to have settled down a bit. Logan climbed in behind the steering wheel and passed over the jelly babies, holding the cola bottles in reserve. Just in case.

The inspector dug his way into the packet, then ripped the head off some jelly mummy's pride and joy.

'Sir,' Logan started the car, 'I think you need to go home, OK?'

More jelly babies were sacrificed, but it didn't seem to be appeasing the volcano. 'McFarlane was in it with Wiseman. The two of them together. Killing and butchering.'

Logan pulled out into traffic. 'We've got nothing on him. And before you go off on one: I know, OK? But look at him: all Andrew McFarlane wants to do is pickle himself in vodka. It's all he's *been* doing since his wife disappeared eighteen years ago. Half the time he wouldn't be sober enough to know what day of the week it was; Wiseman could butcher half of Torry downstairs and McFarlane wouldn't notice.'

'Sergeant...' Insch's voice had taken on that ominous rumble, like a twenty-eight-stone, angry rottweiler.

'I'm just saying.'

'Well don't. Sophie's dead because—'

'You shouldn't be here. You should be at home, with your family.'

Insch slammed his fist into the dashboard. 'I DON'T HAVE A FAMILY!' Trembling with rage. 'That bastard took them. He took *everything!*'

His tea was cold. Logan took an exploratory sip, then spat it back into the mug.

'Hoy!' Steel scowled at him from the other side of the history room. 'Don't be so disgusting.'

'You want another coffee?'

'And would it kill you to scare up some biscuits? Rennie always manages.'

'So get Rennie to make your bloody—' Logan's mobile phone cut him off at the pass. 'Hello?'

Geordie, male, early forties. *'Aye, we've nothin' on the Weight Watchers front.'*

'Who is this?'

'Bloody hell... Detective Superintendent Danby, Northumbria Police: none of the Newcastle victims were in Weight Watchers. Went round all the relatives, know what I mean?'

'Damn.'

'*Aye. Bloody tragic, lookin' at them photo albums all over again. Forgotten what half them looked like. Thought I'd always see their faces, every time I closed ma eyes . . .*'

'Sorry Superintendent, it was a long shot.'

'*I want you to remember they weren't just victims, OK? They were people. With families and friends who miss them. The Calverts raised money for charity. Jack coached kids five-a-side football. Emily won prizes at the local gallery, even got a bit in the papers about it. They didn't deserve what they got. They deserved better, know what I mean?*'

Logan did. He thanked the DSI, and hung up.

'Well?' said Steel.

'The Weight Watchers angle was a dud.'

Steel nodded, then fiddled with her hedgehog hair for a bit. 'You had your one-to-one with our Weegie blamemongers yet?'

'No.' And to be honest he wasn't looking forward to it either.

'Did me today while you were off playing with DI Fat-and-Grumpy.' She tipped him a wink. 'Think that redhead DCI fancies me.'

Logan went back to his paperwork. 'Thought you were getting married.'

'Girl can dream, can't she? Now where's my bloody coffee?'

Tonight it was trout fillets in herb butter with seasonal vege-tables: serves two. According to the packet anyway. Logan stuck it in the microwave and padded through to the lounge to check the messages on his answering machine.

'MESSAGE ONE: *Logan, It's your mother. You know I don't like talking to this thing.*' And then it was straight into haranguing him about hiring a kilt for his brother's wedding. *Beeeeeeep.*

The next message was from Alec wanting to know if Logan was up to anything interesting tomorrow, worried that the BBC were going to start cutting his budget if nothing happened soon. *Beeeeeeep.*

And then it was Colin Miller, voice low and urgent. *'Laz? It's me. I need you tae phone me back soon as you get this, OK? I mean it: ASAP!' Beeeeeeep. END OF MESSAGES.'*

Logan called him back. 'Colin?'

'Aye?' There was something small and snottery wailing in the background. *'Hold on a minute darlin' Daddy's on the phone, but. Laz? Laz, you want to go out for a pint tonight? Please?'* More high-pitched screaming. *'Shhhh, shhhh ... yes, Daddy knows. Daddy'll change it in a second. I'll even bring the stuff you wanted from the paper's archives? Come on man, I'm dying here ...'*

'When?'

'Prince of Wales: half seven?' Another voice in the background, nearly inaudible, but it sounded like Isobel, asking the reporter if he was aware that their son was crying. *'Sorry, Izzy, it's work – need me to cover somethin' for tomorrow.'* Then back to the phone. *'OK, but I can't be there till half seven at the earliest. I've got a family to look after, and that comes first.'*

Thank God the screaming had finally stopped. *'It's not her fault, Heather.'* Mr New sat back against the bars. *'She's frightened, her sister's dead and she's trapped in a strange, scary place all on her own. You can't blame her.'*

'Did I say anything?'

'No, but you were thinking it.'

True.

'So,' Duncan nodded at the plate of cold meat resting in her lap, *'do you think that's her? The sister?'*

Heather picked up another cutlet, bit into it, and chewed for a bit. 'Probably ... tastes a bit ... funny. Sort of metallic.' But at least it wasn't off like those last slices of Duncan. Heather didn't fancy another bout of food poisoning. She tore off a chunk, washing it down with a mouthful of water.

The plate had been there when she'd woken up, head throbbing, mouth like ash. Along with the pills. Kelley said the

Flesher was worried about her – that he'd picked up her unconscious body and laid it on the mattress, then gone to get some medicine. Little round pills that Heather had forced down. They made her teeth feel squeaky, but took the pain away.

She chewed, thinking... 'Kelley? Kelley, are you awake?'

'Do you need another pill?'

'What did He say? When He made you promise: what did He say?'

'That ... that if I didn't get you to take your medicine he'd hurt me.'

'Oh...'

'Heather?'

'Yes?'

'Tell me about Justin again.'

So she did: from the moment of conception, right through to when he was eighteen and off to university to become an architect. The life he'd never have. Then Kelley told the story of her little boy, and how it was all a mistake and the doctors gave him back to her and he grew up to be a famous actor.

Then they sat quietly in the darkness, eating slices of the girl next door's murdered sister.

And then Kelley asked, 'What's she like? Your mum?'

Heather grimaced. 'I never did anything right in her eyes. After Dad ... died, it was as if everything was my fault. She hated Duncan...'

Her cellmate was silent for a minute. 'I ... I lied to you. It wasn't my boyfriend who got me pregnant. I've never had a boyfriend. How pathetic is that? Forty-nine and I've never had a boyfriend...'

'Kelley, it's not—'

'It was my father... Mum died when I was six. And he ... he said he had needs...'

'Oh Jesus.' Heather could hear her crying. She slipped her other hand through the bars, searching for Kelley's.

317

'I ... I cut all my hair off, dressed like a boy.' Sniff. 'But he was drinking so much...' Deep breath. 'Then he had this accident. And ... and he got ... he got even worse.'

'Shhhh...' Heather laced her fingers through Kelley's. 'It's OK. The bastard's dead right? The car crash?'

'No ... Social Services took me away from him when I was eight. I got ... I got adopted by a lovely old couple ... they never hurt me...'

Heather bit her bottom lip, but it didn't stop her own tears. To go through all that, and end up here, in the Dark, waiting for something horrible to happen. Waiting to die. 'Oh Kelley, I'm so sorry.'

'When ... when they ... after the crash my dad came to see me in the foster home... He ... he was so drunk ... I couldn't stop him...'

Heather and Kelley held hands, both of them crying in the darkness as Kelley told how her father would visit his little girl every week until she got pregnant. After that, he never showed up again.

It was strange: before all this – the kidnap, the prison, the Flesher, the Dark – Heather would *never* have cast herself in the role of avenging angel. She was soft and fat and weak. Someone to be ignored, or pushed about, walked all over. But if she ever got out of here, she swore she would track Kelley's father down and cut the bastard's heart out.

Then eat it.

43

The Tuesday morning briefing was a pretty dismal affair – they now had two more victims: Sandra and Maureen Taylor from Dundee. Their flatmate had returned from a long weekend in Edinburgh to find the kitchen soaked with blood.

'Tayside Police,' said DCS Bain, 'have identified the blood as Sandra Taylor's; she was a type one diabetic. It looks like the attack happened some time on Sunday evening. They've emailed up all the details, make sure you read them!'

Two more victims and still no sodding clue.

There was a bit of discussion about whether this was another copycat or the Flesher hunting outside of Aberdeen, and then everyone was given their assignments and told to go catch the bastard.

Back in the history room, Logan sat at his desk, eating a breakfast muesli bar and wishing the Environmental Health hadn't confiscated half the bacon in the city. There was nothing like a bacon buttie to set you up after a night in the pub. Except maybe a steak pie, and they were like hen's teeth these days as well.

He pulled out the folder Colin Miller had given him in the Prince of Wales, and spread the contents across the desk –

printouts and photocopies of articles from 1987 to 1990. A chunk were about the McLaughlins and their disappearance, but most were the missing person and food-poisoning stories he'd asked for. Which were about as much use as Rennie's INTERPOL reports; it was impossible to tell what might be connected and what was just random stuff.

So Logan went back to the articles on Jamie McLaughlin and his missing parents. Why had they never found any sign of the third victim, Catherine Davidson? Directly after the attack, the papers were full of her photo, but as time went by she drifted into the background and the media concentrated on the tragedy of little Jamie McLaughlin. Eventually Catherine Davidson was simply forgotten.

Logan flicked through the sheets again. Colin had been thorough, there was even a piece from before the attack: an article dated the eighth of October 1987 about how Ian McLaughlin had joined the team at Lindsey Arrow and was going to help them become a driving force in the field of Liner Hangers and Well Completion. Whatever that meant. McLaughlin wasn't exactly a pretty man, but then neither was the thin bloke with the Zapata moustache he was shaking hands with. Welcome to the oil industry.

Logan finished his tea and stuck all the printouts back in the folder. At least Ian McLaughlin had got to enjoy his fifteen minutes of fame, all the other Flesher victims got theirs post mortem. Well, except for one of the Newcastle women.

He looked at the death wall, trying to remember who it was, then went for a rummage in the old file boxes by the radiator, till he found a small stack of yellowed newspaper clippings. 'BAINBRIDGE'S BRIDGE IS A WINNER' was the headline, above a photo of Emily Bainbridge, grinning away like mad as she showed off her big oil painting of the Tyne Bridge. She'd come first: a cheque for one hundred pounds and an exhibition planned for the Autumn. She was dead three weeks later.

Three weeks...

He went back to Colin Miller's printouts and pulled out the article on Ian McLaughlin again. Eighth of October 1987: a Thursday. Three and a bit weeks before Halloween and the McLaughlin's death.

'Oh you beauty...' He fired up his computer and went onto the *Aberdeen Examiner*'s website, doing a search for all the current victims, looking for news stories published before their deaths. There weren't any. So he tried the same thing with the P&J and *Evening Express* sites. Then sat back and swore. So much for that theory.

He stared at the screen ... mind you, the papers didn't post *everything* on-line, did they?

He picked up the phone and put it down again. After the Weight Watchers fiasco he didn't want to stick his neck out without something more conclusive than two newspaper articles from twenty years ago. He tried the phone again, dialling Colin Miller's mobile. Engaged, so he tried the *Examiner*'s News Desk instead.

There was some muffled conversation then the Glaswegian's dulcet tones sounded in the background, *'Can you no' see I'm on the bloody phone?'*

'It's your copper boyfriend.'

'I'll boyfriend your arse with my— No Mrs Wilson, I didn't mean you... Aye, I agree, there's no need for language like that, I'm sorry... Aye...'

'You going to speak to him or not?'

Silence.

'He'll call you back.'

Steel dumped another stack of reports on Logan's desk. 'There you go – Tayside say if you want anything else give them a shout.'

Logan stared at the pile of SOC, IB, and door-to-door data. 'I don't even want this lot.'

'Aye, well, we've all got out crosses to bear.' She struck a pose. 'You think it's easy being this gorgeous?'

'You said I was supposed to check up on those Polish police reports.'

'And did you?'

'Yes . . .' Logan realized his mistake as soon he'd said it.

'Perfect, then you're free to do this now, aren't you?'

'But—'

'Ah, ah, ah.' She waggled a finger at him. 'Remember the golden rule: you—'

Logan's phone rang and he snatched at the excuse: 'Hello?'

But it wasn't Colin Miller, it was an annoyed Chief Constable with a Brummie accent: *'Where are you? I've been waiting here for ages.'*

'Waiting?'

Steel asked, 'Who is it?'

'Faulds.' Back to the phone. 'I don't understand, sir, where—'

'Aberdeen airport. You were supposed to pick me up at eleven!'

'I was?'

'DI Steel assured me . . .'

Logan pulled the phone away from his ear and stared at the inspector. 'Thanks a heap.'

She shrugged. 'Oops?'

'I'll be there as soon as I can.'

Forty minutes later Logan was heading out the road to Turriff, with Faulds in the passenger seat and his luggage in the boot. Logan kept sneaking glances at the Chief Constable's face – it looked as if someone had given him a going over. The bruise on his forehead was starting to fade around the edges – dark purple tinged with greeny-yellow, a scab on his cheek, another bruise blending into his goatee. He hadn't shaved for a couple of days either.

'Didn't think we'd be seeing you back again so soon, sir.'

'I can't believe she didn't pass on my message.'

'She's been a bit … preoccupied with the investigation.'

'That's one way of putting it.' He went back to staring at the scenery.

'If you don't mind me asking …' Logan coughed. 'You look a bit … er …' Try again. 'I called when we IDed Kowalczyk on the abattoir's CCTV, but they said you had a couple of personal days … ?'

'You know,' said Faulds, watching the sun-flecked fields go by, 'I heard about your solution to the Leith case. Very impressive.'

'It was a team effort.'

'Of course it was. But every good team has to have a leader, otherwise it's just a mob. I was surprised to see DI Steel giving you so much of the credit.'

Logan shrugged. 'She's not as bad as everyone says.' Which wasn't strictly true, but Faulds didn't need to know that.

The Chief Constable's phone went off just past Fyvie and he disappeared into a convoluted conversation about staffing levels and Home Office statistics. All very boring stuff. So Logan gave up on eavesdropping and let his mind wander instead: what was he going to have for his tea? Would he ever see Jackie naked again? Could he fake diarrhoea to get out of going to his brother's wedding? Whatever happened to Catherine Davidson?

According to the background reports she worked as a dinner lady at her son's school. She liked horses – went riding in Hazlehead Park whenever she could – wanted to go to Spain for her holidays, talked about running a bed and breakfast …

And no one had seen or heard from her since the night Ian and Sharon McLaughlin died.

If you wanted to get rid of a lot of suspect meat there were worse places than a school canteen. Who'd ever know?

'… himself with a pineapple. Some people, eh?'

Logan glanced across at his passenger. 'Sorry, sir?'

'Never mind, I probably shouldn't be complaining about my officers anyway.' Faulds stuck his phone back in its holster as Logan drove them through Turriff. 'I'd forgotten how much I missed this: out on a case instead of stuck behind a desk, or shaking some slimy politician's hand. Must've driven half my team mad when I got back from Aberdeen last time. Poking my nose in . . .'

He watched the market town with its collage of red sandstone and grey granite buildings go by. 'You know,' he said, touching the glass, 'I grew up in a little place like this . . .'

Logan turned the pool car into the road with Alaba Farm Fresh Meats at the end of it.

Faulds peered through the windscreen at the large plastic sign with its grinning butcher pig. 'This it?'

The massed armies of the national press had gone, but a couple of die-hard journalists were parked by the high, chain-link gates, scrambling out of their cars as Logan pulled up at the barrier.

'Do you have any suspects?' 'Will Alaba Meats be torn down?' 'Do you think the Polish community is responsible for the killings?' 'How would you react to claims that this is just an attempt to pin the blame on ethnic migrants?' 'How many bodies have you identified from the remains?'

Logan kept his mouth shut and let Faulds do the talking as they waited for the security guard to open the gate, then drove round to the little office block bolted onto the side of the abattoir. 'Hmm . . .' said Faulds, stepping out into the sunny afternoon, 'the smell's . . . interesting. Sort of a greasy bleach . . .'

The receptionist made them sign in and offered them coffee. Mr Jenkins would be down in a minute.

Mr Jenkins turned out to be a grey-haired man in his fifties, with a paunch that made him look six months pregnant. He showed them upstairs to an office on the second floor, overlooking the car park, and sank behind a desk overflowing with paperwork. 'Forty years I've been in this game. Forty years! And now the only buggers who'll take my calls are the sodding supermarkets.' He waved Logan and Faulds towards a pair of leather visitor chairs that squeaked and farted as they settled into them. 'Don't get me wrong, I'm grateful they've not dumped us like everyone else, but they were screwing us on price *before* all this started. You imagine what they're doing now? Barely worth opening again.'

He leant forward and poked the desk. 'There's been an abattoir on this spot since the year dot. And I'm not talking about the fifties or sixties, I mean since the sixteen hundreds. When I was a kid there was a slaughterhouse in every wee town in Scotland. We used to cut the carcasses in half, chuck them on a flat-bed truck, cover them with tarpaulin and stick them on the next train to London. Didn't even have refrigerated carriages back then. And did everyone die of food-poisoning? Did they buggery. Now it's all factory freezing and EU regulations and health inspectors.'

'If it's any consolation,' said Faulds, 'policing used to be the same.'

Logan couldn't add to that. It'd been wall-to-wall forms and procedural guidelines ever since he'd joined. 'At least they're letting you open again.'

Jenkins scowled. 'Tomorrow. You would not *believe* the hoops we've had to jump through. Sixty new security cameras, twice as many guards, and I've got to have some moron from the Environmental Health on staff full time. And guess who pays for it all: me, that's who.' He picked up a thick wad of paper from his desk and wiggled it at them. 'Every single joint has to be tied back to a specific animal, not just a batch like every other place. Every knife has to be sterilized before you can use it on a new quarter. We used to do fifty, sixty carcasses a day. Be lucky to get through thirty now. You got any idea what that's going to do to our cashflow? Bastards made us throw away every side of beef in the place, *and* all the stuff in the aging sheds. Bloody criminal.'

'Well,' said Faulds, 'to be fair, they did find a whole heap of human remains in there.'

'There was nothing wrong with the rest of the meat!'And so it went. On and on and on . . . Until the receptionist buzzed up to say that someone from the Environmental Health had turned up for a spot inspection.

'It's OK,' said Faulds, before Jenkins could go off on another rant. 'We'll see ourselves out.'

But first the Chief Constable wanted to see where the Flesher disposed of the bodies.

Logan led him round to the ageing shed. The place was spotless – the shelves and plastic bins emptied and cleaned, the concrete floor scrubbed to within an inch of its life. Everything reeked of bleach.

'So . . . ' Faulds did a quick three-sixty, his breath fogging in the refrigerated air, 'how did our boy get the meat in here?'

'Far as we can tell, it was all dumped in small batches, probably when he was getting rid of the bones. When we searched the place we found bits of at least seven individuals, all vacuum packed and slipped in with the other meat. Still waiting on DNA-test results for most of them, but we've IDed joints from Tom and Hazel Stephen, and Duncan Inglis.' He pointed back at the small side door. 'CCTV coverage of this part of the plant's a joke. It's all focussed on the perimeter – if you were already inside you could go where you liked: no one would know. And once it's packed away in here, who's going to notice an extra couple of joints?'

Faulds nodded. 'Show me the bone mill.'

The rendering plant had been down for four days, but the smell still permeated everything, overlaid with the chemical reek of trichloroethylene. 'The question we have to ask ourselves,' said Faulds, staring up at one of the new security cameras bolted to the bone mill wall, 'is how the Flesher managed to get into a working abattoir without anyone seeing him.'

He started up the stairs, making for the hoppers. 'He's a big man. He stuffs the bones and offal in a bin bag – something heavy duty, thick plastic so it won't split – throws it over his shoulder and humps it up here. Can't see him doing that in the middle of the day, can you?'

Logan followed him up to the top of the stairs. 'DCS Bain did a walkthrough.'

'Did he now?' Faulds leant on the railing, staring down into the trough at the toothed screw at the bottom. 'And what conclusion did the great Chief Superintendent come to?'

'The Flesher probably has ties to the cleaning company that does the offices.'

'Clever. So he's got an excuse to be on the premises in the middle of the night, get a vehicle close to the building, and nobody's going to look twice if he's seen carrying bin bags.'

'We interviewed everyone who works for them: full-time, part-time, and casual. No joy. Bain's widened the net to friends and family.'

'Worth a try I suppose.' Faulds pushed himself upright and headed down the stairs. 'But it's not a cleaner.'

'How do you know?'

The Chief Constable stopped and turned to look at Logan. 'I've been chasing the Flesher for over twenty years.' He smiled. 'Who knows him better than me?'

44

The walls pulsed in the darkness, she could feel them, making the air taste of sparklers. Heather lay on her back, one arm thrown across her face, the pressure keeping her eyes from rolling out of her head. 'Kelley ... I don't feel good ...'

On the other side of the wall, the new girl was screaming again. Shouting. Swearing. Demanding to be let out. For a blissful couple of hours she'd been quiet – then she'd told them all about her sister and how she'd opened the door expecting the pizza guy, only to find the Flesher standing on the top step. How everything was covered in blood ...

Still, the calm had been nice while it lasted.

'Kelley?'

'Shh ... I'm here, Heather. It's OK. You just need a bit of sleep, that's all.'

'I think there was something wrong with the meat ...'

Silence.

'What? What was wrong with it?'

'Maureen. The new girl. She said her sister was diabetic. She'd be injecting herself with drugs ... I thought it tasted funny ... Oh God ...'

Kelley reached through the bars and gave Heather's hand a squeeze. 'They inject with insulin. It occurs naturally in the body. I doubt it'd even survive the cooking process. Maybe you got concussion when you banged your head?'

'Maybe.'

The screaming settled down for a minute and Heather breathed a sigh of relief. Then it started up again. 'That bloody racket isn't helping.'

She waited for Mr New to appear and tell her she was being cruel, but nothing happened. Maybe he was off giving Duncan's ghost a hard time? The sulky sod had barely showed his dead face since Kelley arrived. Or maybe it was Heather's fault? Maybe Duncan wasn't coming round so often because she was getting a little bit less mad every day? Now that she wasn't trapped in here on her own any more, maybe she was going slowly sane.

Heather laughed. Then groaned. Then thought about throwing up.

'You should take some of your medicine. He made me promise to give you your medicine if you weren't feeling well.'

'I don't feel well.'

Kelley let go of her hand and there was a scrabbling sound. Then a package was pressed into Heather's palm: tinfoil, wrapped around two small pills. 'You have to take these and get better. If you don't he'll come back and hurt me. Don't make him hurt me . . .'

Heather didn't want to take them.

'*Now, Honey*—' Duncan poked her in the shoulder.

'Where have you been?'

'Heather? I'm right here.'

'*Just take your medicine.*'

'But it could be anything.'

'*Honey, if He wanted to hurt you He could turn you into veal chops any time he liked, couldn't He?*'

'But—'

'*But nothing. You're not feeling well, remember? You banged your head? And if you don't take them He's going to hurt Kelley. You want to make Him hurt her?*'

Heather ran a finger over the pills. 'No.'
'So take your medicine and nobody has to die.'

Operator: *Emergency services, which service do you require?*
Caller (female): It's him! From the papers and the telly!
The Flesh bloke!
Operator: *It's OK madam, we—*
Caller: I saw him! I was looking out the window and I saw
him! He climbed in over the back fence!
Operator: *He's in your back garden?*
Caller: Not my garden, next door! I saw him – he had the
mask and the apron. He went in the back door!
Operator: *Can you confirm your address for me?*
Caller: Seventy three Springhill Crescent, Northfield. Hurry!
Operator: *I need you to stay inside and lock all your doors and
windows. The police are on their way.*

Anderson Drive flashed by the car's windows, the city's lights
glowing in the indigo night. Logan kept his foot flat to the
floor, following in the wake of blaring sirens and flashing
lights. Sitting in the passenger seat, Faulds turned the radio up.
'Alpha Mike Three, this is Alpha Sixteen, what's your ETA, over?'
*'Just coming up to the roundabout onto Provost Frazer Drive so
about—'* the sound of a horn blaring in the background. *'—
Jesus! LEARN TO DRIVE YOU WANKER! Did you see that? Get the
bastard's number plate . . .'*
'Still waiting on that ETA, Alpha Mike Three.'
'Oh, right. Five, six minutes tops.'
'OK,' said Faulds, as they flew through a set of red traffic
lights, 'who's had firearms training?'
Steel shouted through from the back seat. 'Don't look at me.'
'Alec?'
The cameraman shrugged. 'Not the sort of thing they do in
the BBC.'
'Logan?'

'Last Christmas, but I've never been on an actual—'

'Good enough for me.' He picked up the radio handset. 'Control, this is Chief Constable Mark Faulds. Tell the Senior Firearms Officer he's to stay put till I get there.'

'But, sir—'

'I've handled dozens of these situations before. You don't get to be Chief Constable by hiding under a desk.'

There was some muffled conversation, and then the voice on the other end said, *'Yes, sir.'*

Faulds winked at Logan. 'You and I are going to be in at the kill.'

That was what Logan was afraid of.

Springhill Crescent was a strange conglomeration of semi-detached houses, some were harled, but others were clad in dark brown wood, looking like something out of a Norwegian housing estate. Number sixty-two was the left-hand side of a pair, its exterior in need of a good coat of creosote. The upstairs lights were on, glowing in the cold night.

Logan ducked back behind a people carrier two doors down. 'Are you sure about this?'

Faulds grinned. 'You ready?'

'How the hell did you talk them into it?'

'Rank has its privileges.' Faulds ejected the magazine from his borrowed Heckler and Koch MP5 automatic machine pistol, checked the load, and slapped it back into place. Then did the same with his Glock 9mm. He squeezed the airwave handset attached to the shoulder of his black, bullet-proof jacket. 'Team Three, we are good to go.'

A click. *'Roger that, Team Three ... Sir, are you sure I can't—'*

'Yes, I'm sure.' He peered round the side of the huge car. 'Any movement?'

'Negative. Target is still in the building.'

Logan adjusted the strap on his borrowed helmet, pulling it tight under his chin, then wrapped the black scarf around the lower half of his face, like the bad guy in a cowboy film. It smelt of stale cigarette smoke and onions.

Faulds did the same. 'You nervous?'

'Bricking it. You?'

'Stay behind me; you'll be fine.' He patted Logan on the back. 'Flesher's got a knife and a bolt gun, neither's going to go through your vest. OK?'

'All teams – positions for entry.'

'Here we go . . .'

They ran for the front door, staying low through the gate and up the concrete driveway. Team One got there first, standing flat against the wooden wall to one side of the red door, waiting. Logan and Faulds stopped directly opposite. And then a burly figure dressed all in black lumbered her way up the path, carrying a one-woman battering ram.

She placed the striking end against the lock and nodded at Faulds.

The Chief Constable clicked on his Airwave again. 'Team two?'

'Back garden is secure, we're ready to go in.'

'OK, everybody on three, two, one—'

The constable swung her battering ram – BANG – the lock tore free of the doorframe and they were in.

Team one took the lounge, team two burst through the back door and into the kitchen, Logan and Faulds hammered upstairs.

Landing: 'Clear.' Faulds kicked the bathroom door off its hinges: 'Clear.' Bedroom one got the same treatment: 'Clear' Bedroom two: the door banged back off the wall. 'Hands on your head! HANDS ON YOUR HEAD NOW!'

Logan charged into the room after Faulds, the machine pistol heavy and cold, even through his gloves.

A naked middle-aged woman was tied to the bed, covered in blood, screaming behind a makeshift gag. The Flesher stood over her, knife in one hand and a slippery chunk of offal in the other, face unreadable behind that rubber Margaret Thatcher mask.

'I SAID, PUT YOUR HANDS ON YOUR HEAD!'

The Flesher dropped the knife. He was naked from the waist down, his trademarked butcher's apron draped over an exercise bike in the corner, allowing his erection to swing free.

Faulds pointed his gun at the offending member, and the Flesher slapped both hands over it.

'Other head.'

The muffled shouts from the bed got louder. The woman struggled against her bonds, screaming blue murder as Faulds forced the Flesher to his knees at gunpoint. Logan hurried over and untied the silk scarf gagging her.

'Aaaaagh... You bastard!'

'It's OK, you're safe! You're safe!'

Faulds dragged the Flesher's hands behind his back and slapped the cuffs on.

The woman writhed, yanking at the silk scarves tying her wrists and ankles to the bedposts. 'You dirty bastard!'

Logan scanned her naked body, trying to figure out where all the bright-red blood was coming from ... only it wasn't blood.

'He's my husband!'

It was tomato sauce.

The press officer sat at Logan's desk in the history room, with her forehead resting on the Formica and her arms wrapped over the top. 'Oh dear Jesus...'

Faulds leant back against the other desk, still wearing his borrowed SAS ninja outfit. 'When we left she was on the phone to one of those ambulance-chasing lawyers that advertise on the telly.'

The press officer hauled herself upright. 'Why couldn't it have been him? I really thought we'd finally come to the end of this bloody case, and now we've got a lawsuit to deal with.'

Logan finished off his post-incident report and stuck it in the 'out' tray. 'I can't believe she'll go through with it. Can you imagine what the headlines are going to be like? "Police raid kinky serial killer sex games", "Wannabe Flesher caught playing hide the sausage". Not exactly going to get them a lot of sympathy, is it?'

The press officer stared at him. 'They weren't photogenic, were they?'

'Not from where I was standing.'

'That's something, I suppose . . .'

'If it helps,' said Faulds, peeling off his bullet-proof vest, 'I've got that criminal psychologist coming in tomorrow. We could get him to do a piece on why people who dress up as mass murderers for sexual kicks are a menace to the gene pool?'

'Chief Constable!' She was on her feet like a shot. 'Are you suggesting Grampian Police should lower itself to character assassination just to avoid a lawsuit?'

'Yes.'

She smiled. 'Sounds good to me.'

'What you still doing here?' asked Rennie, plonking himself down on the edge of Logan's desk. Half past eight and the station was gearing itself up for another quiet night of underage drinking and random acts of vandalism.

Logan nodded at the pile of paperwork sent up by Tayside Police. 'Trying to catch up on those two sisters who got grabbed in Dundee.'

'I went on a stag night in Dundee once. Ended up in this strip club and—'

'What do you want?'

'Right.' Rennie clapped his hands together. 'Tonight: Archies, pints. Laura and me are off to a costume party later, but we can stop by for a few drinkies on the way.' He dropped his voice to a camp stage-whisper, 'Laura's got this kinky schoolgirl outfit. She put it on last night, and I tell you—'

'Is this going to be one of those conversations where you tell me about your sex life and I fantasize about beating you to death with an office chair?'

'OK, OK.' The constable held his hands up in surrender. 'Jealousy's an ugly, ugly thing.' Pause. 'About you and Jackie: I was thinking—'

'Don't, OK?'

'But you're both mates, I mean I—'

'Just ... don't.' Logan pulled the crime scene photos from the pile and flicked through them.

'I only wanted to—'

'Seriously, you'll live longer if you shut up right now.'

There was a brief, petulant silence. 'You're going to come to the pub though, yeah?'

'Will Jackie be there?'

'No.'

'Then I'll think about it.'

Rennie nodded. 'You can bring your English overlord if you like?'

'You're kidding, right? He sodded off hours ago.'

'Come on, while the cat's away, the mice can sod off to the pub and get blootered.' Rennie jumped to his feet. 'Couple of pints, get you out of this shitehole, spend some time with the living for a change.'

The world twisted and throbbed around Heather's head. In and out, in and out. Sounds came and went in the darkness: the pounding of her heart, her mother's disembodied voice: *'You're just feeling a little under the weather, Darling. You'll be fine. You will.'* A cold, papery hand on her forehead.

She'd been asleep, but now she was awake. Or still asleep, and dreaming she was awake. Feeling drunk and tired and sick. 'I want to see my Justin ...'

'I know, darling, I know. You'll see him one day. When you die. But that's not going to happen for a long, long time. The

Flesher will look after you. You'll see. The medicine will make you all better.'

'Kelley? Kelley?'

'Shhh... Kelley's asleep, Darling. You should be too. You'll feel much better in the morning.'

The screaming outside had started again: Maureen bellowing at the top of her lungs that she was scared and wanted someone to let her out ... Only the words were different. Panicked. 'Please! I'll do anything you want! Please!' More screaming. 'Please! I won't tell anyone: PLEASE!'

Her mother kissed Heather on the forehead. One soft hand cradling her cheek.

'Please! Please don't—' *Crack*. And then there was no more screaming.

The silence was beautiful and rich and dark. Like chocolate.

Heather didn't even mind when the hacking started.

The bar was full of off-duty police officers and students, both sets here for the cheap beer. Logan sat at DI Steel's normal table – in the corner beneath the television – polishing off his first pint of the night and enjoying every mouthful.

'I mean, think about it,' said Rennie, dressed for some unfathomable reason in a dog collar and priestly black, 'how come whenever the Flesher strikes, our so-called Chief Constable Faulds is nowhere to be seen?'

Logan consigned his empty pint glass to the drinker's graveyard that covered the table. 'You're not *still* on about this, are you?'

'Where is he tonight, then?'

'How should I know?'

'Exactly!' Rennie finished off his Stella and plonked it down with the others.

Logan shook his head. 'I don't know where Steel is either, but that doesn't make her Jack the bloody Ripper.' He pointed at the collection of empties. 'Your round.'

The constable stood, pulled on an ecclesiastical expression, and marched off to the bar. Blessing random strangers on the way, leaving his girlfriend behind.

Rennie wasn't kidding about Laura's kinky schoolgirl outfit – she was dressed in an exact replica of the Albyn School uniform, only she had her shirt-tails tied beneath her breasts, hoiking them up to create a vertiginous cleavage and exposing her stomach at the same time. The skirt was so short there was a flash of white knickers every time she moved her stockinged legs. She'd even put her long, blonde hair in pigtails and painted freckles on her cheeks.

Logan had never really got the whole schoolgirl fantasy thing himself – it always seemed a bit paedophilic – but the other men at the table were falling over themselves to laugh at her jokes and ogle her breasts.

Logan barely heard his phone when it went off. 'Hello?' With all the laughing, jiggling and rampant testosterone, he couldn't make out a word. 'Hold on, I'll have to go outside . . .'

The front door to Archibald Simpson was sheltered by a granite portico, held up by huge ionic columns, a perfect little haven for all the banished smokers to light up in. He waded through the cigarette smog to the outer edge, looking into the cold, rainy night as Colin Miller said, *'You in the pub again? Christ knows how your liver copes . . . Listen, I did a search on all the victims, right? No' just the Aberdeen ones: every bugger. They all had a wee thing in the papers three or four weeks before they died. It's like clockwork, but.'*

'You sure?'

'Every last one of them. Gonna be all over the front page tomorrow: "Headlines Spell Death for Flesher Victims!" Continued page seven, eight and nine.'

'Can you email me all the references you found?'

'What am I, your secretary?'

'Oh come on, you wouldn't have a story at all if—'

'*Aye, aye. Bloody prima donna.*' But he promised to send them straight over. '*You up for that curry you owe us this week then?*'

'Khyber Pass, or Light of Bengal?' They were still debating the relative merits of sit-in versus takeaway, when someone poked Logan in the shoulder and said, 'Shift over for God's sake. I'm bloody drowning out here.'

DI Steel squeezed in beside him, then dragged her hands through her sodden hair, shaking the water off all over Logan's trousers as he hung up.

'Hey, watch it!'

'Oh, grow up, you're no' going to melt.' She gave her hair one last pass – leaving it remarkably tidy-looking for a change – then produced a packet of cigarettes from her sodden jacket and lit up. 'How come you're looking so happy? Someone polish your truncheon for you?'

'I've found a connection.'

'Four hours I waited in that bloody doctor's surgery.' The inspector hauled up her trousers. 'You any idea how many buggers are getting themselves tested for HIV and Hepatitis C right now? Thousands. National Health Service my sharny arse!'

'Should've gone to the duty doc.'

'I'm no' letting that bastard anywhere near me with a needle.' She smoked her way into a scowl. 'I liked Doc Wilson better. Might've been a miserable cancer-ridden bastard, but at least he could take a joke.'

Probably not the epitaph the ex-duty doctor had been hoping for. 'Besides,' she said, 'I ... hold on a minute – what connection?'

Logan told her about the newspaper clippings.

'Bloody hell . . . ' She took the cigarette out of her mouth, grabbed his shoulders, and planted a big, smoky kiss on his lips. 'Laz, I love you! Call the station and let them know, then I'm going to buy you a bloody *huge* drink!'

He phoned Control, and by the time he'd finished Steel was waiting for him inside with a double Highland Park. 'Well?' She handed him the glass. 'What did . . .' she drifted to a halt, staring at Rennie's girlfriend as the constable reached the punchline of whatever joke he was telling. Laura threw back her head and laughed, exposing the smooth skin from her throat all the way down into her cleavage. Setting everything jiggling.

'Oooooh,' said Steel, 'that *can't* be legal.' She drifted off into a little reverie . . . 'Yes, anyway, come on. Can't spend *all* night staring at nubile young women's chests: there's drinking to be done.'

'KILLER' SEX GAMS
PARK POLICE RAID

XCLUSIVE
y Colin Miller
iller@Aberdeen-Examiner.com

ULL-SCALE POLICE
l was launched last
t after neighbours
rted the Flesher
king into a house in
nghill Crescent,
hfield.

when police arrived they
ered that the 'Flesher' had
of a different kind on his

couple, who can not be
for legal reasons had
d to 'spice up' their love life
ssing up as Serial Killer and
The husband was wearing
sher's trademark butcher's

mask, while his wif
the bed, covered in fa

Unaware that this
kinky sex game,
firearms squad brok
front door and swa
the building, arrestin
at gunpoint.

"It was a ridicu
police time," said
they'd just kept
wouldn't have bee
was because the h
to break-in to his ov
the garden that his
him and raised the

Noted Criminal
David Goulding
uncommon for pe
their sexual fantas
one of many wa
keep the spark
marriage, but I
anyone embark
Killer/Victim sc

CANNIBAL T-SHIRT
AND BURGERS FOR SAL
SICK PRODUCTS ON INTERNET
By Russel D McLean

How on earth can anyone
find anything funny about the
situation in Aberdeen at the
moment?

But that's what happening right now
– as T-shirts featuring the Alaba
Fresh Meats mascot, Mr McPork, go
up for sale on websites all over the
world.

Sickening

The T-shirts bear slogans like, "I've
Got Some Meat For You, Baby" and,
"Got Any Human Meat In You? No?
Want Some?"

Chief Constable Brian Anderson of
Grampian Police described the T-shirts
as sick and twisted. "These shirts are
basically poking fun at people's deaths.
Whoever is selling these things has no
respect for human life. It's a disgrace."

But the shirts aren't the only product
to step well over the taste barrier, you
can also buy Aberdeen Angus, Duncan,
and Stephen burgers.

We tracked down the 24-year-old
behind the sick site: Justin Noble. "I
really don't see the problem," he told
us, "it's just a bit of fun. It's not hurting
anybody."

That's not a view shared by Paul, son
of Hazel and Tom Stephen who went

The
Alaba
Farm
Fresh
Meats
mascot
Mr McPork
gets a sick makeover

missing last week. "If I ever get my
hands on this b******d, I'll kill him.
How can he think this is funny?"

Adding insult to injury

The Abattoir where Tom Stephen's
remains were found is due to open
again tomorrow following an
investigation by the Environmental
Health Board.

DUNDEE S

UREEN TAYLOR (25) AND HER SISTER
NDRA (23) disappeared from their flat over the
kend, leaving the kitchen awash with blood.

I can't believe it," said their flatmate, "I got back
n Edinburgh and there was blood everywhere, It was
ble. They were lovely girls and wouldn't have hurt
I can't believe this has happened."
ayside Police h

ARIAN H
as MSP Vows to Close Abattoir for

OLISH
MMUNITY
EAKS OUT
XCLUSIVE
y Colin Miller
iller@Aberdeen-Examiner.com

RS of Aberdeen's Polish
ty are to make a formal
t to Grampian Police today
g a number of violent
s across the city.

just want to work and be left
," said one, "the police arrested
men at the abattoir and now
think that this is all the Polish
's fault. That is not fair."
lice sources say that attacks on
mic migrants are up more than
t of three men at

TESTS ARE planned
Turriff this weekend
tspoken MSP Robin
afferty vowed to stop
othing until the
ir at the centre of
rrent crisis is shut
d.

staggering that they've
ven permission to open

His comments sparked instant
complaints from local business
leaders in Turriff. "The abattoir
brings in a lot of money to the
local community," said one
shopkeeper who didn't want to be
named. "The Polish workers get on
really well with the locals and they
always spend money in town. If
the abattoir goes, things are going
to get a lot tougher out here."

The chairman of the local
Rotary Club said, "Mr McCafferty
should engage his brain before
speaking. He's scrabbling after the
popular vote by making knee-jerk
comments like this. He doesn't
understand the impact this would
have on the local economy."

McCafferty wasn't to be

support the MSP's
spokesman for All Me
said, "It's about
understood what it's
preyed upon. Animals
up with this every
lives. Why should it
and eat a cow,
accountant? Both ac
repugnant."

As more and more
Granite City turn to
in the wake of the
human meat in the
have to wonder if an
the meat industry ev

Paul Jenkins, Mar
of Alaba Farm
responded to the M'
saying, "We've b

45

'All right, all right, settle down.' Detective Chief Superintendent Bain stuck his mug on the desk at the front of the briefing room and waited for quiet. Logan sat with DI Steel, two rows back, marinating in the aftermath of a well-deserved hangover.

Nearly everyone in the team had wanted to buy him a drink when Steel told them about the newspaper connection, and Logan had let them.

'You'll have heard,' said Bain, 'that we finally know how the Flesher is selecting his victims.' He held up a copy of that morning's *Aberdeen Examiner*, with Colin Miller's exclusive splashed all over the front page. A ragged cheer went up and Logan blushed.

DCS Bain held up a hand. 'Before anyone breaks out the champagne, think about it: each of the Flesher's victims were featured in a newspaper article before their deaths. *Press and Journal, Evening Express, Dundee Courier, Glasgow Herald, Daily Mail, Scotsman, Sunday Post* ... Do you have any idea how many people read those papers?'

And suddenly Logan's glow didn't feel so rosy.

'Exactly. Millions. This tells us *how* the Flesher picks his victims, but it's a long way from getting us his name and address.

Steel nudged Logan in the ribs. 'Told you.' Which was a lie.

'But,' said Bain cutting through the groans, 'it might give us an insight into the mind of the bastard. Which brings me to item two on the agenda: Doctor Goulding.' He pointed and a man in a sharp grey suit stood and joined him at the front.

'Hi, call me Dave, OK?' Liverpool accent, hooked nose, hair like animal pelt, and a lurid tie that looked as if someone had eaten a whole range of fluorescent paint and then thrown up on it.

'Chief Constable Faulds asked me to come in and present a profile on the Flesher. I've worked with sexually motivated violent offenders for fifteen years, attended training courses with the FBI at their Quantico headquarters, worked as a profiler for the Metropolitan Police . . . '

Steel leant over and whispered in Logan's ear, 'Lived in an octopus's garden, dressed up in women's clothing, had sex with a vacuum cleaner, am in love with the sound of my own sodding voice . . . '

'I was asked to concentrate on three scenarios. A: Ken Wiseman is the Flesher and is working with an accomplice. B: Ken Wiseman *was* the Flesher, but the current spate of killings are down to a copycat. And C: it's been somebody else all along.' He looked at Bain. 'Can we get the first slide up? . . . Thanks.' He turned and checked the screen – a shot of Thomas Stephen's surreal post mortem. 'When dealing with sexual predators, or "serial killers", it's important to start with the effect and work back towards the cause . . . '

Steel got comfortable in her chair. 'Give us a nudge if I start to snore, OK?'

There then followed a long explanation of how the Flesher was killing people in order to introduce human meat into the food chain. According to Goulding, this was part of some deranged messiah complex. The longer the psychologist went on, the more coughing, shuffling and yawning he got from the audience. By the time he was going through the first profile, Steel was nodding off, her head dipping lower and lower each time, till her chin came to rest against her chest and she was gone.

Logan didn't blame her: he was having difficulty staying awake himself. Doctor Call-Me-Dave Goulding obviously thought he was 'one of the lads', but he just kept going on and on and on and on . . .

'Of course,' he said, 'what concerns me about scenario "C" is the lack of escalation. Twenty years is far too long for a single individual to be operating. The sexual thrill should become more and more difficult to sustain as time goes on; the buzz he gets from killing and dismembering is over quicker, so he has to go out and kill again, till he's either stopped, or goes on a spree.'

Logan stuck up his hand. 'What if it's not sexual?'

The psychologist pointed at the screen behind him: chunks of meat on a mortuary table. 'It's always sexual. Sometimes it doesn't look like it, but it is. He kills, dismembers, eats: uses it to fuel the fantasy.' He frowned. 'Probably masturbatory. There was no sign Tom Stephen was penetrated pre or post mortem, and no semen recovered from the head.'

Which was a lovely image.

'But what if sex isn't the important bit?'

Goulding smiled. 'Sex is *always* the important bit. The Flesher is a classic necrophiliac.'

'But you said he doesn't have sex with the bodies, how—'

'Many necrophiliacs are sexually aroused by the *image* of death. The Flesher kills to produce a dead body he can have absolute power over. The act of murder is a means to and end, it's incidental for him. He doesn't sexually abuse the corpse, because that's not what fuels his fantasy. The Flesher practices necrophagy – the mutilation and eating of dead bodies. It's quite a fascinating subcategory of necrophilia.'

345

'But—'

DCS Bain glowered at him. 'If you have any more questions, Sergeant, I suggest you take them up with Doctor Goulding *after* the briefing. Now: moving on.'

'Sorry about that,' said Faulds, when they were back in the history room, 'didn't think he'd be so . . .'

'Boring?' Steel sat back in Logan's chair, hands wrapped around a coffee.

'I was going to say, "thorough", but "boring" works too.'

Logan tore the wrapper off his Tunnock's tea cake. 'How about "condescending"? Or "toss-pot"?'

'Anyway, I think it's a reasonable profile. We should go through our list of possible suspects and see how they stack up.'

Which led to three hours of sodding about on the whiteboard.

Logan: 'How about Catherine Davidson? Maybe they never found her remains, because she was the one doing the killing?'

Steel: 'What a *great* suggestion! Let's see how she fits the profile: oh, wait a minute, she's no' a man. Next!'

Faulds: 'What about Jamie McLaughlin? His friend is screwed up so badly he ends up in prison, but Jamie ends up writing children's books. He's a creative guy. Lives alone. Did a lot of research into the first round of killings. What's to say he's not re-enacting the death of his parents over and over again?'

Logan: 'How does he get into the abattoir to dump the remains?'

That was how they spent the rest of the morning – coming up with alternatives then picking them apart.

Finally, Faulds pushed his chair back, stretched, groaned and said, 'Lunch?'

'Wednesday's haddock and chips in the canteen.'

'Oh God, not more chips. You people never heard of salad?'

Steel bristled. 'And what the hell's wrong with chips?'

'How about sushi then?' Logan grabbed his jacket off the back of the chair and slung it over his shoulder. 'There's a little place down the market that's pretty good.'

'It's not deep-fried is it?' Faulds stood. 'Because... DI Insch – David – I was sorry to hear about your loss.'

The inspector was standing in the doorway, a huge, tent-like overcoat draped over his dark blue suit. 'I need to borrow Sergeant McRae for a couple of hours if that's OK, sir.'

'Actually' said Faulds, 'we're just on our way out for some sushi. Care to join us?'

'I'd love to sir, but I'm on a tight schedule. I've got an arsonist being transferred to Barlinnie this afternoon – Sergeant McRae was part of the initial investigation, so I'd like him there when I talk to the little sod.'

'I see...' Faulds turned to Logan. 'Well, I think we've done a good morning's work here anyway, so if you want to accompany the Inspector, I'm sure we can cover for you.'

Logan looked from the Chief Constable to Insch and back again. Watching any hope of lunch disappearing into the sunset. 'Of course, sir.'

Craiginches: the inspector hunched over the battered table in one of the prison's interview rooms, methodically chewing his way through a family-sized bag of Liquorice Allsorts. Logan stood against the wall, listening to the noises of a prison at lunchtime echoing down the corridor outside, as they waited for someone to bring Ray Williams from the canteen.

'You know,' said Insch, 'I used to really love being a policeman. Thought I was doing some good. And now look at us...' He pulled a coconut wheel from the bag and turned it over in his thick fingers, then stuck it in his mouth. 'Miriam wants a divorce. Going to emigrate to Canada and take the kids with her...'

'I'm sorry.'

'And all because I didn't catch Wiseman soon enough.'

Ray Williams – when he finally turned up – was five foot ten of shifty looks and acne scars, who wouldn't know the truth if it got up and gave him an enema. He sat on the other side of the interview table, fidgeting as Insch asked him about the night a disused factory unit in Dyce spontaneously combusted. The inspector was making a decent show of it, but Logan could tell his heart wasn't in it.

Halfway through the interview, Insch checked his watch and excused himself, returning five minutes later with three polystyrene cups of something that might have been coffee in a former life. It wasn't like the inspector to get the drinks in, but Logan wasn't complaining.

Then Williams did some more lying. No, he had no idea how that can of petrol ended up with his prints all over it. Rags soaked in accelerant, Officer? Me? Must be thinking of someone else.

There was a knock on the interview room door and a prison officer stuck her head in to tell them their one o'clock appointment was waiting next door. Logan didn't have a clue what she was on about, but Insch nodded, thanked her, and said someone would be through in about five minutes, then pointed at Williams. 'You can take this thing back to the cells if you like, I'm sick of looking at his ugly face.'

'Will do. OK, Sunshine, let's go.

'I am not ugly!'

She pulled Williams to his feet and shuffled him out of the door. 'You ever look in a mirror?'

'He's not allowed to call me ugly, is he?'

'Right,' said Insch as the voices faded down the corridor, 'let's get this over with.' He stood, and patted down the pockets of his huge overcoat. 'We should ... oh bugger. I've left the case file in the car.' The inspector glanced at Logan. 'Well: run along then. It's on the back seat and there should be a packet of Jelly Tots in there as well.'

Logan picked himself off the wall and tried not to look too pissed-off at being used as an errand boy. 'Yes, sir.'

The file was on the back seat, but there was no sign of any confectionary. Logan stuck the manila folder under his arm and wandered back into the prison. By the time he'd signed back in and made his way through to the small suite of inter-view rooms, his stomach was growling. Why couldn't Insch have waited till after lunch?

He could hear two men shouting at each other, the sound muffled behind a closed door at the far end of the corridor. One of them yelled, 'Bastard!' then there was a loud crash – fur-niture smashing into a wall. 'I'LL KILL YOU!'

Oh Christ, that was Insch.

Logan dropped the case file. It hit the ground and spilled its contents all over the corridor at his feet, only it wasn't full of statements and reports, it was full of brochures from a funeral parlour: 'SEEING YOUR CHILD SAFELY INTO THE NEXT WORLD.'

'Oh you stupid...'

He ran for the interview room, grabbed the handle and twisted.

Locked.

The whole door shook as something slammed into it from the other side. Logan aimed a kick at the lock, shouting, 'I NEED BACK-UP HERE NOW!' The door didn't give. He tried again and this time it exploded inwards.

The interview table had been ripped from the floor – the bolts that were meant to hold it down sheared off half way. It lay on its side surrounded by smashed audiovisual equipment. A huge pink fist rose behind the tabletop, then plunged down again.

Logan scrambled through the wreckage.

Insch was on the other side of the table, straddling Wiseman's chest, pinning his arms to his sides; he had one hand around the butcher's throat, throttling the life out of him. Another punch. Wiseman's head bounced back off the terrazzo flooring, bright red spurting from his nose.

Insch punched him again. More blood.

He raised his fist for another go, but Logan got there first, grabbing the inspector and hauling him backwards. They crashed into the wall just as a pair of prison officers burst through the broken door.

Wiseman coughed, sending a spume of blood into the air. It spattered down around his face in little neon droplets. He raised his hands to his face – wrists still cuffed together – and retched.

Insch struggled, arms and legs lashing out, but Logan was wrapped around him like an octopus.

'Calm down!'

'I'LL KILL HIM!' A foot went soaring past Wiseman's head. 'KILL HIM!'

The prison officers charged, and between the three of them they managed to haul Insch into the corner, forced him over onto his face and twisted his hands up behind his back.

'GET OFF ME!'

Logan staggered to his feet.

Wiseman was lying on his side, coughing up blood and bits of teeth. His face was a mess – nose flattened, one eye bright scarlet and already swelling shut, lip split, a gash on his forehead.

Insch roared again: 'I'LL FUCKING KILL HIM!'

Logan glanced round. 'Will you shut him up?'

One of the prison officers braced themselves against the wall, holding on for grim death. 'What d'you think we're trying to do?'

Wiseman's shoulders were shaking – not surprising given the going over Insch had given him . . .

And then Logan realized he was laughing. The crazy bastard was actually *laughing*. The butcher forced words out in a red froth of blood and spittle. 'You're fucked, Fatty. You hear me? Fucked!'

And he was right: there was no way in hell Insch was going to wiggle his way out of this one. He was well and truly fucked.

46

Heather stretched out on the mattress, content and full. She gave a little burp in the darkness then apologized, but Kelley didn't seem to mind.

'The pills helped then? You're sounding a lot better.'

'I *feel* a lot better.' She'd woken up to the smell of stew – rich and spicy and full of meat. 'Slept like a log.'

'You looked so peaceful.'

Heather rolled over onto her side and felt for the bars. They were cool beneath her fingers. Cool and constant. 'I wanted to be a vet when I was little. Was going to specialize in ponies and kittens.'

'What happened?'

'Didn't get enough O-levels. So what did I end up with? Answering the phone in a bloody insurance agent's.'

Kelley shuffled closer to the bars. 'I wanted to be a pilot, flying to all those exotic places you only saw on telly.'

'Did you?'

'No. Even tried to be an air hostess, but they said I wasn't glamorous enough . . .'

They lay there in the Dark.

'Do you think it's too late for me to go back to university and become a vet?'

'Course not. And I'll get my pilot's licence! We'll fly all over the world.'

Heather laughed. Then stuck her hand between the bars and grasped hold of Kelley's. 'And if anyone's got a sick pony or kitten, I can look after it.'

'And we can solve mysteries and marry international jewel thieves!'

'And the jewel thieves will really be princes, and we'll live in a big castle. And have beautiful dresses.'

'And drink champagne every night.'

'And be happy . . . ' She smiled into the darkness, holding on to Kelley's hand. Maybe life wasn't quite so bad after all. Maybe everything was going to turn out all right.

'What the hell were you thinking?' The Chief Constable paced up and down the boardroom floor, the light flashing back from the shiny silver bits on his black dress uniform. 'I was dragged out of a meeting with the Joint Police Board because one of my senior officers seriously assaulted a murder suspect. In prison. IN BLOODY HANDCUFFS!'

Handcuffed or not, Wiseman had still managed to get a couple of shots past Insch's guard. A dark red scrape sat high on the inspector's cheek, the beginnings of a bruise beginning to blossom around it. 'He provoked me.'

'He provoked . . . He was in bloody prison!' The Chief Constable picked up a couple of faxed sheets and hurled them across the table at him. 'You made a formal request in DS McRae's name to interview Wiseman as a suspect. Then you made sure the prison officer left him unattended. Then you assaulted him!'

Logan shifted in his seat and tried not to make eye contact, just in case someone dragged him even further into this mess than he already was.

Insch took the blue chill-pack off his knuckles for long enough to pick up the faxed complaint and give it a brief once over. Then tossed it back down again.

'Well, Inspector?' The CC leant on the table, looming over Insch. 'Care to tell us how this handcuffed prisoner *provoked* you?'

'He killed my daughter.'

'He . . .' The Chief Constable slammed his palm down. 'Have you any idea what you've done? Have you?' He turned and pointed at the Procurator Fiscal. 'Tell him. Tell him what you told me.'

The PF had put on her pink tweed outfit today; the cheery colour didn't go with the expression on her face. 'By assaulting Wiseman in prison you've opened up a line of attack for his defence. Now they can claim your actions prove you'll do anything for revenge. That nothing you say can be trusted.'

'Do you understand, Inspector? You've compromised this case.' The CC turned his back on the room, arms folded, glaring out of the boardroom window. 'Everything you say happened in your house is now suspect in the eyes of a jury. Instead of abduction and torture and illegal imprisonment, we'll be lucky to get causing death by reckless driving!'

Insch nodded. Not saying a word.

'I knew it was a mistake letting you come back to work. Consider yourself suspended without pay.' He turned and addressed Logan. 'I take it Ken Wiseman wants to press charges?'

Logan coughed. 'Well, maybe we—'

'Does he want to press charges?'

'Yes, sir.'

'Then we have no choice. Sergeant, take DI Insch down to the cell block and process him.'

'But—'

The CC stopped him with a finger. 'No. No buts. I will *not* turn a blind eye to one of my officers attacking a prisoner. I want him processed and stuck in a cell until the first available court slot tomorrow. Just like any other criminal.'

'Sir, Wiseman killed his daughter, surely—'

'I'm not going to ask you again, Sergeant.'

'It's OK,' said Insch, hauling himself to his feet, 'I'd do the same if it was one of my team.' He stood for a moment in silence. 'Will you have to release him?'

The PF suddenly found the buttons on her pink suit of all-consuming interest. 'We're going to have to talk about that with his solicitor. But it's possible.'

Insch turned and walked from the room.

Logan took Insch's fingerprints and DNA sample in the little breezeblock cupboard laughingly referred to as the 'processing suite' in the basement of FHQ.

'Do you want me to call Miriam?'

The fat man didn't say anything, just picked up the name board and went hunting through the rack of magnetic letters. Holding up, 'DAVID INSCH' so Logan could take his photograph.

Click. 'Turn to the right.' *Click*. 'Turn to the left.' *Click* . . .

'Are you sure you don't want me to call Miriam?'

Insch picked the letters out of his name and put them back where they'd come from, then pushed past, making for the cells.

Logan opened the door to number five, asked Insch for his shoelaces, belt and tie, then got the inspector to empty his pockets into a plastic tray. Five pounds in change. A Swiss Army Knife. A wallet with two twenties, a driver's licence, three credit cards, a Tesco club card, and three photographs: Brigit, Anna, and Sophie.

'I'd . . . ' Insch cleared his throat. 'The photos . . . '

Logan handed them over. 'What photos? I don't remember finding any photos.'

The inspector cupped them in his huge, bruised hand. Running a fat finger over Sophie's picture. 'Thank you.'

He didn't even flinch when Logan closed and locked the door.

PC Jackie Watson was waiting in the corridor outside, looking anywhere but at Logan. 'How is he?'

What was the point of lying? 'Fucked up.' He chalked Insch's name on the board beside the door.

'He . . .' She tried again. 'They're going to throw the book at him.'

'First offence, mitigating circumstances—'

'Strathclyde finished its review. We found significant shortfalls in his running of the investigation. Insch saw Ken Wiseman's name and decided he was guilty. He ignored procedure, didn't followed up leads. If it wasn't about Wiseman he didn't want to know.'

Logan stared at her. 'He's a good officer.'

'My DCI feels there's a case for negligence.' At least Jackie had the decency to look ashamed.

'But he's Insch!'

'It doesn't matter if he's Nelson Bloody Mandela. He cocked up.'

'So you're going to screw him over?'

'*I'm* not doing anything. Strathclyde were asked to review—'

'He trusted you.'

She scowled back at him. 'Don't even try to make this about me. Insch was so obsessed with Wiseman—'

'The bastard killed Sophie!'

'That's got nothing to do with it. I'm sorry, it was a horrible thing to happen, but he was obsessed *way* before that happened. It clouded his judgement.'

'Like you were obsessed with Rob Macintyre?'

Jackie froze. 'I don't know what you're talking about.'

'I covered for you. I *lied* for you.'

Pause. Two. Three. Four. 'We agreed never to talk about that again. It didn't happen.'

Logan took a step back. 'No. Of course it didn't. Nothing happened.' He looked her in the eye. 'You wanted to know why we split up? That's why. That's when it all went to shite: eighteen months ago. Not the baby, not the miscarriage, it was the night that never bloody happened.'

47

The sound of drunken singing echoed up from the women's cells downstairs as Logan handed over a wax-paper cup of coffee from the canteen. 'Busy tonight.'

Insch shrugged, took an experimental sip, and settled back on the blue plastic mattress. The rubbery coating creaked beneath him. 'Don't suppose you've got anything sweet on you?'

Logan dug out the handful of Quality Street he'd liberated from a big tin in the CCTV room. 'Chocolate might be a bit melty.'

Insch helped himself. The ice pack didn't seem to have helped much – the knuckles on his right hand had swollen up like purple Brussels sprouts. He struggled with the green foil. 'They say anything about how he is?'

'Broken nose. Couple of teeth. Cracked cheekbone.'

Nod. 'They going to let him out?'

'Why did you have to—'

'Are they going to let him out?'

Logan sighed. 'Possibly. Probably. I don't know. It's not looking good anyway.'

Insch finally managed to fight his way into the noisette triangle. 'You know he killed Brooks, don't you?'

'We've been onto the Federation: Big Gary thinks they might stump up the cash to get Hissing Sid to defend you. Maybe barter it down on account of diminished responsibility.'

'Diminished responsibility . . . ' The inspector picked his way into a toffee coin. 'I compromised the case and now they'll have to let that murdering bastard out on bail.' A predatory smile crept onto Insch's face.

'Sir? Are you OK?'

'You gave me the idea. If he goes down for thirty years I can't touch him. But if he's free . . . '

'Don't tell me you did this on purpose!'

'Ken Wiseman's going to disappear.'

'You can't *do* that! You're a police officer—'

'Was. *Was* a police officer.' He looked up at Logan, his eyes dark and empty. 'The rules don't apply any more. Ken Wiseman and I are going to spend some quality time together when he gets out.'

Logan backed towards the door. 'No. No way, you're not making me an accessory.'

'You're supposed to be my friend.'

'You're talking about abduction and murder!'

'He killed Sophie. And he killed Brooks, and he killed all those people: hacked them up and—'

'You can't just appoint yourself judge, jury and executioner! There's no evidence he—'

'My wee girl's lying in a fridge in the mortuary with her insides in plastic bags! How's that for bloody evidence?' Insch was on his feet now, his face a thunderous purple in the cell's overhead lighting. 'He'll get out and start killing again. Bastards like Wiseman don't just stop, you know that: it'll *never* end. You want that on your conscience, Sergeant? Do you?'

'No. But I won't be an accessory to murder.'

Not again.

48

'Do you have any idea what time it is?' said the woman on the other end of the phone. *'Everyone's locked down for the night – we're not supposed to disrupt their routines. You'll have to call back in the morning.'*

Logan checked his watch. Nearly eleven o'clock. The history room was littered with the 1987 case file – search reports, post mortem reports, IB reports, court transcripts, statements, psychological profiles, plastic bags full of forensic evidence: blood samples, a knife from the McLaughlin's kitchen, a hook from the derelict butcher's shop where their remains were found . . .

'I know it's late, but I need to speak to him urgently.' Logan stared at the evidence bag sitting in the middle of his desktop: a square of blood-soaked carpet cut from the boot of Ken Wiseman's car. He'd read the analysis over and over again, trying to find something, *anything* that would keep the butcher in prison where Insch couldn't get at him.

The sound went all muffled – probably a hand over the mouthpiece – and then she was back on the line again. *'Give me your number and we'll call you back.'*

Fifteen minutes later, Logan's mobile rang: HM Prison Peterhead doing as promised. There was some back and forth, then a familiar fake English accent said, *'Detective Sergeant McRae, to what do I owe—'*

'I want to know what Wiseman told you about the woman he killed.'

A pause. *'I don't think it would be very ethical of me to—'*

'You said you talked about her. What did he say?'

'Do I get my own chef?'

'What do you think?'

'Then I don't know anything.'

'Thought as much. But then you never did, did you? Pretending you're so damn smart, when we all know you couldn't count to eleven with both hands and your dick.'

'You don't get to say that to me! You don't! I spoke to my therapist and she says you're not allowed to undermine my self-esteem, you're—'

'Fuck you and fuck your self-esteem, Robertson.' Logan hung up. Trembling. Angry. Feeling sick. He grabbed the carpet and headed for the IB lab on the third floor. Calling Angus Robertson had been a stupid idea.

He got as far as the lab door before his phone went again. HMP Peterhead phoning back.

'He told me about it, OK? At night, when he thought everyone else was asleep. He told me about cutting her up. How it wasn't like butchering an animal. How the meat didn't lie the same along the bones. How sick it made him feel.'

'Who was she?'

'He buried everything out by Bennachie. Said it was all lies: he didn't eat anyone.'

'Who – was – she?'

'It was money. I think it was money . . . She had something, or was connected to something . . .'

'Will you focus? Who did Wiseman kill?'

'Something . . . something about . . .' Robertson sounded as if he was on the verge of tears. *'I can't remember . . .'*

A voice in the background: *'Angus, if this is upsetting you, you can stop. You don't have to do this.'*

'I don't know who she is. I used to know. I did! I used to know, but now I can't remember.'

'It's OK, give me the phone.' Rustle, clunk. *'Hello? DS McRae?'*

'Put Robertson back on: I need a name.'

'Angus is upset, I—'

'Oh boo-bloody-hoo. I need to know who Wiseman killed.'

She was obviously trying to keep her voice level. *'He was stabbed a couple of years ago; lost a lot of blood. There were some complications with the anaesthetic during the operation. There are some things he can't remember, it's very frustrating for him.'*

'It's no picnic this end either. I want to know—'

'I think you could show a little sympathy for a human being in pain, Sergeant.'

'A fellow human . . . He murdered fifteen women and raped their dying bodies! Now put the bastard back on the phone.'

'That's it – this interview is over. I'll be making a formal complaint about your behaviour, Sergeant. How dare you—'

'Yeah? Well when he's stabbed *you* twenty-three times, you can lecture me on my bloody empathy skills.'

But she'd already hung up.

Logan stuck the phone back in his pocket – already starting to feel guilty about acting like an arsehole – and pushed through into the IB lab. They'd obviously not managed to fix the little stereo on top of the freezer, because Radio Two was still playing. Three IB technicians in white lab coats and latex gloves slouched around the central desk, drinking cups of tea and moaning about having to still be there in the middle of the night, testing mounds of mystery meat.

Logan dumped the evidence bag full of carpet on the desktop and asked if someone could do him a quick favour.

Samantha – the Identification Bureau's one and only Goth – brushed a long, dark curl from her pale face, and asked if he was taking the piss. 'We've got about nine million hunks of meat to get through.'

'It's for Insch.'

She prodded the bag with a chewed biro. 'What is it?'

'Blood-soaked carpet from nineteen ninety—'

'Oh Jesus. You not think we've got more urgent stuff to test?'

'It's from Wiseman's car: animal and human. They couldn't separate the DNA strands back then.'

Samantha picked up the bag and peered at the rust-brown contents. 'This stuff's nearly twenty years old.'

'Yes, but you're twenty years brighter than they were.'

'You really think shameless flattery's going to work?'

'Twenty years prettier too ... in a scary *Night of the Living Dead* kind of way.'

She tried to scowl, but a smile broke through. 'You're a rotten sod...'

'Come on, bump it to the top of the queue. It's important.'

'I can't—'

'Very important.'

Sigh. 'OK, OK. I'll see what I can do.'

Phone. Ringing. 'Phhhhh...' Logan tried to sit up in bed, but none of his limbs were working. The answering machine must have kicked in, because there was silence and then a *bleeeeeeeep*.

Roll over. Pull duvet into cocoon. Sleep.

The phone started up again.

Logan squinted at the alarm clock: twenty-one minutes past four. He slumped back into the pillows and scrubbed his face with his hands, listening to the phone warble. 'Urrrrgh...'

He padded through into the lounge, just in time to hear the answering machine finish its pre-recorded invitation to leave a message. The speaker crackled for a moment, and then a woman's voice said, *'Bloody hell, ask someone to do you a favour and—'*

He snatched the phone out of its cradle. 'Hello?'

'What took you so long?'

A yawn shuddered it's way free. 'It's half four . . .'

'I managed to separate out the human DNA from the rest of the garbage in your carpet sample, and yes, it was a vast pain in the arse, thank you for asking. Took bloody hours to amplify enough of it to make a viable sample.'

Logan plonked himself down on the couch. 'Mmmph?' Another yawn.

'Ran it through the database. Guess what: no direct hit.'

'Bastard . . . Sorry, I suppose it was a long—'

'No direct *hit, but I did get what looks like a familial one.'* She gave it a dramatic count of five before continuing. *'Want to guess who?'*

But Logan already knew: 'Richard Davidson – he's in Craiginches doing three years for possession, perjury, and aggravated assault. His mum disappeared the night the McLaughlins were killed.' They finally knew what happened to her.

'What? No, Ken Wiseman. *It would have been close enough to look like his blood in the mid nineties when they did the appeal, but it's not. It's female. You're looking for his aunt, mother—'*

'Sister. Kirsty McFarlane. She was supposed to have run off with an electrician eighteen years ago.'

Showered, shaved and feeling like shit, Logan waited for PC Munro to park the pool car, then climbed out into the cold November morning. Half past five and it was still pitch dark, the hollow streetlights glowing like wet gold against the indigo sky.

Munro locked the car and yawned, her breath a thin white cloud as she shook herself. 'Still don't see why this couldn't wait till later . . .'

McFarlane's butcher shop had been given another graffiti makeover – four-letter words sprayed all over the plywood sheeting that covered the broken windows.

'I mean, the guy's going to be asleep and—'

'Just ring the doorbell.'

She shook her head, muttering to herself as she stomped up to the butcher's front door, then stopped, staring at the door-frame.

Logan stuck his hands in his pockets and waited. 'Today would be nice.'

'There's dog shite on the bell.' She prodded the door with the toe of her shoe and it swung open. 'Lock's busted. Looks like it's been kicked in.'

All that graffiti: 'MURDERING BASTARD!', 'CANNIBAL', 'DEATH'S TOO GOOD FOR YOU!', 'ENGLISH OUT' . . . Logan told her to call it in. 'Tell them we've got a B-and-E, possibly in progress. House-holder's life's been threatened.'

'Oh crap . . .' She grabbed the Airwave handset from her shoulder and got onto Control as Logan stepped quietly over the threshold and into the long, dark hallway. The walls were covered in spray paint: profanity, threats, and 'UP THE DONS!'

He stopped at the foot of the stairs.

A faint glow of light broke the gloom from somewhere under the stairs. Logan crept round. It was coming from the internal entrance to the butcher's shop. The door was almost shut, but he could make out a torch shining on a paint-spattered wall. Mumbled singing, the words soft and slurred, the tune unrecognizable.

Logan eased the door open.

McFarlane was dressed up in his butcher's outfit – white coat, blue stripy apron, little white porkpie hat, sloshing petrol from a green plastic can all over the shattered deli counter. He gave a sudden lurch to the left, legs stiff beneath him as he tried to stay upright, getting petrol all down his trousers, and then he was stable again.

'Let me guess,' said Logan, stepping into the devastation, 'you're having a going-out-of-business barbecue?'

McFarlane spun round, petrol and legs going everywhere as he slipped and crashed down on his backside. 'We . . .' For a second he looked as if he was about to be sick. 'We're shut.' And then he was – all over himself.

The butcher's flat was oppressively warm, which only made the smell worse. McFarlane sat on the immaculate couch, in his immaculate lounge, wearing an apron stained with petrol and vomit. He cradled a silver photo frame against his chest, ignoring the cup of strong black coffee on the table in front of him as Logan introduced PC Munro.

Throwing up seemed to have done McFarlane the world of good. If it wasn't for the stink and the bloodshot eyes he could almost have passed for sober. 'I'm ... I'm sorry ... ' He blinked back a tear. 'I didn't know what else to do ... twenty years I spent, building up the business ... I thought if no one got hurt ... I mean it's not as if the insurance company haven't had their pound of flesh from me over the years, is it? ... Place was ruined anyway ... '

'I'm afraid we've got some bad news, Andrew.'

The butcher didn't look up. 'I didn't have any choice ... '

'It's about your wife, Kirsty. We retested the carpet from Ken Wiseman's car boot – the human blood wasn't his, it was Kirsty's.'

McFarlane screwed his face into a knot, clutching the photo tighter. 'She was everything to me. Everything ... '

'PC Munro is a Family Liaison officer, she'll—'

'He killed her.'

'We think so. He told the guy in the next cell—'

'I watched him ... I watched him cut her up ... ' He buried his head in his hands and sobbed.

Logan looked from the vomit-soaked butcher to PC Munro and back again. Trying not to grin. They had a witness – after all these years, they *finally* had something on Wiseman.

49

'Where the hell have you been?' Big Gary grabbed Logan as soon as he got back to FHQ. Quarter past seven and the place had that calm-before-the-storm feeling to it. As if something nasty was lurking just around the corner with a baseball bat.

'The Chief Constable's going ballistic.' Big Gary thrust a copy of that morning's *News of the World* into Logan's hands: 'DI BEATS HANDCUFFED SUSPECT'. 'As your Federation Rep I need to see your statement about what happened *before* you hand it in to Professional Standards.'

'Too late, I did it yesterday.'

'You . . . ?' The huge sergeant grimaced. 'What the hell did you do that for? Thought you were supposed to be his friend!'

'That's why I'm trying to save the daft bastard from himself.' Logan skimmed through the article. 'Where's Steel?'

'Where do you think?'

He started for the door. 'Get someone to pick Wiseman up and stick him in an interview room.'

'No. Hoy – paper!' Big Gary stuck out his hand.

'What do you mean, "no"?'

'One: I'm not your bloody secretary, and two: he's in court first thing – they're thinking about letting the murdering bastard go, remember?'

'Bloody hell ... When?'

'Eight.'

Logan dragged out his phone and started dialling.

Aberdeen Sheriff Court was an imposing granite building at the bottom end of Union Street, sandwiched between the Council chambers and the Tollbooth Museum. They'd convened Wiseman's hearing in one of the small courts – a converted jury room tucked away down a side corridor – and it was a closed session, so Logan was forced to wait outside, nodding at the lawyers he knew, the police officers he worked with, and the shoplifters he'd arrested.

It was nearly twenty to ten when the doors finally opened and someone from the Procurator Fiscal's office stormed out, muttering darkly. Which wasn't exactly a good sign. Next it was a couple of clerks, the Sheriff, and finally Ken Wiseman, flanked by two prison officers.

His lawyer had shovelled him into a grey suit, the formal attire not really going with the collection of bruises and swellings. The butcher's face looked like a mouldy pumpkin, bisected by that white line of old scar tissue.

Logan stepped up. 'Kenneth Wiseman—'

A balding woman stepped in front of him. 'It's OK, Ken, you don't have to talk to him.'

Wiseman pulled his swollen face into something that might have been a smile. 'They fired that fat fuck yet?'

The butcher's lawyer placed her hand against her client's chest. '*Please*, let me deal with this.' She looked back at Logan. 'Mr Wiseman has nothing to say to you.'

'No? Well I've got something to say to him—'

'Threatening my client will—'

'They had fuck all on me in 1990, and they've got fuck all on me now.' Wiseman stepped forwards, but the prison officers took hold of his arms. 'That bastard Brooks fitted me up and I—'

'Kenneth, I must insist—'

'For what it's worth,' said Logan, 'I believe you. Brooks screwed up the original investigation. You're not the Flesher, you never were.'

The butcher opened his mouth to say something, then shut it again, a puzzled look oozing out between the bruises. 'I ... yeah, the appeal—'

'But you're still a killer. Kenneth Wiseman, I'm arresting you on suspicion of the murder of Kirsty McFarlane, also known as Kirsty Wiseman, in February 1990. You do not have to say anything—'

'But ... but you can't ... I was ...' He grabbed his lawyer's sleeve as Logan read him his rights. 'They can't prosecute me for the same thing twice. Double jeopardy. Tell him!'

And it was Logan's turn to smile. 'You were tried for the murders of Ian and Sharon McLaughlin, *not* Kirsty McFarlane. So—'

The lawyer stepped in again. 'I insist you let me speak to my client in private, we—'

'You can have him back when I've finished with him.' Logan turned to the two prison officers. 'How do you fancy escorting Mr Wiseman round to the station?'

The butcher was too shocked to struggle.

Interview Room Number Three was like a sauna – as usual – a thin film of condensation furring the double glazed window, while Ken Wiseman sat and sweated. 'I ... I didn't do anything ...'

It was as if someone had pulled the plug, letting all the cocky bastard drain away, leaving a scarred, scared, middle-aged, balding bloke.

Steel stretched out in her plastic seat. 'That, Ken, is what we in the business call a "fucking lie".'

The butcher ran a hand across his battered face, wrists still handcuffed together. 'It wasn't me ...'

Logan slapped a small stack of paper down on the table – Andrew McFarlane's statement. 'Your brother-in-law says you were drunk. Got into an argument with your sister.'

'That's not—'

Logan read it out loud: '"Kirsty slapped him and he went mental. He wouldn't stop hitting her. I—"'

'That's not how it happened!'

'—tried to stop him, but he was too strong.'

'No!'

'I wanted to call the police, but he wouldn't let me.'

'He's lying!' Wiseman battered his fist off the tabletop, hard enough to crack the fibreglass cast. 'He's lying . . . '

'He dragged her body into the butchery and—'

'That's not what happened!' He stared at the dent he'd made in the Formica, chewing on his split bottom lip. 'We'd . . . we'd been out on the piss. All three of us, up the Malt Mill on a Friday night. Kirsty was hammered – they were supposed to be celebrating their anniversary. She started saying stuff . . . When we got back to the flat, she tore into Andrew: he was a useless tosser; crap lay; had a tiny dick; she was having an affair . . . '

'Then what?'

'I don't know . . . I was hammered. Got a bottle of vodka out the freezer and next thing I know it's three am in the morning. I'm lying on the couch and Andrew's shaking me. He's crying and going on about how it wasn't his fault – she was going to leave him . . . '

Wiseman looked up, then straight back down again. 'She was lying at the bottom of the stairs, all twisted and . . . and her head was . . . She was already cold. There wasn't anything I could do.'

He shrugged, big muscular shoulders rising and falling. 'We panicked. She was dead. And . . . Andrew said we had to get rid of her. That if we called the police the business would be ruined. That no one would care if it was an accident or not. And ... the butcher's shop was right there.'

'She was your *sister*!'

Wiseman started picking at the crack in his cast. 'She was always ... Andrew wasn't just my brother-in-law, he was my best friend... We vacuum-packed the bits and buried them out in the middle of nowhere. Only...' Shudder. 'The bag with her insides got caught on the boot catch. Went every-where. I ... we had to scoop the bits out with our bare hands...'

'What do you think?' asked Logan, when Ken Wiseman was back in his cell.

'He's a silly bastard.' Steel pulled out her cigarettes and stuck one in her mouth, flicking it from one side to the other with her tongue. 'If he'd come clean when they arrested him, he'd've got what? Four, five years for illegally disposing of a body and not reporting a death? Would've been out in three.' She sighed. 'Silly, silly bastard.'

'I meant – do you believe he only helped cut up the body? that she was already dead when he got there?'

Steel shrugged. 'Don't think it really matters anymore if he did it or not. The PF'll do him for murder and he'll get another sixteen years. It'll be his word against McFarlane's, and who's a jury going to believe: an alki butcher, or good old Ken – Murdering Bastard – Wiseman? Anyway,' she fidgeted with her lighter, not looking Logan in the eye, 'I suppose now someone's got to tell Insch.'

And Logan got a nasty feeling who that someone was going to be.

50

According to the custody assistant, Insch's five-minute appearance in the Sheriff Court that morning had provoked a media circus and ended up with the inspector released on bail and into the ever-loving arms of Professional Standards. Which was a bit like being kicked in the testicles, smeared in marmite, then thrown to the sharks. He was still up there now.

Logan got himself a newspaper and a cup of tea, then settled into one of the uncomfortable chairs outside the Professional Standards office. Bracing himself for a long wait with a punch on the nose at the end of it.

'You're an utter bastard!'

Logan looked up from his *Aberdeen Examiner* – 'Grieving DI Attacks Murder Suspect' – to see Wee Fat Alec glowering down at him, HDV camera in hand. 'Morning Alec.'

'Why didn't you tell me you were going to arrest Wiseman? You *know* I'm supposed to—'

'There wasn't time, OK? I only found out at half four this morning.'

'I thought we were a team!'

Sigh. 'Look, Alec—'

The door through to Professional Standards burst open and DI Insch stormed out: face dark purple, little flecks of spittle around his mouth, eyes like angry pickled eggs. He barged past, making for the stairs.

Logan hurried after him. 'Inspector?'

'Not any more!' Insch slammed through the stairwell doors, making them boom off the walls. 'BASTARDS!'

'About Ken Wiseman . . .'

'How many years have I given this place?' He took the stairs two at a time.

'Sir, we ... I arrested him this morning.'

Insch froze. Voice low and dangerous. 'You did *what*?'

Alec finally caught up with them, his camera focused on the inspector's furious face. Logan held a hand in front of the lens. 'Switch that damn thing off—'

'What the fuck did you do?'

'Wiseman was involved in his sister's death. That's where the blood came from in 1990. There was an argument, maybe an accident and—'

Insch grabbed Logan by the lapels and thumped him back against the wall. 'I *told you*! I wanted him out, not behind bloody bars!'

'I couldn't let you—' BANG: back against the wall again. This time Insch let go, and marched off, Alec scurrying after him. BOOM: through the doors. Leaving Logan to slump, swear, then follow on behind.

The inspector bulldozed his way into reception, shoved past a pair of constables and out into the rain. The sky was battleship-grey above the rain-battered granite buildings, making it difficult to tell where the city stopped and the downpour began. Logan splashed after Insch and the cameraman, catching up to them just outside the District Court.

'Wait, you need to—'

Insch spun, wrapped a huge fist into Logan's jacket and threw him to the floor. 'I TRUSTED YOU!' The fat man loomed, bald head dripping, suit slowly turning funeral black as the rain soaked into it.

'It was all Brooks' fault. Wiseman isn't the Flesher, never was.'

'You knew I needed him outside—'

Logan sat up, feeling the cold puddle soaking through his trousers. 'He's not the Flesher. He went after Brooks because he set him up – he came after you, because you helped. If Brooks had done his bloody job none of this would have happened. Sticking Wiseman in Peterhead Prison made him what he is today.' He groaned his way to his feet. 'It was a self-fulfilling prophesy.'

Insch looked as if he was about to burst: face dark scarlet, lips pulled back like a snarling dog, thin breaths hissing in and out between his gritted teeth.

Alec peered round the side of his camera. 'Inspector? Are you OK?'

'You . . .' Grimace. 'You . . .' One hand went to the middle of his chest, fingers splayed. Then curled into a fist. 'You . . .' Mouth open, no sound coming out as Insch's legs gave way.

On his knees. One hand against the cold, wet concrete paving slab, the other massaging his chest.

And then he was face down, the rain bouncing off his suddenly pale head.

'Oh fuck . . .' Logan scrambled through the puddles and stuck two fingers to the side of Insch's throat. 'Fuck!'

'Is he OK?'

'Get the duty doctor – hurry!' Logan pulled out his mobile phone and called for an ambulance.

51

Quarter past four and the traffic was starting to get heavy – the school-run clogging up the side streets with four-by-fours and badly parked Audi estates. Union Street was one long shuffling procession of scarlet brake lights – nose-to-tail all the way, with an unmarked CID pool car stuck in the middle. 'Sorry, sir,' said Rennie as they chugged to a halt, yet again. 'Thought this would be quicker than Schoolhill, it's a sodding nightmare when Robert Gordon's lets out. Should've gone left to Mounthooly . . .'

Logan shrugged – it wasn't as if they were in a hurry.

The rain hadn't let up any – water hitting the pavement hard enough to bounce back to knee height, hiding the ground in a sheen of mist between the crawling traffic and the hurrying pedestrians.

Not every school kid had a parental taxi booked, some marched down the pavement with their schoolbags over their heads, others shared brightly coloured golf umbrellas. A million miles away from murders and heart attacks.

Logan watched a pack of Robert Gordon students stream into McDonalds, a sign in the window proclaiming, 'NOW WITH 100% IMPORTED BEEF!'

Rennie drummed an annoying tattoo on the steering wheel. 'Going to buy a house and ask Laura to marry me.' He turned and grinned. 'How cool is that? Course, we won't get married right away, I mean she's got to finish her degree first. And kids can wait till we're older. You know, like in our thirties, or something . . . '

Logan let him rattle on. Why burst his little bubble?

'Going to honeymoon in Vegas. Maybe get married there too? What do you think? Elvis Presley now pronounces you man and wife . . . or is that too cheesy?'

'Pretty cheesy.'

'Sometimes cheesy is good.'

The traffic ground to a halt again at the junction with Union Terrace. On the other side of the road a gaggle of schoolgirls – all wearing the green jumpers and tartan skirts of Albyn School – waited for the cars and buses cutting across Union Street to give way to the little green man.

They laughed and joked, smoked, listened to iPods, sent text messages to their friends, peered in shop windows . . .

Logan frowned. Then slapped Rennie on the arm. 'Look!'

'What?' The constable glanced across the road. 'Jesus, never figured you for a dirty old man.'

'No, you idiot: *her*. The one with the red and green brolly. Blonde. Does Laura have a little sister?'

'Eh? No, she's . . . ' Rennie was staring at the girls again, face going pale. Without the makeup, tiny skirt and hoiked-up boobs, Laura didn't look quite the same as she had in the pub the other night, but it was definitely her. 'Ffff . . . oh . . . Fuck!'

'What do you think? Sixteen? Higher? Lower?'

'Fuck!'

'Not so much your pretend kinky schoolgirl, as an *actual* schoolgirl.'

'FUCK!'

'You were saying something about dirty old men?'

The intensive care ward was quiet, just the hum and ping of machinery to break the gloomy silence. Insch was wired up to a bank of equipment, little round sticky pads on the pale pink expanse of his chest; an oxygen mask strapped over his mouth, misty with condensation; another pulse monitor on the end of his finger.

The inspector's wife, Miriam, was sitting by his bedside, sniffing into a handkerchief, looking twenty years older than she should have.

Logan stopped at the end of the bed. 'How is he?'

She looked up, saw who it was, then went back to staring at her husband. 'They're waiting to see if ... he needs to be stronger, or they can't operate.'

'We ... ' Logan gave an embarrassed cough, and held up the massive get-well-soon card in the shape of a teddy bear. 'Everyone signed it. We ... ' Another cough. 'You know he's too damn stubborn to give up.'

'It all went so wrong ... '

Brilliant evening. Spectacular. Like a hole in the head.

Vicky clambered out of the car and plipped the locks. Sodding Marcus and his sodding parents and this sodding, GODFORSAKEN DINNER PARTY tomorrow night. All over town looking for organic sodding lamb in the rain ... If Marcus wanted roast lamb with sodding baby vegetables to impress his sodding parents, he could sodding well get out here and help her unload the car.

She tried the front door, but it was locked. 'Oh for God's sake.' As if anyone was going to break in while he was there – and she knew he was in: his car was in the drive and all the lights were on. She tried her key, but it wouldn't turn. The idiot had left *his* key in the lock.

Vicky leant on the doorbell. 'Come on Marcus! Answer the sodding door!'

She took two steps back and scowled up at their three bed-room semi-detached rabbit hutch. He was probably in the toilet making smells and reading Dilbert, or one of his 'post-modern-ironic' lads' mags. Yeah, young ladies getting their boobs out. Very post-sodding-modern.

'MARCUS!'

Nothing.

'Sodding hell.' She turned and stomped back down the drive. Fine, if Captain Useless wasn't going to help her, she'd just have to— She heard the door unlocking behind her.

Vicky turned, hands up in mock rapture. 'Halleluiah!'

Only there was nobody there. The lazy sod had unlocked the door and disappeared back into the house. You know what? *Fine*. She'd unload the car on her own, and if Marcus thought he was getting any sex for the next month he was going to be *very* disappointed. He could go have a post-modern-ironic wank for all she cared.

She threw her handbag over her shoulder, grabbed as many carrier bags as she could manage and staggered back up the drive, her high heels clicking on the wet lockblock. In through the front door. The television was on: some pretentious late-night discussion programme droning on about a book no one would ever read. Why couldn't he watch the sodding Simp-sons like a normal person? That's what she got for marrying someone called *Marcus*.

She stomped down the hall, calling, 'They're your sodding parents, you know. You could help!'

No response.

Typical. She pushed through into the kitchen/dining room. He was such a useless ... She stopped. Eyes wide.

Red.

Everything was red.

There was red everywhere.

The smell of hot copper and sea salt.

Raw meat.

Something that used to be a man was laid out on the kitchen table. In bits. She could ... she could...

Clunk.

The front door closing.

Snick.

The front door locking.

RUN!

Vicky didn't look back, just dropped her shopping and charged straight though the kitchen, heels skidding on the blood-slicked linoleum. She grabbed the patio door handle, but it wouldn't budge. Locked. Sodding Marcus!

Key in the lock. KEY IN THE LOCK!

She turned it and yanked the door open, throwing herself out into the night ... which wasn't dark for long as the back garden security light glared into life.

She slipped and fell, sprawling across the wet grass, and for a moment she was looking back into the kitchen. And came within an inch of wetting herself. It was him, the man from the papers: butcher's outfit, Margaret Thatcher mask, knife.

Marcus's head was staring back at her from under the table.

Vicky scrambled to her feet, grabbed her handbag, and ran.

Down the garden, heels sinking into the sodden turf. She wrenched the damn shoes off, leaving them behind.

Past the shed.

She could hear *Him*: the Flesher was coming after her.

She clambered over the back fence, ripping her jacket as she tumbled down the other side and into a gorse bush, not caring if the thorns tore her skin, just as long as she lived to see tomorrow.

She ran, tearing down the little gully that separated her street from the next one in the development, screaming 'HELP ME!' at the top of her lungs. Until she realized that gave the man chasing her something to aim for.

She concentrated on putting as much distance between them as possible instead.

Mobile phone. She had a mobile phone in her handbag. She had to call the police.

The Flesher crashed through the undergrowth behind her.

Vicky took a sudden dive to the left, into the grass, scurrying behind a huge whin bush. Holding her breath. Praying.

She could see him: a faint silhouette against the orange-grey clouds.

Phone. Where was her phone? Where was her sodding, bloody, fucking phone?

Vicky tipped her handbag out into the wet grass and felt her way through the contents: compact, tampons, purse, brush, credit card wallet, bits of paper, more bits of paper, more BITS OF BLOODY PAPER. Comb. Lipstick. PHONE!

She flipped it open and the screen sent out a little bloom of light. She slapped her hand over the thing, trying to hide the glow. Praying he wasn't looking this way. Jesus, Jesus, Jesus . . .

Nine. Nine. Nine.

Come on, come on . . .

'Emergency services, which service do you require?'

'Police.'

'I'm sorry, you'll have to speak up, you're very faint.'

Vicky cupped her hand over the mouthpiece and whispered 'Police!' as loud as she dared.

Now all she had to do was tell the man on the other end who was after her, where they were, and—

The silhouette stopped, turned left, then right, then marched straight towards her.

Vicky ran.

52

One woman screaming would have been bad enough, but two of them going at it like blue-rinse foghorns was doing PC McInnis's head in. Kingswells was meant to be a sleepy little commuter town, not a septuagenarian war zone: the battle line drawn through a dying leylandii hedge. Both sides were squaring off outside a pair of identical yellow-brick boxes, ignoring the misty drizzle that drifted down from the cold November sky as they screamed at each other.

McInnis had another go: 'Look, can we all please calm down. We—'

'This was a nice place to live before you moved in!'

'Oh why don't you go shove a cactus up your—'

'Ladies, if we can just—'

'Should be ashamed of yourself!'

'Just because *you've* got cobwebs growing down there doesn't mean the rest of us can't have sex!'

'Don't you talk to me like that!'

PC Guthrie had retreated back to the patrol car, out of the rain – lazy bastard – leaving McInnis to play United Nations. 'Ladies, why don't we go inside and—'

'There's a wee thing called Viagra. You should get some for your William, maybe perk the poor old sod up a bit. God knows he could use it.'

'How dare you!'

'If we could all just—'

Guthrie stuck his head out of the car window and shouted: 'McInnis!'

'I'm *busy*.' He turned back to his battling pensioners. 'I need you both to—'

'Someone's spotted the Flesher in Kingswells: three streets from here!'

'Holy shit!'

He sprinted back to the car and jumped in behind the wheel, ignoring the outraged cry of, 'What about my bloody hedge?'

McInnis put his foot down, leaving two smoking trails of rubber behind.

The whole car shuddered as he slammed on the brakes. Lights and siren blaring. First on the scene.

They leapt out of the car and swept the undergrowth on either side of the road with torchlight. Raindrops glittered in the beams like shards of falling glass as the drizzle gave way to proper pelting-it-down rain.

It was a stretch of wasteland between two housing developments, tarted up with a tarmac path and a couple of streetlights. PC Guthrie took a couple of steps into the darkness and bellowed, 'MRS YOUNG?'

'How's she supposed to hear you? Turn off the siren!'

And the night was suddenly quiet – just the drumming of rain on the car roof, the soft hiss of it falling on trees and bushes, and the gurgle of the stream at the bottom of the ravine.

McInnis had a go. 'MRS YOUNG? VICKY? IT'S THE POLICE!'

'There's got to be miles of scrub and bushes out here.'

'MRS YOUNG?'

A new sound joined the *shhhhhhhhhhhhhhhhhh* of rain – distant sirens as patrol cars hammered along the Hazlehead Road, more coming over the back from Bucksburn. The cavalry was on its way.

'Did Control say where she was—'

A woman screamed.

'Over there!' McInnis ignored the path and half-ran, half-scrambled down the slippery embankment with Guthrie hot on his heels, torchlight bobbing across wet grass, stones and bushes.

'MRS YOUNG?'

They slithered to a halt at the foot of the slope, rain drumming off their peaked caps and black jackets. 'OK,' said Guthrie, 'you go left, I'll go right.'

McInnis snorted. 'Bugger that! If the Flesher's out here we should stick together, so—'

'Don't be such a big jessie. There's a woman out there getting murdered, remember?' He stumbled off into the downpour, following the beam of his LED torch. It wasn't long before he was swallowed by the night.

McInnis swore, then waded out into the knee-high grass. This was ridiculous – probably just a hoax, or some kinky sex game gone wrong, like those idiots in Northfield with all the tomato sauce. Nothing was going to happen. False alarm.

He swung his torch across a mountain range of gorse bushes.

'MRS YOUNG?'

He didn't see the patch of mud that sent him sprawling. One minute he was upright, and the next he was lying flat on his back, watching his torch spin through the air . . . It came down somewhere deep inside the prickly bushes – clattering through the branches till it finally hit the ground. 'FUCK!'

A pause, then the Airwave handset on his shoulder started ringing: Guthrie. *'Are you OK? What happened? You need help?'*

There was no way McInnis was going to say he'd slipped and fallen on his arse. 'I'm fine. Dropped my torch.'

'*Moron.*'

'Up yours.' McInnis ended the call and struggled to his feet. Everything was soaked through: trousers, jacket, socks, T-shirt, pants. 'Bloody marvellous . . . ' He could see the faint gleam of his torch leaching out beneath the line of gorse bushes. For a second he considered just leaving the damn thing, but it wasn't as if he could get any wetter.

He edged his way forward in the dark.

The torch was no more than a couple of feet from the outer cordon of spines. McInnis hunkered down and tried to reach it.

Thorns scratched the back of his hand as he fumbled in the shadows. Stupid bloody torch. Come on . . . Branch, rock, something horrible and sticky – please not dog shit, please not dog shit— torch! McInnis grabbed it, thankful no one had seen him make an absolute tit of himself.

And as the torch came out of the bush, its beam glittered back from something dark and oily. Blood. His hand was covered in blood. There was something white further back. It was a foot.

McInnis froze, then slid the beam up: ankle, leg, thigh, buttock . . . a woman, lying on her front, naked except for a pair of control-top knickers and a substantial bra. Her neck had been slashed so deeply the head was barely attached. Very, very dead.

'Oh, Jesus.' He sat back on his haunches. Mouth open wide as the rain hammered down all around him. He reached for his Airwave handset and punched in Guthrie's badge number.

It was picked up on the second ring. '*Aye?*'

'It . . . I've found her.'

'*She OK?*'

Pause. 'No. She's . . . ' he drifted to a halt, all the hairs standing up on the back of his neck. The sound of the rain had changed – the soft hammering of water on vegetation had been

384

overlaid with a new, harder noise. As if there was something else ... *someone* else there.

'What?'

McInnis stood. Trying to pretend he hadn't noticed anything. Oh-shit-oh-shit-oh-shit.

'Where are you?'

He whipped round, snatching his baton from his belt, ready to crack the bastard's head open ... But there was nobody there. Just the rain and the bushes and the weeds and the grass and the darkness.

'McInnis: what the hell's going on?'

Idiot. Scaring himself like that. He turned back towards the bush. 'Nothing. We need to get the IB out here and ...' The Flesher was standing right in front of him.

'Oh,' McInnis could barely get the words out, 'shit.'

And then the Flesher hit him.

Darkness.

'Ah Jesus!' McInnis sat up, coughing, water streaming down his face, a bright light shining in his eyes.

'You OK?'

Everything smelt of blood. 'Where ...?'

Guthrie peered at him. 'Bloody hell! What happened to your nose?'

McInnis shuddered, spat, and held out a hand, getting Guthrie to haul him to his feet. 'How long?'

'Is she in there?' Pointing at the bush.

'How long was I out for?' Another shudder. His nose felt as if it was on fire.

'Not long. A minute? Two? I saw your torch: nearly killed myself getting here. Tore the arse right out my trousers.'

McInnis wiped a hand across his mouth, it came away covered in red. 'He was here: the Flesher. I *saw* him!'

'Which way did he go?'

'I don't bloody know, do I?'

The wailing sirens were getting louder – flashing blue lights bouncing along the road as a patrol car San Franciscoed over the speed humps, making for Vicky Young's address. He could hear another one on the opposite side of the ravine. They could still catch the bastard.

McInnis swept his torch over the surrounding grass and bushes. Three tracks led away into the damp undergrowth. One went up the hill, back towards the patrol car, another headed off to the right – where Guthrie said he'd come from – and the third snaked away to the left.

McInnis staggered into a run, following the trail of flattened grass.

'What about the body? We can't just leave—'

'She's not getting any deader, is she?'

There was a stream at the bottom of the ravine, swollen by the torrential rain. Guthrie slithered to a halt at the water's edge. He was on his Airwave handset again, telling Control where the body was, while McInnis tried to work out which way the bastard had gone.

Upstream, downstream ... no sign of flattened grass on the other bank.

McInnis picked his way around a small pile of boulders, following the course of the stream. Heading away from the road.

'Aye,' Guthrie waved his torch back towards the patrol car, 'down here, we're in pursuit of—'

McInnis froze. 'Will you shut up a minute?'

'Look, I'm only trying to—'

'Shhhh!' There was a clump of brittle whin, six foot further up the slope, its seed husks rattling in the downpour. Not quite loud enough to hide the faint sound of sobbing coming from inside the bush.

Pulling out his pepper spray, McInnis inched forwards. 'Police! Come out with your hands up and no one gets hurt.'

Guthrie crept round the other side. They made eye contact for a second and McInnis mouthed, 'On three.'

One.

Two.

Three: Guthrie grabbed the nearest branch and yanked it back. The person hiding in there squealed and tried to scrabble away, but there was nowhere to go. It was a woman: mid to late forties; only partially dressed – pale skin glowing in the torchlight; no shoes; her trousers ripped and stained, her blouse torn, the buttons missing, the material soaked with bright red blood.

McInnis put the pepper spray away and held out his hand. 'You're going to be OK.'

She squirmed back against the branches, clutching a big leather handbag in front of her like a shield. Her bruised face was twisted and filthy. 'Don't touch me! Please don't touch me! *Please!*'

'It's OK. We're the police. You're safe now.'

'Please . . .'

McInnis straightened up and ran his torchlight across the rain-hammered night. There was no way they could leave her alone out here in the dark while they went after the Flesher.

'Son of a rancid bitch.'

The bastard had got away.

53

'Who stinks like a brewery?' DI Steel, turned in her seat to sniff at Logan. 'You bathe in beer this morning?'

The briefing room was full, everyone waiting for DCS Bain to turn up and hand out the morning assignments. Up till now the discussion had been exclusively Flesher-related: speculation and rumour leaving reality far behind as the tale of PC McInnis's clash with Aberdeen's most notorious serial killer was told and retold.

Logan pointed at the green-faced constable sitting next to him. 'That's Rennie you can smell. He went for the world record vodka-and-Red-Bull-get-pissed-quick-athon last night.'

'Oh, aye?' The inspector grinned. 'And there was me thinking our wee boy looked like shite 'cos he'd been up all night shagging Luscious Laura.'

Rennie went pale, and then bright red. 'Not feeling too good.'

'If you're going to puke, do it in that direction: Laz's suit needs a good clean, he won't mind.'

'No one's being sick on anyone. We—' Logan sat up straight. 'Look out: Bain.'

The Detective Chief Superintendent had finally appeared –
Faulds, the ACC, the Procurator Fiscal, and the DCI from
Strathclyde following on behind. The room fell silent.

'Right,' said Bain, nodding to a constable who killed the
lights, 'Elizabeth Nichol.' A face appeared on the screen behind
him – middle aged, bleached blonde hair with grey-flecked
roots beginning to show, her face a patchwork of bruises.
'Alpha Nine Three discovered her less than two hundred yards
from the body of Vicky Young.'

Click and the photo changed: night time, a woman in blood-
stained underwear lying face down beneath a gorse bush, the
skin tones bleached out by the photographer's flash. 'Her
throat was cut through to the bone, she was nearly decapitated.'

Click and they were looking at a kitchen table covered with
bits of human body. 'Marcus Young.' *Click* – a severed head,
lying under the table.

Click – back to the battered, terrified face of Elizabeth Nichol.
Bain picked up a stack of paper from the desk beside him and
handed it to the nearest constable, telling him to take one and
pass the rest on. 'This is the preliminary victimology report on
our survivor.'

Logan accepted the pile from a queasy-looking Rennie and
handed it on to Steel. According to the cover sheet, the Family
Liaison officer they'd assigned Elizabeth Nichol was the same
one he'd taken to see Andrew McFarlane: PC Munro.

'Read it later,' said Bain. 'The gist is that Nichol went to the
Youngs' house to borrow a cookery book. Mrs Young was out
shopping, but her husband asked Nichol in to wait. She says
the doorbell went fifteen minutes later and when Young went
to answer the door he was forced back into the hall and beaten.
Nichol panicked and ran.'

'Not bloody surprising,' muttered Steel.

If the Chief Superintendent heard her, he wasn't letting on.
'Next thing she knows, she's wandering round the waste

389

ground at the back of the houses in the rain. She comes across Vicky Young's body and is accosted by a man fitting the Flesher's description. They struggle, but Alpha Nine Three turns up and she manages to escape. PC McInnis found her hiding in a whin bush. Her clothes were torn and covered in blood.'

Click – a cutting from the *Aberdeen Examiner* appeared. 'Marcus Makes Merry': a story about how Marcus Young had written a comedy play that was going to be performed on Radio Scotland. 'This article was published three and a half weeks ago. Just like all the others.' Bain pointed at the screen. 'The MO fits, the butchery fits, the description fits, the victim selection fits.'

The DCS smiled into Alec's television camera lens. 'We have a living witness, backed up by an experienced police officer. We have a crime scene that was abandoned before the Flesher could finish. This represents a very real breakthrough in the investigation – we're one step closer to catching this bastard.'

'Aye,' Steel said in a smoky whisper, 'and I'm sure that's a great fucking comfort to Marcus and Vicky Young's families.'

Bain stared at her. 'Did you have something to add, Inspector?'

'Aye, I'd like to widen the door-to-door radius round the Youngs' house – the bastard knows there's police everywhere, he's going to keep running till he's nowhere near the scene. Might even have abandoned his vehicle.'

The DCS nodded. 'Good point: get right on it.'

'Come on, Laz,' she stood, 'you heard the man—'

'Actually,' said Faulds, 'I was hoping to take DS McRae with me to interview our surviving victim.' He smiled at the inspector. 'Hope you don't mind?'

'Mind? Me? Why would *I* mind?' She grabbed Rennie by the collar. 'Come on Boozy Boy, the fresh air will do you good.'

'I meant to ask' said Faulds as they drove out of Aberdeen on the A947, heading north, 'How's David doing?'

It took Logan a second to realize he was talking about Insch. 'Not so good. They need to operate, but...' He shrugged and put his foot down, overtaking a Renault Espace full of ugly children and assorted dogs. 'I don't know ... it sort of feels like he's given up.'

Faulds was quiet for a while, looking out of the car window as the countryside went by. 'It's actually quite pretty, in a never-ending-green-and-brown-slog-of-muddy-fields kind of way... Ooh, look: sheep. Just to break up the monotony.' He smiled. 'Do you like it here?'

'Never really thought about it. Lived here most of my life, so ... well, you know.'

'Have you thought about what you're going to do next?'

'Go through the abattoir security tapes again?'

'I meant in the slightly longer term. I've got a couple of openings coming up in Birmingham. Detective Inspectors – of course you'd be on secondment to start with, and you'd have to forget all this haggis-munching Criminal Justice Scotland Act nonsense: learn PACE, like a proper police officer. But I think you'd make a good addition to my team.'

Logan turned and stared at his passenger. 'A DI in *Birmingham*?'

'Come on: you're intuitive; determined; good attention to detail; you jump to conclusions, but you're not afraid to listen to alternatives; open minded; loyal; and do you think you could keep your eyes on the road?'

'I ... yes ... sorry.' Logan gripped the steering wheel and pulled them back into their own lane.

'I run a fast-track programme for real coppers, not just jumped-up overachievers with law degrees. Up here you could be a DS till you're drawing your pension. With me, if you keep on the way you're going, you could be looking at a Chief Inspector's job in four or five years.'

Faulds left an expectant pause ... and when Logan didn't fill it, he said, 'You're not exactly biting my hand off here.'

'Actually, sir, I was wondering what it'd be like: leaving everything behind. Starting again from scratch. Not knowing anybody.'

'Your family's here, aren't they? You're worried about missing them.'

'Dear God no.' Smile. 'Trust me, that's a bonus. My mum's a nightmare.'

'Yeah, my foster parents were the same. So, if it's not your family . . . ?'

A new life in Birmingham: he could leave all the guilt and bad memories behind. A clean slate.

'Look,' said Faulds, 'sleep on it. I'm only going to be up here for another couple of days, but if you let me know tomorrow I can get the paperwork started. Four weeks' time you could be Detective Inspector McRae of West Midlands Police.'

Logan had to admit he liked the sound of that.

Newmacher had started out as a tiny village, but as with most places within commuting distance of Aberdeen it had contracted a nasty dose of developer's spread: housing estates breaking out like acne as more and more people squeezed into cheek-by-jowl brick-clad boxes.

Elizabeth Nichol had a 1970s bungalow in a little grey cul-de-sac. An unmarked car sat outside the house – the back seat cluttered with yellowing newspapers and empty wax-paper cups from Starbucks. Logan parked behind it.

'Rule one,' said Faulds, climbing out into the sunshine, ' if you're going to be on my team I need you to be goal-orientated . . . Don't look at me like that: I know it sounds wanky, but there's a reason. We don't just bumble about hoping some wonderful clue will fall into our lap; we go in with pre-defined goals.' He pointed at Logan. 'What are we trying to achieve here?'

'See if Nichol can remember anything more about that night. Go over the physical description again.' Logan stopped to think for a moment. 'Find out if there's a connection between the Youngs and the Flesher. Maybe there's more to it than just the newspaper cuttings: he might have made contact.'

'Good. Now lets go see if some wonderful clue will fall into our lap.'

Elizabeth Nichol's house was a cathedral of kitsch. Pride of place went to her massive collection of snow globes from all over Europe: Poland, Moldova, Croatia, Lithuania, Slovakia, Croatia, and a lot of other places ending in 'ia' that Logan couldn't pronounce. They filled a bank of floor-to-ceiling shelves that dominated the lounge.

Elizabeth herself was a small, nervous-looking woman who fidgeted constantly with her blouse: tugging at the collar, brushing off imaginary lint, picking at the buttons.

PC Munro sat in a floral armchair by the window, leaning forward every now and then to pat her on the arm and tell her it was all right, she was safe now.

Elizabeth made them a pot of tea, sat back down on the couch, fidgeted a bit more, stood, picked up a snow globe, looked out the window, 'Would ... would anyone like something to eat? It's no trouble, really, I was going to have something myself. Just leftovers really...' She put the snow globe back with the others. 'Sorry ... it's stupid...' The tears were starting.

PC Munro got up and put an arm around her shoulder. 'It's OK.'

'I just wanted to feel useful.' She sniffed and rubbed at her eyes. 'I'm such an *idiot*.'

'Nonsense, it's a lovely offer,' said Faulds. 'I've got to go have lunch with some boring old fart from the council, but I'm sure DS McRae and PC Munro will join you.'

'Er...' Logan looked at Munro, then Faulds, and finally at Elizabeth Nichol. 'Well ... only if it's not any bother.'

Elizabeth assured him it wasn't and bustled off into the kitchen.

'So,' said Faulds when the muted roar of an extractor fan kicked in, 'down to business: why isn't she still in hospital?'

The FLO pulled out her notebook. 'Discharged herself. She has a thing about doctors and nurses. Won't take witness protection either. Those Muppets were here earlier, trying to bully her into it.'

'Not acceptable. I'm not having the only surviving victim of the Flesher running around unguarded.'

'She doesn't *want* a guard; won't even let us put a patrol car outside the house. She wants to pretend it never happened. As far as Elizabeth Nichol's concerned, if you stick your head in the sand nothing can hurt you.'

'Then you'll have to stay.'

Munro was lost for words. 'You ... what? I ...'

'You're her FLO aren't you?'

'But I'm supposed to be investigating her background, establishing victimology.'

'And do you really think that's more important than making sure she stays alive?'

'What?'

'Nothing's going to happen, but if anything does you'll be here to call for backup. We'll get a couple of cars doing low-profile surveillance – Nichol won't even know about it – they'll be thirty seconds away. You see anything suspicious, you call them in. No heroics.'

Munro tried again: 'Look, sir, I'm supposed to be off at two, I've got—'

'Have you finished the background report yet?'

'I ... not as such, but—'

'Well, what *have* you done then?'

'I did the preliminary report.'

Faulds didn't look impressed. 'You've been here all morning; where's the family history, work record, timeline?'

'I ... it's not easy, OK? She won't settle down for more than two minutes at a stretch. She's nervous. Probably still in shock.'

'Look,' said Faulds, 'you've got an opportunity here to prove to everyone you're not a screw-up—'

'What? I'm *not* a screw-up! Who's saying I'm a screw-up?'

'After that business with William Leith—'

'That wasn't my fault! How was I supposed to know he killed his wife? He said it was the Flesher: everyone—'

'Some people would think an experienced FLO wouldn't have made that kind of mistake.'

'That is *so* ...' She looked at Logan, but he had no intention of getting involved. 'I'm doing my best.'

'That's what worries me.' A friendly smile blossomed on Faulds' face as Nichol returned from the kitchen with two heaped plates of mince and tatties.

She put one down in front of PC Munro, and the constable blanched. 'Ah ... actually, I'm a vegetarian, sorry ... Mind you, half the city seems to have gone veggie these days, don't they?' She pulled on a smile. 'But it looks lovely.'

'Oh ...' Elizabeth picked up the plate again. 'I've got some tins of tomato soup? I could—'

'You sit yourself down,' said Faulds, 'PC Munro can help herself,' he shot her a look, 'can't you?'

Brittle smile. 'Of course, sir.'

Logan balanced the plate on his knee, dug a fork into his mashed potato and swirled it through the mince, coating it with thick brown gravy. Then stared at it.

'It's ...' Elizabeth blushed. 'I know what you're thinking, but it's OK. I got the mince from Dundee. It's not ...' she flapped a hand at a copy of the *Aberdeen Examiner* sitting on her coffee table, 'local.'

Thank God for that.

Logan took a bite. 'Mmm, this is excellent. *Much* better than the stuff we get in the canteen.'

She beamed with pride as Logan got stuck in.

'This might sound daft . . . ' she said to Faulds, 'but you seem familiar. Have we met before?'

The Chief Constable gave a little self-deprecating shrug. 'I was in a TV show when I was younger.'

'Oh . . . I see.'

'Now, Elizabeth,' said Faulds as she started eating, 'I don't want to put you off your lunch, but I need to ask you some questions about last night, OK? The man who came to the Youngs' house, was he taller than me?'

'I . . . ' She pointed through to the kitchen, and the buzzing drone of a microwave oven. 'I told her everything I can remember.'

Faulds scooted forwards. 'The human mind is a remarkable thing, Elizabeth, sometimes memories don't bubble up to the surface till days, even weeks later. I'm willing to bet that together, you and I can get something on the boil.' Flirty wink.

He teased details out of her over the next ten to fifteen minutes, changing the subject from the Flesher to something innocuous – like the snow globe from Krakow – and back again. Constantly shifting. Getting a little more information every time.

Logan gave a satisfied groan and pushed his empty plate away, glad he'd been the one lumbered with making Elizabeth Nichol feel useful.

'Will you look at the time?' said Faulds, peering theatrically at his watch. 'Going to have to fly or I'll be late.' He stood, motioning for Logan to do the same. 'Thank you for your hospitality, Elizabeth. If you think of anything else, you give me a call, OK?' He dug out a business card and scribbled something on the back, then handed it over. 'Doesn't matter how late or early it is.'

Outside, in the car, Faulds allowed himself a smug smile as Logan drove them back towards town. 'You see, that's what being goal-oriented gets you . . . What?'

'Don't you think you were a little hard on Munro?'

The older man nodded. 'That's the thing about leading a team: some people are motivated by the carrot, others by the stick. The trick is telling which is which. You're a carrot, Munro's a stick. Yes, she'll think I'm an utter bastard, but what do you want to bet she's in there right now giving it a hundred and twenty per cent, just to spite me?'

Which sort of made sense.

'Right,' said Faulds, 'when we get back I need you to organize two unmarked cars watching the main road. Anyone turns into Nichol's street, I want a PNC check on the number plate. At least one member of each team to be firearms trained.'

'You think he's going to come after her? Not exactly the Flesher's type, is she? Too thin.'

'True, but I'm not prepared to take that risk. Are you?'

PC Munro waited until the pool car disappeared before she started swearing. Faulds was such a patronising wanker. '"That's what worries me." Git.'

She marched through to the kitchen, determined to show that stuck-up Brummy arsehole she was perfectly capable of getting information out of a victim.

Elizabeth Nichol was up to her elbows in the sink, wearing a flowery pinny with ducks on it, washing up after lunch.

Munro grabbed a dishcloth. 'Can I help dry?'

The woman nearly jumped out of her skin.

'Sorry, didn't mean to startle you.' Munro picked a plate from the draining board. 'You never told me about your family. Any brothers or sisters?'

'I . . . one of each: Jimmy and Kelley.' She was going bright red. 'We're not close.' She sank her hands back into the bubbles. 'Kelley was always the sensitive one. Jimmy . . . well, he was always . . . difficult. I haven't spoken to him since we were little. Doubt I'd even recognize him now.'

Finally they were getting somewhere. Munro moved onto Elizabeth's parents and job – trying to do the same bouncing-back-and-forth-between-subjects trick that Faulds had pulled earlier – pushing a little harder than she normally would. No one could say she'd not been thorough *this* time.

Only it didn't work: instead of providing a steady trickle of information, Elizabeth burst into tears and ran off, leaving a trail of soapsuds behind.

Munro stood alone in the kitchen, listening as Elizabeth scurried up the stairs and slammed the bedroom door. Then the sound of sobbing filtered down from above.

'Good one, Yvonne. Very professional...' She wandered into the lounge and slumped into an armchair. It was all that bastard Faulds' fault: if he thought being a Family Liaison officer was such a piece of piss, *he* should try it sometime. Up to your ears in other people's grief.

She spent a few minutes feeling sorry for herself, then switched on her Airwave handset and made some follow-up calls. Then she brewed a pot of tea and went upstairs to apologize.

After all, it wasn't Elizabeth's fault she'd been attacked by the Flesher, was it? Sometimes people were just in the wrong place at the wrong time.

Sometimes that was the difference between life and death.

54

'Hello? Can anyone hear me? Hello? Please! I'm a police officer! Hello?' The new voice was female, muffled and scared,
coming from the other side of the cell wall. Heather hoped she
wasn't another screamer.

She rolled over onto her side, turning her back on the noise.
'Kelley?' Silence. 'Kelley are you—'

'They'll be looking for me!'

A hand reached through the bars, cool against her cheek.
'How are you feeling, Heather?'

'Bit woozy, not quite plugged in . . . '

'I'm a fucking police officer! Understand?'

'Maybe it's the medicine? You took a lot of those pills yesterday.'

'HELLO?'

'So tired . . . '

'YOU HEAR ME? THEY'LL COME AFTER YOU! I'M A
POLICE OFFICER!'

'Maybe you shouldn't take them any more?'

'WHY WON'T ANYONE ANSWER ME?'

Heather shuffled forwards, till she was lying beside the bars,
resting her head on Kelley's hand. 'I don't want him to hurt
you.'

'PLEASE!' The shouting had turned to sobbing. 'Please . . .'

Heather closed her eyes. 'Do you think she's going to keep shouting?'

'Shhh . . . go to sleep.'

'I don't feel well . . .'

'Sleep. It'll all be OK soon, you'll see. I promise. You just need to get some rest.'

And Heather drifted off to a lullaby of frightened sobs.

Doc Fraser was in the process of peeling off his green surgical scrubs as Logan walked into the mortuary's sterile area. Ten to five and the post mortem was over – all the bits of body cleared away. Which made a nice change.

'How did it go?'

The old pathologist shrugged, and tossed his waxy trousers into a plastic laundry hamper. Stripped down to his vest and Y-fronts – grey socks slipping down his ankles, a smattering of little red blisters visible on his pasty legs – he pointed at the row of refrigerated drawers. 'You want to look?'

'Not really.' But Logan opened the drawer anyway. It was an old man: long grey beard, drink-swollen nose, skin pale and covered in scabs. All in once piece, except for the ugly raw scar left by the Y-inscision.

'Not that one.' Doc Fraser slid the body back into the fridge. 'Filthy Freddie we used to call him: just another poor homeless bastard. It's the same every year – soon as the weather starts to turn, they get high or drunk, go to sleep in a shop doorway and don't wake up. That's the trouble with care in the community – nobody does.'

The pathologist pulled out another drawer. 'Marcus Young. It's fascinating to see the remains so intact, thought we were going to be stuck with slabs of meat and bags of mince on this one.' He had a brief scratch at the sides of his stomach. 'Fascinating.'

'Care to define "Fascinating"? Faulds wants an update.'

Doc Fraser sighed and slipped his socked feet back into his morgue clogs. 'If he'd bothered turning up for the PM he wouldn't need an update.'

'High-powered lunch.'

'Ah, how the other half live. I had a cheese and pickle sandwich with no bloody pickle in it.' He slid the refrigerated drawer shut, then shuffled out of the cutting room, down the corridor and into the pathologists' office. Logan followed him, making the tea while Doc Fraser climbed into a pair of grey trousers and a stripy shirt, then pulled a V-necked jumper over the top.

'Two and a coo for me,' said the pathologist, settling in behind his desk. 'I'd offer you a garibaldi, but someone's eaten them all.' He picked up a pad of A4 and started scribbling on it. 'Marcus and Vicky Young were almost certainly killed by the same knife: approximately eight inches long, extremely sharp. The husband was beaten unconscious, then his throat was cut vertically from here to here . . . ' He demonstrated by running a finger from just beneath his chin all the way down to his clavicle. 'And then from side to side, severing pretty much every major vein and artery north of the heart. He'd have bled out in seconds, especially if he was upside down. Head was removed from the back – which is pretty unusual – in a single cut.'

'Here you go,' Logan plonked a mug of tea on the desk, 'milk, two sugars.'

'Ooh, lovely. Anyway, we're looking at someone who's had a *lot* of practice. It's a remarkable piece of work, very skilled. The skinning alone . . . ' He took a sip of tea. 'I'd say our victim probably went from being a living, breathing human being to lumps of meat in about thirty minutes. No hesitation marks around the joints, no false starts, just clean, economical cuts.'

'What about the woman?'

'Hmm? Oh, she's a different kettle of fish. Same knife, but there's no precision: her throat was slashed, not cut. This wasn't the Flesher's best work. Educated guess: our killer was disturbed.'

'Disturbed?' said a voice from the door. 'That's a bit of an understatement, isn't it? Bug-shit crazy's more like it.' Jackie Watson stood on the threshold, the smile slipping from her face as she spotted Logan. 'My guvnor wants an update on the post mortems.'

'See?' Doc Frazer stuck a biro in his tea and gave it a stir. 'No one wants to attend the things any more, they just want the edited highlights. What happened to professional pride?'

Jackie looked long and hard at Logan. 'If you like I can come back later.'

'Don't be silly.' The pathologist pointed at the visitor chairs. 'Sit your bum down and DS McRae will make you a nice cup of tea.'

And so began one of the most awkward half hours Logan had endured for a long time. At one point – while Doc Fraser was going on about blood patterns – Logan's leg accidentally touched Jackie's. She actually flinched.

Then, when it was finally over, and the pathologist had shooed them out of his office, they stood in the corridor, not looking at each other.

Logan: 'I was—'

Jackie: 'It's not—'

Pause.

She coughed. 'You first.'

'I've been offered a DI's post.'

'Oh aye?' Almost sounding impressed.

'With Faulds in Birmingham.'

'Birmingham.'

'West Midlands Police.'

'I know who looks after bloody Birmingham. Could you have run any farther away?'

'Don't be like that, I—'

'Oh for God's sake! You think I *care* where you go. Fine, bugger off to Birmingham. Abandon everyone.'

'I'm not abandoning anyone!'

'No? What about Insch?' She counted the points on her fingers. 'No wife, no kids, no job—'

'I'm not the one stitching him up in my report! And I'm not the one who disappeared off to bloody Strathclyde for three months.'

'You are such an arsehole!'

Doc Fraser stuck his head out into the corridor. 'Will you two either shut up, or take it outside. This is a mortuary, not a playground...' Grumbling as he shuffled back to his desk, 'Making enough noise to wake the dead.'

'I'M A POLICE OFFICER, THEY'LL BE LOOKING FOR ME!'

'*Jesus,*' said Duncan, settling down on the mattress, '*she doesn't give up, does she?*'

'I'M A POLICE OFFICER!'

'*WE KNOW! SHUT THE HELL UP!*' Duncan shook his head. '*What does she think the Flesher's going to say, "Oops, terribly sorry, didn't know you were a policewoman. Tell you what, I won't make you into burgers after all. You're free to go. Mum's the word?" Pathetic.*'

Heather looked at him. 'Remind me again what I saw in you.'

'*I make you laugh, I'm great in bed, and I do a mean boeuf bourguignon. Oh, and I got you drunk and knocked up.*'

'HELP!'

'*I can't sleep.*'

'*Not surprised with that bloody racket going on.*'

'PLEASE!' The new woman's voice was beginning to go, cracking from all that shouting.

'*She's got to stop sooner or later.*'

'Duncan,' Heather reached for him, holding his hand in hers, 'Duncan I've been thinking ... I want you to move on.'

'*Don't be silly, I—*'

'I mean it. Be with Justin: he needs his father. Look after him.'

'*And leave you alone with the Dark?*'

'I'm not alone, I've got Kelley.' She smiled at him. 'It's OK. I'm not mad anymore.'

Duncan looked down, the light from the hole in his head glowing like a million dying suns. '*I'm scared.*'

'I know, Sweetheart.'

'*If you . . . you know, ever need me, for anything—*'

She silenced him with a kiss. And when she opened her eyes he was gone. Heather got the feeling he wouldn't be back.

Ken Wiseman is Not

YESTERDAY Grampian Police made a startling announcement: "Ken Wiseman is not the Flesher. He never has been."

This raises a lot of questions about the investigation to date − if they mar— — get this, fundamental — —asp— — —hat else— —hav— — — —inr— —by— —ar—

charges dropped, leading to angry scenes outside Aberdeen Sheriff court.

"Early this morning, Ken Wiseman was charged with the murder of his sister Kirsty McFarlane in February 1990," said DI Roberta Steel. "Advances in DNA technology have identified the — discovered in Wiseman's boot — —investigation

— —ted to — —ic. We — —eads at

— to be — visible — —months. — he task? — in the — lt to see — e.

Strathclyde Police are undertaking a review of G— handling of the case. — officially this is just a "pee— one can't help wonder— represents the first step in — investigation out of their ha—

And perhaps that's n— idea. With tainted meat in— chain, and more victim— targeted every week, — Police are clearly out of thei—

Normally they do a goo— the Flesher is anything bu— Surely it's time a national s— set up to look into extrem— like this one. With a cer— force taking on responsi— serial killers and terrorism— we could have a mu— integrated response to

Woman Survives Flesher Attack

THE FLESHER struck again last night, leaving a Kingswells couple dead. Marcus Young was discovered in his kitchen, while his wife Vicky Young was found on waste ground behind the house.

But for the first time since the —pate of killings began, someone —urvived. A woman, who has not —en named, is thought to have been —und not far from Vicky Young's —dy.

According to eyewitness reports —woman was being chased by the —her.

— phoned the police as soon as I —what was going on," said a —bour who did not want to be —d. "It was awful. I wanted to go —nd help her, but my wife —n't let me. We have a small

— survivor was taken to —n Royal Infirmary, where —treated for cuts and bruises. —was phenomenally lucky,"

said one of the nurses, "but has been traumatised by her ordeal. It is probably post traumatic stress disorder. But at least she's still alive."

Police refused to comment on rumours that the woman may hav— seen the Flesher's face i— attack.

"W—

LOCAL FILM-MAKER WINS AWARD

THE CREAM of the safety training video world gathered yesterday to honour the best in their — 'Safeties' are the highest — the most — Aberdeen

— cooped the —: Container —ector for the

— speech he —nd the makers — getting him —ion.

—ut telling people —' said Mr Clark, —ng a story with —cters and plot. —on't have to be a — from one tawdry —ext, they can have —eaning beyond the —ourself killed."

An emotional Zander Clark collects his award

"It's great to see new life being breathed into the industry."

And Zander Clark is no newcomer to the awards scene. His film company ClarkRig Training Systems Ltd. has picked u— numerous industry accolades sinc— it was set up in 1995.

"I've been very lucky to — surrounded by wonderful staff a— —crew," said Mr Clark. "It's th— —that allows

HANDCUFFS

— is attacked at Craiginches Prison

—by a jury of their peers. The — are not meant to be —s, doling out punishments —own.

—pian Police issued a — saying that, "DI Insch's — were inexcusable. We —se with him for his loss, —an't be used as an excuse — a prisoner in our care." —ian Police take this —ry seriously. We will — full investigation and —es if necessary." —sed an instant backlash

incredible. How can they throw the book at a man grieving for his daughter? It's just not fair."

With a growing sense of resentment that the criminal justice system is just that − justice for criminals, not their victims − the people of the North East are getting behind an appeal to raise money for DI Insch's defence.

Local businessman Simon McLeod was one of the first to donate. "It's important that we send a message to people like Wiseman—

—n a thi— —? We— —been —baggy— — way—

—ll g— —pa— —ou— —n— —th— —s,

55

The clock radio cast a green glow across the bedroom: 05:58 –
seventeen minutes before the alarm was due to go off. Logan
yawned, rolled over onto his back and stared at the ceiling. A
DI in Birmingham. Detective Inspector Logan McRae . . . It had
a nice ring to it, like something off the television. It wasn't as if
he had anything keeping him here, not even—

An arm wrapped itself around his chest and Logan nearly
screamed.

There was someone on the other side of the bed, asleep, her
dark curly hair rumpled across the pillow like an explosion in a
mattress factory. And then it all came back: the trip to the pub;
drinks; Jackie turning up with that Janis McKay woman from
Glasgow; him refusing to chicken out and leave, still stinging
from Jackie's 'running away' rant; more drinks; bumping into
each other on the way to the toilets; the long, tipsy heart-to-
heart . . .

There was a muffled snork, a huge yawn, and Jackie was
staring blearily at him. And then she hid her face in her hands.
'Please tell me we didn't— Oh, God, we did, didn't we.'

He slipped out of bed and grabbed a towel off the back of the
chair, wrapping it round himself before clicking on the light.
'Jackie, I—'

'Don't, OK? You don't get to say it this time, I do.' She sat up, hauling the duvet with her, making sure everything was covered. 'Last night was a one-off. Drunken break-up sex, nothing more. It doesn't mean anything.'

Logan nodded.

'Now,' Jackie glanced around the bedroom, probably looking for her industrial underwear, 'if you don't mind leaving the room, I'd like to get dressed.'

'Bloody hell . . . ' Logan stood in Elizabeth Nichol's lounge and surveyed the damage. It was as if someone had gone wild with a cricket bat – the walls discoloured with snow-globe water and little flakes of glitter, the floor covered in curved shards of glass and broken plastic. The TV was battered to smithereens, the sofa shredded, the standard lamp a very non-standard shape. A bloodstain marked the wall by the kitchen door, the plaster-board buckled and cracked around it.

'As far as I can tell,' said the IB's pet Goth, her face as pale as her white SOC suit, 'this was where someone's head was rammed into the wall.' She knelt on the carpet and demonstrated in slow-motion. The dent was just the right size and shape. 'No idea if the blood's the householder's or PC Munro's though. We've called for the mobile DNA unit.'

It wasn't the only bloodstain in the place. There were smears on the balustrade, as if someone had staggered downstairs, trying to keep themselves upright. A spatter of red infected the kitchen floor like chickenpox. Drops of scarlet on the landing.

Every single room had been trashed.

Faulds stood in the kitchen doorway, SOC suited and booted: hood up, latex gloves, blue plastic shoe-covers, worried look on his face. He waved Logan over, leading him though the train-wreck kitchen to the patio doors – where no one would hear them. 'I didn't know this was going to happen! It was a long shot, a safety precaution. Elizabeth Nichol wasn't even his type . . . '

'They might still be alive. The floor's not soaked in blood; he's got to keep them somewhere: a basement, disused industrial unit, somewhere . . . '

Faulds turned his back on the ruined room. 'The bloody media are going to love this.'

'We should think about setting up roadblocks.'

'How the hell did he get past the officers watching the place? They were supposed to monitor everyone going in or out! What sort of useless, halfwit, haggis-munching bastards— '

'This isn't helping.' Logan glanced out the window: still dark, just a hint of pre-dawn light staining the horizon. 'Sun'll be up in half an hour: we need to get a fingertip search organized. Find out how the Flesher got in here.'

Faulds looked at him. 'You're right. We have to focus, lay out a game-plan, strategize . . . ' He closed his eyes and rubbed his fingertips into his temples. 'We'll need a press release: appeal for witnesses, photos of Nichol and PC Munro. We'll tell them that . . . that Munro volunteered to look after a vulnerable witness who'd refused protection.'

'Volunteered?'

'I didn't know this was going to happen, OK? Asking Munro to stay was the right decision at the time – given the circumstances. Yes, in hindsight we should have taken Elizabeth Nichol into protective custody whether she liked it or not, but it's too late for that now. We have to stay focused on how we get them both back. *Alive.* We can play the blame game later.'

The media briefing was a disaster. As soon as the Chief Constable finished reading out the prepared statement the questions started flying: How could Grampian Police let one of their own be abducted by the Flesher? Why wasn't Elizabeth Nichol given proper protection? Who was responsible? Was there going to be a public enquiry?

'Jesus,' said Steel, standing next to Logan – as far away from the cameras as possible, 'straight to the finger-pointing. Tell

409

you Laz, we don't get Munro back in one piece we're screwed.'
She pointed at Faulds, sitting up there on the podium next to his
Aberdeen counterpart. 'You think they'll throw that Brummie
cock-weasel to the wolves? Will they hell, it'll be one of us.'

'It wasn't anyone's fault; Nichol wouldn't take protection—'

'She shouldn't have been given the bloody choice! And we'd
no've lost a police officer.'

Logan frowned at her. 'Not helping.'

'Aye, well ... tough.' The inspector dug out her cigarettes.
'I've had enough of this crap, give us a shout when the dust
settles.'

Half an hour later they were all upstairs in the boardroom,
getting snarled at by Chief Constable Baldy Brian. 'How *exactly*
did the Flesher get both of them out past two unmarked police
cars?'

DS Beattie might have been blushing, it was difficult to tell
under all that beard. 'We clocked every vehicle going in and
out of the street, *and* the two streets either side. PNC checked
the lot: all residents.'

'I want them hauled in here and questioned.' The Chief
Constable must have caught the expression on DI Steel's face
because he rounded on her. 'You have something to say,
Inspector?'

She shrugged. 'Just think it's a bit of a coincidence, don't
you? Suddenly the Flesher lives four doors down from the
Nichol place?'

'*Actually*,' Doctor Goulding, Faulds' pet psychologist,
straightened his horrible tie and waited for their undivided
attention, 'it's not that unusual. Some serial killers start close
to home, then spread their wings. Others select victims from
the people they see around them every day – they stay close.
And others are building up to something. There was a chap in
the States who decapitated older women – only stopped when
he finally got round to cutting off his mother's head. He'd been
working up the courage.'

Goulding smiled, as if that somehow made his anecdote more palatable. 'Given the level of destruction in the Nichol house, I think it's fair to say that our killer's finally lost control. Twenty years he's been operating with impunity, but since Halloween he's been under a lot of pressure. Thursday night he almost got caught; one victim escaped; he had to kill a second and hide her body in a bush; abandon the partially-butchered remains of a third. He's not in control anymore, and that's never happened to him before. So he goes out for revenge, even though he *knows* it's high risk.' The psychologist nodded, agreeing with himself. 'It's taken twenty years, but the man you call "the Flesher" is finally escalating.'

'Aye,' said Steel, 'it's a comforting thought all right. Sure it'll make Munro's husband and kids feel all warm and fuzzy inside.'

'I'm just saying that this is the end game as far as the Flesher's concerned. He's unlikely to come back from this, most likely it's the start of a spree—'

'Jesus, that's even *more* comforting! The bastard was bad enough when he was in control, can you imagine what he'll be like now?'

'HELP ME! PLEASE HELP ME!' Sobbing in the darkness. 'PLEASE!'

'Heather? You awake?'

'With all that racket going on?' She rubbed at her eyes, feeling gritty all over. 'You got any more of those pills? We could both—'

'They made you feel ill.'

'I just want to sleep . . . '

The shouting stopped, replaced by incoherent screaming and the sound of Mrs I'm-a-Police-Officer throwing herself against the metal walls of her prison.

Heather groaned and stared up into the impenetrable dark. 'Kelley? Tell me a story.'

'I don't—'

'Please?'

'HELP ME!'

'I . . .' Kelley went silent. 'I can't think of anything.'

Heather reached through the bars, feeling for her cellmate's hand. 'Tell me about your mum and dad – the nice ones.'

There was a long pause. And then she realized Kelley was crying.

'Oh God, I'm sorry. It's OK, you don't have to.'

A sniff. 'No. I . . .' Kelly squeezed Heather's hand tight. 'Once upon a time there was a princess and it was her birthday. She was twelve and she was going to see *The Aristocats* in the cinema, and have fish and chips for tea.'

'Kelley, you don't have to—'

'They were singing as they drove from their castle in Banchory into the city. The sun was shining—'

'I'M A POLICE OFFICER!'

'The sun was shining and they had the windows rolled down. The princess . . . the princess had been given a big bag of jelly babies for her birthday and she leant forward from the back seat to offer the king and queen some. The king liked the red ones best, and while he was looking for one . . .' She stopped. 'The truck . . . An evil wizard . . .'

Heather could feel her trembling on the other side of the bars.

'It was like being struck by thunder. The noise . . . oh God, it was the loudest thing I ever heard and there was glass everywhere and mum screamed and then everything went round and round. End over end . . .' She squeezed Heather's hand so hard it hurt. 'We were upside down at the side of the road and I can't move and no one else is moving and they're hanging there . . . like bats, upside down with their seatbelts on. And there's blood *everywhere*.'

'Oh Kelley, I'm so sorry.'

'And I'm trapped on the roof of the car and I'm covered with it. Mum and Dad are dead and I'm soaked with blood . . .'

56

Rennie stuck the big stack of newspaper on Logan's desk and crashed into one of the visitor chairs. 'Where's Chief Constable Creepy Crippen then?'

'In with Professional Standards, and don't be an arsehole.' Logan flicked through the pile – P&J, *Evening Express*, *Aberdeen Examiner*, *Scotsman*, *Observer*, a bunch of other broadsheets and a pile of tabloids too. 'Anything?'

'Bugger all. No one printed Elizabeth Nichol's name, never mind her address. Nothing on the radio either, or the telly. Media Department say they didn't release the details.'

'So how did the Flesher know where to find her?'

Rennie sagged so far down the plastic seat he was almost on the carpet. 'Did you . . .' He blushed, looked at the stack of papers, coughed. 'Did you tell anyone about Laura?'

'What, that you're a dirty old man and she's—'

'She's fifteen.' The blush went nuclear.

'Oh you have *got* to be kidding me!'

'I did a PNC check . . . I swear I thought she was older. She told me she was going to university!'

'Yeah, when she's finished her O-levels.'

'I didn't know!' Rennie twitched. 'You can't tell anyone, OK? Please! You saw her: she was all over me from the start! I didn't know!'

'Bloody hell … fifteen …'

'She doesn't look fifteen! You *saw* her – you bought her drinks in the pub!'

'Yeah, but there's a bit of a difference between buying a minor a rum and coke, and painting her with golden syrup then licking it off.'

'Oh God … I'll have to go to court … I'll lose my job! My mum'll find out! What'll the papers say?'

'Probably something classy like, "PC Paedophile Showed Me His Truncheon".'

'It's not funny! What am I going to do? If anyone finds out …' He looked on the verge of tears. 'I didn't *know*!'

Logan took pity on him. 'I looked it up. Section five point five of the Criminal Law – Consolidation Scotland – Act 1995, says you've got a defence if you genuinely believed she was over sixteen—'

'I did! You know I did!'

'And you're under twenty-four years of age when the offence was committed.'

Rennie looked as if something special had just happened in his trousers. 'I'm twenty-three!' He closed his eyes and slid off the chair. 'Oh thank you dear, sweet, fucking Jesus …'

'You're welcome. Now get your arse back up here, we've got more important things to worry about.' He dumped the newspapers on the floor. 'Like how the Flesher found Elizabeth Nichol.'

Rennie scrambled into the seat. 'I never would've touched her if I'd known—'

'Will you bloody concentrate? We've got two women out there who're going to wind up as happy meals if we don't *do* something. So come on: who knew where Nichol lived?'

Rennie scrubbed his face with his hands, relief oozing out of him like a very happy smell. 'I don't... Hospital: doctors, nurses, admin staff. They'd all have access to her patient records when she got admitted after the attack.'

'Good, I want you to get someone up there, see if anyone fits Goulding's latest profile. Who else knew?'

'Police.' The constable poked the desk. 'We knew. Better yet, *Faulds* knew. Where was he Thursday night, eh?'

'Oh for God's—'

'Think about it: we all went to the pub, but he didn't come, did he? He'd be a dab hand at covering his tracks; knows forensic procedure inside and out; he's got all them mystery bruises; and every time there's a—'

'Enough! OK? Faulds is *not* the bloody Flesher.' Logan tossed PC Munro's FLO report across the desk.

'No need to get all—'

'Read it, you idiot. Control says Munro called through an update at two o'clock: Elizabeth Nichol is local, forty-nine, single, lives alone; one sister, one brother. Both parents are dead ... She likes swimming, romantic fiction, and collecting snow globes.'

'No accounting for taste.' Rennie flicked through the report till he got to the photograph of Elizabeth Nichol's bruised face. 'How come she's not fat-tastic? Thought the Flesher liked them self-basting?'

'Wrong place at the wrong time. If she hadn't been borrowing a cookery book from the Youngs, he wouldn't have touched her...' Logan went back to the death board. 'Mind you, Goulding thinks Nichol might be the end of some sort of chain – that she was a 'close to home' victim the Flesher's been working up to.'

A thoughtful expression slowly crawled its way across Rennie's face. 'Maybe the Flesher followed her to the Youngs' and *they* were the ones in the wrong place at the wrong time?'

'Which brings us right back to how does the Flesher know her?' Logan picked up the latest crime-scene photo from the board – Elizabeth Nichol's lounge, covered in shattered snow globes and ruptured furniture. 'There was no sign of forced entry, so she let him into her house. That makes him a friend, or a colleague, neighbour, or family member.'

'Or Chief Constable—'

'I'm not going to tell you again. Steel's doing the neighbours; see if you can dig up Nichol's brother and sister...' Logan checked his notes. 'Jimmy and Kelley. I'll take the workmates.'

Which was easier said than done. PC Munro hadn't passed on any details about Elizabeth Nichol's employers – Logan had no idea who she worked for.

He dug out his phone and started dialling.

Kelley had cried for a while. It was difficult holding her with the bars in the way, but in the end the shuddering had stopped.

Heather gave her a squeeze. 'How you feeling?'

'Better ... I feel better.' She sniffed. 'I've never told anyone about it before.' Sigh. 'I miss them. I really do miss them. They were so *kind*. If I messed up they'd sit down and talk to me. No more cigarette burns or cracked ribs, black eyes ... Dad never raised his hand to me, not even when I broke his coronation mug.'

'They sound nice.'

'HELP ME!' The bloody policewoman had started up again.

Kelley shifted in the darkness. 'Heather? I'm glad you're here.'

'I'M A POLICE OFFICER!'

Heather smiled. 'I'm glad you're here too. Strange isn't it, being glad someone else is trapped in this little metal prison...'

'YOU WON'T GET AWAY WITH THIS!'

'You think she's ever going to shut up?'

'THEY'LL BE LOOKING FOR ME!'

Kelley patted Heather's hand. 'Yes.' And then she moved away from the bars. 'Do you want any more medicine?'

'LET ME GO YOU BASTARD!'

'It makes me feel bad.'

'Sure you don't want any?'

'Positive.'

'PLEASE!'

'Did you hear something?' Kelly's voice was low and urgent: 'He's coming back . . .'

'What do—'

'I'M A POLICE OFFICER!'

'Close your eyes! Pretend you're asleep.'

Heather peered out into the darkness. 'But—'

'Roll over! Away from the bars! Keep your eyes closed, or he'll know you've not taken your medicine!'

And he would hurt Kelley. Heather rolled over onto her side and screwed her eyes shut, lying perfectly still beneath the duvet. A metal clunk . . . and then the groan of un-oiled hinges – the door opening – and light flooded their prison, she could feel it burning through her eyelids.

Some rustling, and then Kelley said, 'She's sleeping.'

The light went out and everything was darkness again, then the boom of the door closing echoed through the metal cell, momentarily drowning out WPC Shouty.

'I'M A POLICE OFFICER! THEY'LL FIND YOU! YOU HEAR ME? THEY'LL . . . Oh God . . . No, please, I didn't . . .'

Then there was screaming.

Heather waited for the bolt gun's '*Crack*' and drifted off to sleep.

57

Logan tried HM Customs and Revenue, but no one would speak to him without a warrant. It was the same story at Elizabeth Nichol's bank, so he gave up and put a call through to the PC they'd left guarding the woman's ruined home – asking him to have a poke about and see if he couldn't find any payslips or bank statements.

Twenty minutes later the constable was back with the name of a haulage firm in Inverurie and a complaint about the number of journalists and TV people crawling all over Nichol's street. *'Had to chase two of the bastards out the back garden. Bit of backup would be nice!'*

Logan said he'd see what he could do, hung up, and tried the hauliers.

'Hello, Garioch United International Distribution Limited, hope you're having a GUID day. How may I direct your call?'

It took a while, but eventually Logan managed to persuade her to put him through to someone in charge.

'Oh for God's sake. What now?'

'Mr Arthur? This is Detective Sergeant—'

'Don't you people have anything better to do? I told your colleague everything, OK? Now if you don't mind, I've got a golf game at—'

'Who did you speak to?'

'A woman. What's her name...' There was some rustling at the other end. 'Michelle? No, Munro. Wanted to know about someone who used to work here. Elizabeth Nichol'

'Used to?'

'We had to let her go a couple of months ago. Shame: been with us eight years... Look I've been through all this already and—'

'What did she do?'

'Driver. Trucks and vans. Used to do a lot of Eastern Europe drops for us, before we lost the bloody contract.'

Which explained the collection of unpronounceable snow globes.

'What else did you tell PC Munro?'

'She wanted a list of all Elizabeth's trips: destinations, clients, dates and stuff. As if we haven't got anything better to do than—'

'You do understand she's missing, don't you? She's been abducted, her house trashed, there's a policewoman missing too: both their lives are at risk. I think that's a little more important than a round of bloody golf, don't you?'

There was an embarrassed silence, and then, 'What do you need?'

'Everything PC Munro asked for, and a list of all your employees too. One last thing: Do you know Ms Nichol well?'

'She's OK. Bit soft at times, you know, all that charity work and stuff. Forever doing sponsored this and fund-raising that.' Pause. 'She really been abducted?'

'Yes.' Logan dug a notepad out of his piles of paperwork and started asking questions.

By the time Faulds put in an appearance, Logan was scribbling things up on the whiteboard. 'Cup of tea?' asked the Chief Constable. 'I got packet of custard creams.' He dumped a Markie's plastic bag on his desk and peeled off his jacket. 'Bloody chucking it down out there.'

Logan stepped back and looked at his handiwork – a list of Elizabeth Nichol's friends and acquaintances. It wasn't exactly

419

comprehensive, but it was all he could get out of the combined personnel at Garioch United International Distribution. At least now they had somewhere to start putting together a timeline of Elizabeth's last movements. He'd put another two columns on the side: one headed 'BROTHER ~ JIMMY' the other, 'SISTER ~ KELLEY' With a couple of question marks under each. Still no word from Rennie.

'I said, do you want a cuppa?'

'What?' Logan turned away from his scribblings. 'Oh, thanks. How did you get on with Professional Standards?'

'Thought my days of worrying about the rubber-heelers were long gone . . .' Faulds peered at the board, 'Who the hell are Garry-otch United thingumy?'

'It's pronounced, "Geeree" – the area round Inverurie – Elizabeth Nichol works . . . *worked* there.'

'Geeree? Then why the hell's it spelt "Garry-otch"?' He went round the office picking up the dirty mugs, muttering, 'Honestly, that's what's wrong with this bloody country: all the road signs are designed to make visitors look like arseholes . . .' on his way out the door.

Logan tried Rennie on his mobile phone – the clank and scrape of cutlery on crockery, some swearing, then the constable was on the line: *'I'm having my lunch, OK?'*

'Jimmy and Kelley Nichol.'

'I'm allowed lunch, aren't I? Even bloody mass murderers get lunch.'

'Did you find them?'

'No. Tried every spelling I could think of but they're not in the PNC, or on the electoral register. Maybe they emigrated because someone wouldn't let them eat their fish pie in peace?'

Logan hung up and tried himself, but Rennie was right: there was no sign of Jimmy or Kelley in the Police National Computer.

He widened the search, looking to see if he could pick up Elizabeth's birth records, but the database didn't go back that far. So he tried her parents' details instead. Munro had left their names – Edward and Sheila – when she'd called in her final update on Thursday afternoon. Probably one of the last things she'd done before the Flesher grabbed her.

According to the PNC, Edward and Sheila both died in a car crash in 1970. So that was no bloody . . .

Edward and Sheila – car crash . . . Logan sat back in his seat and tried to figure out why that sounded familiar. Something to do with Steel and Alec and dead men with humorous facial hair . . . *couldn't have kids of his own so they adopted a little girl from a broken home . . .*

Logan grabbed his phone and went hunting through his notebook, wanting contact details for the little old man who'd shown them around Trinity Hall.

The Fleshers' Boxmaster picked up on the fourth ring: *'Ewan Morton speaking.'* The familiar up and down lilt of a Fife accent.

'Mr Morton? It's DS McRae, we met last week? You were telling me about your mentor—'

'Oh, yes, Sergeant McRae. I've been following the case in the papers. Dreadful isn't it?'

'Your mentor: Edward, what was his last name?'

'Nichol. Edward Nichol.' Pause. *'Why?'*

'And the girl he adopted?'

'Elizabeth? Lovely girl, she was at our silver wedding anniversary and—'

'Did Elizabeth ever talk about her brother and sister?'

'She didn't have— Oh, you mean from before they adopted her. She used to have nightmares about her brother. I remember Edward saying she'd wake up screaming in the middle of the night. From what I gathered he took after their . . . what is it they call them these days? . . . Biological father? She had a pretty rough time growing up, so—'

'Do you know what her original name was?'

The old man was starting to sound a little flustered. *'I . . . no. I can't . . . look, what's all this about?'*

421

'It's important.'

A sigh. *'I think it was someone associated with the trade, but not in the trade, if that makes sense? I know it wasn't another member.'*

'Can you find out for me?'

'What? Well ... I'm supposed to be seeing my chiropodist—'

'Thought you always wanted to help with a murder investigation.'

Ewan Morton's singsong voice grew an edge of steel. *'Don't worry, you can count on me.'* And to hell with his bunions.

The Fleshers' Boxmaster was as good as his word. Twenty minutes later he was back on the phone, sounding out of breath. *'Had to go to ... had to go to Trinity Hall ... Went ... went through all the minutes from ... from 1966.'* He went quiet for a while.

'Mr Morton? Are you OK?'

'Just a little angina ... The minutes show that Edward adopted the daughter of a man called James Souter. He wasn't a member of the Fleshers, but he worked in a slaughterhouse as a butchery assistant.' Another pause, and this time Logan could hear the puff of an inhaler in the background. *'It says here he had an industrial accident – sleeve caught in a bit of machinery, lost most of his arm. The Council took Elizabeth into care and Edward adopted her.'*

Logan was scribbling in his notebook. 'What about her sister and brother: any mention of what happened to them?'

'Erm ... no, just Elizabeth.'

'OK, thanks, you've been a great help.' Logan was about to hang up when he realised there was something he hadn't asked: 'The slaughterhouse where Souter worked, what was it called?'

'It was on the site of that big new place. What's it called ... mind's going ... the one in Turriff? Been in all the papers?'

'Alaba Farm Fresh Meats.' Bingo.

'Aye, that's the one. Never did understand why they couldn't spell "Alba" properly. You'd think someone would have said.'

Logan barged into the main incident room. DCS Bain was deep in conversation with Faulds, while Wee Fat Alec played with his lens cap – on, off, on, off.

Logan marched over and Faulds looked up, smiled, and held out a mug of tea. It was cold. 'Ah, just in time. I want to get your opinion on—'

'We've got a suspect.'

'Oooh! Wait, not yet . . .' Alec pressed buttons and fiddled his focus. 'Aaaaand . . . Action!'

Bain scowled at him. 'What have I told you about that?'

'Sorry. Force of habit.'

'Jimmy Souter: he's Elizabeth Nichol's brother. Their father worked at the Turriff abattoir. Maybe Goulding was right: he's been building up to taking revenge on his sister.'

'What?'

'Mother abandons them; father loses an arm in an industrial accident; Elizabeth gets taken into care and adopted. She got a loving family, he got stuck at home with a violent, alcoholic father.' It hadn't taken long to dig up Daddy Dearest's criminal record: drunk and disorderly, assault, criminal damage, child endangerment, a couple of what they used to call 'domestic incidents' – one involving a frying pan full of bacon fat. It wasn't surprising the mother left. Just a shame she hadn't taken her kids with her.

'And does this Jimmy Souter have prior?'

'We don't know.' This was the bit that Logan wasn't so happy about. 'I can't find him anywhere – chances are he was adopted too, so he'll have a different surname now. I've got Rennie going through all the children's homes in Grampian for any record of him, Elizabeth, or their sister Kelley.'

Bain turned and asked Faulds what he thought, but Logan wasn't finished yet: 'I did a search on the father: James Souter.

He's wasting away in a hospice up the coast, but he still owns a house. It's one of the dilapidated ones that backs onto Alaba Farm Fresh Meats. Number three.'

Bain grabbed a phone off the desk and put the call through to Control: they were going now, and they were going mob-handed.

58

Logan put his foot down, doing eighty on the twisting A947 north out of Dyce, lights and sirens blaring. Three vans – all loaded down with firearms-trained officers – two patrol cars and a couple of CID's scabby Vauxhalls, with Logan struggling to keep up at the tail-end of the convoy. Faulds was in the passenger seat, holding on for dear life, while Alec sat in the back, bouncing from side to side like an unattractive ping pong ball. He'd brought a friend with him: someone called 'Mike' from the BBC, there to watch his back when he went in with the firearms team. As if a dozen heavily armed officers wasn't going to be enough protection.

They went through Newmachar at full speed, then roared up the windy road to Oldmeldrum, tractors and four-by-fours getting out of their way.

Constant radio chatter.

Logan turned it down and asked Faulds to put a call through to Control. 'Get them to send someone out to Elizabeth Nichol's place – she might've been in contact with her brother. Tell them they're looking for photo albums, letters, postcards. Anything that might tell us where he lives.'

Faulds released his death grip on the dashboard for long enough to pull out his mobile phone. 'Why are we always trying to break the bloody sound barrier?' He punched a couple of numbers into the phone and gave a small squeal as Logan threw the car round the last bend and they hammered into Oldmeldrum, the convoy roaring straight through and out the other side.

Past Fyvie, Birkenhills, and Darra without even slowing down, and on to Turriff. The sky was almost black, golden shafts of sunlight spearing through gaps in the heavy cloud, making the little market town glow.

They killed the sirens as they passed the swimming pool, just the flashing lights to warn Saturday afternoon shoppers out of the way – not wanting to give Jimmy Souter too much advance warning.

'Kelley?' Heather whispered into the darkness. 'Kelley, can you—'

The door creaked open, spilling light into the cell, catching Heather kneeling on the mattress, holding onto the bars. She tried to duck, but it was too late: He was standing in the doorway staring at her, the front of His butcher's apron stained dark red.

She turned to ask Kelley ... but Kelley wasn't there – Heather was alone in the little metal cocoon.

There was a wheelbarrow sitting in the dirt corridor behind Him, and Heather could make out a tuft of blonde hair poking over the edge, white and red bones sticking up into the dank air.

'Oh God . . . ' How long had she been asleep?

The Flesher pointed at her, then at His stomach, head tilted to one side in question.

Heather's eyes went back to the wheelbarrow. 'Is that ... is that Kelley?'

The Flesher shook His head and pointed a blood smeared finger down the corridor. Where PC Screams-A-Lot had been. He did the stomach thing again.

'Yes, I'm hungry.'

He nodded, stepped back outside, picked up the barrow's handles and walked it out of view. The wheels squeaked away into the silence.

'Do you think He's killed her?' Duncan stepped through the bars, pausing on the threshold to look up and down the corridor.

'I . . .'

'Be a shame, that. She was nice.'

'Maybe,' said Mr New, *'He's put her in the policewoman's cell?'*

'Why would He do that? Unless He's going to kill and eat her?'

'Good point.'

'He can't: she's my friend!'

'Now, now, Darling,' her Mother said, *'No point crying over spilt milk, is there? Or blood.'*

Heather clamped her hands over her ears. 'She can't be dead!'

'Why not? We are.'

Tears. 'She can't . . .'

'You know,' said a new voice, one Heather hadn't heard before, *'you've still got the knife . . .'* And suddenly Duncan, Mother, and Mr New were gone.

She turned, but there was no one there. 'Hello?'

Just the empty metal cell.

Heather slid her hand underneath the mattress for the forgotten knife. The blade shone pale blue in the dim light that filtered in from the corridor outside.

'There you are,' said the voice, *'all you need to do is slip that into His guts when He comes back.'*

'I've never killed anyone . . .'

'If He's hurt Kelley, doesn't He deserve to die?'

'But I'll be trapped in here.'

'Oh, I'm sure He has the keys on him . . . In fact, is it even locked? You've not checked for ages, have you?'

Heather's eyes drifted across the bars to the heavy Yale padlock. 'Who are you?'

'*Who do you think I am?*'

And suddenly Heather knew. 'You're the Dark.'

'*The knife, Heather. That's how it works. If you want to be my favourite, you have to use the knife.*'

'But . . .' She stepped across to the small gate set into the bars and reached up for the padlock. The Dark was right: it wasn't even locked.

Heather sat down on the mattress, the knife cold and vibrant in her hands. The Dark wanted her to do it. Kill the Flesher and be the favourite. Save Kelley. Take His place at the top of the food chain. Live forever in the Dark . . .

A clunk and He was back, carrying a plate of food that smelt delicious. Liver, onions and creamy mashed potatoes.

He stepped up to the bars and Heather tightened her grip on the knife.

The abattoir car park was nearly full. The sounds of cattle and sheep echoed out from round the back of the huge building, where the unloading docks and pens were. Alaba Farm Fresh Meats was back in business. The convoy slipped past and up the small road on the other side – the one flanked with five dilapidated and deserted houses: their windows boarded-up or broken; gardens overrun with weeds and yellow grass; their red sandstone walls stained and blackened, glistening in the headlights.

The vans bounced to a halt on the potholed road. Then the doors were flung open and armed officers piled out, charging up to number three in the growing gloom.

Logan sat in the car with his fingers crossed, watching as the firearms team took their positions. Alec and his minder from the BBC bringing up the rear.

Warped plywood sheets covered the downstairs windows. The door looked as if it hadn't been touched in twenty years – the paint blistered away by weather and time, until there was nothing but grey wood left. The portable battering ram sent it flying inwards.

The black-clad figures swarmed inside.

Heather wasn't sure where the noise came from, but the Flesher looked up, His dark eyes invisible in the depths of the mask. Staring at the ceiling.

She slipped the knife out from behind her back and slid it into His belly, all the way up to the hilt. Hot blood poured over her hand, making the handle slippery and sticky at the same time as she pulled the blade out and plunged it back in again. And again. And again.

The Flesher didn't even make a sound.

The place was a mess: rotting carpet sending up clouds of dust as the firearms team swept through the building. Detective Constable Simon Rennie lurched into what had to be the lounge, the torch attached to his machine pistol picking details out of the darkness: a mouldering sofa; a couple of disintegrating armchairs; a fireplace full of broken crockery; windows boarded over.

He did the little nimble-toed dance they'd taught him during the firearms course – a swift three-sixty turn that covered all four corners of the room – then off round the furniture while someone else watched the door. 'Clear.'

Voices sounded in his earpiece: *'Upstairs is clear.' 'Kitchen: clear.' 'Bathroom: clear.'*

That only left the cellar.

Rennie joined the rest of the team at the door leading down from the kitchen. It was much brighter in here, thanks to the spotlights on Alec's TV camera, showing up the mouldy wallpaper, rotting table, brown-stained sink, curling linoleum floor.

'OK,' said the sergeant in charge, 'we go on three. Rennie, Caldwell: you're on point. No mistakes and no getting shot, understand?'

'Yes ma'am.'

'On three: One ... two ...'

The Flesher looked down at Heather's hand – wrapped around the handle of the knife – then up into her eyes. Deep within those lifeless rubber sockets, Heather could see something glint as He cocked His head to the side and stared at her.

He stepped back from the bars, placed the plate with the liver and onions within easy reach, turned and left. He didn't bother closing the door.

Heather's legs gave way and she collapsed onto the mattress, still clutching the knife in her blood-soaked hand.

'Honey, are you OK?'

The Dark had been testing her.

It told her to stab Him and she had. It promised she'd be the favourite ... it *promised*.

'Only you look like you've seen a ghost.'

Maybe there was something wrong with the knife? She ran her thumb along the edge, pressing just hard enough to break the skin, and felt no pain. Pressed harder, till the blade sliced through the pad and scraped along the bone. Her blood mingling with His.

'Seriously, you should lie down.'

'He can't die ... He's part of the Dark, he's eternal.'

'Ah ...' Duncan smiled. *'Only just figured that out, have you?'*

Heather held her thumb up, watching the cut surface ooze. 'Blood to blood.'

'I know what you're thinking, but—'

'Now *I'm* part of the Dark. I passed the test.'

'Heather—'

She laid the point of the blade against her stomach, just above her bellybutton.

'Come on, Honey,' Duncan knelt in front of her, *'Don't do this.'*

'Blood to blood.' She took a deep breath, closed her eyes, and plunged the knife in. Once. Twice. Three times. Ripping it back and forth, slashing herself wide open, staining the mattress dark, shining red.

'The knife's not real.'

Stabbing, stabbing, stabbing . . .

A dry hand wrapped around her own, holding it still. *'Heather, it's not real. You're imagining it.'*

She opened her eyes, looked down at her stomach. Nothing broken, nothing torn. Not even a drop of blood on her hands. 'But . . . but the knife . . . the Dark said . . . ' Feeling the tears start to come. 'The knife . . . '

'Shhh . . . it's OK.' Duncan wrapped her in his arms, holding her close.

'But it was real! It was—'

'Shhhhhhh . . . you've gone mental, remember? There never was a knife.' He kissed the top of her head as she cried. *'It's just what's left of your mind playing tricks on you. Like talking to dead people.'* He placed a finger under her chin and tilted her head up until she was looking into his beautiful eyes. *'Even I'm not real.'*

'I don't want to be crazy . . . '

He kissed her, then told her it was too late to worry about that now.

59

The lead firearms officer pointed back towards the house. 'Place has been deserted for years, we've been all over it from attic to basement and there's no sign of anyone. IB can tear the place apart, but I'll bet you pound to a penny there's nothing there.'

DCS Bain nodded, then gave Logan what could only be described as a fucking horrible look. 'Well?'

Chief Constable Faulds stepped in. 'Just because Jimmy Souter isn't here, doesn't mean it wasn't a solid piece of police work. We now have a suspect with a connection to the abattoir and one of the victims. That's a lot more than we had this morning.'

'We're still no closer to finding PC Munro.'

Faulds asked Bain if he could have a quiet word, leading him away out of earshot as the firearms team piled back into their vans and sodded off before the rain started.

'I can see why you're thinking about leaving.' It was Jackie, dressed in her full ninja police gear: black shoes, black trousers, black T-shirt, black stab-proof vest with a black fleece over the top. 'A Chief Constable who's not an arsehole.'

Logan nodded. 'And you're going back to Strathclyde.'

'If they'll have me after this . . .'

They stood and watched as the IB marched into the old Souter house, armed with crowbars, pickaxes, and shovels to tear the place apart.

'Jackie ... I'm sorry.'

'For what?'

'Pretty much everything.'

By twenty to five most of the odds and sods had disappeared – back to the station in time to punch out and go to the pub. Now it was just Logan, Faulds, Wee Fat Alec, the IB team, and an unidentified PC standing guard outside the house in the pouring rain. Whoever it was, they must have *really* pissed someone off to end up with that job.

Rain drifted down in undulating sheets, caught in the glow of the abattoir's security spotlights between the leylandii hedge and the blood-blister sky. The row of bleak, dead houses, slowly rotted in the darkness. Only the old Souter place showed any sign of life: light oozing out through the occasional gap in the plywood sheets that covered the windows; the bang and crunch of demolition as the IB tore out fireplaces and ripped up floorboards. Poking and prodding every nook and crevice for evidence of PC Munro, Elizabeth Nichol, or her brother Jimmy.

'Well,' Faulds shifted round in the passenger seat of their pool car, 'have you decided?'

'DI McRae, West Midlands Police.' Logan turned and offered Faulds his hand to shake. 'Pleased to meet you.'

Faulds smiled. 'Excellent. I'll get someone to start the paperwork soon as we get back to the station.'

The rear passenger door opened and someone jumped in out of the rain. 'Bloody Hell.' It was Jackie, looking like a drowned rat as she pulled off her peaked cap and shook it in the footwell. 'Like going for a swim out there.'

Logan stared at her in the rear-view mirror. 'Thought you'd gone back to the ranch?'

She grimaced. 'Put the heating on, I'm *freezing.*'

He started the engine and turned the blowers up full. Reheated greasy air filled the car. 'Don't tell me you're the poor sod . . . ?' He pointed through the misty windscreen at the Souter place.

The grimace turned into a scowl. 'DCI McKay wasn't impressed by my revised report on Insch's handling of the investigation. Thinks I should've screwed him to the carpet.'

'I thought you had?'

'Yeah, well . . .' She shrugged. 'You were right, OK? Don't rub it in.' She huddled forwards into the gap between the two front seats and cupped her hands over the air vents, complaining that they were still cold.

'You'll get chilblains.'

'Bite me.'

At least she was talking to him again. And then Logan's phone went: DI Steel calling from Elizabeth Nichol's ruined house in Newmacher with an update on the search.

'No postcards, or letters, but the bugger's definitely been here. Found a scrapbook in the spare bedroom – thing's full of newspaper cuttings. Heather and Duncan Inglis, Tom and Hazel Stephen, Marcus Young, Maureen and Sandra Taylor . . . they're all in there, all the little articles from before they went missing, and a lot of the stuff from after as well. "Flesher Strikes Again: Couple Missing" sort of thing. And they're no' the only ones – got stuff in here from Inverness to Eastbourne, and loads of stuff from Fuckknowswhereistan. Eastern European probably, but I can't read a bloody word of it.'

Logan passed on the information.

Faulds asked for the phone: 'Inspector? When does it start, this book? What's the first clipping?' Pause. 'Uh-huh . . . Yes . . . Is it? Good God . . . How many do you think? . . . OK, thanks.' He hung up and returned Logan's mobile. 'Looks as if the scrapbook only goes back as far as 2004. We're going to have to run all the newspaper clippings against every force's missing persons' database.' He rubbed a hand across the fogged-up windscreen, revealing the Souter household in all its ominous glory. It looked as if the IB were giving up, hauling their stuff back through the rain and into their filthy van. '2004 ... Christ knows how many Jimmy Souter killed before that...'

Jackie nodded. 'There'll be more scrapbooks.' She must have seen the expression on Logan's face in the rear-view mirror, because she turned to stare at him. 'What? Souter's a hoarder, isn't he? He'll have every article he's ever clipped.'

She had a point.

'Can you imagine growing up here?' said Logan, watching the IB slowly disappear as the windscreen fogged up again. 'Downwind of the abattoir, everything you own covered in a greasy film. Go to school and it clings to your clothes and your hair. All the kids pick on you because you smell. Then you go home and your alki dad beats the shite out of you.'

Faulds wiped the windscreen again. 'You're not suggesting this isn't Jimmy Souter's fault?'

'I'm just saying it's ... well, not *understandable*, but you know ... it's amazing Elizabeth Nichol turned out as well as she did. Wonder if her sister...' he trailed off into silence.

Faulds said something about search warrants and national appeals, but Logan wasn't listening, he was staring out at the row of derelict houses.

He pulled out his phone and called the station, getting them to put him through to DC Rennie. There was a long pause while someone went to get the constable out of the locker-room showers.

The IB van did a clumsy three point turn and juddered past, the driver waving them a cheery goodbye. The red tail lights glowed like halos of blood as it disappeared down the road, leaving them alone in the dark.

Alec jogged over to the car and clambered in the back with Jackie. His SOC suit had gone a nasty, patchy grey colour, and it dripped filthy water all over the seats as he shrugged out of it.

'Like a demolition derby in there.' He coughed, blew his nose, then checked his camera. 'Didn't find anything though. Probably stick the footage together as a ten second jump-cut montage. You know: tearing the skirting off, floorboards up, fireplace—'

And then Rennie was on the other end of the phone. *'Yo?'*

'What happened to the children's homes?'

'I didn't have time to finish—'

'This *is* important you know! I didn't ask you for fun.'

'OK, OK, no need to get all snippy. Can I get dressed first, or do you want me to go running upstairs in the altogether?'

That was a visual image Logan *really* didn't need. He hung up.

'Well,' said Faulds, 'going to share with the rest of the class?'

'I am a carrot. Rennie is a stick. What if—'

'No wait ... hold on ...' Alec got his camera going. 'Aaaand ... Action!'

'Would you stop doing that?' Pause. 'The whole street's deserted – what if Jimmy just picked one of the other houses? He's been smart enough to get away with this for over twenty years.' Logan killed the engine and reached across the Chief Constable for the glove compartment, looking for the torch. It was buried right at the back in a graveyard of empty crisp packets, and by some strange miracle the batteries actually worked. Logan clicked it on and shone it through the clear patch of windscreen at the row of dilapidated houses.

'You're joking, right?' asked Jackie from the back seat. 'We're not seriously going to—'

Logan popped open the driver's door and stepped out into the drizzle. 'You can stay here if you like. I'm just going for a quick look around.'

'But we haven't got a search warrant. You can't—'

He closed the door before she could start swearing at him.

Five seconds later Alec was out in the rain too, his HDV camera tucked under his jacket to keep it dry. 'Just in case ...'

436

60

Logan swung his torch along the row of dilapidated houses. The beam sparkled against the rain-slicked grass and broken windows. He turned his collar up and picked his way between the potholes to the middle house – number three – now festooned with blue-and-white POLICE ribbon, like a shabby, unwanted birthday present.

'What do you think, Alec – one, two, four, or five?'

'I'm bloody freezing.'

'You're such a girl.' Logan fought his way up the weed-clogged path to number two, rainwater trickling down the back of his neck. The front door was locked, but the wood was so rotten that a firm push was enough to tear the lock out of the frame. The door creaked open on rusty hinges.

His mobile rang as he stepped into the gloomy hallway – Jackie wanting to know what the hell he was doing.

'I'm poking about.'

'We don't have a warrant for "poking about" – Faulds says you have to get your arse back in the car.'

'I'm not going to be long. Just want to take a quick look through the other houses. There's a police officer's life at stake, remember?' She said something rude and he told her it would go much quicker if they got off their bums and helped.

There was some muffled conversation and then Jackie was back with, *'OK, fine. Be like that. We'll all go tromping through the rain so* you *can satisfy your bloody curiosity.'* So much for being civil.

Logan didn't rise to it. 'Thank you. We'll do numbers two and one, if you and Faulds do four and five—'

'Care to tell me what we're looking for?'

'No idea.'

Five minutes later he was back out in the rain again, doing his best to ignore Alec's revolting monologue on the perils of eating a whole family-sized bag of Fruit-tellas in one sitting. Torchlight spilled out through the broken windows of number five. Jackie and Faulds might not be happy about searching the place, but at least they were giving it a go.

Number one was the last building on the deserted street. It was slightly bigger than the others, with a garage tacked onto the side, but the roof sagged like a mouldy hammock and the front windows gaped black and empty.

God knew who owned these ghost properties, but they wouldn't be selling them anytime soon.

Logan pushed through the wrought-iron gate – the squeal of metal on metal following them up the path as it swung slowly shut.

A disintegrating sign was fixed to the wall by the front door, 'THE LAURELS' picked out in fading black paint on scabby grey wood. Logan's torch drifted across the wet sandstone and through the remains of a bay window: crumbling plaster and tattered wallpaper, a mantelpiece littered with bits of collapsed ceiling.

The door was locked, and this time giving it a shove wasn't enough. An old bench sat engulfed in a clump of dead brambles, but when Logan tried to drag it under the bay window it fell to pieces. 'Damn . . .' He looked up at the hollow window frame, then back at the cameraman shivering on the top step. 'Want to give me a leg up?'

Inside, the lounge stank of damp and mould, the floor sagging alarmingly as Logan landed on the squelchy carpet. Alec's head peeked over the windowsill. 'It safe in there?'

'I'll let you in the front door.' He picked his way around the edge of the room, out into the hall, and up to the front door. A big rusty key stuck out of the lock, jammed nearly solid. Logan worked it backward and forward till the seized-up mechanism gave with a squeal, then dragged the door open.

Alec peered inside. 'Doesn't look promising, does it?'

'We'll start upstairs.'

Heather sat cross legged on the mattress, the plate of liver and onions going cold in her lap. Not that it wasn't good – everything He cooked for her was good – it was just that she didn't know what was real anymore.

He was on the other side of the bars, sitting with His back to the rusty red metal wall, His face an expressionless rubber mask.

She took her knife and fork and cut another slice of liver – caramelized on the outside, delicate pink on the inside – put it in her mouth and chewed. Moist and rich and tender. Heather had never eaten policewoman before.

'Are you . . .' She tried to remember the name of Kelley's brother. 'Jimmy?'

The Flesher tilted His head to the side – that cat-like gesture He always did, questioning.

'Is she OK? Kelley? Is she . . .' She bit her bottom lip, not wanting to say it: *is she dead?*

He placed a hand over His heart. Then pointed at her plate of food.

'Yes, it's lovely.' She took another slice, heaping it with mashed potato and fried onions. 'Can I speak to her?'

Silence.

'She's my friend.'

A nod.

439

'Please don't hurt her.'

The Flesher reached up, took hold of the rubber mask, and pulled ... then froze, the mask half on and half off. There was a noise filtering down from somewhere, like electronic music being played far away. He slid the mask back down over His face and stood, then pulled a long butcher's knife from His apron. It looked exactly the same as the one Heather had been hiding.

Only this time she *knew* it was real.

'Hold on a minute ...' Logan stopped at the top of the basement stairs, pulled out his warbling phone and pressed the green button. 'Hello?'

Rennie, sounding excited: *'I did it! I rule! And rock! Rock and rule!'*

'Have you been drinking?'

'Children's homes. I went through every bastard in Social Services till I got some doddery old bat who remembered something about a wee girl getting taken into care after her dad lost an arm in a slaughterhouse. You may now worship my—'

'What about the other kids – Kelley and Jimmy?'

'God knows. I was lucky to get that much out of her.'

'What bloody good does that do us?' Logan started down the stairs, his torch's beam supplemented by the lights on Alec's camera. 'We already know—'

'Ah, this is where my genius comes in. She didn't deal with the case herself, but she knows a man who did. We ...' Silence. *'... time with ...'* Hissing. *'... night?'*

'Hello?'

Tsssssssssssssssssssssssssssssss '... lo?'

Logan froze on the stairs, then took two steps back up. 'Hello?'

'Hello? You still there?'

'What did he say?'

'Didn't speak to him, thought you'd want to do that yourself. His number's oh, one, two, two, four ...'

Logan pinned the phone between his shoulder and his ear, dug out his notebook and copied it down. 'Thanks.'

'*And now, Ladies and Gentlemen, Simon Rennie has* left *the building!*'

'Oh no he bloody hasn't.'

'*What? Oh come on, I—*'

'Just hang around till I've spoken to him, OK? I might need you to follow up on something.' He hung up before Rennie could start whinging, and dialled the number.

'*Hello?*' An old man's voice.

Logan asked him about Elizabeth Souter. There was a long and thoughtful pause. '*Nope, doesn't ring a bell. Sorry.*'

'Well how about Kelley? No? Jimmy Souter?'

'*Jimmy Souter? Now there's a name I haven't heard in a long, long time. You wouldn't believe the trouble one person can cause. If anything got broken, vandalized, set on fire, it was always Jimmy Souter's fault.*'

'Any idea what happened to him?'

'*Elizabeth and Kelley ... now I remember – we all breathed a sigh of relief when someone adopted her. Can't have been easy for the family, but I understand she turned out pretty well.*'

'What happened to Jimmy?'

'*Hmm? Oh, I suppose he just went away, like all imaginary friends.*'

Logan frowned at the phone. 'Imaginary—'

'*Kelley Elizabeth Souter was a very disturbed young lady when we took her into care, Sergeant. I understand she named "Jimmy" after her father. Any time she did anything wrong it was always Jimmy's fault.*'

Thirty seconds later, Logan was back on the phone to Rennie.

'Just shut up and listen, OK? There's a fax on my desk from Garioch United something-or-other, I need you to cross-reference all the dates and locations with those incidents you got from INTERPOL.'

441

'But that'll takes ages, I'm—'

'You've got it all in HOLMES, haven't you? Just run a search. It'll take twenty minutes!'

'All right, all right. Jesus.'

'And call me back soon as you've got anything!'

'What do I tell Bain?'

Logan started down the basement stairs again. 'Just let him know . . .'

'What ab . . .' Scrrrrrrrrrrrrrrrrrrr '. . . ed? Hello?' Hissssssssssssss '. . . in tr . . .'

He hung up. At least that would buy him some time. The DCS wasn't going to be too pleased when he found out Logan had sparked a nation-wide manhunt for Elizabeth Nichol's childhood imaginary friend.

The basement was cluttered: tea chests full of mildewed clothing; cardboard boxes of paperback books, bloated and blackened by damp; disintegrating furniture; rusty bicycles.

'Fuck!' Alec spun round, the spotlight on his camera raking the debris. 'Was that a rat?'

Logan picked his way into the middle of the rotting maze. The building might have been sandstone, but the basement walls were granite. No wonder there was no signal. He peered into one of the boxes: Mills and Boon, Catherine Cookson, Barbara Cartland . . .

Alec did another panicky pirouette. 'I bet it's rats. I bet there's hundreds of them down here . . . feeding on the abattoir's leftovers . . .'

'Will you calm down?'

The cameraman shivered. 'You never read James Herbert?'

Logan ran his torch across the walls again. 'Is that a door under the stairs?'

'Probably just a fuse-box, or something. Can we get out of here before something eats us please? I fucking *hate* rats.'

'Tell them your Fruit-tella story, that'll put them off.' Logan fought his way round to the door and opened it. 'Bloody hell . . .'

There was a long dirt corridor on the other side, stretching off into the darkness, at least twenty foot long. Logan stepped inside. The floor was almost shiny, worn with years of use. He swung the door back and forth on its hinges a couple of times. No sound. Not even a creak.

Alec stumbled through the piles of mouldering boxes and peered over Logan's shoulder. 'What?'

The corridor had a strange smell – not the rancid tang of rendered tallow, but something cloying and floral. Air freshener, or incense. Logan ran his torch along the corridor's rough walls. 'Get back up the stairs and call Faulds. Get him and Jackie over here now.'

'What is it?'

But Logan was already creeping forwards into the dark, telling himself that he was just going to the end of this bit and no further. Just in case.

Twenty yards in and the tunnel took a sharp right turn. He eased himself up to the edge and peered round the corner. Another short length of corridor had been dug out of the dirt, but this one had a blanket, or a curtain draped over the end, forming a makeshift door.

It was probably nothing ... these houses had been here for decades. Since the 1890s at least. This could be an old air-raid shelter, or somewhere to hide an illicit still . . . . Whatever it was, Logan was *not* going in there on his own.

When the voice sounded at his shoulder he nearly screamed.

'They're on their way over.' Alec whispered, camera at the ready. 'You think this is where he keeps them?'

'We'll find out when Faulds and Jackie get here.'

Alec nodded, looked around, then said, 'Sure you don't want to take a quick peek?'

'Certain.'

'But what if PC Munro's in there? Shouldn't we be, you know, saving her?'

'Go charging into an unknown area with no backup and no plan? You mad?'

The cameraman pursed his lips and made sooking noises. 'They'd do it if this was a film. Don't you want to be the hero? Ride in on your dirty big horse and save the damsel in distress in the nick of time?'

Logan stared at him. 'And get her, you, or me killed in the process? We're waiting till Faulds and Jackie get here and that's final.'

'You don't have to—'

'Shhhhh . . . did you hear that?'

A woman's voice. Muffled somewhere on the other side of the curtain.

Bloody hell.

And then a scream for help.

Oh shit . . . Logan pulled out his little cannister of pepper spray and charged through the curtain into a low room: chest freezers on one side and—

He didn't even see the blow coming.

INTERIOR: *A low-ceilinged room lit by three flickering fluorescent lights. The walls are panelled with rough wood. Camera pans hard left, jiggling, the lights leaving hot yellow streaks as the autofocus catches on: DS McRae is slumped back against a chest freezer, blood on one side of his head. A man crouches over him, dressed in a butcher's outfit and wearing a rubber mask of ex-Prime Minister Margaret Thatcher. The man has a knife in his hand pressed against DS McRae's throat.*

VOICEOVER: Oh God . . .

[the Flesher stares at DS McRae for a moment, head on one side, then lowers the knife]

VOICEOVER: Oh God, oh God, oh God . . .

[the Flesher stands and turns to face the camera]

VOICEOVER: Oh God . . .

[picture shakes as the cameraman backs up, then turns and runs]
VOICEOVER: *[panting and swearing – the sound of fabric rubbing against the microphone]*

Alec ran for it, too scared to feel guilty about leaving Logan behind. Back through the curtain, puffing already – why did he have to be such a fat bastard?

'Oh God, oh God, oh God, oh God . . . ' Shut up! Shut the fuck up and RUN!

He could hear the Flesher coming after him, closing the gap. OhGodohGodohGodohGodohGod . . .

Alec burst through the door back into the basement and slammed into a box of crappy romance novels. He went sprawling – the camera flying out of his hands, clattering against a pile of mating bicycles. The light blinked out, leaving him in darkness.

OhGodohGodohGodohGodohGod . . .

He scrabbled to his knees, fumbling forward, trying to find the stairs, trying to find the way out before—

The door under the stairs opened, spilling pale yellow light into the crowded basement. The Flesher was here . . .

Alec bit his lip and tried not to cry.

Keep low. Don't make a sound.

A creak, the sound of a foot scuffing the floor: the Flesher moving between the stacks of boxes and mouldy debris.

Quiet. Not a sound. Don't even breathe.

Something brushed his leg and Alec flinched, staring terrified into the gloom. Oh God, please don't let it be . . .

A pair of black eyes glittered back at him – teeth, claws, naked pink tail.

RAT!

Alec screamed.

He scrambled backwards, kicking out. Fucking rats! Jesus fucking . . . There was someone behind him.

OhGodohGodohGodohGodohGod . . .

Alec looked up into that lifeless rubber face. 'Please . . . '

The Flesher grabbed him by the collar and dragged him, kicking and screaming, back through the door and into the darkness.

61

'Unnnnnnnnngh...' Logan rolled over onto his side and threw up on the hard dirt floor.

'Are you OK?' Faulds stood back, nose wrinkled against the smell.

Logan coughed, spat out a bitter mouthful and struggled to his knees; Jackie dragged him to his feet then held him upright, her body warm against his. 'What the hell were you thinking, charging in here on your own like something out of bloody *Die Hard*?'

His head was swimming. 'She was screaming for help. What was I supposed to do?'

'My God...' Faulds had opened one of the chest freezers. 'It's full of *meat*...' He pulled out a chunk of frozen breast, the areola pale purple in its clear plastic vacuum pack.

Jackie let go and wandered over to the far wall. 'There's some sort of grave in the corner... "Here lie the mortal remains of Catherine Davidson, beloved companion. Died 14th September 2001." What the hell's that supposed to mean?'

Logan closed his eyes for a moment, then peered out at the low room. The whole place had been lined with chipboard – the wood swollen and peppered with mildew. A large stainless steel butcher's table sat against the opposite wall, a set of knives displayed above it on a pair of magnetic strips. The curtained-off entrance Logan had rushed through lay open, showing the dirt tunnel back towards the house. Another pair of curtains partially hid an opening beside the butcher's table, and a third pair hung at the far end of the row of freezers. 'Where's Alec?'

They found him behind curtain number two. It was a kitchen – the walls covered with the same grimy wood, the floor with chunks of faded carpet. A pair of red Calor Gas bottles sat in the corner, hooked up to a spotless gas hob and oven. 1970s-style work surfaces and cupboards lined the room in shades of dirty cream and faded mahogany.

The whole room reeked of blood and garlic.

Alec was hanging upside down in the middle of the room over a tin bath full of dark red, his skin so pale it was nearly translucent. He was still warm.

Faulds swore, then turned on Logan. 'Why the hell did you bring him down here? He was a civilian!'

'I didn't know . . .'

'Do you have any idea what the BBC are going to do to us? It's going to be a PR disaster!'

'Alec, you silly, silly bastard . . .'

A circular hole sat in the top of Alec's head, dripping pink and grey gloop into the bathtub full of blood.

'How could you let this happen?'

'I didn't *let* anything—'

'No? Well you managed to save your own—'

'I ate her mince, OK? That's why.'

'What?' Disgust pulled at Faulds' face. 'Whose mince? What the—'

'There is no Jimmy Souter – he doesn't exist. It's Elizabeth, it's *always* been Elizabeth. She fed those kids human flesh and they got to live.' Logan turned his back on the cameraman's dangling corpse. 'When she made lunch yesterday, I ate the mince...'

He pushed through the curtain and back into the butchery, feeling sick again.

The third curtain – the one beside the chest freezers – was all roses and birdies, faded to a greasy, mottled gray. Logan took a handful and ripped it down.

It was another tunnel, stretching away beyond the soulless light of another fluorescent strip. Less than six feet down, two sets of metal doors were sunk into the wall, as if someone had buried a pair of offshore containers. One blue, one red: the paintwork pockmarked with rust.

Logan hauled the red doors open on groaning hinges.

Definitely a container. The metal box was about the same size as Logan's bathroom, with a set of rusty bars running down the middle, empty except for a mattress, a duvet, a chemical toilet, and a set of pulleys bolted to the ceiling.

The blue container was a different story – instead of the pulleys it had an A-frame made up of scaffolding poles. The floor was spattered with dark red droplets that glittered in the gloom. A pile of black clothes were thrown in the corner. The red container smelled of disinfectant, but this one stank of fear and blood.

Jackie stepped carefully inside, her black shoes making sticky noises as she worked her way across the floor and picked up a chunk of fabric. 'It's a police uniform.' She went hunting through the trouser pockets, coming out with a small leather warrant card holder. She flipped it open and swore.

Logan stood in the doorway. 'It's Munro, isn't it? She was a vegetarian...'

'Fucking hell!' Jackie kicked the container wall – BOOM – the echo was swallowed by the dirt corridor. 'Fucking, bastarding hell!' Another kick.

'OK, OK. Enough.' He grabbed her by the arm and pulled her out into the tunnel. 'How long did it take you to get here? When Alec called? Ten minutes? Fifteen?'

'Something like that. We had to break down the front door.'

'And you didn't see anyone leaving the house?'

'Of course we bloody didn't. Don't you think we would have said something?'

Logan nodded, went back into the butchery and picked up his torch. Dead. He shook it a couple of times and a thin light flickered on. Good enough.

If the Flesher didn't go out through the house there was only one way she *could* have gone. Logan lurched past the containers and on into the darkness.

62

It seemed to go on forever – dark and oppressive, smelling of earth and decay, with an undercurrent of meat. The tunnel took a sudden right – an old wooden door blocking the way. Logan stopped with one hand against it, trying to tell if there was someone waiting for him on the other side.

He had no intention of finding out the hard way.

'This is a complete and utter cocking disaster.' It was Faulds, muttering his way down the corridor, following Jackie and her torch.

She stopped when she got to the door and ran the beam over Logan's face. The light was blinding, making him feel sick all over again.

'Argh, Jesus . . .' He held a hand up over his eyes.

'You're bleeding. And you look like shite.'

'Ow!' Logan flinched away as she prodded the side of his head. 'Thanks, I love you too.'

She stared at him. 'No you don't. That was the problem, remember?'

Faulds pushed his way to the front. 'We shouldn't leave all that evidence unguarded.'

'Tell you what then,' said Jackie, 'why don't *you* stay behind, in the dark, on your own, in the Flesher's lair, while we go looking for the bastard? I'm sure you'll still be alive when we get back.'

'Are you . . . ' Faulds looked as if he were about to pull rank, but Jackie was right: there were only three of them, splitting up wasn't an option.

Logan grabbed the old Bakelite handle and pulled the door open . . . exposing a blank, white wall.

'Oh, that's just brilliant,' said Faulds. 'Dead end. And while we're arseing about here, the Flesher's getting away.' He turned. 'Watson, I want you—'

'Hold on . . . ' Logan gave his torch another shake and ran the jaundiced beam around the blank, featureless surface. A couple of small hinges ran down the left-hand side. 'It's a door.'

It took a bit of fiddling, but eventually Logan got the thing to open. There was a store room on the other side, full of shelves and cleaning products. Jackie pulled out her extendable baton and clacked it to full length. Then inched into the room. 'Clear.'

They followed her past racks of bleach, disinfectant, and tubs of antibacterial hand-wash. The door at the far end was more traditional. Jackie turned the handle and stepped out into a corridor: white walls; suspended ceiling with fluorescent lighting; stainless-steel flooring – the kind with raised diamond patterns to stop people from slipping; the distant rumble and squeak of machinery; a radio playing something innocuous; the almost overpowering smell of lamb.

Logan looked up and down the corridor. 'Left or right?'

'Left. If there's a radio there's people.' Faulds set off towards the noise with Jackie hot on his heels, leaving Logan to trail along behind. Every step making his head swim. The smell, the noise and the bright white walls weren't helping. Probably a concussion and—

His phone blared into life, adding to the waves of nausea. He fumbled it out, still marching after Faulds and Jackie. 'What?'

It was Rennie, talking so fast it was nearly gibberish: *'I did it! It was a right pain in the arse, but I did it! Every time Elizabeth Nichol was driving her truck on the continent there's at least one hit from the INTERPOL files. She's the Flesher!'*

'Get a firearms team out to the abattoir *now*. And an ambulance.' Logan stopped for a second, eyes squeezed shut, leaning against the wall to stay upright. Mouth suddenly full of saliva. Not going to be sick, not going to be sick.

'That's why we've not had any bodies for eighteen years: she's been killing her way round Eastern Europe. Bain says—'

'Shut up. Fuck's sake . . . Roadblocks – every route out of Turriff . . . ' Maybe it would be better to throw up now and get it over with?

'You OK?'

'No.' Logan hung up, pushed off the wall, took a deep breath, and hurried after Faulds and Jackie, the mingled sounds of Northsound Radio 2 and heavy machinery getting louder with every step.

He limped around the corner into a steamy room that reeked of lamb. A pair of mechanized belts ran along the ceiling. Sheep carcasses creaked and swayed their way down one side – fully wooled at one end, skinned and gutted at the other. The opposite belt carried stainless-steel poles, each with a little basket on the end; severed sheep heads staring out of them, looking mildly surprised by death, their innards draped over a spike underneath. All going round to the tune of Blur's 'Parklife', like some macabre merry-go-round.

Faulds and Jackie were in here, the Chief Constable trying to get a man in a bloodstained overall to understand English by shouting at him. Finally the man seemed to get it and pointed at a doorway next to a plastic bin full of lungs.

Logan pushed his way through the crowd of abattoir workers just as Faulds stepped into the corridor. 'Armed backup is on its way.'

Faulds stopped and turned. 'I want this place evacuated. We're not putting any more civilians—'

He didn't get to finish the sentence.

The Flesher appeared in the doorway behind the Chief Constable, knife in hand. There wasn't even time to shout. The Flesher wrapped her arms around Faulds in a lover's embrace – a knife blade flashed in the overhead lighting. It disappeared into Faulds' side, just below the bottom rib.

He looked down at the arm wrapped around his stomach and the bloody hand holding the knife. 'P . . . please . . .' His face went white.

The Flesher yanked it straight across Faulds' belly and out the other side. Less than a second start to finish.

Bright-scarlet oxygenated blood pulsed out into the room. Someone screamed, but all Faulds could do was open and shut his mouth. He fell to his knees – innards bulging out, still held together with connective tissue – the stink of punctured bowels and severed intestines barely noticeable, just another slaughterhouse smell.

The workforce ran: shouting, swearing, getting as far away from the blood and guts as they could. The Flesher disappeared into the crowd.

'NO!' Logan scrambled over to Faulds. The man was in shock. His face pale and glassy, hands shivering over the hole in his belly, not touching anything . . .

'Come on, you're going to be OK, You're going to be OK!'

No he wasn't – there was blood everywhere, she'd nearly cut him in half.

Jackie shouted over the sounds of panicking abattoir workers: 'YOU! STOP RIGHT THERE!'

Logan scanned the room; she was over by the line of skinned and gutted sheep, facing off against the Flesher. The knife flashed out, but Jackie slashed her baton across it, sending the blade clattering to the metal floor.

The Flesher lunged, shoving a hollowed-out carcass into Jackie. She staggered back against the wall, slipped on the bloody floor and went down hard.

A small pause and the Flesher pulled out what looked like a lightsaber, twisting it apart and slipping in a small green cartridge as Jackie struggled to get up.

Logan yelled, 'IT'S A BOLT GUN!'

Snap and the thing was back together again.

He tried to get up, but Faulds had a death grip on his jacket, mouth moving soundlessly, eyes wide, gasping for breath.

The Flesher swung the bolt gun at Jackie's head.

Everything seemed to go into slow motion: the gun cylinder arced down; the song on the radio changed to Tom Jones, 'It's Not Unusual'; Jackie threw her hands in the path of the bolt gun, trying to protect her forehead.

The end of the barrel hit her right palm, forcing it back against the left, and CRACK! The bolt fired. Jackie screamed. Bright red spattered across her face.

The metal rod had gone straight through both palms.

The Flesher stood for a moment, then tried to pull the bolt gun out. Jackie's hands went with it. 'AAAGH FUCK!'

Twist to the left, then the right. More screaming. 'FUCKING HELP ME!'

Logan struggled out of Faulds' grip and scrambled to his feet. 'FUCKING HELP!'

The Flesher gave one last tug and the bolt slid free, just as Logan barrelled into her back. They hit the wall with a crash and the bolt gun went flying. For once Logan came out on top: he balled up a fist and slammed it into Margaret Thatcher's rubbery face. And again. And—

Jackie shouted, 'Look out!'

Something solid battered across Logan's shoulders, sending him sprawling across the gutter that ran down the centre of the room. There was a woman in pink-piggy pyjamas standing over him, clutching a metal pole.

She looked incredibly pale: grey circles around her eyes; hair all matted and greasy... But Logan knew he'd seen her somewhere before.

She raised the pole again, and he curled up into a ball, arms wrapped over his head, teeth gritted against the blow ... only it never came.

The woman in the PJs dropped the pole and helped the Flesher to stand.

Logan rolled over and tried to push himself upright. His left arm gave way, fire screaming across his shoulder. He fell back against the blood-slicked floor. Groaning.

Up. GET UP.

He tried again, hauling himself up using the eviscerated carcass of a sheep ... it was still warm.

The woman threw her arm around the Flesher, and together they hobbled away. Logan took two steps after them, then stopped, turned back and looked at Jackie. She had her hands cupped in her lap, head thrown back, teeth gritted. Her whole face was painted scarlet, tears washing little pink trails through the blood. He sank down beside her, using the wall for support. His whole left arm was burning now, throbbing in time with his head.

'You OK?'

She glared at him. 'Do I fucking look OK? I've got holes in my hands!' Grimace. 'Ah Jesus it hurts!'

'I'll get an ambulance.'

'No you don't – you go and you catch that bastard!'

'But Faulds—'

'He's already dead.'

Logan glanced over at the Chief Constable's body. The man's eyes were open, staring at the ceiling, his chest still, his blood-soaked hands limp at his sides, his stomach a gaping hole...

Jackie tried to grab hold of Logan's filthy suit jacket, but her fingers weren't working. 'You let that bastard escape, I'll bloody kill you.'

63

Logan lurched along the corridor, clutching his left arm to his chest, following the Flesher and her accomplice as fast as his wobbly legs would go. The burning sensation was slowly giving way to a worrying numbness. Dislocated or broken, either was better than a bolt gun through the hands, or getting cut in half.

A pair of double doors at the far end led through into the cattle area: a tall, warehouse-style room with another mechanical conveyer built into the ceiling. Only this time it wasn't sheep dangling five inches off the floor, it was cattle: hanging head down, their rear hooves chained to the belt ten foot above Logan's head. He'd seen plenty of cows in the fields around Aberdeen, but he'd never realized they were so *huge*.

An elevated walkway ran along the twisting path the carcasses followed; men and women in blue and white overalls, Wellington boots, and hardhats; strange bits of equipment; the stench of rendering fat and hot copper and raw meat; gouts of greasy steam drifting out of circular holes in the floor.

There was music playing in here too, but no one was working – they were all staring at Logan in his blood-soaked suit.

A hydraulic noise, then a faint buzzing, and then a huge bullock fell out of a slot in the wall onto a knee-high plinth. It wasn't even twitching as someone in a long green apron shackled its back legs and winched it upside down to join the line.

'Which way did they go?'

No one could hear him over the clank of machinery and the roar of Tom Jones.

Three quick slashes to the throat and the bullock's blood gushed onto the killing floor, bright red.

Logan tried again. 'WHERE DID THEY GO?'

The man in the green apron pointed down the line – past where the emptied, skinned cattle were being sawn in half with an industrial band-saw – at a small area tacked onto the end of the cavernous room.

Logan lurched into a run.

The little alcove was full of plastic bins and metal racks: lungs, livers and tongues handing from stainless steel hooks. He slithered on the wet floor, bounced off the wall and round into a foetid recess where three industrial-sized spin-dryers shuddered away to themselves. A stunned woman stopped in the middle of stuffing a cow's stomach into one and watched him stagger past.

A door banged shut up ahead. Logan tore through the Den of Dung and wrenched it open just in time to see a pair of pink pyjama legs disappearing at the top of a flight of steps.

He hurried up after her, bursting out of the door at the top and into the deep, metallic rumble of the bone mill.

The Flesher and Pyjama Woman were scrambling up the stairs to the top hopper – the one they'd found Thomas Stephen's head in. Logan grabbed the handrail, shouting over the grinding noise, 'STOP, POLICE!'

It never usually worked, but this time it actually did; by the time he'd got to the top they were waiting for him.

Oh shit.

He went for his pepper spray, but his left arm wouldn't work. Trying to move it was like jamming red-hot knitting needles into his shoulder. He fumbled for it with his right hand, then aimed the canister at the Flesher's face. 'I need you to lie down on the floor. Now.'

The woman in pyjamas shook her head. 'You can't.'

'You too: on the floor.'

'Jimmy's only doing it to make us pure.'

'Jimmy doesn't exist, it's...' And that was when Logan finally realized why she so looked familiar. 'Heather Inglis...? You need to come with me, Heather. It's over. He ... *she* can't hurt you anymore.' Back to the Flesher. 'On the floor NOW!'

And then the Flesher stepped behind Heather and hefted her over the greasy handrail that ran around the lip of the hopper. Heather squealed and grabbed onto it, holding herself in place.

Logan risked a quick glance into the big, slope-sided metal bin. It was nearly empty, the last few bones disappearing as he watched – ground into bite-sized chunks and dumped into the next hopper down.

He held his hands up, placatory. 'It's over Elizabeth. By tomorrow morning your face will be on every television and newspaper in the country. There's nowhere you can go.' He inched his way forwards, eyes scanning the bone mill's walls. Looking for the off switch.

'Come on Elizabeth. You don't want to hurt Heather: she's eaten the food, hasn't she? She's pure.'

The Flesher raised a trembling hand to the mask and peeled it off. It was Elizabeth, but at the same time it wasn't. Her face looked different from before. It wasn't just that her nose was broken, bleeding, or that her left cheek was swollen, it was as if the rubber mask wasn't the only one she was wearing.

She threw Margaret Thatcher's face into the hopper. Logan watched it bounce off the far side, then slide down into the rotating metal teeth; they tore it apart like a slice of wet bread.

459

'Come on, Elizabeth, you don't really want to do this, do you?'

There was a long pause, and then, 'No.'

Heather turned and looked at her, letting go of the handrail with one hand to touch Elizabeth's cheek. 'But I do, Kelley. For you.'

Logan crept another step closer. 'Heather, come on, don't do anything stupid. You've survived too much to throw it all away.'

Elizabeth leant forward and kissed her on the cheek. And then Heather jumped.

'FUCK!' The hell with inching – Logan leapt, snatching a handful of her pyjamas as she hopped off the railing and into thin air. He was off balance, dragged forwards by her weight as she fell. His stomach slammed into the guardrail. Pain, sudden and immediate, tore across his scarred stomach. He opened his mouth to shout, but all that came out was an agonized wheeze.

No strength in his fingers.

Logan tried to grab her with his left hand – his shoulder screamed at him as something inside gave way.

She was slipping.

Their eyes locked. Heather looked strangely peaceful as she fell the dozen or so feet into the hopper. Her feet hit the sloping wall and slid out from underneath her. CLANG: backwards onto the grimy metal. Her left foot jerked into the air. And then fell into the rotating teeth.

The only noise was the rumble of the metal driveshaft.

Foot. Ankle. Shin. Then Heather started to scream, pushing against the wall with her remaining foot, pyjamas drenched with fresh blood, hands scrabbling for purchase on the sloping sides.

The door through to the protein processing unit burst open: Jackie, her hands curled against her chest. She stopped, rooted to the spot, staring open-mouthed at the stuttering bits of leg falling into the lower hopper.

Logan forced himself upright and staggered across to the cut-off switch, slamming his palm down on the red button. The grinding noise whined to a halt.

He clambered over the rail and dropped down beside Heather, shouting at the top of his lungs: 'GET A BLOODY AMBULANCE!'

The Flesher was gone.

Tributes pour in for murdered BBC filmmaker

COLLEAGUES and friends of murdered BBC documentary maker Alec Thorogood paid tribute to his skill and dedication today.

"He was the consummate professional," said producer Frank Martin, "he was one of the best in the industry. I can't believe he's gone."

Last year Thorogood won a BAFTA for the observational documentary *Scaffies*, which depicted the lives of bin men working in Fraserburgh. At the time of his death he was working on *Granite City 999* (due to be broadcast on BBC Scotland early next year) following Grampian Police as the _____ crimes in Aberdeen.
_____ killing aga_

ABATTOIR IN FOOT & MOUTH COVER-UP

BURIED CONTAINERS USED TO HIDE EVIDENCE

By Russel D McLean

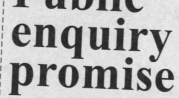

Environmental Health inspectors have found evidence that the containers used by the Flesher were buried by Alaba Farm Fresh Meats in the 70s to hide a foot and mouth epidemic from the government.

The abattoir's Managing Director Paul Jenkins has been detained for questioning.

Diseased cattle

"I can understand why they might have thought it was a good idea," said local farmer, Stephen Robertson, "it would have devastated the local community if all the cattle had to be destroyed. Th__ _____

Three containers, thought to contain up to twenty carcasses were buried in 1972 to hide the evidence from vets and inspectors. This was just five years after the devastating outbreak of 1967 which left the farming industry crippled.

Arrogance

"The management at Alaba showed a staggering degree of arrogance. If this outbreak had spread it could have caused a nation-wide epidemic."

And yet the secret lay undisturbed for nearly thirty years, until another epidemic hit the North East of Scotland.

Police believe the Flesher, who allegedly grew up near the abatt___ __

LOCAL COU__
__IN HOLI__

ELGIN COUPLE __e won the holiday of a __time after buying a __le ticket at the __meldrum sports day.

__e prize was sponsored by __rows Offshore to help raise

James and __ delighted at __ the all-expe__ Seychelles i__ said Barbara __ for 12 years __ a holiday sin __ forward to it __

__PED IN THE DAR__

__le of What Happened to Catherine Davidson is S__

__d speculation.

__ grave, dug into the tunnels __g from the Flesher's home __abattoir, had been well cared __th a bunch of plastic roses __eddy bear placed against the __made headstone.

__re lie the mortal remains of __rine Davidson, beloved __nion. Died 14th September

__herine Davidson went __g on the 30th of October __ That means she was held __e by the Flesher for nearly __en years. Kept locked in the __nd fed on human flesh.

__ body was exhumed by __ogists on Tuesday and taken __ police mortuary for analysis.

__ appears that she died from __al causes," said a police __esperson. "We can't release __rther details at this time."

son, Richard Dav__ serving time in C__ has applied for l__ mother's funeral __

"I was only __ mother was tak__ father couldn't __ fell apart," said __ thought she wa__ hear what happ__ she had been. __ does that to __ being?"

Although p__ know the ide__ killer they h__ details.

"It's a lega__ DCS Bain, he__ say is that __ police author__ and alerted __ INTERPOL."

The Fleshe__

Public enquiry promise

MSP Robin McCafferty vows that there will be a public enquiry into the events of Saturday night, when a BBC cameraman and Chief Constable Mark Faulds of West Midlands Police lost their lives.

"How can we possibly allow Grampian Police the opportunity to sweep this under the rug?"

The criticism comes after it was revealed that one officer, DS McRae, bungled the opportunity to detain the Flesher.

"All our officers have a duty of care to the public," said DCS Bain, head of Aberdeen's CID. "DS McRae

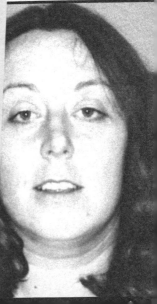

Six Months Later

Heather dries her hands on a kitchen towel and limps over to the fridge. Twenty-eight weeks and they still haven't managed to get her a prosthetic that fits properly, but that's being ungrateful, isn't it? If it wasn't for Aberdeen Royal Infirmary she'd have lost the whole leg.

According to the clock on the microwave it's half past five. An afternoon in May – probably blazing sunshine, but in her little Fittie house it's black as the grave. The neighbours might not like that she's boarded up all the windows, but they don't say anything on account of her 'ordeal'. Dead husband, one leg, not right in the head . . .

Stockholm syndrome – that's what Mr New called it. That's what the hospital's psychologists said as well. None of them understand.

Heather drops a chunk of lard in the pot and adds the sliced onions.

All this time and they still don't know where He is. But *she* does. Sometimes Kelley sends her a postcard from somewhere exotic like Prague. Heather keeps them in a secret box where the police will never find them.

'Dinner going to be long then?' asks Duncan, his little blood halo glowing in the darkness.

'Hours and hours.' She says, 'You can open a bottle of wine if you like.'

Three tablespoons of paprika when the onions are soft and translucent.

He wraps his arms around her and leans in close, smelling her hair. *'Mmmmm. Gorgeous.'* He kisses her neck and she giggles.

'I know what you're thinking, and you'll have to wait till I've peeled the potatoes.'

'Damn potatoes.' He steps back, leaning against the working surface, head on one side, questioning. A little physical tic he's picked up from the Flesher. *'Do you still miss Justin?'*

'Yes.' Into the other pan go the chunks of offal: heart and kidneys, browning on a high heat. For some reason she couldn't cope with Justin being alive – it just didn't seem right for him to be walking about when she knew he was dead. 'But I'm sure Mother's looking after him.'

The browned meat goes in with the onions, followed by a tin of chopped tomatoes, some white wine and garlic.

'You never cooked this well when I was alive.'

'That's because you were always so bloody precious about your boeuf bourguignon. I thought if I did anything fancier than fish fingers you'd be telling me I wasn't doing it right.' She grinds a few twists of pepper into the pan, adds a dash of salt, then sticks the lid on and puts it in the oven. One hundred and twenty degrees Celsius for two hours. And by that time she's drunk half a bottle of wine and the whole house smells wonderfully meaty and rich.

Heather changes into her good frock, does her hair, lipstick, and eye shadow. It's not every day she has someone for dinner.

She doesn't bother with the table anymore. Just puts their plates down on the carpet in the lounge, next to the mattress from the bedroom. It's the only piece of furniture in the place, except for one of the dining room chairs – for her guest – and a single candle that flickers on the mantelpiece.

It hadn't been easy, tracking down James Souter. He was so small and frail in his tatty little dressing gown, sitting in his room in the hospice. Shivering and terrified.

Hard to believe he was the man who'd done all those terrible things to Kelley.

And now look at him, all nice and quiet, tied to his chair, skin pale as bone china. Chest hollow and empty. The stump of his missing arm all shiny in the candlelight.

Heather digs her fork into the paprikash and pulls out a chunk of meltingly tender meat. Yes, James Souter was a nasty bastard, but his heart's in the right place.

And very tasty it is too.